The Black Envelope

The Black Envelope

NORMAN MANEA

TRANSLATED BY PATRICK CAMILLER

YALE UNIVERSITY PRESS ■ NEW HAVEN & LONDON

A MARGELLOS
WORLD REPUBLIC OF LETTERS BOOK

The Margellos World Republic of Letters is dedicated to making literary works from around the globe available in English through translation. It brings to the English-speaking world the work of leading poets, novelists, essayists, philosophers, and playwrights from Europe, Latin America, Africa, Asia, and the Middle East to stimulate international discourse and creative exchange.

First Yale University Press edition 2012.

Originally published in Romanian under the title *Plicul Negru.* Copyright © 1986 by Editura Cartea Românască. Copyright © 1995 by Norman Manea. English translation copyright © 1995 by Farrar, Straus and Giroux.

Yale University Press books may be purchased in quantity for educational, business, or promotional use. For information, please e-mail sales.press@yale.edu (U.S. office) or sales@yaleup.co.uk (U.K. office).

Library of Congress Control Number: 2011939658
ISBN 978-0-300-18294-1 (pbk.: alk. paper)

Set in Electra and Nobel types by Keystone Typesetting, Inc.
Printed in the United States of America.

This paper meets the requirements of ANSI/NISO Z39.48-1992 (Permanence of Paper).

10 9 8 7 6 5 4 3 2 1

The Black Envelope

IN THE KIOSK WINDOW, the lovely curled head of a spring morning. Small black eyes. Crimson lips, pink-enamel cheeks.

"The newspapers! They're just coming. The papers will be ready in a second."

The men huddling around the window came to life.

The girl moved back inside the kiosk to arrange the stacks of papers. The pavement was no longer large enough. There were pedestrians darting everywhere, casting impatient glances to left and right—wave upon wave of bustling ants. The line for the paper grew longer.

"I haven't got any more *Flacăras*," announced the soprano. "And this one is the last *România Liberă*. You can whistle for *Filatelia* and *Pescarul*—they're real vintage wine. No, I haven't got *Rebus*. Maybe tomorrow."

The tall, pale man moved beside the lamppost with a bundle of fresh papers under his arm. He opened them up and began skimming through.

"What could have got into them?" grumbled a little old woman leaning on the rubbish bin. "Newspapers—lining up for the paper, would you believe it. Stupid brats. As if they'd find anything out by reading them. I tell you, sir, they're the same. All the same! Money down the drain, I say."

But the tall man with white hair, beard, and mustache, all perfectly trimmed, did not hear her. Nor did he hear the tapping of heels on the asphalt or see the rainbow skirts fluttering in the breeze or the brief glitter of golden stockings. The gentleman neither heard nor saw anything, absorbed as he was in leafing through the papers.

"That's what people are like. They forget quickly," the elderly voice continued. "We've got this lovely country, this heavenly climate. But you can't do anything with just nature, you bunch of good-for-nothings! It's man who does everything, with those brains of his. That's why we've got into this mess. Look at them, they've even forgotten the winter. They've forgotten the horror of it. They don't even care—they're off goggling at women. People forget quickly, sir, I'm telling you."

The man did not hear. Disappointed, the old woman stepped sideways toward a wrinkled man who kept shaking his empty shopping bag.

"Too true, too true!" muttered the aged hunchback. "My wife died on me this winter. It was because they didn't give us any heating. They kept us in the cold all winter—not even any hot water. She had heart trouble, so the cold finished her off. Yes sir, how people forget! They don't give a damn," the old man erupted in the direction of the elegant gentleman leaning against the post and absorbed in his reading. "Look at them! Minds like sieves. You can do what you like to them and they'll forget it. Just give them a little pleasure —a fine day, a pretzel—yes, they forget as soon as you give them a pretzel and a bit of sun. That's what people are like."

The smart-looking man did not seem to feel that the stranger's fury was aimed at him. Probably he did not even hear. He gathered together the bundle of papers and tore himself away from the lamppost.

The compass of his legs opened wide. Beanstalk strides, but slowly, because he was rather short of energy.

A happy street, it was true. Picturesque Bucharest, feminine and sprightly—just like the petit Paris of old. If only there were not this poverty and gasping all around, and this clumsy, artificial happiness. Happy spring. Happy, forgetful people. Happy papers, too. Optimistic, pedagogic, ever holding forth about the future, the radiant future, whoever might be around to see it.

The kitchen table. Bread, milk. The white starched tablecloth. He had to get up at the break of day to find some bread and milk.

Two steaming cups. Coffee substitute with milk—a substitute because real coffee was so hard to come by. Anyway, old age is itself a substitute. And our entire country a nation of senior citizens. Slices of hard black bread thinly smeared with plum jam. But the spoon, knife, and plates sparkle like new. Everything is clean and fresh. Windows open to let in the elixir, the venom, the illusion. Spring, spring.

Mrs. Gafton thumbed through her newspapers. She put her glasses on, took a sip from her cup, glanced at the title pages, then gave up. Anyway, she never has time to read except in the evening, after all the chores are done. She pushed the pile toward her husband at the end of the table.

"At least our climate's still wonderful. What if we only had winter? Or only summer? Harmony is so important! And we've certainly got it here. How lucky we are!"

Her husband looked hard and long at her.

"Yes, in fact someone was saying that just a while ago, in the newspaper line. Spring is a gift of nature! Not youth any longer, but still a rebirth, eh? A real provocation."

His wife took off her glasses, put them on the heap of papers, and looked down into her cup. After a few moments of silence, she began to whisper. Yes, whisper.

"Do you still know when Franz Joseph died?"

"Eh? What's got into you now?"

"I don't know, just a bit of nonsense. I'm mixing things up. Well, you used to say he was a tolerant emperor."

The husband smiled. He was familiar with these morning antics. Signs of tenderness and support for his studies. She did not ask him anything about his work; she knew it would only annoy him before he set off for the library. Anyway, he always talked about it again in the evening.

But in the morning she usually found various coded expressions to indicate that his work obsessed her, too.

"In fact, I was thinking: when did Caesar, Nero? I mean, when did they . . . ? And what about Franco, or Salazar? Mussolini I know—it was in the spring, wasn't it? And it was the same with the Führer: he set fire to himself in the spring. But that other guy with a mustache, the Georgian, he croaked in March. I couldn't possibly forget it. Is it the siege of spring? Or like a whirlwind. Something unstoppable."

The husband tugged at the pile of papers, laying his gold-rimmed glasses beside the cup. The woman primped her hair, gray and tight at the back of her head.

"Yes, a siege, as you say. The onslaught of change. Something uncertain, unstoppable. Let me read you a little story from today's paper. Just let anyone say nothing ever happens here."

He smoothed the corner of the tablecloth. The woman stood up, breadbasket in hand. He looked at her. The day's moment of peace. Breakfast gave him strength. It was a calm reference point at the start of a new day, before all the running and jostling around, the lines, library cards, letters to the authorities, more lines.

"Listen: 'The facts, as we will briefly relate them here, seem to have been taken from a film about the Ku Klux Klan or some gang of witch-hunters. The hunting of witches in the neighborhood.' Listen, don't you want to listen?"

The woman arranged the cups and tableware in the sink. Moving slowly, halfheartedly, she tilted to one side as she limped with her left leg. But then she came back and sat down. Her pale plump hands again rested dutifully together on the immaculate tablecloth.

"So they burst into the woman's apartment. And then, what do you think? They set fire to it. Can you imagine? Because she loved animals, do you hear? Because she had cats or dogs, or who knows what she had. Just look at the pretext on which they did it, and the means they used. The woman's name and address . . . Don't you see? And So-and-so, who claims to be on the local council, is in league with the instigators, with the other tenants in the block. You see the connection, don't you? Do you see how it all fits together?"

His wife stared at him without smiling. She was used to his

obsession for linking the day's events to his research in the library. She knew his habit of returning again and again to things that happened forty years ago. This time, though, there was something special in his voice. It seemed like a crowning moment, a final and decisive test that she did not understand. But she did understand his excitement—a kind of unexpected victory and, yes, panic. A long-suppressed panic that both confirmed his expectations and gave him new life, as it were.

An hour later, then, Mr. Matei Gafton was asking the librarian for more volumes than usual and, for some strange reason, stood with a blank look for a long time before touching the piles in front of him. But he did check them, carefully. Decree No. 966 of April 7, 1941, introducing harsher penalties for the crime of high treason and espionage. Plumyene and Lasierra, *Les fascismes français*; General Ion Antonescu, *The Basis of the National-Legionary State*, September–October 1940; Lucrețiu Pătrășcanu, *Under Three Dictatorships*, reissued, Bucharest 1970; *The Graziani Trial*, Rome, 1948–1950; Decree No. 966 of April 7, 1941, prohibiting the marriage of civil servants with foreigners or Jews; *Nazi Conspiracy and Aggression*, Washington, 1946 . . . He knew them all: they no longer satisfied him. The epidemic spread, the confusion—so many deceptive little hopes, until the invisible trap snaps shut and it is too late, with nothing more to be done. Yesterday the disease was still next door or at the next door's neighbor; today it is inside you and it is too late. The roots of evil are in each prisoner not just in the butchers. Hunters and victim, fire, a kind of lynching, and the pretexts do not matter in the slightest: it could have been anyone at all.

It would be too simple an explanation, really too simple. That spring is to blame? Spring, like forty years ago? A delayed encounter of which you are no longer capable, exhausted from adapting to so many snares, at every moment. The pretext—who would believe it—was cats!

"Are you leaving already?" The blonde behind the library counter was evidently intrigued.

He shrugged his shoulders, feeling guilty.

He sauntered along the boulevard. Spring. Words. Spring made up of words. Trotyl. Dust. Red. Cherry. Delicate buds as in an advertisement. A dog and a cat. Blows, fire, hooligans, crowbars, destruction of the apartment, the blaze. Earth, air, water, and fire. Oxygenization, aphrodisiacs, aggression, the venom of loneliness. Spring, roll of words.

He sat down on a bench in the small dusty park. Words: the mind is forever producing words; you hear them flowing all the time inside you. Destruction. Fire. Crowbars, blows. Spite. Red. Crematorium. Mayflies. The look and the body of mayflies. Magnetic encounters, the grating silk, morbid idylls, night breeze. The fancies of tiredness wrapped him in words, as in a protective film. Absent moments—he knew the danger of such senile flights.

Maybe he should go to Tolea's, to show him the magazine. Tolea's reactions are childish and unpredictable: they mimic vitality well and even radiate a kind of therapeutic irritation. He might start shouting or cursing, or set the magazine alight, or quite simply throw him out as an intruder. Well, it's hard to say who the intruder is. After all, Tolea, not he, is the tenant. So yes, it would be good to visit Tolea, especially since I don't do it very often; the tenant would have no reason to complain. Not very often—but then the last time was just yesterday.

He had knocked timidly. No answer. But Tolea was home. He felt that Tolea was in but did not want to open the door. He knocked again, once, twice, then cautiously opened the door. Mr. Tolea Voinov barely turned his head. He seemed to recognize the intruder but did not honor him with any gesture. The man remained at the door, unsure whether to enter. The waiting lasted only a moment. The host cut through the air with his legs and bounded straight up to the guest.

"So, old fellow! Just as well you've come."

Bowing down to the ground. Then a step sideways to make room for the eminent guest, who decided on the only possible course: he smiled. He looked at the professor and beamed. Yes, the tenant was the same. White ribbed trousers, white sweater, white tennis shoes. Shaven, bald, fresh. Yes, there was no mistaking him. He sat down on one of the two chairs in the tiny room.

"I've got bad news."

"Thank God!" The professor crossed himself. "Let it all out, then. I'll offer you a coffee as a reward. Get it off your chest, *panie*! You'll have a real coffee, *hundert prozent*, not like the piss that's drunk in our multilaterally developed society. If the news is serious—I mean, bad—you'll get a super-coffee, straight from Allah's kettle."

He circled around the pigsty, among books, ties, notebooks, shopping bags, and like a conjurer fished a thermos and cup out of thin air. There was the coffee. A big, green, full cup on the metal table between the two chairs.

"Just for me?"

"I've already drunk a tankful; my pistons are racing away. Sip it slowly—don't rush. Relax while you're getting the calamities ready. I'm all yours today, Citizen Matei. You found me in—my tough luck."

The guest sipped, smiled, put it off.

"To make it easier for both of us, let me do the explaining," the professor began impatiently. "Let me tell you what it's about. Otherwise you'll keep beating around the bush all the way to Katmandu. Come on, out with it: you need this room. I've got to free the burial chamber. Yes?"

The guest nearly choked on his drink.

"No, no, not at all. What I was going to say was that big staff cuts are in the offing. What's in your file will count. As in the fifties. That's it: losing your job isn't a joke. And as you see, there's no longer any way I can help you."

He spewed it all out and breathed a sigh of relief. A long silence followed—a kind of crumbling, a loss of contact.

Finally, the professor's voice. Sharp, rejuvenated.

"As a pensioner you take an interest in all sorts of monkey business, isn't that right? I've heard that you write to the authorities every day. Is it to atone for your sins of the fifties? You were a journalist in those days and you scribbled any old lie they wanted, plus a lot they maybe didn't even ask you for but which you believed. Now you're trying to make up for the past. So you write demands, appeals, suggestions. You criticize and notify and propose. A volunteer, a really stubborn journalist! Brave, ready to help us poor sinners. You were saying that political files are back, like in the fifties? But that things won't repeat themselves? Then why don't you write all that down? Nowadays courage is not such a big thing, and the pension arrives every month. You help us sinners, isn't that right? Maybe you'll find me another job. After all, a century ago you were at the Polytechnic together with my brother, now an Argentinian citizen living in that madhouse called Buenos Aires. One of the most beautiful in the world, says our friend Marga. And he knows about these things, working in a madhouse himself."

The guest was bent over, the cup still in his hand. But Tolea was not looking at him.

"What do you want me to do? To ask your Argentinian colleague for help? To ask my charming brother? For charity? The boss has gone kaput, you know. What's to be done? Swimming pool, car, farm, house, bank accounts, holidays—it's all very tiring. Shall I write to him about childhood years, the fireplace, the parental home? Tears will flow and he'll be off to see a psychiatrist."

"Come on, don't exaggerate. It seems he's already written to you."

"Of course, of course, I've had nothing but delights. Correspondence! Abroad! Capitalist countries! Military-fascist dictatorships! Relatives who were drawn from the country by the mirage of money and an easy life, and who send us their convertible charity at Easter and Christmas. I'm just a substitute, Comrade Gafton! A relic of the past dressed up as a scapegoat. That's the word they used in the political seminars, wasn't it? But who knows? You might offer me some compensation that leads to a job. A paid hobby. Not paid like your new occupation, which is really unpaid heart-searching. What do you say? Will you take me on?"

"I don't understand. I don't understand a thing."

"So you don't understand. Well, if someone doesn't understand, it has to be explained to them, right? Do you remember the 'great tragedy'?"

Gafton remained silent. He shifted his weight from the left to the right side of his body.

"The family tragedy! Death, sir, that's the only type of tragedy there is. Death. The Great Scriptwriter hired us for that, didn't he? So, death . . . You do remember the funeral? I mean, what happened with Father—then?"

"Yes, of course I do," the guest quickly broke in.

"Goo-ood, so you remember. What was it: suicide, murder, accident? Or don't you remember anymore? Maybe you don't. You had a different name—everything had a different name."

"How's that? What do you mean?"

"How's that, how's that! Look, surely you're not going to tell me your name was Gafton in those days. Or am I wrong? Well anyway, let's skip the details. So now you're a journalist working from home."

"From where did you—" The journalist blushed, paled, reddened, all of a sudden.

"No harm done, *panie*, nothing to be ashamed of. Some will-o'-the-wisps can be nice and innocent; they're not all mean and vile. Your recent one, like the first, is humanitarian enough. It's just more congenial, because it's useless and unpaid. So now you write as a correspondent of the masses. Goo-ood. Letters instead of articles, right? Right. Like those Latin American policemen who decide to form their own gangs to have a crack at the villains—but as private individuals using police expertise. Good. Only you also have other passions. I was going to say manias—excuse me. So you investigate! You examine the past to forget the present, or to understand it better. Of course, it's not my business. But it is also, or could also become, mine. I mean, why don't we concern ourselves with the same period, for different purposes? Only I'd be paid for it. What do you say?"

"No. I don't understand what you're after."

"What I'm after? To get excited about something, that's what. To find a conjuring act. A game, a hobby, as they say in the capitalist paradise. Not to be bored any longer! Even death is not a greater tragedy than boredom. The Old Scriptwriter likes us to amuse him, doesn't he? After all, that's why he created us.

"So, could I take part in your great work? I'm drawing up my family tree and also looking into the mysterious chapter in its story. What do you say? Others don't know what I'm like, but when I think of the hearth back home, of my childhood years, I'm ready to start writing the memoirs of my decimated family! Will you pay for my help, then? How about it?"

It became quiet again. As the silence continued to grow, the professor felt he had probably gone rather too far.

"Let me make you another coffee, sir. I haven't anything else to offer. You don't drink or smoke, I know, and I can't offer you one of my ladies, as they've got the day off today. But a genuine coffee—in our times that's a real provocation, believe me. Almost an attack on social harmony. Just think: a kilo of coffee on the black market costs a whole month's wages."

The other man did not reply. The window was darkening as evening fell. His movements grew slower, his voice less distinct.

"No." The voice could be heard at last. "It's late and I don't sleep well anyway. Let's talk about your job, rather."

"Pah, what is there to talk about? I understand that you can't help me. You're not the official journalist you once used to be, so you can't work shoulder to shoulder again with mad Marga, the loonies' doctor, to save me and take me away to the famous capital to work in the sought-after post of receptionist at the Hotel Cunty. I'm sorry, I know you're not so keen on slang. Let's say Hotel Pussy—that's the popular expression."

"Yes. It won't be easy to find you a job. But that's not the most difficult problem."

"Well, if there's a more difficult one, we're really in for it! In fact, I'm just starting to correspond with Argentina."

"It's the business with that hotel. But you know what things are like there. The staff, the various connections and obligations."

"Ah! So you know the network, I see. You must have worked in that branch as well! After all, you've practiced all the trades, including that of professional revolutionary, haven't you? Isn't that so? Tell me, isn't that so?"

"Stop playing the fool. No one will believe you were a receptionist who knew of nothing but work and wages, day shift and night shift, for a fortnight at a stretch. A receptionist at that hotel is not the best of recommendations. Or only if you want to be taken on as a flunky. You know what I mean."

"Sure I do. It means we can't go on discussing in the dark, comrade. They mustn't think there's a conspiracy, Comrade Gafton—that we're taking advantage of the dark."

Suddenly the light came on, another one of Tolea's tricks. A candle-thin bulb, held by a metal clasp attached to the table leg. A weak light, just enough to outline the Roman-consul face of the receptionist. Perfectly shaven, almost too pale.

"Now that you mention it, m'sieur, you're going to end up in really hot water with those freelance journalists' letters. A petitioner for the good of humanity! I didn't understand that business with your name, either. Why should you be doing good under a changed name? After all, my ancestors or yours changed their name for quite different reasons, didn't they, eh? Aliens that we are, isn't that so?"

No answer could be heard, not even a whimper.

"Was it all for effect that you took your wife's name? Precisely after the war? Because she'd had one of those brothers, a Heil Heil man, but she herself was innocent? And in the fifties you risked your spotless record as an apostle just to defend the principle of objectivity! Is that how you justified it to yourself? Like that, Herr Gafton?"

Nothing from Herr Gafton, not a word. Or rather yes, there did come a whisper. "I thought you might try some translating for a while. You can still find a connection at one of those cooperatives that do technical translations. Or even at a publisher's. It would help out until something else comes along."

"A translator, goo-ood! *Traduttore traditore,* or however it goes. We all translate, it's become the law of survival, hasn't it? Good. We're all replacements and translators, no?

"But what about the translator's file? His *curriculum vitae,* his police record? His mother, father, brothers, and sisters, political affiliations—kept particularly for special cases! Argentina's a special case, isn't it? The Argentine circus: generals who are continually visiting this country because we're sister Latins and sister menageries, isn't that so? And then, *gospodin,* what do you know about the post of receptionist at the temple of fornicators? There's no way you can know, *panie.* For the time being we are killed by messengers, by intermediaries, not by the Chief Star and his Saints. Petty auxiliaries, substitutes—even me. A substitute, sir, you know what I mean only too well. It's a world of substitutes, this circus of ours. Any tenant on the flattened planet knows it already. Anyone knows it, my dear sir. Even you do, I'm sure."

The professor remained in the weak candlelight, while Herr Matei received in darkness, and in silence, the words streaming from the tenant Anatol Dominic Vancea Voinov, called Tolea.

After a pause for breath, Herr Matei finally replied.

"As a matter of fact, I came here to suggest—why hide it? If you need some—to be blunt, if you need some money. I'm not a man of wealth, you know. Still, I came to offer you—I would be able—I'm prepared to—"

"As a loan, eh?"

"Well, of course. Otherwise . . ."

"Goo-ood. Perfect! As a loan, I accept. Look, *Panie* Matei, I accept. I agree about the loan. Any time, any way, any amount. I was afraid that when you left I might find an envelope stuffed with crisp new notes. You're still sitting in the dark there. You could easily slip me your delicate gift without being seen. I don't like philanthropists, you know. I'm glad you don't belong to that dubious category. You're even a little stingy, Mr. Gafton, sir. I hope you don't mind that I was watching. I confess an unshakable respect for this imposing sign of seriousness. Meanness is a serious matter: it deserves every honor! Only simpletons think it's a defect. It makes me all the more moved by your offer, you realize."

The professor was speaking very fast, his eyes turned away from the other man and almost glued to the black window. The sentences seemed to ricochet from the glass in which the darkness of night was reflected. He half felt that his guest had stood up and was right beside the window, that Gafton-the-beanstalk was already on his left, bent over an invisible shadow. He felt, or maybe he didn't—and anyway, he didn't care—that the blockhead had already turned around, slowly, that his smooth pate was like a bright sphere beneath a thin aura of rush light. Yes, he had moved the clasp and lightbulb to a shelf so that its holy light fell on the bald head, and now he was looking astonished at the beanstalk, as if he had only just discovered his presence.

"Have I annoyed you in some way, sir? Is it my shameless good humor? It's just harmless playacting, really. You should ignore it. Don't worry, I'm not such a bore as to pester you with my melodramatics. As for the loan, make it some other day. When the time comes. When we start our walks down memory lane."

Then he fell silent. Probably he was gathering strength for the last bombshell. And his voice became grave, calm, low, without any sharpness.

"You know, sir, I don't care about anything. I really don't care about anything. Do you remember my father? He thought he'd escape. Philosopher! Sorbonne! *Magna cum laude!* Pah! and he built up a stock of wine—to escape. He thought he'd escape: wine is an ever necessary fuel. Including in days of wrath—especially then. Just look at how everyone jostles in lines to get some of that stinking sawdust-and-garbage wine. The receptionist at the Hotel Vancea doesn't care whether he escapes or not! I don't care about anything, remember. But that one did. Philosopher, Sorbonne! When he realized what awaited him in the paradise he'd gone back to, he went into hiding. Relations, money, wine stocks—we'll shake all that off. That's what the philosopher thought. He didn't escape, as you know; he didn't escape. And as for me, I don't care even if I do escape somehow. I really don't, you know. My indifference is harder than diamond! It is a diamond indifference, sir, harder than the heart of His Majesty the Chief Scriptwriter, hidden everywhere, never to be found. Everywhere and nowhere, a fine old trick."

He had suddenly opened the window. The darkness rushed in— swift, perfumed, cunning. A sudden lashing. The professor tottered, raised himself up, and took his guest by the shoulders.

With an air of boredom he had gently pushed him toward the door, into the night. And that had been only yesterday.

"You're back?" the library blonde murmured in astonishment.

Pensioner Matei Gafton gave a smile of complicity. He was a regular customer, as they say. But although he spent much of his time at the library, he hesitated to give any explanation. "Yes, I've given up the idea of going home. I'd only disturb my wife, who'll be giving private lessons there until this evening. And my friend and neighbor was out looking for the Great Scriptwriter." The reader smiled at his own joke, happy to be back with the joys of reading.

"I had a bit of a rest in a park. It's an aggressive spring, I'd say," added the distinguished reader, timidly and conspiratorially, as he went toward his usual place at the back, beside the window.

Soon, therefore, columns of books and old newspapers were rising high on Mr. Matei Gafton's desk.

The Activity of the Ministry of Internal Affairs under the Regime of Marshal Ion Antonescu, published by the Dacia-Traian National Society of Book Publishing and Graphic Arts, 1943; the *Decree of October 1940 on the Reorganization of Romanian Sport;* the *Decree of October 1942 on Propaganda, Danger, and the Existence and Interests of the State,* 1940, 1942, 1943; *Romanianization commissioners, penalties for high treason, death for deportees who surreptitiously return to Romania.* Yes, it was all there. The *decree prohibiting marriage with foreigners or Jews;* the *Graziani Trial; the introduction of harsher penalties for high treason and espionage,* to which he had settled down; the *Appeal of 65 Romanian intellectuals to Ion Antonescu in April 1944 for the withdrawal of Romania from the war.* And then, of course, there were the papers and, oh yes, the books. The librarian already knew the menu.

But the studious pensioner did not feel like doing any more research that afternoon. Spring was sabotaging his reading and study. The room was deserted—just a few elderly maniacs. He might be considered one himself, with all those index cards and quotations for a work that no one had asked for, expected, or wanted. His head ached. No, he could not do any work today. Let spring take the blame: the restlessness, the migraine . . . a delayed encounter not suitable for captives who have long been broken in. That bewildering upheaval—a mirage in which you could not have any confidence.

Without meaning to, Mr. Gafton put his hand on his forehead to wipe away the perspiration. A whirlwind, yes, an invisible fire in the sky . . . He bent over the open notebook, his mind made up to start writing. "Ethics and justice must be the principles of both the legislation and the life of a new society. Public servants, right from the bottom to the top, should be the first to respect them. Just one example: the package received through the mail a short time ago from a former colleague. Well, I checked the contents against the Argentinian invoice note and some of the items on the list had disappeared." Yes, he recognized the words with a certain disgust. He tore up the sheet and threw it into the wastepaper basket. Here is another full page, the draft of another letter. "As you see, I don't practice anonymity. I take responsibility for my little demands and suggestions. They may be little, but they are important. What depends on us must be corrected, improved. At least what depends on us. I have already informed you of the wretched quality of the elevators bearing the sign ELEVATOR. Well, the day before yesterday . . ."

He was sick and tired of it, he had to admit. And yet he could not give up these beautifully handwritten messages by which he told the world of his existence, perseverance, and failure.

He looked into the distance, no place, before again bending bitterly over the words. "At the pound, dear comrades, they do something that not only animal lovers consider impermissible. By law a period of three days is allowed for owners to claim missing animals. The only way of knowing whether an animal is in captivity is to visit that institution. But entry is prohibited, and in vain do people stand at the gate waiting to pay the fee to recover their missing creature. Comrades, this defiant trampling on the basic right to . . ."

IT WAS LATE AFTERNOON when Dr. Marga heard about the article in the popular weekly.

The patients had gone out onto the hospital grounds. The doctor was sitting on a bench. He took off his glasses, rubbed his forehead, undid his smock, and tried to relax.

His thin stripe of black beard dripped with perspiration. He wiped it with a handkerchief. He tried to forget his tiredness. He crossed his short arms over a jutting belly and stretched out on his back. His hands were soft, his shoulders, too, but his short legs turned leaden. As he unwound, he gave himself up to a sweet dizziness.

His assistant brought a mug of cold tea and a paper cornet full of tablets. The doctor again passed his palm over his beard and put on his smoky glasses. He swallowed the fistful of tablets and slowly sipped some tea.

"You're exhausted," she said. "You're much too hard on yourself."

"Too hard—huh! We manage, as they say."

"You smoke too much. You eat any old how, and you don't get enough sleep. You must know that the heart . . . You have no right. You break all the rules, like a patient who doesn't have a clue."

"Ah, but I do know. Suddenly is the best way to go."

A long silence followed. The wily, hypnotic breeze; a long, invisible peacock's tail in the pale sky. Yes: the buzzing of mayflies, the insurgent spring with its mad provocations, as if coming from another age, another world.

The assistant was contemplating the sky, not looking at the doctor.

"Let me read you something so you can see how far things can go."

Her short hands, with fingers laden with rings, took the magazine from under her arm and opened it up. Marga did not seem to be listening. But the woman's voice became stronger and stronger.

" 'Those who tried to do something were abused by the hooligans. The forces of order were alerted . . . They arrived on the scene, advised everyone to calm down, and went away.' Did you hear that, Doctor, they 'advised.' As if . . . ? What more is there to say? Listen to some more: 'The wrecking of the apartment continued. The militiamen returned, again appealed for calm, and went away.' Did you hear? They 'appealed' . . . 'The representatives of order returned a third and last time. The gang left only when they grew bored and tired.' "

Marga seemed not to have registered when the voice came to a halt. The woman waited impatiently for some effect. The voice had indeed stopped, but the listener did not react. He seemed to be dozing. No, he wasn't dozing.

"I think we've got a guest," the doctor was heard to whisper.

Coming up the drive was a petite lady in a brown costume. She had a deliberate way of stamping her feet as she walked. The nurse recognized her at once, of course, but continued to read without paying her any attention. " 'Incredible, but that is how things happened. In broad daylight, under the eyes of a whole neighborhood and—' "

But the doctor had already stood up. He arranged his glasses on his nose so that the missing eye could not be seen and smiled. The young lady also smiled as they shook hands. The assistant looked up from the page for a moment and went on with a certain irritation.

" 'As we write these lines, such-and-such apartment . . . in such-and-such street . . . looks like after a bombing raid, a fire, or some natural disaster' . . ." The plump assistant, Ortansa, turned to the doctor without looking at the visitor. She pursed her thick, heavily painted lips.

"Remember, the victim ran from her home! The newspaper people say she's sleeping at friends' and relatives'. The victim is afraid that the attack will be repeated . . ." It was not clear whether this information was in the text or was a personal addition.

"So that's what things have come to! It looks as if we'll now have the poor woman as a client. It's the victim who comes to us, not the crazies who wanted to set her on fire. They've nothing to worry about, you know. No one locks up the really mad ones, as they should." By now she was in a fury. She looked at the two nonchalant listeners as if they were implicated in the affair, encompassing them in a more general discontent.

She leaned across the bench and picked up the saucer, teacup, and empty cornet. But then she remained there with them in the lap of her smock. She sat down, spread out, looked at the thin violet clouds, and smiled. Twilight, clouds chasing through the spring sky. But the doctor did not seem to notice, having eyes only for the newcomer. Irina understood, smiled. He took her gently by the shoulders and guided her toward his office.

A long, twisted day, a day that turned her to the point of dizziness. A few times she had felt the need to collect herself in the quiet of a church, but in the end she found herself in Marga's office. It had still been morning when Irina arrived at the bus stop, under the sway of a refrain whose jarring time induced a kind of idiotic trance. *From the point of view of death . . . point point point . . . point of maximum vision, the perfect clear lucid night, the absent dead, like the living . . . the fixed end point, illumination and blindness.*

The words returned as a magic spell. A kind of senile impulse, a barely visible point, returning, returning, both extremity and center at the same time. Illumination and blindness, yes, a phosphorescent needle of nothingness, the perfect clear night, the absent dead like the living. Yes, that was it.

Sounds—thick delicate garrulous voices, bubbling. Somewhere, far off, she heard the theater of the world. Trucks, trams, wheels whipping the asphalt with a roar, anarchic voices, a traffic policeman's whistle, a tin can turning somersaults, an ambulance siren, the muffled hysteria of people lining up for newspapers and potatoes and toilet paper and aspirin.

She opened her eyes: a drowsy convoy of children from a kindergarten was lining up at a crossing near the park.

A daytime creature, that's what I used to be. Night scared me. A cunning and barbaric swamp. I used to be sunny and earthly, ready to clutch at anything visible, alive . . . When oh when did everything change? Now I'm completely given over to the night, my only refuge. The time and geography of night have replaced my days. Now, in the midst of a torrid blindness, it would not even be possible to recognize my face.

The traffic lights had changed from red to green. The children's column moved off. Little smiles, hands tightly squeezing one another. The stocky woman teacher gave the signal for singing to begin. A long, thin babbling, drip drip, soft, weary, anaesthetized. A sleepy convoy of tottering shadows.

Irina again shut her eyes, violently pressed the lids, reopened them. She crossed the road and walked up the paved slope toward the park. She sat down on the first bench, under a vaulting arch of branches.

She took the newspaper from her pocket and opened it: *Viaţa Noastră*, the national newspaper of the Association. She could not take her eyes from the red-lettered banner that she had known for years, or from the slogan above it: *Workers of the world, unite!* It was printed in every paper and magazine in the country, in every office, school, or hospital, seen countless times without ever being seen. This time she read the clarion call, once and once more—as if she were experiencing for the first time its urgent, vigorous meter that demanded a response. What would happen if . . . ? She woke up, murmuring in amusement. Unity, urgent unity. What if . . . ?

"The complex tasks of the Association. Directives and guidelines of the General Secretary concerning the role of the mass organizations and state institutions in implementing the general policy."

She turned the page: the cheap paper nearly crumbled; the ink was already dirtying her fingers.

"The title of the Association's best locksmith. Homage to the beloved leader. The celebration of labor. The photographer emeritus of the Association. The training of members in the spirit of socialist ethics and justice." She moved on to the next page. "Two decades since the Ninth Congress. Professionalism and integration of the disabled into production." And on and on. "Relations of friendship and cooperation with similar associations in other countries. Football championship at the Association of the Disabled. The spirit of socialist ethics and justice. The struggle for peace and the broadening of external relations. The testing of defective pupils. Demands of the socialist economy. The protection of labor. Photographic exhibition at the Association's Jubilee. Integration of the disabled into production. Homage to the beloved leader . . ."

A kind of drowsiness took hold of her—torpor, lassitude, a lazy, slothful sourness. She would have liked to put her palms on a holy wall to feel its coolness, to ask: "Are we worse than the rest?" and then to keep waiting for the echo of the empty words. Yes, she would have liked to glue her palms together on a hermitage wall and to pose unanswerable questions. But she woke up to the sound of voices close by.

"A hyena, that's what she was, bombarding the director with hundreds of demands, screaming at meetings that he was betraying the working class. Jesus, what a demagogue! And then, just two days before the annual holiday, he called her in. He was like a wounded bull. You're worse than Tunsoiu, he shouted at her . . . You don't know Tunsoiu? She was promoted a long time ago to the ministry. An illiterate, a careerist—she used to send people to do her shopping and asked for little gifts, and she took money from anyone . . . And that's what he shouted at her: You're worse than Tunsoiu! I helped you, saved your family life, promoted you up the ladder, defended you against complaints, sent you abroad, buried that story with the driver. But you turned your office into a filthy hole, a public toilet, where anyone could throw up when they wanted to. The screaming could be heard out in the corridor."

Irina crouched motionless over her handbag, as if she had not sensed the young ladies sitting down near her. Nor were they aware of her, so taken up were they in discussing the story.

They did not sound unpleasant. The nearer of the two women seemed to have a wave-like, rippling voice. The one on the other side of the bench had a strong, deep timbre, and Irina imagined her in sweater and jeans.

"So the director shouted: 'Out! Get out, do you hear?' After that I think he got scared, too. After all, Bretan does represent the Party. That's what she presents herself as: the Party. You could say it was very courageous to kick her out. But things could turn out badly; we could really be up the creek."

Irina slowly stood up and walked away. The little sparrows fell quiet. "Are we worse than the rest?" the void was ready to ask her. Yes, she would have answered, and then she would have said no, not knowing which of the two replies was the sadder, and she would have ended up with a Don't know harsher than either and recalled the impious games of the ant heap: the production of butter, the riveting of boats, the stitching of uniforms, dancing, speeches, hair-pins bicycles wigs records ties trains tins bras guns cards, the inventive competition of human futility.

"Ooh-oo, Irina! Long time no see!"

A man tapped her on the shoulder.

Irina was leafing through a guide to medical plants at a street bookstall. Old cures, seeds and herbs.

He was tall, beardless, and pale. Thick lips, large nose, a spreading bald patch, glasses. A cocoa-colored suit, coffee tie, milk-white face.

"But I don't remember you wearing glasses then," she mumbled in confusion.

Ştefan Olaru, top of his year in the engineering faculty, an ambitious man whose hard work and application won him the first place that should have been someone else's, but that someone else was too careless and disorganized. So Ştefan, shortened to the diminutive Fănică, had lived first with tiny Laura, for whom lovers still came to blows, then briefly with Nora, and then, surprisingly, had married Salomeea, a lanky maiden who quickly turned out for him a couple of myopic, podgy babies, and whom he then left for a young handball-playing engineer, beautiful, solid, lustful, and after her no one really knew. Fănică the vain—industrious and efficient. Who knows, maybe he had managed to turn his qualities to advantage.

That's right, they had not met since they were quite a bit younger, and she remembered Tolea and the doctor and Gafton and the lunatic who still visited her dreams.

"Still reading?" the man observed with a bored air. "You haven't changed at all. Isn't it supposed to be a sign of unhappiness?"

Irina put down the pamphlet she was holding, let him look at her, looked at him attentively.

"Have you got over unhappiness, then?" she asked in turn.

"Not quite! But I stick to the classics. As for the new lot, I can't make head or tail of them. Life is simpler—much simpler. It asks and gives. A clear code."

"Has it given to you? You seem content."

"There you are, you can use the big words, too! It comes from reading. But what does all that mean—content or discontent? After all, we're intellectuals, aren't we? Do you want me to complain that I've got an ulcer or that I can't find any meat or cheese or needles? Or that like everyone I've spent the winter in an unheated apartment? No lemons or toilet paper, crowded buses? Is that what you want us to talk about? Well, I'm sorry, I won't stoop so low. You see, intellectuals still haven't understood that . . ."

Irina smiled. She thought Fănică had forgotten that a moment earlier he had been speaking in the name of that dishonorable category. But Fănică realized at once.

"A contradiction? You think I contradict myself too quickly? Well, there's no contradiction, you know. The number of educated people has grown enormously here. The peasants and workers have changed, thanks to machines. And what are intellectuals really nowadays? Doctors, engineers, lawyers, teachers, political organizers. Don't laugh: yes, political organizers today also belong to that category . . . So all these are intellectuals! And not the characters who jabber away in cafés. It's an important new class which regulates the activity of society. So what can I say? I do interesting work, things are nice at home, what else—shall I start whining?"

Fănică seemed to move even closer, so as to be more convincing.

"I've also done quite a bit of traveling. Five years or so ago they started sending me all over the place. I've seen what people are like over there. Sure they've got food and cars and contraceptives. But they're not any happier, you know! Their happiness is in bad shape, believe me! At least we've got decency here—and that's a precious quality! Of course, I'm not saying it's hunky-dory here; I know why you're smiling. But we haven't lost our decency! And what isn't possible isn't possible. Life is short. Look, we'll whirr around for another ten years or so and then phhh! that's the end of us."

Irina was fascinated. She looked at him with the clear wide-open eyes of a calf.

"Surliness, hm, yes. Look at those surly ones." Comrade Ştefan Olaru pointed to a group of people in front of the bookstall, to the street, the world, the universe. "Yes, and you're pretty surly, too! Why is that? Do you believe in the generations to come? And do you think that what they're like depends on a clean conscience? Here and now! That's the only proper code, you know."

Irina looked at her watch—ah, she'd forgotten, she wasn't wearing one.

She smiled, blinked rapidly, with new life. She no longer feared Fănică's questions. "Things are nice at home!" "Intellectuals, political organizers." "It asks and it gives, here and now, phhh, that's the end of the generations to come . . ."

Fănică baby didn't care. His code wasn't new and he wasn't the only one to invoke it.

But Mr. Ştefan Olaru suddenly became hurried. He consulted his watch, he had things to do—of course, he was also wearing a watch. For a moment he continued to rock from one foot to the other. "You mean I've joined the upstarts?"

She had to, didn't have to answer—who was to say?

"It's more interesting, believe me. I don't like losers, declassed types. It's much more interesting on this side of the hierarchy! Not just more profitable. More interesting."

Irina rejoined the flow of the street. Old people with shopping bags, schoolchildren dressed in slickers, policemen in and out of uniform, housewives racing from shop to shop, line to line, urchins concealed in passageways, the hot dusty air of the daily gallop. Bulldozers, cranes, excavators. Everywhere the city was being demolished, everywhere invaded by caterpillar tracks, thudding blows, and the noise of collapse. Thick smoke and black clouds from the tar works, gray waves of dust from the cement trucks. The constant roar, the prefabs and pipes, the designs for collective happiness.

Irina lost herself among the neighborhood blocks, in a cloud of smoke and odors. She was struck by the inscription in front of a brick building. Yes, this was where she had dreamed of finding herself—in front of this door, in front of this inscription. She read and reread the inscription on the gold-plated rectangle. VETERINARY CLINIC. She glued her hands to the cold wall and remained with her eyes shut for a long time. Then she opened them again and saw a wide-open door. She went in. Completely deserted. She moved along to the end of the corridor, then came back. She pressed on the handle of the first door to her right and entered a long room. Two rows of large kennels—dogs. She had time to glimpse a doleful setter, cowering, with its chin covered in festering red sores. She turned toward the door and came across the housekeeper. The woman had been watching her all the way from the front door, with her hands on her hips. Fleshily built, wearing a white coat and slippers.

"Have you come to a patient?"

A strange formulation, and it did not seem either ironic or hostile. She was almost an old woman. Large black eyes, white curly hair.

"No . . . I . . . just to . . ." Irina tried to smile as she took a step back.

"Dr. Pompiliu isn't here; he's at a congress. He'll be back on Friday. If you have an appointment for—"

"No. I just wanted to—"

"Well, please come into the office," the older woman decided. She had already moved on ahead. She seemed to have a limp, or perhaps she just staggered a little as she walked. She went into a third room. The visitor read on the door: DR. VETA APOSTOLESCU, UNIVERSITY TEACHER.

The woman went to the far end of the office, where she bent over and put on a pair of spectacles. So not the housekeeper but . . . The academic made a sign for her to enter.

"Have you got a problem?"

What could she invent, what should she ask? About the disabled best friends of disabled man, mute, deaf, deaf-mute?

"How quiet it is here! Are those saintly dogs really mute?"

"No, no . . . they're just drowsy. It's the drugs. They suffer. And we've got thick walls, so you can't hear any barking. Otherwise—"

The pause grew longer. Fog. Some filament had to be switched on. Anything at all.

"Are there such things as mute dogs?"

The academic straightened her glasses. She looked with suspicion at the uninvited guest who was so keen on talking.

"Why are you interested?"

Irina, confused, took some time to answer, and her very hesitation produced a miracle. The doctor became considerate, ready to help if—

"Tell me, tell me what has happened."

"Well, I work at—how shall I put it?—I work at the Association. But that's not really the point. I can't think how to—A friend of mine. That's what it's about—friends. Friends used to speak of such a case. Maybe from birth, or perhaps something had happened—"

"A mute dog, you're saying?"

"Well, sort of. I think that—or maybe she was wrong, I don't know. Is it possible?"

The university doctor stared her in the eye. The pause was so long that she seemed to have lost any desire to answer. "There is a type like that. In Australia."

Irina remained silent. So did the elderly vet. Nothing could be heard from the drugged dogs, but then the building had thick walls.

"The dingo dog," resumed the academic.

Another long pause, until the veterinary apostle Apostolescu decided to offer a short lecture in popular science. The star Veta looked bored, as if she was reciting a long-familiar text. Veta of all people! Looking down from the moon on a simple-minded little ninny who did not have a clue about the basics. "It's a mute dog, but it has very good hearing. At first a normal domestic dog, it turned wild and soon multiplied in the huge spaces of Australia. It's a ferocious beast—a creature of the outback. It doesn't bark: it doesn't make a sound as it lies in wait for its prey, in total silence." Veta was sternly and distrustfully watching her audience, not at all convinced that it was worth the trouble. But she seemed unable to resist the pleasure of giving instruction.

"Such ferocity isn't found even among wolves. It kills even if it is sated. Two dogs can kill a thousand sheep in one night. A thousand! Without making a racket. It doesn't bark. It lies in wait, attacks and kills without making a noise. It suffers in silence and dies in silence."

So there were cases of mute dogs, then—perhaps because of specially hostile circumstances? At certain times and places, things might happen to man's best friend which— Could the friendly doggie carry a disease or condition which— But Irina did not want to keep adding to the possibilities, especially as Veta was calmly continuing with the lecture.

"Research is being carried out on the dingo in special reservations. If the dog is removed at birth from its habitat and placed under different conditions, it develops normally without any murderous tendencies. I mean, more or less normally. It becomes an extremely submissive dog. Yes, they can be tamed if they are taken from the wild. They display a mute, submissive tameness. Quite shattering!"

Oh yes, I see, mumbled the visitor, yes, of course; Irina went on nodding in accompaniment, yes, yes, the old woman confirmed, yes yes, when she had already begun to slide back along the corridor toward the door, to the repetitive stuttering refrain that matched the rhythm of her steps.

She could hear the old woman's spectacles dropping, probably onto the glass surface of her desk. It was a glassy gloomy sound, yes, a silver xylophone, and suspicious little whimpers and the harsh sound of spectacles on desk glass. Thinned kettledrums, .clink clank, the spectacles, the knife, the silvery night breeze: yes, Irina walked away from the brick cube enveloped by the soft perfumed waves of darkness, but it was still daylight, powerful and aggressive, with thousands of ravenously open mouths and holes.

At some point she reached the city center. A tram rattled into the stop on Rosetti Boulevard. The step was too high and her dress too tight. In irritation she gave a little push on her leather handbag, straining and clinging to the bar, and she was up.

The tram was nearly empty, just a few passengers. In front, a disheveled, scabby-cheeked young man was reading a magazine, all the time making agitated movements with his legs. She put her hand to her throat, closed her eyes as in a dizzy faint, and wiped the sweat from her cold brow. When she opened her eyes again, the young man had vanished. Probably he had got off, although the crumpled magazine was still lying on the seat in front. Without realizing, she picked it up automatically with a rapid, absurd movement of her hand. Her eyes met the sensational headline: the first few sentences lashed out at her and immediately vanished; all she could see were a few traces. As if the tracer fire had left behind only discontinuous signs, which still pulsated like a red lightbulb. "In the morning the female tenant of the apartment . . . Climbing the balcony, the windows . . . broke into the house, tied the woman up, pulled out the telephone . . . Under the balcony they lit a bonfire . . . The tenant, her cats, fists, fighting . . . The broken windows, the fire . . . the bound woman, her burned cats . . ." The words became real as soon as she spoke them to herself.

Words—their sharp, vigorous presence. Sunday, March 8, 9:30 a.m., the attack on the apartment in such-and-such street, the fire, the roughing up of the cats and the pensioner. A moment in the life of the magazine, in the life of the world. Was it just a snapshot from the onslaught of spring, unchained force attacking a chained object nearby? A certain meeting on a certain day in a certain tram car, just as the new trance, spring, was bursting with excretions and aromas.

She managed with difficulty to remove her hand from the back of the seat. She got off at the next stop and made her way, shivering, on foot to Dr. Marga's. An hour of rambling talk, as between friends. That was how people discussed with Marga, perhaps because in the end his profession was also friendship, nothing else. She left feeling tired, relieved, secluded from the world.

A gray film floated over the day's agony. Before her opened the welcoming seas of the night, which gives us the forgiveness we have been seeking, and gives us back our selves. A fine dust settled on her eyes and lips. Suddenly that shudder, that shaking of her shoulders, as if the crust that had kept growing in the course of the day were now breaking up with a thin, silvery sound.

She really did shake, as if being set free. Her shoulders jerked from the currents of chill night air. She crossed her arms in an effort to gather strength for the prancing void of the night, for its extremity of illumination and blindness.

Finding herself right in the opening of a metro station, she went down the steps. A concrete grotto with a neutral geometric plan. The red signal came on. The train glided smoothly into the station; its doors drew open.

What a day, ooh, what a day!

But she did manage to find her way to the refuge.

Gradually she shook off the weight of the strange day as if extricating herself from a suit of armor. Recovering the right to become alive with a secret dimension of your own. In other words, real—which is to say alive, again alive. Oh, joyful pain of the great and good night, give us back to ourselves.

A VIOLET SKY. A bluish silhouette with a pack of whelps. A bitch's head, if you looked closely enough; it was nothing other than the oblong head of an angry bitch chasing the night sky, followed by clouds coming from all sides and covering the nocturnal sea. And somewhere, sometime, the ghost of the murdered father, forty years ago.

His hand trembled on the cup's enamel rim. Tolea gripped the handle, lifted it slowly, and took a sip. The coffee was cold, as usual, having been left for hours in the pot until whenever. As if he were not alone: as if he felt around him the presence of Marcu Vancea, who had been killed or committed suicide forty years before. It had already happened to him several times; it was happening more and more often that he saw him, felt him nearby.

As they head for death, so do I head with them for death: that's the premise. To see how I and my fellow countrymen present ourselves at the moment of the supreme embrace. One appointed morning, when you no longer hope for anything and you suddenly rediscover nature in its boundless indifference. One appointed morning of glistening spring, when we forget for a moment the guardians' faces and the dirty streets and souls, and we lift our eyes to the empty golden sky.

Finally at peace—happy, and free from the panic of our tiny cell. Then, bang, heart attack, surprise! The murderous fraction, the last tangent, the end of it all.

It is night, creative night. At last the action is going to start! He knew it would be a highly ambiguous action, Operation Spring.

All at once the gentle night breeze enveloped him. He suddenly remembered Toma the pursuer. Miserable informers are not even servants of the devil: they don't have such a high rank, no, they're just fish in the swamp called the present. Wretched fish in the swamp, with souls and diseases and fears and pleasures of the swamp. What can his mission be, in fact, that mask called Toma? Why does he appear when you are not expecting him, after days on end of expecting him all the time? Is this a race of barbarians? Are the barbarians coming at last, as the old man Cavafy whispers? They will come because they came and multiplied a long time ago, gradually occupying not only the tumbledown fortress but the souls, diseases, and fears of the mice population. And the barbarians never stopped coming, never stopped interfering with the honorable rodent citizens. That is what the barbarians and their barbarianized prisoners became—a huge mass of hungry, cunning mice ready for the great fiestas of collapse. All of them attracting attention, with a scar wrinkle at the tip of their eyebrows. A barely visible sign in which one could read the tic of a sly and degenerate species—the winking of an eye.

At some point he finally fell asleep, lost in the oneirosphere of night.

The airplane rocks gently, and the man gently leans over to his left toward the little window. The seats vibrate slightly; a brief current of alarm shudders through the plane's metallic pike-belly. The passengers look at the distinguished tourist, as if his behavior is the real test of how the flight is going. They look excitedly at their watches and then worriedly at one another. But the elegant foreigner does not show the least sign of unease. He looks at his neighbor, a slim, dark young man with an inoculation-type scar by his left eyebrow. He stretches out his hand toward the little table fixed to the back of the seat in front. But the stewardess leans over to serve him herself. In a long voile dress, with a silver tray in her hands. Naked beneath the purplish voile. Long white hands. A bronze bust, red lips. Rings of violet facepaint. She bends toward the turkey ear of the tourist. The voile dress flutters. Glossy breasts with their pea-mouth in the middle. But the senator appears not to notice. He smiles into infinity, listening enraptured to its music in the head-phones placed over his ears.

Tolea is awake, has drifted off, asleep again, who knows.

The city was in darkness. Dirty winding little streets now swallowed up in obscurity. Just some dim yellow blots in the distance. Sick orbs of a sick city sunk in nightmares.

Silence. Now and then the steps of guards sound with their metallic cadence. Occasionally the night toxins can be heard in the sighs of a drunk, like the bubbling of a diver stuck in the thick oil of a bottomless crater.

Riotous, chaotic groans, a short green flame, cursing and alcohol. And again the unlit silence and the hobnail boots rhythmically striking the asphalt. The darkness grinds its teeth as rays of light suddenly spring up. Metal plate, wheels, and screws are banged; there is a massive sickly noise of something starting up. The monster moves off: its headlights sway in the thick black ocean. The crippled truck lurches about and noisily fills the desert—a gigantic deformed savage moving unsteadily forward, breaking up the darkness bit by bit. The edge of a rusty roof. Thickets of rubbish. The handlebar of a bicycle. A doorway with a broom resting on its handle. Another door, with a statue. The statue glimmers for the twinkling of an eye. The door is framing the nude, the statue. Under the golden stream is the man's naked body. Large forehead, metallic pate. It's Dominic, it's Tolea, it really is! The driver wakes up properly; his hands tremble as they clench the steering wheel. He looks back to catch another glimpse of the phantom. Yes, the vision is still there: a naked man in the doorway. And it is Mr. Dominic, that scatterbrain from Hotel Tranzit! Quiet unmistakable. The appearance of the noisy vehicle does not disturb him. The driver brakes, stops, and switches off the lights, so as to recover his senses. The street disappears. The same endless silence. He turns the ignition key again: the engine starts up, the lights come on. As the rattletrap moves off, the driver nervously rubs the wart at the corner of his eyebrow.

There is a crackling of levers, metallic claws, and screws, a bursting of air bubbles, brass tools, and springs.

The dinosaur moves slowly backward, crawls over to the curb on its right, and finally completes the reversing maneuver. It goes back along the lifeless street, then stops. The door is wide open. But there is nobody in its old wooden frame!

The driver strains his eyes as he looks through the dirty cabin window. No, there isn't anyone in the door. After switching off the engine and lights, he lies there in wait . . . But Dominic is no longer in the doorway. Dominic is asleep, naked, on the narrow sofa. He tosses about as he dreams that the driver is lying in wait, and sweatily tosses about in an attempt to escape. Two thin phosphorescent streaks—that's all. The driver can no longer be seen—only the two luminous lines of the driver's phosphorescent eyes follow him from afar, from the cabin of the truck. He is there at a distance, watching with stubborn hatred, nervously stroking the weird sign at the corner of his eyebrow.

The city is desolate. The night, the oozing putrefaction. Now and again the measured step of security guards. Or the spasm of an owl striking rooftop aerials. The little electric owls whirr for a long time, with rapid flashes. The rattletrap is swept off somewhere into the pitch-black depths. The air opens enormous black wings and, at the same time, huge nets to collect bats and airplanes and suddenly rejuvenated phantoms. The airplane keeps darting from side to side, to escape the talons following behind it. The inside is clean and functional. Geometry and luster.

The man gently leans over to his left, toward the square of a steamed-up window. Large blue round eyes, giving nothing away. A suit with a white handkerchief in the lapel, a tie, a long wrinkled neck, staring eyes.

The seats shake slightly: anxiety passes thinly among the ranks of the passengers. They all turn to the elegant Westerner, looking for signs of danger in his important face. The tourist is calm and unflurried. The plane rocks gently, and the man again gently leans over to his left toward the little window. Once more the seats vibrate; there is a brief current of alarm through the plane's metallic pike-belly. The passengers again look at the distinguished passenger, as if his behavior is the real test of how the flight is going. They look excitedly at their watches and then worriedly at one another. But the elegant foreigner does not show the least sign of unease. He turns to his neighbor, a slim, dark young man with an inoculation-type scar by his left eyebrow. The spitting image of the stranded truck driver! That prehistoric, batrachian truck, in the slimy shipwreck of the night . . .

Unable to settle down, the passengers fiddle with handkerchiefs and paper tissues, wipe their perspiring brows, crowd into the smoking area, watch out for the few coded gestures of the distinguished guest, and look at their watches as they rub themselves nervously in their seats. The aircraft banks slowly, from right to left, left to right. The elderly gentleman with white hair and expensive clothes leans from left to right, right to left, toward the window, toward his neighbor, again toward his neighbor, but the conversation with his traveling companion, or guardian, cannot be heard. "We are approaching the capital. Mentioned in documents from the fifteenth century, it is a junction of air routes, eight main railway lines, nine through roads." The announcer's voice shows no sign of unease. The travelers appear calmer as their heads obediently straighten. "It is a Romance language of the Indo-European family. The largest port is credited with 40 million tons a year—on the site of the old Greek colonies." The old man again leans toward the humble orderly. He says something to him, but the voice does not take audible shape, as if it is sucked up and destroyed before it can become sound. The young man replies with large hurried gestures, out of keeping with his tight provincial suit and with the guest's rare and slow movements.

"The country is a republic. The President is head of state and commander in chief of the army; he appoints and dismisses ministers and leading personnel in the administration; he establishes the status of diplomatic missions, accredits and recalls diplomats, receives letters of accreditation and recall, establishes the nomenclature of state secretaries and the names of towns, districts, and streets, lays down the citizens' rules of behavior and the system of allowances and retributions, and signs international treaties." The information flowed clearly and decisively; not a sound could be heard other than the firm voice of the announcer. "The stimulated birthrate is 18.6 percent. A majority of the population lives in the lowlands. It is a socialist republic, with a single party. The country's President is also General Secretary of the single party, with 20 percent of the total population. The law prohibits contacts with foreigners. The currency is equivalent to 0.15 rubles and 0.2 dollars. There are universities, libraries, daily press, and radio. And television for four hours a day."

The tourist is voicelessly chattering, while his companion makes gestures of agreement with his hands and eyebrows. Actually, he even seems to say something in reply to the soundless phrases.

"The natural relief is well balanced: one-third mountains, one-third valleys, one-third plains. The rivers radiate outward from the center of the country. There is forest vegetation on a quarter of the surface. A temperate continental climate. Oceanic influence in the west, Mediterranean in the southwest, and continental in the northeast. There are tourist areas in the mountains and by the sea, as well as monuments of feudal art."

The white-haired gentleman stretches out his hand to the little table to the right of his seat, but the stewardess is in position and leans over to offer him the elixir. A silver tray on which brown, yellow, and green glasses are vibrating. A loop of blond curls. Long white hands. A long voile dress. Naked beneath the transparent material. The customer does not appear to notice. The frame banks to the left and the passengers wince in their seats.

"The population first appeared with Bronze Age civilization. Waves of migrating peoples . . . war with the Ottoman Empire . . . rulers from the Greek aristocracy in Istanbul. We are in the proximity of the capital, which has a density of more than ninety inhabitants per square kilometer. Life expectancy at birth: sixty-seven years."

The stewardess, without moving, watches and waits for her client —the elegant senator, pastor, lord, butler, or whatever he is. Wavy white hair, a narrow wrinkled brow, pink complexion, moist eyes, large ears, protruding nose, slightly open mouth, starched collar, dark-red tie, lips measuring out soundless words . . .

Not a sound. Smooth silent flight. Like movement on the spot, in the belly of a silver whale, stone-still in the great aquarium of the sky. The tray with juices, aphrodisiacs, and poisons. White green yellow glasses, but the man from Mars does not notice. The mannequin keeps leaning over, with her naked breasts on the tray and that lightbulb in the middle . . .

The man with a mustache on the pensioner's right cannot take any more. He pulls a yellow square from the pile of cards on his table, holds it up to view so as to jolt the tourist awake, and then turns in irritation to his subordinate.

"He can't hear a thing, girl, and he's left his batteries at home! I'm telling you: his hearing aid isn't working. And God knows why, kiddo, he's on a diet; even tits are out."

But the gentleman does stir and tries to fix the tiny transistor earpieces, to take off the headphones and put on the earpieces. And he does see the bust, yes, he finally notices the statue of Aphrodite— and, of course, he is very interested, he really is; there is a dry gulping sound in his throat, viscous saliva, strangled mumbling, the snake-like tie, and again the soundless battle of the crustacean mouth, until his neighbor understands the command and conveys it to the mannequin, who by now is standing paralyzed, with her breasts on the tray, deafened by the shouts of the man with the mustache. Only she appears to hear them, while the passengers remain impassive and seemingly unaware of anything at all.

"You load of dolts!" shouts the accompanying agent, not just to his guest, but also to the unfamiliar world that he represents. "You're blind, blind as hell! You blind dolts, you stuff yourselves with all that information, all those relays and rockets. But you don't understand a thing! And me? And us? Speechless, sir, quite speechless! The angels have taken away our voice. My bosses have taken mine as well as Lieutenant Aphrodite's, as you can see . . . And all our sleeping people are just waiting for you to come and save them! You, with your flying fortresses and your arrogant chewing gum."

The foreigner nods pastorally, without understanding a word. Yes, the foreigner does look like a pastor. He looks with disappointment at the defective earpieces, which he checks once more without success. The little capsules are now hanging on a golden chain over his impeccable silk shirt front. He smiles with satisfaction and looks contentedly at the glass of milk lying on his table. Milk is what the missionary ordered. Milk is what the maternal agent Aphrodite has given him, and now she is agilely working to point her completely available body toward him—her glossy breasts, her electric button, her hips of gold. The customer smiles as he puts his hand out for the glass of milk. Just as he touches it, the alarm sounds in the aircraft. Gunfire is shaking the walls, the bodies, the seats—enough to raise the dead. An infernal alarm, the end of the world.

Anatol Dominic Vancea Voinov jerks dizzily to stop the inferno. The telephone is right beside his bed. The alarm clock right beside his bed. No, that isn't it. His hand is trembling as it searches for buttons, cutouts, keys. The bell . . . that long tinkling of metal wings, the air, the asylum bells sounding reveille. Yes, it is morning; the windows are shaking from the louder noise of the new day.

TOLEA HAD LEARNED FROM his friend and neighbor Gafton that redundancies were likely in many enterprises. He shrugged his shoulders apathetically. Then he heard that as much as 40 percent of office staff would be affected. He smiled and switched on the transistor lying on the desk of his colleague Gina: Monte Carlo, his favorite station.

Then someone started the rumor that such-and-such a comrade director had already been replaced by another comrade director; that certain networks were being dismantled and new links and combinations established. He looked on impassively at the hysterical reactions of his colleagues at the Hotel Tranzit: the bookkeeper, the barman, the switchboard operator, the cleaning woman were all glued to telephones trying to discover the ins and outs. He raised his eyebrows, in a superior kind of way, when his four-eyed colleague told him the criteria that would be used for layoffs. He merely lifted himself slightly on tiptoe, straightened his colleague's loose tie beneath his made-in-China shirt collar, and went to the window to contemplate the spring fever.

Gina tried to distract him by reading something from the morning papers.

"Listen to this story that happened yesterday. 'On the pretext that in privately owned apartment number . . . on the ground floor of the building there was a dog . . . or several dogs . . . and a cat . . . or several cats.' Well, what do you say?"

Stretched out on the armchair, with his feet perched American-style on another chair, his head on the ceiling, his eyes shut, Tolea did not appear to have heard. Was he meditating, or calculating, or reminiscing? He flicked away the alarming news, like some annoying seasonal insect.

"There now, do you hear? Pretexts. Where are dogs and cats going to have to live now? In the forest, in the wilderness? What do you say? Isn't it well written? Listen: only in forests, on mountaintops and ocean reefs. What are those reefs supposed to be? Yes, it's a strong article. I wonder how it was published."

It may have been at that moment of just-listen-to-thisness that the strange idea flashed into Tolea's mind. The idea of playing a trick— something the public would not expect, something that would liven him up himself. For he was bored: Professor Voinov was bored to death.

In a world where everything seems programmed, even chaos, chance, or surprise, you've got to defy logic and bewilder people. You've got to make the fools believe that you control secret links to which they have no access.

Thought after thought kept passing through the skull of receptionist Anatol Dominic Vancea Voinov, known as Tolea; his brain circuits were working nonstop, in *perpetuum mobile*, and without a doubt it would have been possible to pick up signals from them. Especially as spring—oh yes, it was a real illness, spring, a real onslaught. At last something real and powerful, for which the numbed mice no longer showed any reflexes.

"The instigators—tenants from the block! I ask you!"

The receptionist seemed to have awoken.

Suddenly the word "instigators." Perhaps he had remembered his father . . .

And well, the heir will demonstrate that when all the games appear lost, a new one has to be invented, however bizarre it might seem, however futile it might be. So we are going to do things the other way round, *mon père*, completely the other way! We're not going to commit suicide, *mon père*; no, no, we won't follow your scenario. We'll just study it, act it, face up to it, that's all. Otherwise, without a mission impossible, we won't hold out against the spring or the boredom. Not even against the tedium of multilateral sycophancy.

Tolea jumped up from the armchair, alone at the center of the world, on the great stage with nobody else on it. *Personne, niemand, nikovo.*

"What's the date today, honey?"

Hard to say whether he was speaking to himself or to his colleague Gina.

Anyway, he knew what he had to do. He'd ask for a short holiday. They'd all be flabbergasted. To leave the place of struggle at the decisive moment, when the strings are being pulled and the broadsides delivered, when everyone is trying to save their precious little skin? He'd go to the mountains, solve some crossword puzzles—perhaps also the puzzle of Mr. Marcu, *le père de famille*. He'd go on holiday when no one expects to take one. Such imprudence would show that receptionist Anatol Dominic Vancea Voinov, known as Tolea, has special links; that he's not afraid of the pathetic office workers' neuroses; that he's master of the situation. Meanwhile, already from tomorrow, he'd start to recall all the most unfavorable details of his life story: the bourgeoisified brother in Argentina, the aristocratic Teutonic sister-in-law, even the cosmopolitan exploiter of a father or the sister who had gone back to the Bible, yes, even her.

"I asked you a question, honeybunch. I asked you something, my little chick. I asked you what's the date. What's the date today, sweetheart?"

So, March. Perfect! End of March, a sign of horny Aries. Perfect! Tolea turned the collar of his black shirt, the crease of his black trousers.

"If you can't get what you want, said Terence, want what you can get. Have you heard of Terence, Doña Gina?"

Colleague Gina smiled: she was used to Tolea's larking about. Unlike others, she did not think it was arrogant, not at all; she even rather liked it, really she did.

"And what about Baronius, have you heard of him? The erudite Cardinal Baronius! You must have. In fact, I'm sure you were re-reading him just last week. Do you remember his monumental history of the Church, the *Annales Ecclesiastici*, from 1602? Do you remember how he opens his description of the tenth century? Of course you do. 'Behold, a new century is beginning, known as iron because of its baneful severity, as lead because of the prevalence of evil, and dark because of the dearth of great authors.'"

Tolea stared at Miss Gina as he waited for her to reply, happy that he could have a friendly chat with such a well-educated listener. Her mean-street smile was a fine stimulus for his challenging lectures.

"And the extraordinary Gerbert, Pope Sylvester, what do you think of him, of his Roman imperial idea. Both remembrance and a hope of consoling the great sorrows of the world. *Genere graecus, imperio romanus.* Greek by birth, Roman by empire!—that was the dream they all had. He dreamed of world empire and absolute renunciation of worldly vanity. 'A regime needs poetics no less than maxims of statecraft.' Gerbert, our fantastic friend from Aurillac! Whose legendary knowledge assured him terrible renown as the prince of sorcerers in league with the devil. Do you remember, my little cauliflower? Do you remember the phrases he used in his letters? Cunningly embroidered yet full of love. Full of love, my little frog. '*Dulcissime frater, amantissime.*' Do you remember? *Dulcissime, amantissime . . .*"

And Tolea again adjusted the collar of his black shirt, the crease of his black corduroys, bent forward and . . . evaporated, just like that. Yes, all of a sudden he left his place of work and sighs. He did sometimes vanish suddenly, for one or two hours more or less, to tramp the streets, doze on some park bench, or get up to who knows what tricks.

He had disappeared, then. At some point he may have returned to the side of cherry blossom Gina, in the hall of the Hotel Tranzit. What is certain is that he spent the evening at Dr. Marga's, where he seems to have got drunk after some time; he could no longer re-member whether he had slept there or eventually found his way home—which is to say, to the apartment of his friend Gafton, where he had his own little transit cell.

Anyway, he had slept badly, disturbed by dreams of huge metal-lic birds desperately tossing about in a completely empty space, colorless and noiseless and without end.

He had started in fear at daybreak, to stop the ringing of the alarm clock or telephone. But it had been nothing, after all—just a dream, a nightmare. He did not go back to sleep: the street hubbub was already pouring in, and the windows shook from the noise of buses and trams. He pulled his dressing gown from the back of the door and went up to the window. Right in front of the house, a huge prehistoric truck had broken down and was blocking the traffic. The hooting and braking of cars as they drove around the monster added further to the din. Mere trifles! Nothing could lessen the joy of having once more emerged into the realm of day. For Tolea nights were stupid and tormenting snares best unremembered; he would have liked not to think of them, however many enigmas they might contain. No, they did not exist, they immediately scattered to the winds. Oh, if the new day could be the only reality of his life! Spring, winter, autumn, or summer—it mattered not. If only the night could be a forgotten parenthesis, an aphasiac disorder!

The morning light had dutifully fallen on the sofa's white bed-spread. On the sofa, Tolea stirred the instant coffee at the bottom of his cup. Slowly, slowly . . . Soon, then, once again at the place of atonement. "Hasn't the professor arrived yet?" woodpecker Gina would ask, this morning, too, if Tolea was late. Yes, let him be late: he did not feel at all like hurrying, so he slowly, very slowly, stirred the dark powder at the bottom of the cup. Gina would be arranging the accounts book, the pencils, the stools, the cushion on her chair, the telephone in front of her. Gina drank coffee at work, as everyone did, although it was impossible to buy coffee anywhere. No sooner had she arrived than Gina would disappear behind the office window and return with a freshly filled cup in one hand and her greenish orange dark-red blouse in the other, having forgotten that she was still wearing only a bra. She bent over the books, arranged the pencils, and only after some time pulled the blouse over her shoulders. It was the moment at which she blushed briefly, provocatively.

"Has the professor really not come yet?" the little mouse of an employee would, as usual, be asking as she did up the last button on her blouse. But no one would answer: the good-for-nothings had already donned their blasé masks. Gina, the comrades had decided, should be seen and not heard. Let the little gypsy girl remember her place!

In vain did she try to ingratiate herself by sharing their hostility to the buffoon. "Hasn't the professor come yet?" But their sullen indifference did not allow for such complicity. "Hold your tongue over there. Leave him be—the loony's got his reasons." But if she forgot to point out that he was late, then it would be they who had a go. "Ah ha, our little wanderer is in for some big trouble! He can forget all his connections, all his bird talk, all his airs and graces. That won't do him any good. They're going to start checking up on him—his relatives abroad, his bourgeois family background, not to mention the windbag's own present life. And as for his morals, we know enough about our colleague's little foibles. We know about acts punished by the law. By the law, no less!" That was Titi, of course, starchy and oblique, with his delicate silver glasses and bony face, now thrilling to the subject. Corkscrew Titi, as he was called—but in the end less dangerous than the taciturn and seemingly tolerant Gică "Fatso" Teodosiu. Both passed with their noses in the air around pretty little Gina. Not because they disliked her or had some particular grudge. No, just out of the petty malice of people in a cage. "Watch out: call me when the ones in room 218 come down. Keep 33 reserved for me until three o'clock. No one goes into 105, not even for cleaning.

When Olimpia comes with the coffee bags and the cartons of Kent, put everything to one side. You don't ask anything, and you don't pay a cent. I'm at the head office from ten to eleven. If anyone asks, I'm in a meeting. Unless it's Comrade Pastramă—in which case let me know at this number." The day at work: adapting to necessity; the torments, the humiliation, and above all the equivocation. A cheerful and ugly equivocation, so you can swallow the shit and forget who's watching your digestion—and your mark of contentment, so you forget about Titi and Gică and Gina.

Tolea had left the bathroom and was lying on the sofa with a book in his hand. He prepared his role, working out the bits of impertinence and the quotations that would irritate his colleagues at the Hotel Tranzit. Maybe someone had brought a bottle of whiskey for Comrade Teodosiu. Perfect: well, Gică old man, a comrade left that smoky bottle for you. Or maybe the optician Corkscrew had arranged a room for some boss man or other. Perfect: at twelve he'll be coming with a slim little lady in a red silk dress; fine, no one will disturb them; fine, we won't interfere—see nothing hear nothing say nothing. But we'll drive you nuts with Terence and Baronius and Otto III. The Saint: the idealistic politician. "In turn he offered to Romans the spectacle of his holy majesty and the aspiration to complete solitude in a hut of clay and reed." The Holy See, electric chair, apocalypse . . . twilight of the world . . . *mundus senescit.* And love, of course: the reign of love on earth, for a thousand years, *frater, dulcissime frater,* a thousand and one years, *amantissime.*

His neighbor Gafton had gone into the bathroom: he could hear Matei Gafton coughing and grunting. "Under the formidable pressure of the vast nomadic hordes . . . people had to go among the Romans to find safety and even food . . . We must admit the benevolence and even wisdom of the emperors who accepted those nomads . . . what historians call the infiltration of the barbarians." Recite that to the barbarians? "*Fruges, non viri,*" as brother Gerbert,

the dulcissimus, said. "The fruits of the earth, yes, but not people"—
that's the kind of aphorism that should interest Corkscrew and
Gina, yes, or rather there's room for speculation about such nonsense, really there is; brother Gerbert, *amantissimus*, has a head full
of dross and long rigmaroles. He threw down the book and put on
his black corduroys and black shirt: his uniform. That was how he
appeared at the Hotel Tranzit: in work uniform. That is, in mourning clothes. He had several pairs of trousers and ten or so black
shirts: they could be made of cotton, linen, jersey fabric, silk, so long
as they were black. That was how Professor Anatol Dominic Vancea
Voinov reported for work at the Hotel Tranzit reception.

He put on the black overalls as if they were a suit of armor. Yes,
that was it. At least that was left, the defiance, and he did not complain that that was all it was—of course not. Night had scattered—
that was the real victory. The calendar was made up only of days,
coming one after the other. Night was a shapeless swamp, mere
nothingness, a black hole. Thank God he had escaped again. You
can never be sure you'll reach the frontiers of a new day. What a
wonderful event was the day—oh yes, Don Dominic Vancea was
ready. The story was beginning again: the cacophony, the miracle of
the day would be returned to him. Dressed in black, freshly shaven,
head gleaming like the polar moon, hands in his pockets, lips pursed
to whistle. "Disillusionment itself is a fire, and reality is a waking
dream. The good luck to die before the death of one's passions"—
yes, Maître d'Aurillac, that's right. A dry brow, upright and solid like
that of a Roman senator. Roman the baldness, and the eyes as well.
He's at the door, ready to leave. He takes the key from his pocket,
along with a large red handkerchief. In his black work clothes, and
in his white clothes of idleness and life, a handkerchief is always
included. Preferably red. White, black—sometimes a white one, a
black one. But 5 percent red, as nature requires. Nature and aes-
thetics: 5 percent red. He slowly wipes his bald patch. Today, too,

he's late: again they'll growl at him when he arrives. More proof that nothing has changed, that it's all the same, everything in its place.

Everything in place, *dulcissime*, we can leave. Here we go, *amantissime*, we're starting again.

The repeated sound of the bell. No, not the bell. The telephone was ringing. He staggered between chair and table to pick up the receiver.

"Toma. My name's Toma . . ."

Hesitation, then silence. Yes, he remembered the voice, and he also remembered the name of the man who had already tried several times to speak to him. A polite languid young man, this Toma. How's that for the new block manager! As if people didn't know who these double employees are and who they work for.

He had appeared at the door one morning out of the blue. A decent-enough face, a pleasant voice, and by the time you wake up he's already inside—like the ones who wreck apartments and set fire to cats. Polite, smarmy—and that's that, he's got his hands on you, even if you haven't any dogs, cats, or canaries. It's other matters that interest him. "May I come in? And might I bother you for a chat some other time?"

The swine! But now he'd finally given as good as he got, on the telephone. At least now there'd be a day or two of respite. Then the siege operations would inevitably start again. And why? What was the reason for them in the end? Simply because he didn't have any contact with the neighbors? Or because he didn't go to tenants' meetings or paid the maintenance charges six months in advance so as to keep out of the management's way? No, those weren't the only reasons: there must be others, of course there must. That had been obvious at the incident on Saturday evening, when the careful manager, returning home after midnight, had found the lights still on in the ground-floor canteen. He had gone in and headed straight for the table at the back of the empty hall. What are you doing here? Nothing. I'm looking around. Don't you know it's the foreign students' canteen and tenants aren't allowed to use it? I didn't know, but it doesn't interest me either. At this time there's no canteen here: it's an empty hall. And what are you looking at exactly? His tone of voice no longer bore any resemblance to the time when he had tried to cringe and sweet-talk his way to a longer interview. It was the dry, official tone of a guard who has surprised a villain long under observation. And what exactly did you say you were looking at? A long time passed before he replied. I'm looking at the hall. There once used to be a bar here—the Bar Levcenco. During the war and before. The functionary did not seem surprised at what he had heard. He pulled up a chair and was obviously preparing to discuss the matter. But he gawked as the tenant simply stood up and left, without even glancing at him.

Confusion, memories—the ghosts of the Vancea legend, which have been trailing him all the time recently, of which he has been thinking constantly for so many months, which have been summoning him again and again. And now the little flunky of our times, Comrade Manager Toma, or whatever his damned grade is.

He had taken a card from the pile on the table. Cavafy. "For some a day comes when they have to say the great Yes or the great No." Pages, circled text, arrows. His name, Marcu Vancea, crossed out, rewritten, underlined. Monday, Tuesday, Wednesday—nights with their whispers and breakdowns and phantoms, the capricious play of thoughts.

Had Toma's phone call been a joke or a warning? Remember, he appears when you're not expecting him, like the first time. "At once he sees who has Yes within him ready/and saying it thither goes," so warned the Greek from Alexandria. He moved the book from table to nightstand, from there to the top of the radio, then to the sofa. "Why is there this apathy in the Senate? Why do the senators stand

around and not legislate? Because today the barbarians will arrive."
It is quiet: lazy shadows in the playing daylight, emaciated faces
slinking along the dirty, darkened streets. The door seemed to shake.
A pale youth with soft wavy hair. Very long mustache and a timid
smile. Small scar by the eyebrow, thin murmur of a voice.

"You know, I'm Toma."

Let him prove his identity, make him. He was holding a maroon-
colored rectangular piece of cardboard.

"Come on, that's me—it's an old photo."

How old can the picture be of such a young condottiere? He was
already sitting in the armchair opposite, already making his con-
fession: artful, humble, badly paid.

"I hope you weren't angry. I wanted to get to know you. In fact,
you look like an uncle of mine. I haven't got a father: I grew up in
orphanages."

Throw him out? Or just fall asleep, quite simply, overcome by
sloth and disgust, while the professional delivers the aria?

"You know, since I was put in charge of the administration, we no
longer pay anyone from outside: we've got someone who actually
lives here."

A thin, shy voice, small yellow teeth, narrow, anemic cheeks,
with an exaggerated mustache and that inevitable scar.

"I'd like to know about your plans. I wouldn't take advantage, but
I would like us to get together from time to time."

So, just a pathetic angler for humdrum loot. So was he, Tolea,
worth no more than this general-issue snoop? He felt offended—
really! A taste of vomit filled his mouth and nostrils.

From the balcony he could see the dark empty square. Occasionally the jet of light from a vehicle. After midnight complete silence.
The Bar Levcenco, on the ground floor of the block, had died forty
years before, lost in the night that was still swallowing up the city,

decade after decade, slice after slice—the night in which the Vancea
family came back to life and demanded to ask the old questions
itself, the ones from decades ago.

Yes, he already knew the two sequences in which they would
return; ten times he had seen and noted the two scenes.

First sequence: Late August, war. Placid evening, stifling intense
heat. The Vancea family dining room, white with a high ceiling. A
long festive table covered with damask. Eight glittering sets of tableware, three lengthways on either side of the table, and one at each
end. The dinner guests are still in their rooms, where for some hours
they have been waiting for the head of the family to appear. SONIA in
the bridesmaid's dressing room with her magnificent MATUS, the
lame giant. TOLEA is glued to the radio, listening to London. MIRCEA
CLAUDIU is leaning over the head of the icy ASTRID to check the list
of purchases for the wedding.

DIDA is alone in the dining room, worried at the uncustomary
lateness of her ultra-punctual husband. She is alarmed and fears the
worst, but still does not have the strength to talk of the incident she
witnessed the previous evening. And now waiting tensely, ready to
speak—about what? Would she be able to tell them about the legend of her marriage to MARCU VANCEA, about the time when he had
been blinded and struck dumb by the Andalusian apparition with
bitumen eyes and an angular cheek of white marble? The slender
young lady, just by appearing on the scene, had transfixed the man's
heart beyond repair, even though he had long since completed his
erotic apprenticeship. Then the flight to Paris: the garret, acts of
folly, poverty, the library, a doctorate at the Sorbonne, the return,
the first child, the moment when the illustrious scholar decided to
become the owner of a wine depot. Yes sir, what work for the philosopher Marcu Vancea to plunge into—for that serious, elegant,
seductive man, suddenly shaken in all his certainties—and he per-
suaded his brother, Bob Vancea, to leave his hospital, clinic, and
faculty in a hurry and withdraw to a little country hospital lost amid

the snowdrifts and valleys. Maybe as a kind of protection . . . Should she tell them of how the philosopher occupied himself with worldly matters, with raising the children? Of how he tirelessly fed them like a wet nurse, washed and amused them, not just suggesting books and uncertainties? Should she tell them that she herself had always remained a kind of child of Marcu Vancea's?

But who could she tell of that which sometime afterward, at long last, had been canceled out by the dark storm of the present? Tolea had to be kept safe from emotions: after that terrible bicycle accident something had snapped in the once studious and well-mannered adolescent. In vain had Marcu Vancea tried to hide from the boy the consequences of that stupid incident. It was anyway impossible to conceal them: a schoolboy unintentionally hit a confused, half-blind old woman with his bicycle, but the court, well directed by her relatives, decides that the boy must pay huge damages; Marcu therefore has to sell the house he has only just bought. How could she hide such public facts? And how could she burden Tolea now with the panic of the latest news, which he might well see as the sequel to that wretched incident which had suddenly shattered the family's peace and heralded the greater dangers of the approaching years?

She could not even tell Sonia, who by now was too much in thrall to the messianic fantasies of her beloved Matus. Mircea was the only one she should try to tell of what had happened the previous evening—perhaps the evening before, she was no longer sure; or perhaps it had happened on two successive evenings. Yes, Mircea alone would understand and try to do something concrete, straightaway. Should she tell him that yesterday evening the strong, sharp-witted man called Marcu Vancea had suddenly been *old*? Ghostly pale, exhausted. Nothing was left of his perfect armor, his ceremony of controlled gestures, his sparkling eyes and clear voice which, just two weeks ago, had seemed the same as ever, without any hesitation to signal the danger. Yes, two weeks ago, when out of the blue he had introduced a new employee to his wife—a kind of suspicious "deputy," if such a thing is conceivable, a partner even, you'll see, and don't think that those could be Marcu Vancea's words. A *help* for "the more difficult months ahead"—that's how he had put it. Such solutions would never be resorted to! The preliminaries for the annual wine exhibition always found him ready and on top of all the details. But even on the strange evening two weeks ago when he introduced that unlikely "partner"—who looked more like a spy or a guardian that someone had thrust on him—even on that evening full of foreboding Marcu Vancea still appeared unchanged: high forehead without wrinkles, an easy sober bearing, natural steady gestures. But then, also on that evening, Dida noticed a pile of unopened letters and suddenly remembered a series of bizarre signs from the recent period: too many phone calls, unfamiliar voices claiming either to be hurt that they have not yet received an invitation to the exhibition, or to be disgusted that *your dirty business* is working too smoothly, as they put it, "your dirty business in these times of lofty patriotism."

For two weeks, then, Dida had not budged from her husband's side at the depot. She had neglected her home, forgotten about Tolea, Mircea's wedding, and Sonia's agitation, forgotten everything as hour after hour she watched beside Marcu Vancea in order to see and understand. And yesterday evening, or maybe the one before, a client or acquaintance or agent had appeared at some point—it was not clear when, who, or for what reason. Dida had just gone out, and when she returned, no more than an hour later, Marcu Vancea could no longer manage to sign his name. Imagine, he couldn't sign his own name! Bewildered, terrified, covered in perspiration, as he looked at a sheet of paper that he was unable to sign. He no longer remembered his signature. And it was nighttime, getting later and later, and Marcu Vancea was already an old man.

The brilliant doctor of philosophy from the Sorbonne, determined to live through the storm as an obscure wholesale agent for wine—always a necessary occupation and especially in hard times—

and convinced that his brother would survive hidden among the mountains looking after obscure patients, who would give protection because they needed him, even he would not have been able to explain the sudden collapse of his meticulous strategy.

Suddenly an old man no longer able to ward off the inevitable? Just because he had received some kind of dark message? The thought departed and returned—a brief luminescence, the red-hot point of a needle. Yes, she should tell all this to Mircea.

Dida slowly turned in front of the window to face the wedding table. She actually turned to the slow rhythm of the words: yes, Mircea could be told about it. And incredibly she smiled, beaming like a simpleton. As if under a spell, idiotically. So many memories out of season: despair and panic and yet a kind of diffident, fatalistic reconciliation lacking in energy, like a shallow consolation—caught up in the aura of the legend, the secret incandescence, of the magic cavalier who, until yesterday evening, had been her beloved Marcu Vancea; safe from the eyes of the world.

Having turned to face the festively lit room after so many hours of shocked stillness, Dida Voinov met the eyes of Mircea Claudiu himself, the son who had probably been watching for some time, in silence, how she kept pressing the palms of her hands against the window frame, as a last, reassuring physical contact with reality. A bald young man, with long sideburns on a rosy round cheek, could be seen in the edge of the mirror. Short eyebrows, large marshy eyes. Yes, she remembered the boy—a tidy pupil, effortless prize winner, and good at sports. The headmaster had not suppressed his stupefaction: "Our eminent Mircea Claudiu! Just think, madam, he has stolen a classmate's wallet! A handsome sum, my dear lady. It's incredible! Who would have imagined it? Unbelievable!" But the eminent Mircea Claudiu had smilingly admitted it, without a moment's hesitation, looking straight into the headmaster's eyes. Nor were those yet the years of material difficulty that would follow Tolea's bicycle accident, when Mircea had to start working in his spare time as an architect's draftsman because his family could not pay his school fees and expenses.

Yes, and it had been the same unbending Claudiu on the morning when the architect's wife, a friend of Dida's, with makeup over the deep bluish patches under her tigress eyes, had suddenly burst in. The tyrant! she sobbed inconsolably. Dear Mircea Claudiu, the eminent polytechnist whom she literally *adored*, no longer wanted to see her. In fact, he had *belted* her, no less. It had happened before, because she had flouted convention and gone looking for him at friends' houses, bars, and even at the university. Yes, she couldn't help it: she had flouted the convention of *never ever* going in search of him. But the darling lover had *belted* her, thumped her about without saying a word. "Belted," "thumped": strange words in the beautifully arched mouth of the worthy lady, unused to rising early but now rushing so soon after dawn into the arms of the culprit's mother.

The inscrutable son followed his mother with unfamiliar, searching eyes. Should she speak to Mircea Claudiu about the murky happenings of the past two weeks? Or to his icy Astrid, whom he already resembled too much? Dida again turned around slowly, showing her back to the witness as she looked in the direction of the window.

She had accepted the pose only because her beloved wanted children. Indeed, her husband had given his progeny both time and importance beneath the ever perplexed and easily troubled gaze of the beauty who had unenthusiastically given birth to three children and then grown up herself among them as a kind of fourth offspring of Mr. Marcu Vancea.

Where was Vancea? Where had he broken down and why? Where might he be called back from? The sky was no longer anything other than the dull gloomy cloud of the window in which the long-awaited one did not appear. Her son's rapid movements could be heard behind her. Dida realized that Mircea Claudiu was changing jackets to go out, as on every evening, with his haughty partner. Again, she smiled idiotically, lost in the nightmare of the window.

When she again turned toward the festively lit room, another two weeks would have passed. An evening of celebrations, this time on Sunday. The festive table covered with damask.

Second sequence: Without the dinner setting at the head of the table. After the *funeral* and after the *wedding*.

A farewell meal in honor of the young couple, who will leave Bucharest in just a day's time. The young wife cannot bear the Balkan atmosphere of petit Paris, "the garbage and jokes of this drunks' market." That is what the cold Astrid Vancea said, with ruthless sincerity, impatient to return to the civilization of Braşov, which she mentioned by its German name, Kronstadt.

Dense silence. Strong cold light, crystal glasses, silverware, porcelain, stillness of the tomb. *Unity of place, time, and action?* You will each bear another mark of defeat, the dead man had probably thought . . . and his voice was now being heard again. Defeat—that is, the inevitability of fate—which he had kept trying to mollify, buy off, postpone. But Dida Voinov lost track of her own thoughts. A charred statue; the words had died.

A small group of characters, a brief history boiling in the much-heated cauldrons of History, in the soup of planetary slaughter? A dinner setting for the schoolboy Anatol Dominic Vancea Voinov, the timid prisoner of chance. He had been whistling heedlessly above the bicycle's gleaming handlebar when he was struck down by the stupid black scarecrow of chance. The boy had kept twisting his adolescent guilt into knots, until that sudden bang two weeks before which drove him blindly night and day through streets and valleys, sleepless, tireless, on an empty stomach, to find a witness, an answer, an absolution from all that had happened.

A setting for his beautiful sister Sonia, queen of the Bar Levcenco, target every evening of a constant stream of love letters, flowers, visiting cards, coming from every dinner table. A cheerful, incorruptible prey, a kind of exciting lure to the bar, reappearing, laughing, fluttering her black plaits, feverishly dancing until dawn, when she would retire pale as a Shulamite exhausted by triumph and fear.

Until about six months ago, when the lame and witty Matus, skeptical missionary, terrorist, and drunkard, appeared on the scene. Good-natured but with rigid projects that mixed together biblical metaphors and an overwhelming secular, pragmatic vitality. His puerile intoxication and irresistible masculinity were the ruin of the happy little sister, flower of the accursed family, beauty of beauties and angel ready to burn her wings in the newcomer's fire.

Old china plates, heavy silver cutlery, thin crystal glasses: all the decor of *the end*. So that everyone should remember—including the German woman who had recently married the son of the wandering Jew, and also including the adventurer Matus, ready to carry his fantasies and his sweetheart into the hypnotic infinity of the East. They are all celebrating a funeral repast of disintegration, this festive collapse. The proud possession of the moment—that is all we can strive for, poor Marcu Vancea had thought. Already perhaps the seal of defeat was borne by them all, not only by the ghost of the one who had just departed from their midst. Mother, widow, mother-in-law could not recover word or voice, lost in the apathy of the blood-red evening as in a long-awaited amnesia.

Only the bridegroom proved hyperactive, giving directions to the cook, arranging the wife's chair, stroking the mother's hand, smiling to sister and brother, careful to fill the silence with words and gestures, cheerfully and competently holding forth about his future job with the reputed German industrialist from Braşov who had become his father-in-law, about the furnishing of the home (a whole floor given over to the newlyweds by the family of the great Friedrich Wolf), but also about the course of the war and BBC commentaries, about the activity of speculators, martial law, the race laws, the Byzantine ways of the secret police, the cruelties of the Russian winter, the latest gossip about love affairs at the opera, the starvation among the peasantry, the racially motivated deportations, the blackout, the banquets given by the diplomatic corps, the vanity of the marshal dictator, and and—Engineer Mircea Claudiu Vancea Voinov knew everything there was to know.

The post-wedding and post-funeral dinner, prolonged until daybreak by the skill and hard work of the new head of the family, who takes care not to mention the empty place and what everyone has been thinking all the time without saying it.

An empty place, one setting short. The family reunion will drag on, through thick and thin, until daybreak. With difficulty will they gather the strength to break what has long been broken. Early morning, in the street. The two couples—the Astrid Mircea Claudiu Vancea family and the future Sonia Matus Calinovschi family—are standing on the wet platform of the tram stop. Late revelers from the Bar Levcenco ceremoniously greet the princess who has disappeared from their fox-trot-and-champagne parties. A sure sign that another day really has dawned.

In the dining room, mother and youngest child are silently looking at the uncleared, deserted table.

A hazy hour: the bluish dawn invading the Bar Levcenco on the ground floor of the apartment block. The jolly old Levcenco madhouse is dead as well; it has been for many decades.

The window moistened with dew. The trams started up in the street. Dull grinding movement.

A DARK DILAPIDATED CAFÉ. The eccentric, distinguished vaca-
tioner is waiting with his legs crossed. Wide-open check jacket.
Dark-red silk scarf sticking out from the collar of his black shirt.
Huge black sunglasses. On the chair next to him: a suede jacket and
an umbrella. By the chair a small leather suitcase full of colored
labels—the first hour of a short break in the mountains, the first
coffee with milk. Coffee with milk, wow! It's not quite so extraordinary in the mountains, where there are cows, milk, butter, sour
cream: you should be able to get a coffee with milk at least. Or at
least one without milk. A black coffee, anyhow, that standard coffee,
that coffee substitute made from chick-peas, barley, cornmeal, or
whatever. Or a tea, at least a tea. Russian, Chinese, English—or at
least camomile, mint, lime blossom, whatever.

The distinguished guest did not stand up, did not storm out of the
fake café in which there was neither confectionery nor cakes, just
endless rows of jam and the same tired old bags of cookies. He did
not request the book of complaints or ask to see the manager. He
nodded politely at every piece of information and every refusal—
thank you, we haven't got any tea, thank you, there isn't any coffee
or any milk, thank you, we're out of cakes, we don't do soft drinks,
thank you, the mineral water's finished, thank you, thank you very
much, always with an obliging smile, bent over that glossy magazine, a perfect gentleman! Calm, relaxed, belle époque, a colonial
dandy come for a few moments to confer style and fame on the
forgotten tourist resort, the pearl of the Carpathians.

And so Anatol Vancea, according to his identity book a receptionist at the Hotel Tranzit in Bucharest, remained like that for roughly
two hours, impassive, legs crossed, in the fake café near Sinaia

railway station, waiting—for what? no one could have said. Globe-
trotter's luggage beside him, decadent color magazine in front of
him, waiting, for what? Twelve o'clock, midday, the opportune
hour. He was on holiday: with no thoughts, no memory, nothing at
all. He was nothing at all, as he wanted to be.

When twelve o'clock approached—the time for room check-in
all too familiar to any hotel receptionist—he would therefore head
straight for the hotel. He would utter in an artificial voice the number of the reserved room, 326, go up the stairs, have a shower, and
expire for a few hours in a deep, prehistoric slumber. The second
day, Tuesday, would vanish like the first, in secret. Film, excursion,
sleep: who could say? On Wednesday the weather would turn cold:
overcast sky, thick black clouds. A walk to the bookshop. On Thursday a trip to the castle, some reading, a stroll around the country
houses, through the town and park, to the post office.

Sunday in the mountains has a side that it keeps to itself, as if the
day is making fun of you, sniffing haughtily as the hours drift by in a
kind of hostile, smoldering provocation. You can pack slowly, without hurrying, as on any old day. You haven't the least idea where you
are going; you don't know the time of the train or the place; you put
yourself, as agreed, in the hands of the void.

Tolea Voinov spent only one boring week in the mountains. A
confused, sleepy wait unsure whether to call itself Irina.

Fine weather. The sun takes the forest out of the mists and brings
it up close, restores its nobility. The old boyars' houses are still in
place, though ailing and humbled, but the atmosphere, the atmosphere—identical faces, limp, half-finished gestures! Rotten, putrid
sleepiness, in a huge cask of stale vinegar, carrots, and manure. No,
he hadn't been able to take it. Not the memories either—no, everything had been at another time. It had been May, another age, yes,
another time, long ago, like yesterday.

Irina's laughter. Waking up in the evening on the terrace of the
villa—the lunar tide. Long, long silences, until his tongue grew dry

from waiting. One afternoon, walking up the asphalt bend toward the town . . . Hands raised toward the man's shoulders.

He had not forgotten the incident, even though a thousand years had passed. A topsy-turvy moment, there in the street, where the asphalt curved toward the town—it was there that they had spun around toward each other. Then a kind of unease, as if the afternoon had broken off and was hanging just on the edge of the idle hour. A heavy, poisoned silence, submerging you in its green silt. You begin to totter, and somewhere you hear suspicious pings of unseen lizards. The lips of some teenagers hurrying by—that was what it had been—could not be removed from the ridiculous sequence; they continued to totter mutely, like senile old people fallen back into the minds of children.

Irina went into the food store, having asked him to wait outside. At the bend where the town was left behind, at the very spot where that little nothing had occurred, he seemed to wake up. He had turned to his partner—Here, let me carry a bag, I see you've got two—turned to Ira, taken the plastic bag from her left hand, also the one from her right hand, and they had gone on side by side without talking. They had reached the villa where Irina was staying, a narrow spruce building with a roof of brick tiles. They had walked up the steps and gone down into the hall. Ira had taken off her anorak: she was wearing a large white sweater made of thick wool over her stiff jeans. In one hand she was holding a bottle of red wine, in the other a glass painted with little blue flowers, and a rustic mug.

"There are only two people still lodging here in the villa, and they're not in much. They've got relatives in town and spend a lot of time with them."

She had half-filled the mug. The wine soon trickled down to his limbs with its pleasant, enervating warmth. At a certain moment he had taken the bottle from the floor and covered it with the empty cup. He had touched her elbow, cupping it in the palm of his hand: Let's go upstairs. No no, Ira had put him off without conviction. He had pulled her gently, she was already on the brink of the stairs; they had gone up. A tiny little room, a narrow bed like at school, a washbasin, a large attic window through which the moon was entering.

He pulled her toward him, impatiently, clumsily. Let me undress myself—the jeans had slipped off, and on top of them the white catlike sweater. Ira had kept on her long undershirt. A small, simple slippery body—Not like that, let *me*—burning skin. He had hurriedly lost himself in the narrow body, electrified by the evil light of the moon. Shy dizzy awkward. Ira, her head resting on legs pressed together under the partial cover of a thick blanket, had lit a second cigarette. He was looking nowhere. Then he found the solution: he left that very evening. He had to pack his things and catch the nine-thirty train. Irina had slid off the narrow divan, among the crumpled sheets.

You don't need to come with me. Well, as a matter of fact, I feel like a bit of a walk in the fresh air; it doesn't necessarily mean I'm coming with you. I wouldn't mind at all if you did: I'd like to have your address anyhow. Behind them rustled the discarded, assembled, and again discarded clothes. They had passed by the hotel for the traveler to pick up his suitcase. They kissed, like old school pals, in front of the train's open door. Ira held out a thin strip of red paper: her address. She laughed in a relaxed way; a wisp of hair fluttered stupidly on her forehead. Parched white lips—the train had left.

Alone in the compartment, Tolea refused to go over the failure again. It's the same with all women: the first time, whatever happens, is always haste, insecurity, evacuation. He in her—for a short time. Copulation gymnastics, a performance, growth in the birthrate? Confused magnetism—from which, if you were lucky, you might pick up the abrupt, violent glow? A sudden rediscovery and sudden denial, yes, that was it, a discharge—he preferred not to remember. No, he didn't want to remember the emotions, the shyness, the helplessness: no, he no longer had any desire for complications!

But it was not difficult to remember. He had first met Ira years before, in his small town in the provinces. It was full of young people from Bucharest, engineers architects doctors, sent to help in the modernization of the old historic town.

Irina had worked for a while doing technical drawing, then as a shop-window dresser and as a nursery-school teacher, all the time awaiting permission to take her final exam at the architecture school, from which she had been unexpectedly expelled just before the end of her course. She, too, was part of the circle around the young high-school teacher Vancea. The future character Tolea was already a character. And how! The Professor, as he was known, would fume and fret, perfecting his acrobatics, his flippant jokes and wordplay, his friendly banter and arrogant, offhand quibbles.

He had met her one day in the street: How are you, Irina, isn't that your name? That's right, Professor, I didn't think you would remember it. The young woman who was nearly an architect, Irina Ira, followed him for a while, long enough, one street on the left, a second burning with fury. The young high-school teacher Anatol Dominic Vancea Voinov—snobbish maestro of provincial rebels, a kind of academic oddity of the small town! He was not even ten years older than all those young people, mostly ex-students of his, swarming around his somersault displays, all those school pupils students engineers doctors making rings around gramophone records, magazines tape recorders paradoxes bottles pipes, in the midst of which the thunderstruck Tolea played the role of chic, blasé clown in strident polyglot tones. Even in Russian, which he was still teaching at high school: that language, made to feel so repugnant and oppressive, had become a provocation, a pleasing oddity, in the rictus of his ham actor's mask. There had only been time for a few silent meetings, occasions of foreboding and evasion, in the half year until she suddenly left town. But they had kept in touch by letter, and at some point he had gone to see her in Bucharest.

It was mid-December: Ira was wearing a new overcoat made of a thick blue camel's-hair material. The city had put on some color as it played the child. Lamps, sweets, fir trees—they jostled each other in the merriment of lines on which tiny snowflakes fell as in a holiday album. Streets filled with a bright, festive light. When they reached her house, Irina invited him in. Let's go on up, my sister isn't home, nor is my father: he left for good a month ago, after my mother's funeral. Now and then we get a picture postcard and a few lines—he's back with the woman he was living with for a long time before.

They listened to music, drank some liqueur—that vague feeling, a kind of dizziness, on the beautiful evening of their meeting again. It had been all silence and evasion, nothing else. The idyllic pastel image of winter, with its cheap, inhibiting festivity? Or did the intensity of her scared eyes intimidate him? He had simply postponed any contact. And then, at some time or other, there had been a symmetrical image: Ira in summertime, on a swing. Touched up, happy. The stupidity of those childhood interludes. And again those suddenly charged eyes, promising too much. And again a chance to avoid, in fact, the secret links of touch.

Frightened by the excessive promise, the exaggerated preliminaries?

At some point he had received a brief summons from Ira, who was already working as an architect at the site of a sumptuous new station at Braşov: Come with me to the sea for a fortnight. The coward did not answer, but he knew that he wouldn't be able to keep avoiding her for long. In the autumn he couldn't stop himself: he rang her, come what may. It was her younger sister, engineer Silvia Isabela, who answered the phone: Ira was married. When how why—well, it just came to her all of a sudden, as if she wanted to escape from something that was pursuing her. The friend of a girlfriend of hers, Dr. Bănăţeanu, asked for her hand. She didn't sleep a whole night, nervously fidgeting around, and in the morning she said *yes*. They've moved from Bucharest, but they come here from time to time; I'll pass on the message. Bang bang, just like that.

Comrade Gică Teodosiu was right: spring in the mountains catches you and breaks you, don't forget it. A good thing that he did not wait until May, when the moon's golden hoof has a different step and its thorn enters so deep that you can no longer pull it out. A good thing you ended the holiday early, *professore*: May would have caught you in a twilight intoxicated with aphrodisiacs. There, on the bend leading up to the town, you would somehow have encountered the *fata morgana* . . . On that day, long ago, you had gone up the wooden staircase holding her small frail elbow in the palm of your hand. The dense twilight, moon growing in the window, rushed contact, the light switching on and off, snapshots, too high voltage, disaster. A romantic sequence, good only for farces. Romantic farces, that's all: long rigmaroles with sighing and sickly feelings.

They eventually met again, after time had got all twisted up again. A cold rainy dusk: do you think you're going to escape this time, too, that the trains, addresses, and phantoms will get muddled up, that you will put things off again? But after a few months he rang the doorbell, just for the hell of it, at the address on the red note she had given him at the station.

"I was sure you wouldn't come . . ." And actually he had steered clear, walking a few times around the house to postpone it. "You can take off your raincoat. You're not going to stand like that in the middle of the room, or are you?" The apartment, newly whitewashed, was still being redecorated. They went onto the terrace, beneath the crown of the old tree. They touched. Irina pulled away in a gesture of fright. They returned to the empty room and sat down in facing chairs. They looked at each other. Her thick, dry lips, verdigris eyes, hoarse voice. As they looked at each other, her eyes became clouded, dilated, weighed down. A kind of painful trance. Her small hands touched him. They slipped hesitantly under his shirt. Quietly, trembling all the time. Her eyes delving deeper, pained, on fire. He still had time to see the white window frame, the heavy crystal glass reddened from dense and languid wine. Then burning—or perhaps something else, a kind of dizziness. Her small hands slid down further and further. They reached the fiery center, unleashed the blood, pumped wildly and furiously, like a battering ram. Vibration, trance, lips, breasts, struggling hands—the blood striking wildly, again and again, deeper and deeper. Had she kissed anyone before, had she ever kissed another man? Complete concentration, as at the beginning of the world . . . The miracle, the miracle of rebirth had finally happened.

A hidden force, *professore*, an incomparable force concentrating passion, that's what it was. Irresistible, hypnotic induction. They dragged themselves to the bedroom, sighing, ill in each other's arms. The pain of desire pulled him into her, deeper and deeper, with both hands, deeper, again and again, sobbing, her face twisted out of shape. She had covered his eyes with her hands to stop him from seeing her. "Don't look at me, don't." But he saw her and continued to look at the tears flooding down her small pale cheeks. He was on her and in her, clasping and feverish, but he still followed the tears as they fell incessantly toward her parched lips. Unconsciously she mumbled: "No, don't look at me—please don't," clasping and overcome with joy and fear. Naked beneath the sheet, they remained fixed for a long time in each other's embrace. "No, they can't take this away from us," Irina whispered faintly, militantly, jerkily. "They can't take this away. It's all we've got left—the only thing," she stammered, lightly sobbing in lament and pleasure on the pillow, where her wiry, coppery, unmanageable hair lay. "I knew that you . . ." She waited for him to continue. Not for nothing had he avoided meeting her—but it had been to no avail.

Her hands trembled as they touched him, electrified him: again the blood roared, clothes flew in the air along with the crumpled sheet; she pulled him into her, deeper and deeper, stammering between sobs: "No, don't look at me, please don't." And that torrid trepidation, the tears, the spasm, the salvation. "So you've come after all . . ." She laughed as she opened the door a few days later.

And at once she pulled him toward her, into her, deeper and deeper into the torrid lava. "Don't look at me, don't," she gaspingly sobbed, now healed in the desperate disorder of their embrace, which revived him and scared him and healed him. At some point, frightened, he had made an attempt at depressurization. She had just returned from a trip and he also left town for a while; she was ill and he was going on holiday—pretexts to make the meetings less frequent, to attempt the sobering up, the loosening of the bond.

A thinned-down, poisoned twilight. Torrential downpour. He was sleepwalking in the streets, not knowing where. He had no umbrella and the rain was streaming over his forehead and neck. His clothes were soaked: he was wrapped in a mantle of water. The deserted street. He had awoken on the pavement beneath a tree, looking toward the terrace. One minute, five, ten, and—Ira appeared. She stopped, bewildered, in front of the balustrade. She looked into the street, saw the errant shape, and understood—they both understood. He pushed the metal gate and went up. In the doorway, in a thick, long, white shirt, Ira was shaking with fever.

Her small, tense, convulsed body. "I felt you were out there . . ." The hysterical despair of a child. A pagan ritual resumed with ferocity. She flung the sheet aside, as if it were on a humble mast kneeling wrung and powerless at the foot of the short bed. "I'm leaving: I must go. Now, right away." He repeated robot-like: "I must go. Right now. Immediately. There's no other solution." And she did not hear and did not reply. He dressed hurriedly so that there would be no time for words. She did not look at him, sat motionless, without even blinking, on the narrow coffin of a bed. Then the door had opened. He was again in the yard, in the street, in the rain. He huddled up and lifted the collar of his wet jacket. Without meaning to, he lifted his arm and saw his watch. He looked at the dial, at the circling minute hand. Half an hour! That was all: half an hour, an eternity. Hidden again beneath the trees on the pavement, he looked back at the terrace across the street, where he had been just now, a thousand years ago. In the mist and rain of the night he could hear around him the bustle and voices of passersby, the routine of people taking each other's place in the rush toward their burrows, exhausted by the masquerade that had swallowed up another day.

If the subordinate Vancea Voinov had delayed his ozone replenishment until May, as the wise Gică had advised, then who knows, the happening might have been reborn with a different name . . .

"Some unidentifiable episodes of my life kept making me guilty, although I didn't feel it in any way. I started university again a few times: but something new would always appear in my file and they'd throw me back out. I was eventually on the point of graduating when again they . . . After marriage two broke down, I really couldn't pick myself up anymore. There was a moment of defeat when I suddenly directed my fury onto the outside world, toward those who kept watching me and pushing me to the margins. It wasn't very clever of me to have handed out that text. Too big a risk. I might even have gone missing for good. Then, at the moment before the fall, a hand reached out to me—or rather, a claw. I clung to it, stupefied, exasperated, gone wild. It was Comrade Popescu. Comrade Orest Popescu saved me: he even offered me a job and a salary."

She tensed up in the darkness. Her hand slid along, catching the edge of the table, of the bed. A chaotic danger that she did not want to name. She tensed up, concentrated, stretched out her hand. The fingers passed gently over the man's cheek and chest and manhood: the words jerkily speeded up; the movements grew quicker, up to the trepidation of a single reintegrated body and of tears which naturally fell again and again with each spasm. "Don't look at me, please don't." The embrace, like a reddened claw. And the whimpering, the stammering afterward. "They can't take this away from us. Not this. The great savage mystery." Savage, yes, and frail, in those sobs of lament and pleasure.

The voice had broken off, overwhelmed, and some time later started up again in a perverse and frightened contortion.

"One step from those dangers beyond return. And again I was on the brink of graduating, for the third time. I asked my friend Ianuli for his advice. I've told you about him, haven't I? The legendary Greek. The pure, fanatical hero not yet touched by the dregs all around him. They bought and sold his legend for a knockdown price. The life of a rebel and martyr, not like that of your usual hustler. It's hard to say which masquerade is better: the opportunist or the true believer. Anyway, he still had enough connections to help me. Again I went to the provinces for a while, until the heat was off—although I knew I was married to my file forevermore. Like the Catholics—until death do us part. I wanted to come back, but I couldn't get it fixed. And so again I thought I was a rebel, again I exploded. And they gave me another demonstration of what happens next. Then Comrade Orest Popescu offered his services. I accepted. With a morbid fury, to take revenge on myself."

The city had given up the ghost. Only the tree rustling above the terrace was a reminder that it's no use hiding: there are witnesses and substitutes all around; the comrades of Comrade Orest reach into every corner; their invisible threads have already penetrated even here, to the bed of illicit pleasure.

Irina leaned over the bottom edge of the bed to take the pack of cigarettes. She lit one and arranged the child-size pillow beneath her head. Her slim, diaphanous fingers squeezed the cigarette until she reached the glowing end. "He'd found in me a cure, a dream, a fixation—that's what Comrade Popescu said. He was prepared to let himself be tyrannized over if that was what amused me. He was a tyrant himself—unstable, possessive. He gave me a hand with nothing really. Or maybe perhaps: the subordinate institution. His own little kingdom in a republic of countless kingdoms big and small. And what an institution! The ASSOCIATION! The association of the underworld, of the underdeveloped, of underhand meanings. The association of deaf-mute silence! If I didn't know that that, too, in fact, is only one company. Behind it, under and above it, there is the NETWORK. The NETWORK is everything. The company, the goal, the structure—none of that counts, even in the case of such an exotic company; the important thing is always the way it relates to the system. That was why Comrade Orest Popescu was actually more important than he seemed, and the company much more cunning than its strange profile made it appear. I didn't run away from the sinister experiment. I remained, hoping I would destroy myself quickly. We never know just how much of the poison we can absorb."

It was not obvious when she let herself be carried away by the nightmare—as if the script and the role had been rehearsed so much that she no longer needed anyone else to take part.

"In fact, he even talked of divorcing his wife. No one at that strange institution guessed anything. But my family knew. Then Father gave me the ultimate weapon. They knew each other too well—so I was in a position to act the great rejection scene, with a plausible scenario. That is, I presented him with a surprise. I told him I couldn't agree to making things 'permanent,' whether legally or otherwise. Not because of the age difference or because I didn't like the partner. Those were not insignificant reasons, of course, but they could have been disregarded in our little play with so many obscure codes. No, what I said was that I had heard about his activities during the war. It came as a bolt from the blue, as I expected, but at the same time did not expect. He was stunned. He knew from where I'd found out about his great secret. In captivity, before assuming an identity more in keeping with the new times, he had already begun another operation—the operation of replacing his own self with the expedient one. Substitute men, like substitute bread, clothing, or books, weren't invented today or yesterday."

She was no longer smoking. Paradoxically the intensity calmed her down. The intensity did not come from the telling of her story—not at all. It was as if the acute hidden terror, huge and always there, was appeased by the very facts that she related. As if the unknown which had always terrified, and of course still terrified, her lurking vulnerability became bearable when it took on concrete shape.

As if reality, however terrible it proves to be, is much more ambivalent, more soluble, than the terrors you imagine or expect.

"In the camp, because they were prisoners of war—of the anti-Soviet war—they were each given two little cubes of jam a day on one slice of bread. He was struck off to supervise the operation. Well, seeing how overpassionate he was getting about me, Father eventually told me the whole story. As a final weapon for putting pressure on him—dangerous, of course, like everything else concerning him. His whole being was one of darkness and masks. Father had kept clear of him after witnessing his rapid rise in postwar politics—quite spectacular during the early years. Nowadays, in comparison, he was pretty low down the hierarchy, important only because of the obscure and extraordinary contacts, both old and new, that he had with the NETWORK.

"So anyway, he'd guarded the starvation rations in the camp. And he made sure he raked off the customs duties, so that he and a few others could survive."

She had taken her hands from under the sheet and stretched them out to him, relaxed and parallel to each other. Small, pale, childish hands. The sleeplessness of a feverish night, pleading to be cured. Hungry, delving green eyes, darker and darker, pleading to be cured. The sheet creased up, like her sad mouth parched by expectation. The ball of linen was cast aside, the embrace sighed—self-abandonment and tears.

Much later, after night had come, she regained her thick, disconsolate voice.

"He's someone given an early start in skulduggery, this fellow creature of ours. Evil as a chance for survival. So I hit him where it really hurts. But he took the blow and he's still getting along okay, with the same thirst for life as we have, no? What do they want to prove to us, over and over again? That we're evil, or treacherous, or weak-willed? And that we're really like a bunch of saints, after all—is that what we keep proving? Hunted rebels, apprentices in illusion! Sick people thrashing around in the ephemeral and the precarious?"

During the night she had twisted again in the same impotent whining. But what if she herself is also an unconscious . . . perhaps she, too, is . . . He had left with the weight of that last string of words. Sick people caught in the ephemeral and the precarious. There would be time enough in the future to keep turning them around and around, *professore*. Each new May bends differently the wind of those dubious questions, so like our dubious times. You should have had the patience to follow your suspicions, *professore*; you wouldn't have got bored! Or the boredom—the worst affliction of all, as you are fond of saying—might well have diminished. You would have kept meeting new knots and traps; events would have doubled and tripled their appearance; you would have been rewarded for your patience.

It may be that the episode would have acquired a name, a direction, if you had not been able to find a suitable train to escape on. But you would have needed patience, curiosity, and a certain modesty, *professore*. The modesty of dialogue and of its dangers, *professore*.

You might not have been bored in its syncopations and snares. You would have found that the beginning of a new day brings back the same wrinkled plaster face called Orest, the same phantom quietly waiting at each gong of the calendar to remind you of the cave in which you crawl.

Time macerates all obsessions, as you well know, *professore*. Even Comrade Orest Popescu grows weary under the omnipotence of time: the passion becomes mediocre while the hatred becomes a routine, a kind of mimicry necessary to keep up appearances.

"You ask why I don't find another salary, another job, another town. It would be possible, no doubt. Things aren't like in the fifties anymore. Yes, I'd find a job all right. Even if he continued to hunt me with his legion of professionals, cunning and vengeful as he is. But I, too, have the right to see the play till the end—now, when it has got so unclear and threadbare. Something real and concrete—it helps you to think more constructively! I find I can follow the scale of the degeneration better if I have a goal that I know in detail. Then I have something in flesh and blood that is immediate and accessible. And above all, ambiguous. Is this also where the sense of the abyss appears? In the ambiguity which makes us accomplices, which always holds out to us the mirror and the trap? So as to demonstrate the precariousness of it all? To humiliate us? By delivering us, O Lord, to guilt and despair and our surfeit of weaknesses—by destroying us, destroying us."

You see, *professore*, our fellow creatures are wary of talking about fear and suspicion. Not about boredom, though, as you well know and exemplify every day. Like that, you would also have discovered their painful interpenetration, called Irina. Women keep reminding you of something always put off and always hurt, as your friend Marga would say. Vampires, grasping claws, fetters, fly traps, chain loops, wedding rings—you remember how you used to educate your young companions about their future women partners. No precautions of any kind, Professor? Didn't you take the simplest precautions demanded by the suspicion that already surrounded you and would soon be used to punish your insolence. Actually, there were better strategies than the one of hawking the same old sarcasms to show you feared nothing because you respected nobody. You're still doing it now, this wet evening, in the dusty compartment of the train carrying you back from your mini-mini-break. The haughtiness, the spleen, the pipe, and the little silk bag, your airs and graces with your humble fellow passengers—the same old masquerade.

Look, after Mr. Bănăţeanu's divorce and after old Eusebiu's divorce and between one divorce and another and one marriage and another, the ghost Irina reappears. She comes close, very close, but never close enough to try to make you connect, as our Dr. Marga still hopes. Her stern, delicate face concentrates a kinetic energy in which you could finally become entangled and even, in Marga's view, be cured. Listen again to the echo of that other age, feel the pain once more, like that time when you crashed to the ground from the glistening handlebars of adolescence.

The rhythm of a truth from which it is not possible to escape forever, *professore*. Irina would have helped you to rediscover it, perhaps. And to lose the ham actor's mask beneath which you have been hiding for too long, and behind which you still hide when old Marcu Vancea finds you and summons you night after night to see him again, to give birth to him again.

CHEST OUT! HEAD UP, seeming not to notice the other heads around. The star of the street, towering over it with no thought for the audience. Red scarf, under the open collar of a white shirt. Among signs and shop windows, the day-colored comet: the master pedestrian, available cheat. The roles all payable to bearer, already prepared. The tittle-tattle, the backbiting, the jokes, the pedantic quotations, the banter. Soft, gentle trampling underfoot, ever so carefully. Thick-soled shoes, plush, the kind in which you sink pleasantly and yet also have a firm grip. The duck's foot settles elastically over its full width, lazily, unhurriedly curves and raises itself, shuffle-shuffle, one step after another.

Misshapen, tottering like a duck. Free; hurrah, how free I am! What do I care, na na na! Never ever too busy, *mon cher*. Free, m'sieur, because we don't let ourselves be eaten up. Huh, we've a real raw deal ahead of us, there's no escape: but it doesn't bother us. Na na na, boredom pirouettes tantrums, no? Call me, *ciao*, stuff them, *ciao*, see you soon, anytime, sure sure anytime notime, of course.

But the eye is watching. Watery, without color. Suddenly green gray blue. The lashes blink fast fast. One frame, then another, at great speed. He sees them, oho! he sees them very well. He lies eagerly in wait: he suddenly records films develops stores their faces. They are in the air, in the sky, among the shadows of the street which sleepily rolls along, a starry chimera in which you move crazily forward, without moving. As if everything were true, close, here—so that you can touch smell see crumple pieces, the pieces, and so break absolutely everything, grinding your teeth, hopping about for joy, and set it alight: ash, dust, air, circus. As if it were true, oho! if everyone everything really existed, if if if. Including the conjuror, the tinsel, the mask, the mime. The cynic, the arrogant jester, the impassive swallower of swords and disasters, with his big shaven head of a Roman consul. If they only existed, if if if, if he and they existed now, when he sees them, sees them again, dreams of them, without wanting to, as usual as always, anytime notime, boredom pirouettes tantrums, no? Yes, he sees them, all of them.

Here is the first: the electrician fallen from the pole. Small lips, red eyes, hatched yellow forehead. Sailor's vest. Thick, huge, bluish fingers. The hunter of leeches. That's what he called them, leeches. An old cure, the circulation of the blood. He collected them from the street, from parks, cinemas, museums, swimming pools, anywhere. He drugged them with civilities and the gear of his old Taunus car. Then suddenly, as at an unexpected traffic light, he braked. Eye-to-eye contact. Without warning, brief and direct: Okay, let me give it to you, I'll make you happy. Let's go to my place—I'll fill you up, make you happy, you'll chase after me like a crazy woman; that's what you're all like, crazy. They did not resist—out of three one fell. Afterward the real madness: letters, phone calls, threats, whining: you're not allowed to prolong the madness, boss, so ended the patient's story, you're not allowed to, damn it, sweeties are wild beasts, leeches are wild beasts, that's what our dollies are, wild beasts.

Here is the next: the monk converted. Long white beard, pale sunken cheeks. Long thin diaphanous hands, and that kind knowing old-fashioned smile. "In the name of Joseph, Vissarionovich, and Holy Stalin, amen." In vain do they explain things to him and give him pills: he cannot accept that the greatest strategist of all time, the best friend of children, the mastermind of science and the magic arts, the most beloved earthling, no longer exists—has simply snuffed it, like all earthlings. When he was arrested, thirty years ago, the father of the peoples sat night and day in his brightly lit pulpit at the Kremlin, deciding night and day the fate of each mortal. They arrested the poor monk for his unswerving faith in the hereafter; they tortured him until he suddenly began to pray nonstop—to Saint Joseph of the Kremlin. Today no one can convince him that Saint Vissarion Vissarionovich really has disappeared, that his Name is even prohibited, dangerous to pronounce, although his huge shadow guards and constantly activates our cave of deaf-mutes. Today he still mumbles his prayers and crosses himself in the name of the most beloved father and the most beloved son and his immortal holy spirit. He nods distrustfully at every piece of information or advice, at every injection he is given. Yet sometimes he appears overwhelmed by the insistence of his well-wishers. He smiles archly and mutters into his immaculate beard: "What does the name matter, what does it matter?" But then he immediately falls to his knees, frightened and guilty, begging forgiveness, amen, and calling on the Great Departed to give him protection, amen.

Here she is: elegant, Frenchified, painted as in the times of the whoring King Carol. The former beauty, frail and exotic, of fun-loving Bucharest, petit Paris of yore; the former aristocratic lady of great wealth, unable to hold up under interrogation, sobbingly denounced her former spouse, the former leading international lawyer, and put her signature beneath the aberrations of which he had been accused. And today she continues to write ever crazier denunciations, even though the poor man died in prison a long time ago.

Here she is: huge sleep-filled eyes, heavy black plaits, nun's habit. Flower girl, dancer, spinner, what could that splendid gypsy girl be? No way an engineer! Top of her year at the electronics faculty, the pride of her neighborhood, joyful, beautiful, saintly, married to a fellow engineer who was then posted for two years to Syria. Waiting with pent-up tears, desperate to see him again: wailing, cooing, screaming. The fat, garrulous husband does not hold up under interrogation: he jokingly admits his indiscretions: two years alone, what was he supposed to do? He wasn't a eunuch but a man, yes, like other men. Shock, hospital, injections, divorce, hospital: no prospect of recovery, decreed tiny Marga. She got involved for a month or two with one man or another, but it never lasted; she was just a crumpled rag, the poor thing, said the great doctor of madmen.

And here is another: a short fleshy peasant of uncertain age. After they took away his land and forced him to join a collective farm, he refused to work on any other strip than the one that used to be his. He toured all the prisons of the fifties, but all he could do was repeat the same name: Ioana, Ioana, the name of his best-loved cow.

Look at this one: a nagging woman. Small, wooden, cloudy head. Fear, stuttering. A dull, sluggish way of speaking. It used to be the ideal marriage, Doctor; the difficulties just brought us closer together—the war, his foot wound, the Fascist terror, everything, the hunger, illnesses, postwar hatred, all strengthened the ties between us. And then came the arrest, when they took away our boys. Suddenly he caved in, the mountain of a man crashed down to earth— just like that, you don't even have time to recover your senses. And I'm certainly not all there anymore: I can't think properly, Doctor, I can't keep still.

And now: the gentle, witty giant with no memories, no feelings, who gaily, intangibly crosses the streets, parks, public conveniences, strewing funny stories, questions, roars of laughter and indifference, as is indicated by the board around his neck bearing the diagnosis in large red letters: EUPHORIA WITH PUNNING TENDENCIES.

Finally, the ghost of the last patient: the shy, delicate teenager lost in books, a perfect copy of Tolea a millennium before. He cannot pull himself together after the bicycle accident and the disappearance of philosopher-wineseller Marcu Vancea and the trial over that road accident with the old wreck of a woman, and the trial to expel the teacher he had become, and the trial of the times of life passing too quickly, which suddenly jumbles together trials, punishments, and boredom.

There they are: the assorted extras of the great farce. Men, women, children, soldiers, priests, vagabonds, peasants, prostitutes, ministers, gravediggers, engineers, poets, every category of mask and substitute, the great silent army of the vanquished, the patients, the last relics of normality unmasked by fate's thunderbolt and incapable of remaining indifferent, refusing health and indifference and normality.

How to recognize them? They come and pass hurriedly by him, always hurriedly, looking at the ground and wearing the mask of tired children.

A provocative spring afternoon. The streets are full of the child-ish smiles of the patients he has met there, in the waiting rooms of truth. Bearers of the peculiar incubation or madness, handsome lunatics of the great disasters, the salt of the earth, the last knights of normality, as Dr. Marga says. Intricate codes, nightmares, head-aches, visions, tears, fainting fits—of normality; all of them, main-tains the lunatic who acts the healer of lunatics.

How shall I recognize them, stop them, go home with them so that at least for that evening I am theirs, with them—so that I can gather them together, one and one more, and we can send word to everyone: this night, our night! Our night: all crammed in a vast groan that soon becomes a roar—hysteria, laughter, our laughter, our infinite planetary roar that not even the sky can encompass. Our humble, proud, incurable solidarity: normal people! That's all, the nobility of the last sick people capable of recording the world's disorder, the tearing and the gnashing of teeth, unknown to those who break their back maintaining the rhythm of the play that is continually in search of its end. And friend Marga wastes his time with us wretches, schizophrenic orphans on a schizophrenic planet. If he thought about it, he, Tolea, the schizophrenic orphan, was almost the same age as Mr. Marcu Vancea, whom the Great Script-writer in the sky drove to his death one spring night forty years ago. All of a sudden he went rambling through streets and through fields beyond them, killed or killing himself—who knows anymore?—in the hypnosis of that black spring night.

Suicide or perhaps murder, who can say? and what would be the point anyway except for his Argentinian brother, who did not run far enough, since he could be reached there, too, in the nostalgia of senility, reminiscing about their father floating in the sewers of a town devastated by terror. And so the memories reached his paralytic Argentinian brother—memories of those far-off days when he went to buy himself some white wedding gloves, while his father's corpse floated down as a gift to the cesspool collectors at the sewer's mouth, among all the city's waste matter.

If, on this young spring night, he were to gather together all the patient-brothers—hundreds, a thousand, several thousand—each with a torch in his hand on the slope that protects the collectors' trough up to the exit into the cold black river, so that for a moment he could look at each one, hundreds, a thousand, looking for a moment at each one, just for a moment. In the end he would recognize that one from long ago—yes, he would remember one like that. Time, in its cyclical movement, reproduces such markings to near-perfection; the map of human suffering must surely repeat such features.

He would recognize Marcu Vancea as he was forty years ago. He would read the warning on his mask of a frightened, hunted, aged child. He would be able to take a good look at him, as he didn't have time to do then, and even forewarn him—what for? No, I wouldn't warn him, I'd just examine the hasty way of doing the preliminaries, the rough sketch for a real study in simulation up to or rather beyond the fatal threshold, so that Señor Claudiu could see how conscientious was the slave paid with those wretched dollars of his, which had passed across two oceans and twenty seas and two hundred hands before reaching the noncounting account, because that's how Anatol is, always unlucky and loony and penniless, like his crazy country, in which there is not a penny and never any good luck.

Off the boulevard to the right, then again to the right. A quiet cross street. Trees, unheard buzzing, shadowy silence. The heavy iron gate, solemn steps. A princely building, bolts, lancet arches, stone wood steel, austere windows, pillars, and chandeliers, surely we know the decor. He pressed the doorbell on which the name Dr. Marga was written. Would Auntie Jeny already be standing hidden behind the door, a patient now the doctor's nurse? Would she be waiting as usual on the other side?

"I've brought you a flower, Granny. A yellow carnation—I couldn't find any roses. Because, you know, there are no longer any flowers in this country, except for heroes."

"Oh, poor me! You're the only one who keeps this black soul of mine going"—and she would wipe the palms of her hands on her blue shorts, again and again, and then suddenly bend from the waist to kiss her benefactor's hand.

"What are you doing? I've told you before I'm not the Pope. Come on now, stop groveling like that: let's sing that *doina* which you say tears you apart and puts you together again"—and the young gentleman Anatol would look hard at old Jeny so as not to forget her black, unsocketed eyes, her pale, puffy cheeks, her stumpy hands shaking all the time as if from the cold. Let's go, Madame Hyperthyroid, stop laughing like a fool and let's sing that *doina* that will set your soul aright. Don't put your hand to your mouth when you laugh, Madame Parkinson; stop blushing when you laugh—it's not your teeth that are the problem. You may have teeth missing, but that's not what you're covering up. It's because of what the exploiting classes got you used to—they haven't disappeared, you know, far from it." The young gentleman Anatol would sit on the carpet, as Auntie Jeny closed her eyes in the armchair. *Oh, darling Johnny,* the song began.

A wafer-thin voice, a frail child, a barely noticeable trace, beneath bushy black eyebrows.

Oh, darling Johnny,
would that I could sow your name

Her rough hand stroking the orphan's bald patch. Slowly her voice rises, slowly and thinly the song's tear falls: *Oh, darling Johnny, would that I could sow your name in every garden . . . in every garden . . . so its sweet smell . . . reaches every pretty belle.* It went on and on until, as usual, bedlam broke loose. Tolea leaped to his feet screaming *Rock Rock Rock Again:* twisting dizziness shouting, until he whirled the patient into the kitchen—*Right, let me see the moussaka!* "Right, let me see the moussaka! That's not pepper: it's those green sleeping tablets. And those other ones are for dreams, and the others for the dead. Don't you worry, I know it all right." Rock Rock Rock Again, so that the plates and forks and saucepan and jars, and the table full of remedies spices syrups all quiver and shake for the greatest suffering of all, as great as the garden of the Mad Lord, because this is my fate, sweetheart, that I can find peace here only thanks to the doctor's kindness, bless his soul.

Nothing to be heard: not a sound. As if no one is in, not even the patient acting as governess. So Mr. Anatol Vancea Voinov rings again, for a long time.

The door half opens, very slowly, with maximum caution. It's not Jeny—that's not her style. No, of course it isn't Jeny. It's her male equivalent, the sluggish patient. A pale shy pensioner. Dusty uniform, soft-mannered valet, shortsighted eyes of a domestic frog.

"Ah, it's you. Yes, please come in. The doctor hasn't arrived yet. But Dr. Marga will be here soon. You can wait."

He flicked the switch and light blazed everywhere from the large chandeliers.

Ah, it's evening already! As if it wasn't spring but late autumn, when it gets dark early and the night is hungry to swallow you up.

Mr. Dominic sank into the leather armchair. He turned his shining head toward the full bookshelves, the table and tall chairs, the office, the armchairs—enough room for everything and some left over to walk about, as in a reception room where the guests have not come.

The valet reappeared, pushing a small trolley on which a bottle and glass were vibrating—clink clonk.

"Ah, but, I don't drink, you know."

Valet Vasile did not allow himself to react in any way. Or perhaps he smiled, idiotically. Do you hear, he smiled! But in fact he didn't even smile, how could he have? After all, nothing was visible. Just a breath of air on his shiny yellow face—a barely perceptible trace of artful distrust and mockery. As if he had smiled only mentally, a broad, satisfied smile of which nothing appeared on the surface. Really nothing: not a word came from Vasile, known as Bazil—no such stupidities from him. Maybe Tolea had got the idea that he was guilty of something, who knows? What's this smile—we're not at the circus, are we? Dr. Marga usually says, Don't let me catch you monkeying around or finding fault with anything, it doesn't suit your station, Vasile, you are Somebody, the High Authority of the other world, like you don't see these days in our parts; you must respect your station, don't compromise yourself with anything human—you're a statue perfectly trained to honor its mission, that's all, and it's more than enough. Valet Vasile did indeed return perfectly deaf and mute, with scarcely visible movements. A pile of glossy foreign magazines had appeared on the trolley beside the glass and the bottle of Courvoisier: *Playboy, L'Express, Paris-Match.* Look, the magnificent Romy Schneider has lost the son she adored; fancy that, she also had a son; access to popular tragedy, would you believe it; bravo, Vasile, you know your job, I take my hat off to you, come here and let me shake your paw.

But Vasile had disappeared. That was what his position demanded —perfect discretion. The slyboots! He doesn't want to answer, the schizoid doesn't want to answer: that's how Dr. Goody-Goody, heart of gold, trained him to be. Would you believe it: the country is dying of hunger and fear and cold and darkness, but the lights are glowing at Goody-Goody's as at the Palace. We've got everything here: we even read foreign magazines, and we're waited on by patients dressed up as valets. After all, that's the patients' role—to bring what they don't have, Courvoisier and *Playboy* and our daily cheese; to get hold of everything so that Goody-Goody's in good spirits, so that he gives them tablets and certificates and pensions, because I know you've got an invalidity pension, Mr. Bazil, don't deny it; it know everything, I know you've got a screw or two loose, but otherwise you're fine, in every other department you're perfectly okay. Here's to you, come and let me shake your paw.

Had Mr. Dominic somehow stood up to offer his hand? Time had passed: who could say whether he had stood up or hadn't.

"But it certainly takes a long time to answer the bell in this palace!"

The bell had been ringing for who knows how long, whistling whistling or whatever, very long and thin.

Dr. Marga pressed the guest's shoulder with the soft palm of his hand. Dr. Marga was looking reproachful. Why on earth has he got that sly look in his eyes? Ah, the bottle. What's a man supposed to do? There's no one you can breathe a word to in this desert, only the poor Frenchman Monsieur Courvoisier took pity on the low spirits of the child Tolea.

"Have you been here long?"

Who was asking whom? It seemed that the doctor had asked the question, but it was by no means certain. Tolea also seemed to have muttered something, surprised that Marga was already wearing his red silk smock and holding a thick pipe in his mouth, as if he had been at home there all the time beside the leather armchair, looking indulgently at the stranger. It was a poor imitation, a poor performance. In vain did Goody-Goody try to imitate his patients; he actually did it like a beginner, without any luster at all. It was an affront to the lunatics, it really was, an insult they hadn't deserved.

"Have you been here long, Tolea? I thought I asked you something."

No, he hadn't been there long, but how can you answer such an idiotic question, when Dr. Loonyson measures time by the liquid in the bottle, as if friend Courvoisier were an hour glass!

So Mr. Dominic had forgotten to answer the question. He was up to something of his own, trying to make the doctor say first what he had to say and then get his own bit in.

"What the hell, Tolea, that's not what we agreed to. It's not wine, you know. I keep telling the dimwit to give people only wine. But I don't know why, whenever you come he gets the bottles mixed up."

So Vasile's supposed to have done it on his own! The scene's the same every time, as you know only too well. You've taught him perfectly how to pour that criminal dishwater down my throat. It must have been Metaxa, yes, because Messrs. Hennessy and Courvoisier are much more sophisticated and well mannered, not like that neoclassical hussy. Yes, now I'm sure it was that whore Metaxa. And you even pretend to be astonished, paternally, certifiably, you pretend to be astonished as usual, as if I didn't know your little game.

So Mr. Dominic had answered only after a long delay, and then not as he usually did. No, this time something must have happened for Mr. Tolea to answer like a little lamb, would you believe it.

"Well, now you too are . . . I've got all kinds of things to raise. As if you didn't know!"

Whereupon Dr. Marga immediately drew up a stool alongside Mr. Tolea's armchair. He leaned toward him, like a mother, a real mother—that's always what the doctor did. Exactly like that, always.

"So what's up, Tolea? What's happened?"

Of course! "So what's up, Tolea? What's happened?" That was how he sweet-talked him each time. Now Merlin the Magician was coming to the boil, as always. "So what's up?! What's happened?! You're like a driveling old woman, that's what you are. You bore me stiff, you know, you're driving me mad with boredom!" Those were the words with which he usually exploded, exactly the same words he always used to answer Marga's opening question. But the reply was slow in coming; the explosion was delayed this time.

"Well, what's up . . . what is there . . . drop it. But where's Bazil got to? Who the hell brought that Metaxa whore here?"

So that's how it is! Mr. Tolea is totally plastered. Something real bad has shaken you up this time; it's a good job the doctor gave you some liquor, that Dr. Marga gave you the strength, that he's got everything properly prepared as usual—the bottle and the glass and the magazines and the sweet talk; he knows everything, does the good doctor.

Anatol Dominic, known as Tolea, looked sulkily at the bottle. Um! The metal top was lying sensibly enough beside the bottle. Mr. Dominic frowned at it, jumped forward a little from the armchair, and cautiously took hold of the bottle. He poured some into the palm of his left hand and replaced the bottle on the table with his right. Then he poured some from his left hand into his right, and wiped his bald patch with both. Yes, he poured the drink onto his bald patch and rubbed it in with his palms, left and right.

"Goo-ood, it's all gone now . . ." as he screwed the top on the bottle.

He looked again at the bottle, dreamily. A thimbleful was all that remained at the bottom.

"What can I do? You know I don't drink: I wouldn't touch the stuff even if you cut me into little pieces. Only when I come here to Uncle, to the resuscitation room. Very rarely, you must admit. Once in a hundred years, at the end of the century. Now in the year 1000, at the end of the century and of the world. The end of the world— that is, the beginning; an iron world because of its severity, a leaden world because of its wickedness. A dark world lacking in authors, *dulcissime frater*, that's what it is."

He searched one of the pockets of his velvet trousers, took out a ball of thin, shiny paper, and held it out to Marga. But Marga did not notice, or did not want to notice, as he went on cleaning his glasses. Tolea solemnly placed the piece of paper on the table, next to the glass.

"What's that smell here? What the hell is it? Maybe that old woman had made moussaka again."

"There isn't any smell. You're imagining it."

"What do you mean! It's enough to knock you out. The hag must have put some tomato juice in it as well. I told her last time she should never do it again, never put tomato juice in moussaka!"

"You're raving. There isn't any moussaka. And Jeny isn't around: she had to be admitted to the hospital. When spring comes there's no avoiding it. She always gets like that in spring. I had her admitted yesterday."

"Aha, so that's it. You've had her locked up. Goo-ood. But why hasn't Bazil shown his face?"

"Bazil's having a bath. His head ached and he was beginning to stutter. It's not a good sign. You know what his crises are like; they come back sometimes. The bath will help pick him up."

"He's actually in the bath? In Goody-Goody's bathtub? No, I must be hearing things. Tell me the truth: is he really having a bath in the great doctor's tub? Are you an apostolic missionary, an ambassador of the Red Cross, or the Green Crescent, or the United Organization called the Losers' Charity? Or are you a rabbi, Dr. Marga, a rabbi's son? Didn't you say once that you psychiatrists are like rabbis? Or maybe you're a Buddhist, Uncle Marga? Are you Tao; yes, you must be Tao, or Zen or yoga—what are you? I bet you're a mason—is that it? Yes, James Mason, the killer disguised as the Holy Woman among lepers."

"You don't know Vasile. He's the cleanest man on earth. He cleans the bath centimeter by centimeter—and then he has a go with alcohol as well."

"Of course, and with sulphamide, too. Come on, old man, tell me: they've finally taken away your right to practice, haven't they? They finally caught on, they must have—the swindle stank to high heaven! Philanthropic, sure, like all swindlers, I know. But they've taken away your thingamajig, admit it, and that contraption for

listening to hiccups and those dissertations on hocus-pocus hypnosis and hara-kiri; they've liberated you from them, haven't they?
Look, I've been here for an hour. The phone hasn't rung once. And
I've been here an hour, more than an hour. The phone's dead, sir,
dead. There's no longer a line outside the confessional, Uncle; the
patients have gone; your conjuring trick has been taken away.
Come on, be brave for once and admit it."

"But it does ring. Listen, it's ringing now: they haven't found me
out yet."

The telephone really was ringing, and it was not hard to predict
the conversation.

"Yes, old pal, I've seen the results of the tests: don't worry, it's
going to be all right." Or: "Of course, madam, those are side effects
of the treatment; everything's quite normal, you'll see." Or: "Why
are you crying, Comrade Engineer? You're perfectly sane. Come
and talk it over: things can be done—of course, they always can."
And so on: candies, sleeping pills, fumigation, just be patient.

"Of course, madam. No, it's no bother. Yes, I spoke to him again
yesterday and asked him. Come for a check-up after a month—after
a month. It's an irritation, that's all, just some allergic reaction. Take
th tablets, of course. Yes, you can ring in the evening—any time in
the evening."

Bearded Marga swung his red smock and turned to face tipsy
Tolea. But the telephone rang again.

"Speaking. Don't be silly: I was expecting you to ring. Alternately
—as I wrote on the prescription; alternately. You have my assurance,
Comrade Colonel, my signature. Absolutely certain. We'll have
good news, very good."

Before returning to his seat on the stool, the plump doctor again
wiped his glasses with the skirt of his smock. His large clear eyes
could now be seen: the blue real one and the blue artificial one—
you couldn't tell them apart. Then they could no longer be seen
again, as he put the smoky glasses back on.

"You'll stay for dinner, Tolea. We'll have another chat."

"If you remember who was invited then."

"There you go again. Nearly forty years have passed since then, Tolea! Even if I was completely normal, I'd still have the right to forget. But I'm not completely normal. This job has got to me, too, you know."

"Quit the whining: it bores me stiff. Just one at least—just one witness, that's all. I'm not doing any harm: it's just a hobby—infantile behavior, as you put it. But I do want to see them again. Particularly one of them, you know which one. Just to see him. Otherwise I'll get bored and die. I can't take the lyrical boredom of spring. I'm telling you, I'll die otherwise."

Mr. Anatol Dominic, also called Tolea, leaned toward the table and picked up the ball of paper. Then he stepped forward, as if he wanted to hand the message to the doctor—to hand him the letter. The doctor did not notice the movement: it must have been in the line of his glass eye. Dominic opened up the paper, as if to read what was on it. A letter, no less, he said, trying to summarize its contents.

The doctor exhaled as he registered the news.

"Goo-ood. What can I say? In the midst of a world crisis, you're the only one whose shares are rising. Maybe Señor Claudiu has been pining for his kid brother. Money expresses affections, as you know. He must have been thinking of you. He's a delicate, sensitive soul—the money proves that, I can tell you as a professional."

"I still don't believe it, and in fact I won't until I see the money. I know my dear old brother," muttered Tolea. He took from his other pocket a creased envelope that had been stamped many times. He put it on the table next to the bottle, but in doing so he knocked the ball of paper down beside the stool. Mr. Dominic looked absent-mindedly in the direction of the tall, narrow, castle-like windows, the book-lined walls, the huge lampstand in the center of the hall, the glass squares of the roof, the checkerboard squares of the floor.

Mr. Marga was standing silently at the window. Tolea did not see him, or saw him no longer. Nor did he see Bazil. The voiceless doctor was puffing and blowing; Mr. Dominic did not see him. Bazil had revived, a statue in front of the door—Mr. Tolea did not see him. Deathly silence, no one saying a word. There must have been some sad news in the letter, some memory or sorrow, who knows?

They are no longer looking at each other, as if they are not there. There is no way Tolea can have noticed when his host makes a brief sign. The valet disappears: he has never been there: when could he have been there, since he is no longer visible? Tolea is far gone, as if he has suddenly lost his wits. Eyes staring, mouth wide open, he looks as if he might be unconscious. But he shudders when Marga slowly lifts him up, holding him under the arms. He looks at the doctor attentively, vacantly. Marga grips him behind his shoulders and gently pushes him toward the end of the hall. There are two steps at the end of the hall—a kind of podium, like a stage beneath the spotlight in the ceiling. There, at the end, dinner is being served. They are together, on the two tall chairs on either side of the long table, at the far end of the hall.

The chandelier in the middle has vanished, into the darkness. The homely corner is lit only by the white lamp globe, like a spotlight beamed onto the white tablecloth. Silver cutlery, napkins, large glasses, small glasses, with their thinned-down crystal sound, small large deep plates—it seems as though Tolea, too, is eating.

From time to time the plates are changed and new courses served. Vasile picks up the napkin that has fallen by the chair. Tolea straightens his back; Vasile lays the napkin over his knees. Five, ten minutes, an eternity, the year 1000. Tolea does seem, however, to have bolted something down. Again Vasile bends and picks up the napkin: he shakes it and opens it out. Mr. Dominic sits up straight and the napkin reappears on his knees. Somewhere there is a ripple of music. The napkin falls and is replaced. The soup bowl disappears and a steak appears—or maybe it wasn't steak, or maybe the steak wasn't up to much. Another dish appears, the white napkin reappears.

Tolea is not speaking: he doesn't drink and he holds his tongue. He seems not to hear the doctor's habitual stories, not to be there at all. Even when he finally resumes the conversation, he seems to be absent.

"So, it was moussaka after all. That old dog Bazil! He put tomato juice in it, but it isn't bad. The numbskull can even do that, then."

"Vasile cooks superbly. But Jeny doesn't let him. You should see how he irons clothes. Quite extraordinary—like an Englishwoman at the queen's court. And when he cooks, it comes out perfect. But with him it doesn't have the same therapeutic effect as it does with Jeny. Although it does do him good, I'm sure. I told you, housework keeps them occupied: it calms them down."

"Not to mention the tips, of course."

Mr. Dominic raised his glass of red wine. He brought it to his lips, but then changed his mind. "I'm on holiday. I don't know if you know. I've got a short holiday which could become long."

"You told me on the phone. You've been away, too, no?"

"I soon came back. You can't find anywhere proper anymore. Dirt, pathetic food that's unavailable and expensive. Lines wherever you go. No light in the streets and no heating indoors. And patrols everywhere—armed patrols, like when, you know . . . So I came back to enjoy myself at home. At least it's cheaper—searching for that photographer who's not a real photographer. Maybe you could give me his address; I can't find him. You mentioned him to me once, but probably you regretted that you'd shot your mouth off. You regretted it and you haven't wanted to talk about it since. You knew I wouldn't be able to find him."

"It's come over you again, has it? Back to all that nonsense after two or three years? You're bored, I know. That's what's wrong with you: boredom. But what do you want, for God's sake? To see those fossils again? Nothingness—that's what they are now. Ashes, earth, holes in the ground. And those who survived have got one foot there, in paradise. Look at me."

Old Marga laughed, they both laughed. Tolea motioned behind him, in the direction of the trolley. "Read the letter. You'll see it's not just a question of boredom and distraction, although they shouldn't be ignored by any means. Look at this last letter. I knew he'd get around to it, because sooner or later the memories would overwhelm him: he'd want them to be warmed up, fresh, with salt, with poison, with all the spices of the death that the paralytic is courting these days. So he pays me in convertible currency, Doctor! That's how I'm on holiday. Paid. The alms he sent me a year ago were actually an advance. I could sense he had something up his sleeve."

The doctor stood up, put his napkin beside the plate, gave the patient a smile, blew out some smoke, paced a few steps up and down with his hands behind his back. Then he walked up to the little table, where he could see the ball of paper and the envelope on the floor—looking, not looking.

"Don't exaggerate: he's been sending you money for years, since he found out about the trial. Or anyway, since he found out you've got problems. Otherwise you wouldn't be able to manage. Not a lot, of course, but it adds up over all those years. And you never answered him, did you, Tolea? You never thanked him, never wrote a line. So . . . unless it's another one of your tricks, you can give him a promise. It might even do you good. You'll have something to take your mind off everyday worries."

"What music, Doctor! What cassettes!"

"Well, after all, it's your sister-in-law's letter; you can't tell who thought it up. And then if it doesn't suit you, you can just not answer, as you've always done. Even if the sum is incomparably bigger this time, there isn't necessarily a connection between money and what the sick person is asking for. It could be more like a suggestion, you know; he may not actually be putting any demands on you."

"Who gave you this wonderful tape, sir? It's really something else!"

"Coco, my colleague in surgery, brought it back from a trip to Cuba."

"Cuba? What are you talking about? That is a fantastic tape. Music from the year 3000, old man, the fourth millennium. Death on a cassette tape."

"Sure, Coco knows what's what. And the Cubans have got some fine music, too. Death is everywhere, you know, like music."

"Look, it's stopped. Play the other side, will you?"

"I'd say you should accept the challenge—whether or not it's true that Mircea Claudiu suggested it to you. Accept it—but don't count on me. Maybe they're also exiles over there, sick at heart, you know how it is. But anyway, you've got nothing to lose in the end. If it amuses you, go ahead; any distraction is a good idea. There's no way I can help you, though. Let's be clear about that. Try Gafton: he knows a lot of stories, and he's just waiting for someone to listen. He's also worked on the newspapers and has some connections— which you don't exactly."

"Yes, I do!" growled Mr. Tolea, who was arranging the new tapes and staring at the red eye on the panel of the cassette player. Then time became confused: the doctor had evaporated at some point, the music was on its last legs, there were fewer and fewer lights, the clock had struck, again and again, with no one to hear . . . You see, Mr. Bazil, we've got business to attend to. Tonight . . . Mr. Tolea whispers in Vasile's ear, in two or nine hours or so, when they wake up next to each other on the carpet, looking closely at each other and nodding like two old men, now one now the other, as if continuing a conversation from times of old.

Friend Vasile keeps quiet and looks. Submissive, patient with everyone.

"We patients have arranged to meet there at the outfall—near that miserable little village. Some twenty kilometers away, where the sewer empties into the river. They're all coming tonight, you'll see . . .

"I'm not sick anymore, Mr. Tolea. That's what the doctor says: I'm not sick anymore. You're healthier than lots of people, he says. You're healthier than me, Vasile, that's what he says. Dr. Marga says so."

"That's right. You can believe it, too."

"Yes, my kidneys and my eyes and my heart. Especially my heart, because poor Dr. Marga's heart is not too . . ."

"You feed him too much in the evening: he'll croak from it one of these days."

"Only when you come, sir. But it'll end badly. You don't know how to drink, Mr. Tolea: these are strong drinks. Even though I'm healthy myself, I wouldn't have the courage to . . ."

"How's that, Vasile? After all, you're healthy—not like the doctor."

"Yes, I am. And d'you know what the doctor said? He said: If only THE COMRADE were as healthy as you are—you know who he meant! Comrade Jabber-Jabber, Dr. Marga calls him."

"No, I don't know. And God help you if I did. How does Goody-Goody speak? How does he dare talk like that about . . . we know who . . . how does he dare? And you, Vasile, how can you dare to be compared with we know who? Haven't you any pride left at all, any respect for this poor little country of ours?"

"Yes, that's what the doctor said. If that one was as healthy as me, we'd be much much much . . . what shall I say? . . . um, much happier. But stop shouting like that: it's not allowed. You know it's not allowed and it won't do you any good at all, really."

"There's nothing the least bit wrong with me, m'sieur. All I want is to go to that rendezvous of yours. To listen to you all there. To hear what it was like. Because it's being repeated now, you must know that. You're a brainy guy, Vasile; you can see that it's all happening again, can't you? But let me tell you the truth. You're the only one I'll tell it to. And the truth is, I don't care. I do not care! Not a moment's thought, that's me: I haven't a clue about anything. Everything leaves me cold; it all passes me by. That's my secret, Bazil, I'm as thick-skinned as they come. Do you hear? Thick-skinned and flighty. That's my secret."

And Mr. Tolea seemed disgusted with what he was saying—which meant he was wide awake. He had a sneer when he spoke. He spat out the words, as if they were mere scraps quite unlike what had remained hidden inside.

"Call me Lucky Luke. That's how you can pamper me, Vasile; I'll allow you to tonight. In my class they used to shout out, Bolero. They'd make fun of me—bring me down with a crash, you could say. They'd keep blowing up the balloon as far as it went. And when I was about to get into the basket, pshhhh . . . the gas escaped. Just as I was getting into the balloon, pshhhh . . . They'd all heap scorn on me—with both their eyes and their mouth, as is the habit in this land of ours."

He blew his own trumpet, Mr. Tolea did; that's how he was made. His clothes, his chatter, whims, and stories all served to demonstrate what a great and important guy he was. But he had suddenly realized that if he spat out his words like that—in disgust, with his lower lip turned up—it meant that—

He had suddenly fallen silent. Suddenly silent, and as yellow as a lemon. That's what he's like. Once it comes over him, he loses all interest. He has no appetite for anything, as simple as that—there's nothing to be done about it.

Bonehead Vasile has stopped in the doorway leading from the cloakroom. Stopped there like a dummy. Tolea had sensed it. Without moving and without looking, he had felt that Vasile was no longer nearby on the carpet, that he had sneaked away and was standing over there, a statue, like a dummy.

He wanted to turn and look at him standing with his back to the door: he wanted to swing around and look at him. He didn't care: Mr. Vancea didn't care about anything or anyone, and yet he felt like swinging around to look at bonehead Vasile standing stone-still in the frame of the door. To look, bored, at Vasile the dunce. He couldn't, he couldn't turn around: he was stricken with paralysis. From fear, the fear of being turned into stone perhaps. The only light still glowing was the tiny one on the cassette player. Tolea could have turned around: there was no danger; he had no reason to be afraid of Vasile. But he was rooted to the spot, unable to budge, even when he heard steps approaching. He did not move—and what solemn steps he suddenly had, that sly, servile schizophrenic. The punishing step of a prosecutor. Like a punitive and unyielding father—his old dead father—that was how the madman approached.

Vasile had halted behind Tolea, glued to the curved spine of Professor Anatol Dominic Vancea Voinov.

Not even the doors were creaking anymore. The world had stopped breathing. The end: the year 1000. The duffer Anatol Vancea was cowering, as if he had lost all his sap. It lasted a long time, a short time—hard to say. Vasile sneaked away, giving himself airs in front of Mr. Tolea. The professor was pale in the face, with bulging eyes that saw nothing whatsoever. Mr. Tolea did not even have the strength to look, to whine, to lift his hands in front of his eyes and drive away the apparition. He did nothing; he just looked at great Bazil. Deathly pale, but conscious. He wasn't drunk: he had the same mocking expression on his face that he always wore. But he was white as a sheet. Poor Tolea looked with babyish eyes, without blinking and without seeing.

Vasile was dressed in the doctor's brown raglan from England. Yellow silk scarf around his neck, bowler hat on his head. Very long, fluffy gloves. The full dress that Marga wore when he made a show of himself. The hairy raglan had a breast pocket under the left lapel, containing nothing more and nothing less than the starched white handkerchief of Goody-Goody, the madmen's doctor.

The spitting image of the doctor! Great Bazil was the spitting image of the short, fat, and delicate doctor. And he was smiling, Old Nick! To say nothing of the fact that the dunce's smile was enough to freeze your blood. With all those big, perfect, yellow teeth. Mr. Bazil left the hall disdainful and smiling, like some real big shot!

Tolea had covered his eyes and lowered his head onto his chest in exhaustion.

. . . Not a soul in the streets. It took a very long time to get out into the fields. An infinite, immeasurable instant. At the little wooden bridge on the edge of the village Vasile stopped to straighten his hat—incredible! to straighten his hat. The moon was sleek and golden, Mr. Vasile Moussaka blanched and sharpened, as if he was performing a role too harsh for his lofty magical powers. One last step, to the edge of the concrete slope at the sewer's mouth. Lines or columns of torches awaited him, greeted him. Thin, longish torches —perhaps only candles, in fact, but looking like torches.

Vasile was smiling. When he took the torch candle from the first person's hands, he smiled. He took it and blew on it. The childlike face of the elderly patient abruptly disappeared, along with the flame. Mr. Vasile smilingly went up to the next one. The pious neurasthenic with disheveled hair. He blew his candle out, too. Then the fat woman with green hair and the devil's look in her eyes. Then the next and the next. When he was about to blow on the candle of the trembling, shaking, powerless boy, they all suddenly went out as if a signal had been given.

As if a signal had been given, everyone in the endless row—in the columns drawn up way into the distance—suddenly extinguished their candles. They all disappeared. Mr. Vasile remained alone, torch in hand. He smiled with satisfaction. Torch beside the tail of the raglan coat. Perfect silence, perfect night. That annoying creak of rusty doors could be heard again. The material began to burn, from the raglan's tail up. Then the gloves. Then the yellow silk scarf. Vasile still had a smile on his lips when the howling music and the tom-tom started up.

Numbskull Tolea was paralyzed; there was no one to stop the music. Smoke, magnetic apparitions, the smell of burning and ashes. Only Tolea saw them. Alone, as alone as a dead man, and he did not even have the strength to blink.

THE LIGHT IN THE room turned violent, artificial, hostile. He switched it off. He moved away from the window; the room seemed to have been pacified. The soft half-darkness had tempered the gloom within and the light outside, in a kind of acceptable complicity.

At some point—when exactly?—the hazy shadow had sneaked through the door.

"It's me, Toma; we know each other. I hope I'm not disturbing you."

The familiar voice: well trained, polite. The spy's voice; the voice of the night.

"Are you reading? What is it? Ah, that paper. The business with the old woman, the cats, the fire. Does it interest you? Does it really? We were supposed to see each other—perhaps you remember. I have taken the liberty of, well, just a few minutes. I wouldn't want to intrude on your time—I promise."

The *professore* did not know whether it was in his own voice that he answered.

"It's Ianuli again, is it? It's him you want to ask me about? Well, I don't know him. Yes, I know he's friendly with Irina. Yes, yes, Irina Radovici. No, not in the sense that . . . No, just a friend, I know. I've heard of him, so have lots of people. But I don't know him personally. All I can say are the banal things everyone knows. Everyone knows the Ianuli legend."

Mr. Vancea fidgeted around looking for his cigarettes, but he could not find them. The room was floating in a gray mist; he could not even find suitable words to speak.

"A withdrawn type, not the same as he used to be. That's what people say."

"Very withdrawn, I've heard. And ill, very ill—so they say. He's grown old and sick, and he's got a family, all kinds of worries . . ."

"Yes, the family. Do you know the missus?"

"No, not in the slightest" came the hurried reply.

"Absolutely not at all?"

"I've just seen her a few times in the street. We've never spoken to each other."

"Sure, sure. They've got a boy as well, haven't they? I mean a young man, a student already."

"He's not Ianuli's. He's her son from a previous marriage. Not exactly a marriage, but it's not important—anyway, from a relationship."

"We know: it's not important. So in your view this hero is washed up? Is that what you think?"

"I don't think anything: I don't know him. And anyway, you know him better than I do. He's your typical hero. A revolutionary! You must know him better. He embodies—no?—symbolizes . . ."

"So now we're getting there. You've put your finger on a very sore spot, I can tell you. Does someone like that remain fascinating? Do you think so, eh? But there's a danger as well, you know. It's not your street-corner discontents but these big-time ones who pose a threat, I can tell you. They're past treatment! Heroes of the struggle, sure— good for spectacular upheavals. But what then? They need to understand reality, the world of the concrete—which is always relative. Prophets driven by ideals become, become—you know what I mean. It no longer counts whose side they were on or would like to be on, I can tell you. Where is the devil? In those obstinate monks whose eyes are fixed on an obsession? Or in their opposite: the adaptable crowd, the apathetic jokers?"

"I wouldn't know. I'm not a theologian or a psychologist or an ideologue. I'm a cripple, the most crippled of all, my dear patrolman. Just let me sleep—sleep and be quiet."

"Is Comrade Ianuli also substituting for someone? Is it myth, illusion, utopia? Or mystery, conspiracy? Or what the hell is the Ianuli legend substituting for? How can it still be peddled today, in a world where everyone is numb? Does it fetch a good price? Is there still a demand for it?"

"I don't understand. I don't understand what you want."

"The believers, the rigid, maladjusted ones—are they the real danger, or the crowd of gawkers?"

"A danger for whom?"

"You keep avoiding a reply. You understand me only too well, I know. You understand only too well what we're interested in, why we want to know your opinion. Could Ianuli ever become the same as before? I mean, could he move to the other side of the barricades? All those firebrands, schizoids are the same, in fact, I can tell you. All frustrated! That's the criterion that could be used to pick them out. Frustrated, schizoid. Thirsting for power! They're given pretty names from lullabies. But let's look at it from a different angle. What about yourself? Is there an idealist inside you? A rebel, a true believer? Would you enlist for the struggle, shall we say?"

"I haven't got enough qualities, or enough—defects. I'm contemplative and sedentary and set in my ways and, and—Well, I simply wouldn't covet the honor which—"

"But are you the opposite? Untouched by anything? The slippery one who whistles and hops about?"

"Absolutely not. I'm not sufficiently—"

"Well, you were saying that in everyone there's a bit of everything. That people are different, often opposite, and that's how it should be—but everyone has other individuals inside him, potentially. That would mean, I suppose, that in a certain situation he might become, if only for a short period, he might become—"

"Huh, I haven't said that yet. I never said anything like it—so don't go around saying I did. Who taught you that stuff, eh?"

He was on the point of shouting, but his voice had cut out some time before. The questions had also stopped: the silence had grown longer and longer, turning into weariness. He waited for the torture to begin again, but the pause continued: the silence became lassitude, drowsiness. He should have switched on the light, but he didn't have the strength.

Dawn found him exhausted. The directions for a meeting—is that what I'm looking for? How will they, will I, meet death? Who will be the one singled out? How does the road lie ahead toward the future, that is, toward death? We don't have any immortals or any posterity. An age without immortals and without posterity? How do the past, our parents, the premise meet up again? That is, the future; that is, death. He kept muttering without a break, as if he had become senile. And he was pale, old, wasted by insomnia.

A puffed-up fool, that's all there is to him. A substitute in a world of substitutes. But a crackpot who lashes out and hits the glasses by mistake can also, presumably, knock the alarm circuits. That's what our Tolea is good for. Stupid pranks may give rise to unintentional difficulties, defections, revelations; the clown may revive things sleeping in the depths. We push him into the teeming shadows, till he starts thrashing around and screaming, like the loony blighter he is. Bubbles eddies sparks. Perhaps movement will be triggered by mistake. The shock to set the engine going, that is what he has been imploring for so long.

On the morning when the plot finally began, he looked younger than the age supposedly required by the action. The ex-teacher Tolea Voinov, self-selected as the bait, the trigger, the muddlehead, still looked youthful. Young Anatol, dressed to match the young and alert season.

The challenge, *professore*, the challenge! Proof that there's still a chance for the powerless, even when everything appears crushed. I'll prove it, I swear I will! I'll put up a tiny obstacle, a teeny-weeny poisoned obstacle. Maybe I'll hit the center of the Monster. Maybe I'll blind the Jabberer, the Cyclops. Maybe I'll poison Goliath with my little flower. He had raised his empty glass as if to offer a toast. His cigarette was burning his fingers. But he had still collapsed again—stupefied, exhausted. The shadows of the room and his thoughts and the hours had once more become entangled; dusk had again arrived. He would have liked to stretch out on the sofa for a few moments, but no, it's no good on the sofa, he'd find Toma the spy there, uninvited. Better like this, on my feet, at the night-darkened window. Or on the chair, perhaps there. You can grip it firmly, tighten your belt, push hard against the back of the chair so that you can no longer be dragged up. Yes, it's good like that: he had closed opened his eyes. It grew darker and darker: he shut his eyes and the setting suddenly lit up in the solemn and sumptuous courtroom. The Council for Model Culture and Disabled Education. The Committee for Neurotic Refugees.

The Office for Thought Security. Five, six polished men. The one at the head of the table had just passed his little white freckled hand through his thin fair hair. He had opened the file, closed the file. Like the others, he had two files before him. The red file and the green file. He opened now one and now the other. He looked at his colleagues, who repeated the movement. They opened the red file, with the bulky manuscript. They leafed through it attentively, as the High Commissar also had done, and lifted their eyes as the Boss had lifted his. Then they opened the green file, the one containing the defendant's background, full of thin sheets of paper covered with codes and invisible ink and the Toma correspondence. They said nothing as they read, looked at each other, raised their diseased eyebrows, looked at each other. The scar briefly glowed with a phosphorescent light. The blond girl had breezily waltzed in, already in her sixth month. Blushing, she had put a small glass of water on the table, beside the young man who was perspiring as he read the indictment. He had smiled. "Yes, okay . . . now it's something else." The man wearing glasses had reached the end of the first page. He moistened his thin bluish lips in the holy water. When he hit the ashtray with his Irish pipe, the heads rose from the stained sheets of paper. A moment's deliberation was observed. The first on the left mumbled something, and the others became extremely attentive. "I've had enough; I've had enough of this lot," the fat bald-headed man repeated, yielding the argument. Opposite him, the first on the right cheered up and smiled. "Yes, let him go away—as far as possible. We'll give him his chance in the bosom of Abraham and purify the colony." Now they were chanting in turn, leaning fondly, excitedly, over their neighbor's file: "Clear him away from us all, the dirty je-je-jackal"—in a low chorus. The head of the table tapped his nails on the table glass. "Yes, let Old Trouble go away with his diseases and his sick ideas. The law requires us to give him a chance. So, a vote of censure with a warning. A warning to quit the premises." The young prosecutor at the head of the table straightened his glasses and started to read the indictment again.

Nothing more could be made out. Voice abolished. The batrachian masks prattled out words without sound, winking with their eyes. All that could be seen was the shiny pallor of the masks, the phosphorescent scar above the eyebrow. At the door Tolea, the accused, was pale and sweating. He did not know how to plant himself better in the cockpit, so as not to make a noise and be discovered. For some time he had been on the monitor in the frame of the door. No one had seen him yet: he was coldly perspiring, his heart struggling guiltily, his feet becoming wet, his arms hanging limply down. No, the anxious, frightened face of the alien who had to be got rid of did not disturb the judges. They were working with dispatch, and the murmur of their united voices, the low tone of the gay refrain, could be heard once more. "Je . . . je . . . jackal. Jacko Jacko has got to go." The papers rustled, twisting and turning; the refrain rippled with excitement.

The alien was rooted to the spot in the doorway, together with his chair. Completely drained. In vain did they all stare at him now. They looked at him scornfully, persistently, with a feeling of boredom: tirelessly. No, no, tired! Suddenly, as if commanded to do so, they wiped their foreheads, their phosphorescent eyebrows, their stifling masks. They had become too hot! The spring sun had tired them, look! They had covered their sockets, eyebrows, the scar: nothing could be seen anymore; the dazzling star dominated the room.

So the wreck woke up perspiring in the vernal excitement of a new spring morning. He spent a long time rubbing his forehead, temples, and eyelids, and awkwardly relieved the pressure of the tongs of the chair in which the night had nailed his arms.

There was no longer any point in the action. Just another vanity, another black mark in his file, which would never reach the eyes of anyone except the high custodial authorities. No action materializes in this fictitious world of signs and substitutes. So Tolea decided: don't delay for a moment longer! Because: wanton, vain, puerile, culpable, fictitious. Because because because . . . Therefore: not one delay!

It would get going immediately, there and then. Against the grain! In the morning—against the grain, pampered, in revenge.

The action: that very morning.

HE HAD BEEN AWAKE for a long time, but he still felt listless, stupefied. He opened closed his eyes, stretched out his hand to the alarm clock that had not sounded. His hand trembled on the rim of the clock, then fell back by the crumpled sheet on the floor at the edge of the bed. He had been sleeping naked, uncovered. He remembered that during the night he had probably gone onto the terrace to get some fresh air. It had been a restless night, burdened with strange dreams that had been chased away along with the darkness. He felt tired and clumsy. Only after an hour or so did he recognize the untidy table, the open window, his pair of slippers. Eventually he went into the bathroom, then lay exhausted in the armchair, then swung among the chairs. His mind started up with difficulty, stopped, procrastinated, started up again.

On the table was the long envelope with stamps and postage marks. He saw and recognized it, and seemed to begin speeding up. He was in a hurry, yes, in a great hurry. Suddenly he was speeding along crazily, and then he ground to a halt. On holiday, yes, he was on holiday: but where can you go in the season of uncertainty which is now just a pink haze? After an hour it became sultry and in another three it was whistling with gusts of ice. At Anton's, at Toni's, yes, at Dr. Marga's—among our crazy fellow creatures there was always something to set your blood moving faster. Yes, at Marga's, at Mr. Bazil's, at Old Maid Moussaka's, I'd find some of everything there. But I've just been there, I think; I was there three days or so ago. I spoke to Lord Marga about the letter and my little sister-in-law from Argentina and the foreign currency account in the name of receptionist Vancea. Yes, I'm sure I was at the Hysteria Cabaret and I danced the Tango Macabre with the famous Bazil Beelzebub and the Radiant Angelica, yes yes, and it was evening and night and morning, actually.

Costume already laid out on the chair: red socks, white pullover, white velvet trousers.

Lying naked on the sofa, the star still hesitated. The windows rattled as a bus went by. Look, the real world still exists: it has started up again, a bus is passing right in front of the window, the windows are vibrating, Mr. Dominic is receiving the signal and is in a hurry to get inside the day's routine sounds. At twelve minutes before ten o'clock, the tenant Anatol Dominic Vancea Voinov, known as Tolea, left the building. He retraced his steps twice, as if to mislead someone tailing him. He checked the taps, cupboards, window, and gas valves—or perhaps only pretended to close them again. Scatterbrained and fastidious, perfect in the role.

He looked left right and crossed. TOBACCONIST, DAIRY, TAILOR. "They're all here, close by. As at the beginning of the world. If only we could look with detachment, historically." He turned after the corner, passed the tram stop, kept moving away, and went into a small side street.

Dwarfish silence winding through humble, sloping, Oriental courtyards. Very occasionally, a long green strip of branches winks over the walls. Little rounded gardens alongside piles of garbage; thorny red rosebushes next to heaps of rags, boxes, bags—picturesque, patriarchal, canceling boundaries. To the left the drive opened onto the refuge of a villa manqué. Gates, pillars, balconies, the conceited haste of the parvenu, the nostalgia of a style, the speed of the heterogeneous that must prepare to compromise with the barbarians, the corruption of forms, the assault of rottenness . . .

He went up from the dirty little street to the Hill of the Metropolitan Church. At a short distance the market, the bustle of traders. Then the corridor of Lipscani Street, once the fairy scene of dealers, now completely hushed, slumbering in languor and dirt. A few moments in front of the little church of Ionikie Stavropoleos. The graceful façade with its baroque verve, in contrast to the austere, limpid, geometric interior. He passed beside the palace, stopped before the Atheneum, and looked at the frieze on the arch, still glowing with forgotten crowned heads. On the left, a new construction—a massive white block. Shells from the earthquake three years before, filled with the concrete of the new foundations. Apathy, remembrance. The new model cages, their constricted functionalism. Two rooms kitchen and bath. Couple child refrigerator television. Reproduction of the same sordid honeycomb struggling to make ends meet . . . Mr. Dominic Vancea put himself at the mercy of idle meditation, alibi of whatever surprises were being prepared. "I feel as if I were preparing to commit a murder, or for the great love of my life, or for revelations that have kept being put off."

The eccentric pedestrian advances without haste, slowly looking around him. A delicate spring morning: you become its unassuming condottière, torn from lethargy for a still obscure mission that Fate is producing for you beneath the sky's huge pink hat. You become— finally finally!—the lever or puppet of the epic, bang bang bang, scooby-dooby-do.

And so Dominic Vancea, aged over below fifty, employed as multilingual receptionist at the Hotel Tranzit and at a persistent initiation into the delights of carnival, is sauntering with thin but even steps down Victory Boulevard. The pedestrian on this calm spring morning seems to have no definite purpose, not even when, for the umpteenth time, he carefully searches the back pocket of his white velvet trousers.

He stops for a moment: yes, the envelope is in his pocket, where he put it. He remains undecided, then begins to turn back. He appears to change direction. But after a few steps he abandons the abandonment. Yes, he has finally remembered the quotation that has been obsessing him for the whole walk: "Only what cannot be turned around and brought back to a prior state constitutes a true event." That was indeed the quotation. He can't recall the author's name, but it doesn't matter: the memory exercise is enough to satisfy him.

So, the morning is starting up again. No, it is continuing; that is, coming true. TOBACCONIST, DAIRY, TAILOR, Calea Rahovei, Metropolitan Hill, Lipscani Street, the Atheneum, Strada Batiştei, Strada Vasile Lascăr: now the pedestrian is coming into Rosetti Square. At the crossing he again searches for the envelop in his trouser pocket. No, he won't turn back: he seems determined to set a real event in motion.

Before pushing the metal gate, he took a large white handkerchief from his pocket and wiped his perspiring face. As he removed the white silk, Dominic Vancea's smooth firm face reappeared, now refreshed, from beneath the conjuror's rectangle—a Roman consul's head, as bald as if he had shaved it. Clear forehead, sharp eyes, straight, perfectly shaped nose, thin lips. He seemed to know the routine: enter quickly, self-importantly, with a distant air; don't give any breathing space for someone to check your identity. Quite perfect—the man on the door did not even have time to salute.

He went slowly up the narrow, twisting, dirty staircase and found himself in a dark corridor. Half of a bathroom, packed with stands and boxes, could be seen through a half-open door. It looked like a private lodging for several families. He entered a large open room, then passed a long table covered with red cloth to go into a similar room, smaller and rounder in shape. Four desks with some distance between them, and a typist's worktable to the left of the door. Comrade Orest Popescu? the curly-haired blonde repeated in a simpering voice. Comrade Popescu is away at a briefing, and his deputy is in the organizing meeting. Meeting? Huh! What kind of meetings do they have? Surely we're not at— But frank questions are not permitted. Vancea's eyes stared, then he immediately pulled himself together, anxious not to appear taken aback.

The typist gestured toward the window without looking up from the keyboard. Yes, in fact there was a chair by the window. He sat on the chair, facing a solid, dark-haired man with a tie that was throt-tling him.

"You've come for the Year of the Disabled . . ."

"Well, I'd have liked to . . ."

"You must discuss it with the Executive first. I'm not allowed to give any kind of information. If she calls me in and says, Look, daddy—that's what she calls me, daddy, or sometimes Iopo—discuss it with the comrade. If she tells me that, then of course—"

"I'll wait, then: I'm not in any hurry. Will it go on for long?"

"Depends. It started just now. Maybe it won't go on for long."

"And you say it's a meeting? What kind of a meeting can they be having?"

"Well, the Executive can speak normally. The president and the vice president, too—like us in fact, as you see. But that's not to say, I mean, it makes no difference. We're all united—we're all one with the actual members."

He looked like a foreman in a factory, tired, punished with hav-ing to wear a suit and tie and having to get involved in things that were too complicated and frightening for him.

"Maybe you'd like to read something. It passes the time, so you don't get bored. Here are some of our publications. And our stat-utes. Maybe they will interest you."

Tolea put the pile on his knees and took out the little brochure: STATUTES. "A public organization . . . which exists to train people for the political, economic, social, and cultural life of the country . . . for the work of construction . . . Socialism and Communism . . . its members are citizens . . . living within the country's borders, deaf, deaf-mute, and hard-of-hearing, whose hearing loss is measured at more than 40 decibels . . . Also citizens who are able to hear and who support the Association may become members, in a proportion no higher than 10 percent."

Dominic Vancea looked up at the office worker, who was keeping him under close scrutiny. They stared into each other's eyes, as if communicating in some code or other. The visitor fidgeted on his chair in embarrassment. The office worker opposite him no longer appeared so weary—or so out of place in his role. For now the role suddenly struck him as unclear, as if those suspicious eyes, by scrutinizing the mimicry of reading, should have been able to guess at once whether the stranger did or did not deserve to be trusted by the sect.

"The numbers have increased," he muttered, as if to himself, though still keeping a close watch. The intruder looked down at the statutes, but the guide continued to mumble.

"We have recorded a growth of more than 30 percent in the last five-year period. Forecasts for the next ten years show that we will achieve growth of—" A deep, soft, whispering voice—such was the activist's way of speaking.

"The right to elect and be elected, to take part in discussions and to make proposals," Dominic read in the brochure. The lines were beginning to dance in front of his eyes. "The Association is organized according to the principle of centralism. Leading bodies are elected from the bottom up; decisions are taken from the top down. The minority bows to the majority. Failure to comply—" He looked up and met the dark eyes trained on his bald head. Dark eyes, dark, bushy, knitted eyebrows. Dominic Vancea confronted the watching eyes. He tried without blinking to make out the scar by the dark-haired man's left eyebrow. A faint mark, like a scratch, could be a sign or could be just a scratch—how was he to tell?

"Failure to comply with the statutes is sanctioned by criticism, reprimand, formal warning, censure, and expulsion"—recited the dark-haired man facing Dominic, with a smile on his lips. He was smiling! Why was he smiling, with those big yellow teeth? Dominic looked again at the eyebrow, at that scratch from a nail or razor blade or insect or whatever. He laid the brochure aside and took the first of the Newletters. *Viaţa Noastră, Our Life:* that was the title of the Association's paper, printed in big red letters.

At the top of the page: WORKERS OF THE WORLD, UNITE! VIAŢA NOASTRĂ, ORGAN OF THE COUNCIL OF THE ASSOCIATION. Then the front-page headlines. HOMAGE TO THE BELOVED LEADER. EULOGISTIC POEM. POSITIVE BALANCE SHEET, MORE EXACTING DEMANDS. PLENARY SESSION OF THE CENTRAL COUNCIL. He looked up. The office worker was no longer smiling. He looked down. "The conclusion of the Five Year Plan marks another major step in building the multilaterally developed society, the achievement of new, higher quality in the work and life of working people. The wise, clear-sighted leadership, the Leader's precious directives and guidelines, dynamize consciousness and mark out the broad and intricate process of the construction of the multilaterally developed society. At the center of activity is man himself—created by the conditions for the multilateral affirmation of the human personality, which is an expression of the revolutionary humanism characterizing the Association."

Dominic looked up, looked down, turned the page of the newsletter. "On the fourth Sunday of the month we celebrate the international day of the deaf, a splendid occasion for a balance sheet. Each member must display a greater sense of concern and act resolutely to achieve growth in labor productivity, tighter discipline, and constant improvement of the style and methods of work. The Best Locksmith competition. The Best Sportsman competition. The 'Song in Praise of the Fatherland' literary competition. The International Year of the Disabled. The care taken by the Party and state to create the right conditions for work and study. The football match between the teams Silence C. and Silence P.—a fine occasion to test technical-tactical capabilities and physical training. After the end of vocational training, the young man wanted to follow a course at evening college. Recognizing his qualities, as well as his exemplary conduct, his local organization accepted him into the ranks of the

Party. Sorin is making every effort to ensure that his performance at work matches the confidence shown in him."

Dominic looked up. The office worker was smiling. His dark unblinking eyes were trained on him. And the blue eyes of the man with disheveled hair in the middle of the room, and of the bespectacled man next to him who was furiously smoking a cigarette. Only the sweet little typist clicked away without pause, her role being to cover the silence, the sequence with the rigid office workers who did nothing but keep the intruder under observation.

"It's not an ordinary public association, any old collective of—do you know what I mean?" resumed the whispering guide, Comrade Daddy or Iopo, or whatever the comrades called him. "It's a model, do you understand?" And he nervously rubbed his eyebrows—both ruffled eyebrows at the same time, with both hands.

"Many people, oh yes, too many, could be taught a thing or two. They should learn from—from our members, I mean. They're not distracted by anything during working hours. They don't talk, don't hear, don't listen; then can't gossip or tell jokes. Nor do they waste themselves on all kinds of trifles. They spend the whole time concentrating on their work—tidy, disciplined, and loyal. Above all loyal: that's what matters most. Without any frivolity, without jokes or any of that nonsense. Double-dealing, grumbling, all those whims which—"

He stared straight in Dominic's eyes, severe, distrustful, accusatory, and yet he smiled. He smiled! A weird smile was stuck to his lips—impossible to tell whether it was scornful or malicious or idiotic. A rigid smile which ended up scaring him. Dominic again looked down at the paper. "A call for socialist competition addressed to all branches. The stages of affirmation. Labor—an honor-bound duty. Discipline—as much discipline as possible," but he couldn't escape the sound of the guide.

"They're conscientious, extremely conscientious. They keep their minds on their work, carrying out instructions to the letter. They're punctual and see through to the end what they are entrusted with. We had an exemplary case of a woman comrade who for ten years has been head of a machine shop at the Brotherhood Shipyard. A shining example. What more can I say!"

Had the others also smiled that uniform smile printed forever on their mask? Dominic was just on the point of looking up when the guide's voice suddenly became higher, rising above its usual pitch.

"Ah, here is the Executive. It means the meeting of the executive bureau is over. Now you can talk to the comrade herself."

Beside the typist stood a short, modestly dressed housewife. Thick gray skirt, knitted blue jacket. Spectacles, long nose, sparse tangled hair. She held out a small, moist hand, with nails cut down to the flesh.

"No doubt you've also come because of the new law. It's a state measure. I can't discuss it."

The voice was hoarse, rusty, but calm and weary.

"You know, all I want is to—"

"If you want to know my personal opinion, my private, not official opinion, because I'm an employee here representing the Association, my opinion as a human being, shall we say, well, come along inside and we can talk it over."

She invited him into an enormous long room with a long table against the wall, draped with red cloth and flanked by ten or so chairs. At the end a small desk, full of books, with one chair behind and one in front. Dominic quickly sat down without waiting to be asked. The woman remained on her feet for a moment, as if to get the interview over with as soon as possible, but she eventually sat down as well.

"Yes, the Year of the Disabled. We've just been told not to use that expression anymore. Sure, it was a decision of the UN—the United Nations Organization; but our leading bodies think it is inappropriate. We've been instructed to avoid the term. The editor of our paper was also at the meeting, to be officially informed of the latest directives. The expression is unsuitable: it gives rise to too many comments and generalizations and, well, that's that. So that's what you're here for. The new law is not necessarily connected to this Year of the—well, let's call it this UN Year. It's a long story, and I have to say that I myself, speaking strictly personally, as a human being, think they've made a mistake."

"You know, madam, I've actually come to—"

She shuddered, feeling both angry and flattered at the unexpected word "madam," one she was not used to hearing. But it encouraged her to sit back in her chair and to slow down the monologue.

"Yes, to be quite frank, my own view is that it's a mistake. The years of general training shouldn't be reduced. There are difficulties, I know: the economic situation, of course. But even if the number of school years is reduced, there shouldn't have been a cut in the years of general training. What this means in practice is that our members can no longer go to a better school. Nor will they be able to get anywhere as workers. If they don't have enough years at school, they'll stay stuck on the first rung they are put on. That's how pay grades work here, as you know. Everything depends on your education; if you don't have any, then you stay at the bottom, no matter how good you are. Just think: I did horticulture. And I ended up here. This is where the comrades put me. You know how it is: duty is duty."

Dominic looked at her attentively. The Madam Executive was flattered to receive so much attention from the distinguished stranger.

"It's a pity Comrade Orest Popescu had to leave. He's our president, as you know. He could have told you more."

So the high-class tailor Orest Popescu is not at his command post; he must be moving among the masters. Comrade Reserve General Orest Popescu! A tailor by vocation—and quite brilliant at it according to ones in the know—who lost his voice and so many other qualities there at the front, but learned how to survive at any price, any price. And then, after being discharged, he kept rising and rising, thanks to the comrades he served. General in the reserve!

But if you look at the paper *Viaţa Noastră*, there is no trace of a cult for the general who leads the hard-of-hearing infantry. He must be a sly old fox, that blockhead who hasn't even lost his voice. In fact, nothing gets lost: everything is transformed—signs, substitutes, and invisible networks.

"What are you thinking?" the florist, the horticulturalist, said gently.

"Oh, you know, I'm thinking about what you told me. Comrade Popescu—you said that Comrade Popescu would have more—"

"Well, not necessarily, because I know the situation, too. In fact, he doesn't have time to cover everything. Anyway, he represents us at the top and passes down the line we have to follow. And he represents us very well, as you know. The comrades in the top leadership have a high opinion of our president. But what were we talking about? Oh yes, that law reducing the number of school years. Mmm, it's certainly a problem. You know, we're supposed to be a model organization; we enjoy special attention from the leadership bodies. We regularly report the situation and our results; we're greatly appreciated at a high level. But however understanding the members are, however submissive and disciplined, there still has to be a minimum of—how shall I put it?—encouragement. You know what happened last month with your colleagues."

Dominic kept perfect control, deaf and mute at the surprise.

"Mmm, that's what journalists are like; they think they've caught the big fish this time. What with this Year of ours they've really gone to town: that the number of school years is being cut from ten to eight; that we have no clubs or stadiums or subsidized trips as in other countries; that our members have to meet in the evening in front of the Association or in the courtyard. You've seen what a huge yard it is: the building used to be a large boyar's house. The members fill the yard every evening and kick the door so hard it breaks. Is that what's called a protest? Such a violent and sudden action? It's true they're very sensitive. Sure, they'd like there to be more talk about themselves, about their achievements and our organization. That's true. But how can we possibly explain our special status to journalists? Of course there are difficulties; things aren't easy. We hosted the World Championships, and we came out champions, you know. But when we had to go abroad, we weren't able to: we weren't given passports. Yes, there are certainly difficulties. But we don't have to kick up a rumpus about them, to give ammunition to the slanderers. It's no good journalists getting all excited to land a punch. I told them right from the start: don't get so worked up, think carefully about what you write if you want it to be published. That's what I told them, without going into details. Our special status, the special attention we receive, our duties, an exemplary model! I warned them. Not a word. And it's proved true. Nothing of what they wrote has been published! Not a word. But those unpublished articles have done a lot of harm to us on the executive bureau. Comrade Orest was summoned to Party headquarters and given a talking-to. And since then we've had one meeting after another, so that we can't think straight anymore."

Dominic Vancea was listening too attentively, and the Executive Secretary of the Association was watching his nonexistent reactions. She looked him straight in the eye, he looked her straight in the eye; she passed her small hand across her forehead, tired at the effort of explaining, while he suddenly rubbed his eyebrows like a madman. What could have happened for that strange gentleman to rub his eyebrows with both hands?

"I only wanted to trouble you for a few—"

"I'm sorry, but I really have to go. It's two already and I've got to be back by three. Some comrades are coming with instructions for us; there's going to be a new and urgent operation, which has to be launched at every level of the Association. The Code of Socialist Ethics and Justice has to be debated in every branch and every cell— in every organization, with every member, at every level."

"Debate the code? But the members are—" the journalist who was not a journalist found himself imprudently muttering. "In fact, actually—" The detective quickly tried to correct himself. "Actually, you know, I only came here to—"

"I'm sorry, I'm late as it is," the comrade repeated in irritation as she stood up. "Go and see Comrade Ionel; tell him I sent you. Comrade Ionel—the editor. Go down the corridor, turn left, and go out into the yard. Go through a door with a little green curtain. That's where Comrade Ionel is: he does the paper. He'll give you a few copies. The paper will give you an idea of our activities. It's a special paper: it's not sold in kiosks, and it's only for members. So, into the yard, where there's a small office with Comrade Ionel, the editor, and Mrs. Irina, who does the dummies. As soon as you go down—a door with a little green curtain. Comrade Ionel is an old hand here. He knows everything: he'll fill you in."

She had already put on her worn brown overcoat, already donned her woolen hat.

"You've got to have nerves of steel, you know. Our work's not easy, not easy at all, and our status, our aims, our— Yes, Comrade Ionel will tell you everything. I've got to rush. I'll hardly have time to give my daughter something to eat. Then back at three for the drilling session."

She threw her enormous bag over her shoulder, pulled straight her crumpled green scarf, and scuttled away. Yes, the Comrade Executive had scuttled away.

Detective Vancea went into the main room, greeted Daddy Iopo with a smile, then went down the corridor and turned left into the yard.

He stopped in front of the door whose window was covered with a little green curtain. He went through into a small dark room with two desks. A lightbulb was glowing in the ceiling. Editor Ionel was pale, huddled, speckled with paper.

"I was talking to Comrade Popescu. She sent me to ask you . . ."

"Popescu is the president: Comrade Orest Popescu is the president. The Comrade Executive is called Boca. Well, tell me what it's about."

"I believe you have here a list of all the members."

"I don't deal with the records. Of course there are proper records. We have files for every member. Tens of thousands of files—a special archive. It can't be looked at. Only people with special authorization have access to it. But if Comrade Boca sent you—well. If the Comrade Executive approved it, then go along to the archive. In the Cadre Department. That's where the archive is, too. There are files for everyone. Thousands of files, all in perfect order. You'll find whatever you're looking for."

Detective Vancea did not want to give up Comrade Ionel; he was his only chance.

"I'm looking for one in particular. He must be around sixty years old. A photographer. He used to be a photographer. I've heard he worked as a photographer: maybe he still does. Octavian. An old acquaintance. Octavian, yes, that's certainly his first name. But I don't remember his surname. Guşa, Duşa, Vuşa, Păpuşa—I'm not exactly sure. But it's certainly Octavian. If you have a listing by occupation . . ."

"Of course, we also have a listing by occupation. By age, by social origin, by occupation, by work performance, by education, by family life, by sport—yes, yes, even by sport, that's important. Every aspect is covered. Life at work, life in any organizations, political formation, military training, specialist training, emergency training, intervention training. Yes, we do have some photographers, as far as I remember. A few have even worked with us on the paper. I know those people better. And the others can be found in the listings—of course they can."

But just then the door opened. Flashback, with sighs. "Oh, it's you." "What the devil!" "*Mamma mia!*"

So the visitor was no longer in the charge of all-knowing Ionel. Comrade Ionel confined himself to giving him the last two issues of *Viaţa Noastră*.

"Here, they might be of interest to you. Mrs. Radovici will take you upstairs for the information—I see you know each other. Irina, make sure you tell Iopo that the Comrade Secretary has spoken with the comrade. So Iopo should put him through to listings: he should be shown the occupational listing, that's all. Nothing else. No need for the files. Just the occupational listing. Iopo will understand what it's about."

Pushing, laughter, frolics. Keep pressing the old buttons. "What a surprise, Ira! Is it really you? I'd completely forgotten. You know what I'm like." "It's normal, Tolea, quite normal. Yes, I'm here in the mousehole, as you knew perfectly well. In this poisoned hole for mice."

So Mr. Vancea came to the tram stop again. He waited impatiently for the tram, climbed aboard, found a free seat by the ticket seller, opened the newspaper. He leafed through the pages; the phantom Octavian did not appear, nor the president Orest Popescu, nor the name of Irina Radovici. What could Ira be doing at that creepy Association? Designing special-announcement boards, posters, or graphic displays of its achievements and tasks? Or producing dummies for festive issues? And why the same old hatred of the comrade general and tailor in the reserve, Popescu? Has she still not shaken him off? And where could Señor Octav have got to? Why weren't his portrait and eulogy among all those leaders and model workers? Mr. Vancea kept reading and reading, bent over the pages, although he had long since got off the tram.

The photographer Octavian, then, does not appear in the foreground; he prefers to lose himself in the blurred mass of the sect's members. He must be used to mute efficiency, among so many exemplary members of the model organization. Just miming and code? Was he, in fact, just acting out his basic character as it already revealed itself forty years ago? Opaqueness, deception, seclusion, lack of humor? Rage against the frivolous, complicated, shabby world which manages to muddle through in the end? Hatred of the beauty he covets, the intelligence that humiliates him, the goodness in which he does not believe? Is the Model Association precisely the ideal occasion, the ideal mask? A way of carrying through the dark *initiation* into which he threw himself in youth? The legion of frustration? Mystery and imprecation and wounded vanity?

Mr. Vancea shifted his weight from one foot to the other, searching the paper in which he found no answer. Its language perfectly resembled the model used by every paper available up and down the country; not the slightest difference could be glimpsed. Did the special status operate under the banal cover of perfect adaptation to the surrounding environment? Had the model seed bed of the underworld been created so as gradually to complete the sect's organization, to consummate its potential for intervention? That would certainly suit the photographer Octavian. But what about the others? How do they receive and how do they understand the standard instructions? Does the amputated structure still have any resources of ambiguity? Or are they just model operatives, always focused on the immediate goal and the minimum necessary for successful completion? Armored in their own isolation, in which there are no deviations, detours, or postponement, no playful jokes, no backbiting or disputes, no hesitations or dilemmas? Just the gruffness of the instruction, the elemental act. But what about festive recitals, the taste for spectacle and mirage? What about their immediate, and essential, needs?

Don Octavio ought to explain how he has changed or fulfilled the times in which he has evolved. He would like to offer suggestions about the future in store for us. A minimum of communication: muteness, sign language, pictures, merely figurative imagination.

But what about unforeseeable reactions, strangled instincts? A wild, random outburst at an uncontrollable moment, when the crowd suddenly begins to hop and skip and shout, to destroy everything on the way? Should there be advice, requests, and dialogue only for centuries gone by, for those whose hearing loss did not exceed 40 decibels? Even that is a diversion, probably, a false provision in the statutes. Diversion, diversion, network, network, mumbled Detective Vancea, swaying from one foot to the other in front of the telephone booth.

He looked incredulously at the newspaper, on which he had noted down two addresses and telephone numbers. How could they speak on the phone, those exemplary deaf-mute members? Or maybe their children do the speaking? Does Octavian, too, have children? Has he adopted one to make the double game more sophisticated, as the operational plan requires?

He went into the booth and dialed one of the numbers. It rang and rang. "Maybe it's another number. Have I gone soft in the head? Was it her number instead of his that I wrote down—Mrs. Radovici's? Who isn't Mrs. anymore, she's Irina again. Irina—again Irina."

After half an hour the detective repeated the attempt. He no longer had the newspaper in front of him. He had lost it, of course, but he could still remember the number. Or could he? Tolea's memory was like Tolea himself.

MRS. VETURIA GAFTON WAS not very audible, or visible: it was not easy for her to be seen by neighbor Vancea. But she existed without a doubt, in everything, all the time.

The absence of the tiny lady became like a permanent feature, coded and mysterious. But when she finally appeared, she seemed to contradict the magic through which she had taken on flesh and blood. An absolutely concrete and perfectly ordinary apparition: Mrs. Doctor Gafton. Not only did the banality of her presence not contradict, it actually heightened the insidious power of her absence. That power suffused the vibrating silence and the sound rhythms of domestic messages; it imperceptibly radiated through the whole household, strangely and constantly migrating—there was no way of confronting it. A vast, faint pulsation—until it suddenly burst forth in the gurgling of the tap or the shaking of the window in a storm, in the leavened madness of long summer afternoons of blazing heat, in the languor of red wine in glasses, in the diaphanous invasion of dandelion fluff spinning sweet whirlpools of nothingness in front of a suddenly opening door, amid an unheard sighing of hysterical walls.

Morning movements of the Gafton couple in the bathroom? It did not necessarily mean that Dominic had actually heard a brooch dropping in the washbasin or the xylophone of slippers striking the tiled floor. Was it a sound that clearly belonged to the realm of the immaterial? Not at all! Just the diffident steps of a skinny pensioner, the rustle of towels being changed, grunts, comb and brush and shaving implements, and the clinking of a razor against the mirror. Which did not mean that his spouse was not beside him or had not been or would not be.

His wife communicated her existence in a quite unconventional manner. Dominic picked it up in the long fizzling of the curtains, the buzzing of a fly newly stirred, the shiver of a sudden breeze—they all seemed to lay bare her indistinct breathing in every corner, from where a stimulus or subterfuge warning would issue cyclically, like a heavy blinking of the eyelashes of nothingness . . . Perhaps indeed, on that sunny Tuesday morning, Mrs. Veturia really had asked as usual: "Did the professor shut the door?" Or: "I think I heard the key. Has the professor left?" Or anyway, something similar.

But the words had remained in the swollen air of silence. They had not managed to become sounds: they kept gathering energy, deferred in potentialities. Until Thursday, until Friday . . .

Yes, only on Friday morning, when Dominic returned to pick up his umbrella. It had started to rain in large thick drops, and he came back from the door to take his umbrella. Only on Friday morning, when he turned the key in the lock and came back to take his umbrella—only then were heard the grinding words that had started up a few days before.

The customary words of Mrs. Veturia reached Mr. Dominic only on Friday, in the barely felt interval between the two turnings of the key. The lock stammered, as if tired of so much complicity: "He's left. I think the professor has left."

The words persisted for a long time, multiplying through mutual attraction in new associations. "Did he take the letter? I think the professor has taken the letter." If you wanted to at all costs, you could even make out such couplets. A murmur. Far away, close by, hard to tell.

Judging by his distressed state, the professor was already in possession of the letter on Friday. He thought he could make out the whining of the rusty lock; he read the gray shadows of the wet sky, where silences became stuck and expectation unraveled. He picked up the fixed, phosphorescent gaze of the mouth of the waste pipe at the corner of the building, the refuge of the street's roaming tomcat. All that was left of the feline bundle, screwed like a cork into the bend of sheet metal, was its electric eyes: the gleam of a searching melancholy, a greenish blood-red pulsation in which neighbor Veturia was concentrated for a brief moment of contact. Simulacra all around, heads of cardboard and ashes! Ambiguous intersection of the moment's relays, poisoned boredom, deferred hysteria, masks—the masks ready to deliver you up, apparently through inattention, to the fangs of a meat grinder. At the professor's desk and in the pulpit, in barracks and offices and alcoves and residences and stadiums, on rostrums and at desks and in the cells of evasion, the masks were lying in wait: to find out, to pass on, to play the compulsory game.

But fear not, Brother Dominic: what more could be discovered about you than is known anyway? The bulky file is not much thicker nor so catastrophic, compared with so many like it that appear more innocent. The spies are themselves spied upon: suspicion and fear generate themselves, but distort their emission at the same time.

The complications seemed much smaller in the case of the Gafton family. If you know all there is to know about those living around you, the fear somehow diminishes, doesn't it? Shy Matei, the dreamer of universal harmony, sacrificing himself in the interests of social hygiene, writing petitions to set the administration on the right path and historical studies for the younger generation, which ought to be thirsty for truth if it were not thirsty for more pressing daily needs. The vessel called Veturia, a plump and smiling woman who looked as if she had always been gray-haired, limping gently on her left side, had grown used to forgetting times of old by giving lessons in French English German piano and embroidery. Resigned to her modest job as laboratory assistant, she had used it with discreet tenacity to find out everything happening around her, so that in the end people began to call her doctor. And not mockingly, but with the highest regard.

What more could Mr. and Mrs. Gafton have discovered that they did not already know about scatterbrained Anatol Dominic Vancea

Voinov, whom they called Tolea, when their spare room became vacant and they took him in as a lodger? Nothing. They knew for certain the minutest details of his daily existence, the tenant said smilingly to himself in front of the receptionist's desk on which he had—who knows when?—thrown the cosmopolitan envelope that he pretended not to notice.

His colleague Gina watched closely the professor's impassive face and the panel holding the keys to the rooms of sin, a panel to which he turned from time to time, as if he had not even seen the spectacular object on the table. She would have loved to guess whether the rogue lost in reverie was actually thinking about the message in that important envelope decorated with so many stamps and postage marks, or whether he had no idea of what he had imprudently left in sight of all and sundry. Reverie, strategy, drowsiness—who knows? The confusion of a rheumatic morning, the tomcat screwed into the waste pipe muttering confused warnings, the key turning rusty words in the rusty lock . . . His watch moved on with short ticks, like the scratching of a needle. Eleven, exactly eleven, four five six seconds, the seconds perish, look, eighteen sec seconds, scattered to the winds. Look, time scattered to the winds, thirty, thirty-one and -two and -nine, scat-tered, finished, the minute has melted away.

Eleven o'clock and two three four minutes. At this time which has now passed, at this time, eleven o'clock and six minutes and one three four fourteen seconds, Mr. Matei will have finished his first period in the line for daily bread. Was he already at the library? Perhaps immersed there in the last world war, slowly advancing with a determination to avoid the haste and subjectivity of which he had been guilty in his years of combative youth.

And his goodly spouse? Probably ready to receive her first students of the day. Since her retirement, virtuous Veturia had found a profitable way of hibernating. Former colleagues had given her the necessary contacts to teach Arab students some summary notions of grammar, the usual patterns of conversation, the language of medicine. A kind of recompense for the years when she had served, in silence and resignation, people obsessed with their career and money and promotion up the ladder. On leaving, she had offered the collective the chance to square the account in an acceptable manner. They had been pleasantly surprised at her initiative. They thought she was at peace with herself, dozing between lingerie drawer and jars of pickles. They had used her ruthlessly for so many years, more and more forgetting any sense of guilt. Good old Veturia: it was she, too, who now offered them the occasion for belated generosity, a kind of rapid forgiveness of sin. A brief and convenient gesture which disturbed no one and was of benefit to all. It was like permitting a retired janitor to see his lodge again, even, if he wished, to be on guard there on Sundays when the institution was closed and the real janitors had a day off. They had immediately agreed: how could they refuse shy Auntie Veturia?

So the doctors at the university sent their retired colleague a flow of Arab students who were having difficulties with the Romanian language or with some of their examination subjects. They advised her to be careful, of course—advice which sounded like a joke in the mouth of finaglers whose affairs she knew only too well. Caution was necessary, as overcautious Veturia knew best of all.

She had decided not to accept any money for the lessons, but even so, she felt the dangers of a lightning popularity which, as events would prove, was likely to be inevitable anyway. Patient and old-fashioned, reviving for newcomers the image of some anachronistic aunt from their homeland over the seas, prepared to overlook impudence and laziness and boorish behavior, always carefully dressed, with hair, hands, and round face scrupulously looked after, the plump yet still vigorous old lady had rapidly won both renown and a sizable clientele. The name Veturia, mangled in the most amazing phonetic inventions, was quickly popular among the Arab students. Nervous, suddenly breaking out of a kind of gentle torpor, they eventually came under the control of that calm domestic power. Initially taken aback, exasperated and mocking, they became ever more attentive, submissive, ready to confess to that imperturbably functioning household oracle—in loose, fragmentary avowals that displayed an abrupt intimacy. At such moments Auntie found things to do in the sideboard, limping carelessly between chairs, as if she would never have guessed that a student was still lingering in the room. But after a few weeks the hostess would herself steer the discussion back to that confused subject about which no one thought she had the least idea—and this in the middle of a lesson on anatomy or verb conjugations.

Oh, how many postcards and letters of thanks did Mrs. Veturia receive from the four corners of the earth!

She did not accept money, nor did she reject kindnesses. Convertible trinkets, exchange values facilitating survival. More than once in childhood Veturia had witnessed the philanthropic exercises of exalted society ladies. And having reached retirement along a path of humiliating accidents, the so-called madam doctor was not at all immune from those reveries of high society which, stimulated by a still alert memory, themselves activated a chain of recollections now that everything had turned upside down and grown ugly, as accepted criteria had become inverted and feelings brutalized. To be offered philanthropically, from a dirty pocket, a crumpled cigarette which (to cap it all) you actually need; or a wretched tablet, wrapped like babies' sweets in colored cellophane paper, without which you really cannot last out the day! She had been habitually polite with the arrogant salespersons in stores where nothing was to be found, or indulgent with a lazy and churlish typist, or impassive in the face of cursing bus drivers ready at any moment to leave you in the street, or diffident in the presence of a snotty little boy using his father's card, or even his own, to obtain special privileges. So she had accepted the sly philanthropy, caricatured in hurried and condescending gestures on the part of future doctors from distant and unfamiliar regions. Their transit-lounge trophies—cigarettes, transistor radios, drinks, stockings, cassettes, chocolate—were only a cosmopolitan confirmation of the inevitable: of the fiddling practiced throughout the world; the outrage that disfigured the present and deserved only the skeptical smile of indifference. Surrogates and perishable mass-produced goods from the planetary fair! How will Mrs. Veturia put the cigarette in her mouth . . . As for the drinks, she got dizzy even from the rum mixed drop by drop into the cream filling of her cakes. But she could not have denied the pleasure of arranging the cartons, the bottles, the spectacular jars. Her eyes shone guiltily, as if those colored objects were a shield against everyday banality. Fortified, ennobled—as if they made her a real person again, defended by such puerile enrichment; as happens to children when they receive gifts beyond the reach of their social class and cannot contain their wonderment.

Veturia could not have identified the moment when some student threw a gleaming carton of cigarettes or a potbellied jar of coffee onto the table. Even after she remained alone in the room, she managed not to notice the object for a long time. Again and again she passed near the temptation—until she was no longer able to hold off the poison blindness doom of a base pleasure that she did not wish to know but could not struggle against. Then the inevitable shiver passed down her: the devilry took over and she threw it into the back of the cupboard.

Several days went by. The door of the weapons safe opened wide, grinning, creaking, swinging, pinging, and sneering. The culprit blinked with excitement, paralyzed in front of the toys. An idiotic smile twisted her already creased mouth, her lips parched by impatience. She went right inside the guilty cupboard for a thorough classification and arrangement: the shelf with the Kents, the shelf with the olive oil, the cosmetics, the chocolate and coffee and chewing gum, the bottles, jars, and boxes. She did not need to hear steps behind her to feel that her Matei was already standing in the door.

He would watch her, of course, silently, and damp with perspiration. Veturia continued with her business of selecting and ordering. Then, finally drawing herself up straight, she would turn to her husband—who would be standing dazed in the same position—and offer him the most serene face, with smooth forehead and a smile carefully planted on her round and placid cheeks. "We really need all these little knickknacks, Matei. Oh dear, they do come in so handy! Otherwise who would glance at us anymore, old as we are! If you give Old Nick a pack of Kents, you've got him on your side for a good year. And Jezebel, too—a bit of face powder will solve a lot of things. She even brings me detergent, as you see."

Each time the words rushed over Matei with the same effrontery, so that the petition he had just come to read to his wife shook in his hands. As if his text had suddenly been superseded by an oral version arguing the exact opposite. What of the lofty principles that he repeated every day in his rhetorical battles? "We really need all these little knickknacks, Matei. We're old people: we haven't any children. What if we fell ill—heaven forbid? At our age those great humanists of yours wouldn't even let us through the hospital doors. You've seen how things work at that whore of a chemist's. And what if our shower broke down? We'd still end up going to Stringpuller Satan. With one packet of Kents we've got ourselves some peace of mind. Nowadays that foreign trash can help with any of our troubles."

Dear Matei rolled up the sleeves of his pajama jacket. No, he was no longer a hero, no longer the young man defiantly taking—he of all people—the ostracized name of his wife. The name of a family of reactionaries and Fascists and exploiters! He, the one eternally persecuted, had refused the vengeful persecution of others and even assumed that blacklisted name. And he had paid dearly for that rush of pride. No, he was no longer the foolhardy man of old, even if he still kept his ideals alive with all his failing strength. So he was determined, absolutely determined, to take his old-fashioned ideals and withdraw into his workroom.

After an hour or so, when she had finished her labor of classification, Veturia appeared in Mr. Gafton's study. She bent over the
sheets of paper lying scattered on the table. "After a brief period in
which the quality of matches improved, reasons for dissatisfaction
have again appeared. The phosphorus-tipped sticks are acceptable,
but the strip on the box which makes it possible to light them is too
thin and tears at the first strike. I have written before about this
problem. It is astonishing how little time the effects of the criticism
lasted. The match factory should take a more responsible attitude to
the quality problem and respect the undertakings it has made." A
few blank lines followed, and then the draft of another letter, apparently more important, since the opening had several times been
crossed out and started again. "We refer to the report in your paper in
March of this year. Let us, then, recapitulate the facts about the ill
treatment of the woman who looked after animals in her apartment."

It was hard to tell whether he had or had not heard her come in.
Dominic could imagine at such moments that Matei would not
move from his position in front of the window, moments no different from those in which they met for a chat, each preserving his
own strategy.

Dominic gave no sign of knowing what happened on the ped-
agogical mornings of Veturia the invisible. And Mr. Gafton resumed his narratives of the Second World War, without making any
allusion to the tragedy of the Vancea family or to his own revolutionary conversion in those days of wrath, even though they were im-
plicit in the subject. "There'd be no point in asking me to focus on
everyday life. What was a betrothal, or a funeral, like in those hard
times? How did the authoritarian language of distrust permeate
ordinary speech? It's hard for me to remember such details. But the
events I'm concerned with played a decisive role, and this can be
imagined in the existence of the man in the street. So let us recall
those few days before the invasion of Poland."

Given such familiar notice, you could not for long continue

soaring through the clouds. You were forced to cast a look at the terrestrial wilderness; to observe, somewhere amid the bustle of drunken ants, a copper needle with a rusty head; to recognize the figure of a man—our freckled, skinny friend Matei himself—swaying in time with his own sentences, just a few steps from the apathetic listener.

"You know the scenario. Two-stage operations. An internal reform was proposed to Austria, then it was claimed that she did not respect it. The Sudeten Germans placed demands on Czechoslovakia; then a decision was made to support the Slovaks, supposedly oppressed by the Czechs. Finally: an ultimatum. That was the Führer's technique of making gradual headway!"

In vain did the listener try to close his ears and leave the ground again; he always came crashing down like a fly, right in front of the Atlantic liner of Gafton's imposing foot, size 46.

"Let's go over it once again, Professor. Sir Neville Henderson, the British ambassador, is summoned by the clownish corporal on the evening of August 29. The Germans demand Danzig, but also the Corridor, until Wednesday, August 30. The ambassador's telegram reaches London on August 29, at 22:25. It has to be decoded, then another telegram is coded to the British ambassador in Warsaw."

Matei knew it all. But it was about something else that Comrade Gafton really wanted to speak. Not about Sir Neville Henderson. He would have liked to prove his perfect honesty when he had joined the struggle against the Nazi butchers: that would be his excuse for having agreed to do what he did even after they were defeated; it would be the explanation and the excuse, *frater, dulcissime* . . .

"Toward midnight on the evening of August 30, Sir Neville Henderson proposes to Ribbentrop that the German plan be delivered to the Polish ambassador. To no purpose. What happens next, on August 31, 1939, you probably know. At 9:50 Sir Neville makes a telephone call to Coulondre, the French ambassador in Berlin, and warns him of the gravity of the situation. At ten o'clock the reply is received from Paris: the Polish government accepts and will confirm in writing that it is prepared to hold direct talks with the German government, and undertakes not to deploy troops during the negotiations if it receives the same guarantee on the part of the Germans. At 21:00 Radio Berlin broadcasts proposals which, as a matter of fact, are quite reasonable. The plan, states the German communiqué, has been rejected by the Poles. Yet the Poles had not even seen these proposals."

The speaker's attempts to gauge a reaction were of no avail, any more than were the efforts of colleague Gina at the Hotel Tranzit reception to read the professor's mask, at eleven o'clock on Friday, when Tolea, looking at the keyboard in front of him, was deep in thought about images from his last meeting with neighbor Gafton. Absolutely nothing did Matei detect; nothing were the persistent green eyes of Gina the cop able to make out. "You know what followed. But perhaps you don't know how the first of the accelerated conversations at the end of August actually proceeded. On August 25 Hitler was calm, haunted by melancholy, at his meeting with Henderson. He regretted that Germany had become a barracks. That's what he said. He did not want to go down in history as a warmonger. He was an artist. That's what he had been and that was what he wanted to become again! He was dying to withdraw from political life."

"Herr Adolf an artist? Absolutely not. Zilch! The artist was priestly Dzhugashvili, not painterly Adolf. The Georgian understood the power of ambiguity, its quite limitless power. And he encouraged people to measure up to it: to become anything, with no limits as to race, sex, belief, or other such nonsense. He understood that the victim can become a butcher if he doesn't actually want to, and that it's a game which has no limits. If that cretin of yours had really been an artist, he would have understood that. And if he'd understood it, the game would have been different. What a dilemma the chosen people would have had then."

Had Tolea actually spoken those words? Had he interrupted his neighbor Gafton's speech, or was he merely interrupting it now, mentally, as he recalled the scene?

"What if your old deadbeat Adolf had offered limitless scope for changing one's skin? Then you'd have seen dilemmas, conversions, overzealousness, sudden turnarounds in the situation. Then you'd have seen what a noble wild beast is that humanist fellow creature of ours as he scurries to save his hide. Maybe Adolf would have won the game—who knows?—if he'd been an artist. But no, he didn't understand his great chance, the great experiment. He was no artist, really he wasn't. There's no comparison between him and the priest from Georgia. No comparison, Matei, believe me. That one was an artist, all right! He even knew how to make use of the other one's tricks, of anything he could turn to advantage: nationalism, internationalism, atheism, religion, anything at all. Look around you, Matei, old man. What a fantastic combination! Look around at the mind-boggling work that's been done. Just open your eyes and look around."

But Tolea had remained silent, probably. He was not in the habit of interrupting the rhetorical pleasures of neighbor Gafton; he usually preferred to doze with his mind elsewhere. Neighbor Matei measured his speech without any haste, leaning from time to time toward his apathetic listener. He knew that Tolea would not interrupt him. And he was used to his bored smile; for a long time now there had been nothing new in that arrogant hotel receptionist's smile, and in fact, it did not bother him at all. As he took aim at some imaginary audience or other, Mr. Gafton sometimes gave the impression—for anyone disposed to notice the fine accents and devices of his score—that he thought of himself not only as the narrator of the events he kept reading about in the library but as an actual protagonist, maybe even Henderson. Yes, Sir Neville, Sir Neville Henderson, that was it, no?

"Do you think I'd be too subjective to study those years properly? Well, you're wrong, Tolea, quite wrong."

The hesitant pause did not last long; it was merely a rhetorical effect, of course.

"Why can't we discuss openly what happened? Why is the subject covered up in this country? Why here? Why is it impossible to talk about the genocide, the victims—you know what I'm referring to. Is it that I wouldn't be objective if I were allowed to speak? Well, I would, I can tell you!" All that remained was to force out every proof and more of his absolute objectivity. "I can understand some of the justifications which— Yes, I understand, and I'm not just thinking of the fact that at first the madman exploited a certain resentment at the humiliating peace treaty of 1919. The same kind of thing was there even at Nuremberg. Do you remember Jodl, eh? The duty to the people and the fatherland is higher than any other! And he added: Would that in a happier future it can be replaced by a duty toward humanity. Has it been replaced? Has the happy future come, as the textbooks and speeches proclaim?" Suddenly a new and surprising idea carried him away. "Did Herr Hitler describe himself as an artist? Then why didn't he allow Jews to become Nazis? It would have been an interesting experience, no? How would the play have developed in that case? Remember Italy and Mussolini before the racial laws: who was backing Mussolini then? No, it wasn't our artist Herr Hitler! In fact, he couldn't agree to try out something like that! He'd have felt wasted, cheapened. No, he wasn't curious enough, nor playful enough."

So finally the idea got through Mr. Matei's skull, too. He quickly became worked up; he could hardly wait to get carried away: "Do you remember Sir Hartley Shawcross, the British prosecutor at the trials who said that they had no precedent in history? Why? What was his reason for saying that? The judgment on a war and an ideology had to show not only that the guilty were receiving their punishment but that good was vanquishing evil. It had to give voice to the simple man of our times. Do you hear that: the simple man of our times! You might think you're at a course in Marxism-Leninism!

Well, you're not. It's a sir who's speaking, consider that. The simple man of our times, and I make no distinction between friend and enemy, that's what Sir Hartley Shawcross said. The simple man of our times! To show that he's determined to place the individual above the state. Well, did the simple man prove it? Can he place the individual above the state—is that what he wants? Tell me, tell me what you think. Is that why we're not allowed to discuss History openly?" Neighbor Vancea did not reply, of course; he did not even hear the challenging question.

Does talkative Matei mean to suggest that he has always fought for a just cause, and that even now he has not lost his courage? That his passion for History extends to the present, covering the fate of all those struck down by History, both yesterday and today? He spared no effort to achieve a sign of interest or approval, even after he had convinced himself that the chances for the future did not lie with Tolea Voinov. "Do you remember the so-called system technician who was acquitted at Nuremberg? He it was who called Hitlerite totalitarianism the first dictatorship of modern times. In fact, Speer also gave explanations for it, as you know. The dictator, he argued, no longer needs people with great qualities to work for him. Information technology offers ways of mechanizing the activity of subordinates, so that they do nothing but docilely carry out orders."

But Tolea was silently dreaming, sleeping: he did not take the trouble to give any sign of being there. He was convinced that neighbor Gafton's logorrhea would eventually sweep him on toward the taboo subject.

"You were right, Mr. Vancea. Among the paintings that Carol II took out of the country there was also a Titian. Of course, this was not directly connected to the events that were to follow."

Oh yes, it was. How could it have been otherwise, since you are no longer talking about Sir Neville and Sir Hartley and Jodl and Speer but about our own unlikely parts, with their ultracoded laughter and tears, which are missing from the map of the world.

"The year 1940, as you know, was one of the preliminaries. Moral degradation, corruption, demagogy. There's something attractive about a playboy on the throne, isn't there? At least from the perspective of the tragedy to come. There were forty-one paintings according to Leo Bachelin's catalogue: a lot of El Grecos, but also Veronese, Caravaggio, Van Dyck, Rembrandt. There's also one small Titian, you were right. *Saint Jerome*, the Bachelin catalogue, location 66. Saint Jerome kneeling before a crucifix suspended on the rocks. Beside him a cardinal's hat and a holy book. Cloudy sky, steep slopes, blue sea in the distance. The moment appears to precede the torture of the body. It is a replica of the painting in the Balbi Gallery in Genoa, of which there is another copy in the Louvre . . . Theft, royal theft, of course. The masquerading, the falsification that precedes barbarism. But it really cannot be compared with what followed; it just paved the way for it. Paved the way for the cancer that can no longer be checked. If only there had been a code of behavior; if only we had lived in a different world which— By the way, you've received an envelope . . ."

Yes, that was it. He had to get there in the end, to confirm that not by chance had the letter been handed to its addressee by the Chronicler of History himself, neighbor Gafton.

Dominic usually found his letters slipped beneath the door of his cell, either by the postman or by neighbors. This time the envelope had appeared on view, on the table in the hall. And Mr. Gafton made sure he drew his attention to it: "You've got a letter from a long way away, Mr. Vancea." He was not embarrassed, then, to show that he had examined the envelope, which had remained for several days on the hall table without being collected by Dominic Vancea. The considerate neighbor had therefore slipped it under his door. And now he remembered again that the incident had not been forgotten. He had tried to act as if he didn't care, to avoid looking at the envelope for days. But it had been no use in the end: such strategies had broken down, *dulcissime frater*. In the whole tangle of facts brought to the Gafton Resuscitation Chamber, there is also your life, Old Scatty; it's shown by this envelope from afar, all the way from Argentina, from your brother, who hoped to escape the History of our balloon flattened at the poles and in its feelings. In those days a lot of people changed not only their name, like neighbor Gafton, but also their soul. Times long gone? Present times, *frater*. Without a past, no present, yet we are only present. As for the present past—we can't get away from it. It's shown by this elegant envelope covered with stamps and postage marks, coming from afar and long ago. Present, here, now, inevitable. Quack! Windbag! He tried to hypnotize the keys on the board in the Hotel Tranzit. Time: 11:51 and 13 seconds. Impenetrable before the elegant wrapping from Argentina. As if he were not looking at it, as if he had not been the one who left the envelope on view, on the desk. In vain does his slippery colleague Gina keep twisting and turning, accidentally touching the registers, sorry, accidentally touching the clown—electric touch, excuse me, oh dear, what a fragile, glassy elbow, oh excuse me. Mistake, futile contact. Her provocative, crafty eyes: surely they will find something out, anything. Not a chance, dear hunters! Your prey knows the game and he quite enjoys it. Not a chance, not a chance: the buffoon is wearing armor and lives on the moon.

COMRADE OREST,

Source Mushroom is not available for the time being. She's in bed with a bad flu. I don't think it's a lie this time. I rang her in a rough tone of voice; I know that scares her. She wants us to meet as soon as possible, to know for sure that everything's in order. So we'll leave Mrs. Mushroom for a week to recover.

Yesterday I visited Uncle Mihai at the Association's nursing home. It's better for him there. It may also be better for me, as you say, that I don't have to see him every day. He's the most important person in the world to me, I know. My real father, I know. I never knew the other one; we're the only relatives each of us has got. Do you remember the failure of his first brain operation, nine years ago? That famous lisping surgeon cut through to the nerve and that's where the calamity started. Euphoria! Euphoria, with punning tendencies—that's what those stupid doctors called the illness, and that was what it was. Constant merriment, total amnesia. A special circuit: the scalpel has only to touch it and we start being in paradise, like the man of the future . . . He traipsed the streets all day, spoke to everyone, went in everywhere: cinemas, shops, fire stations, public baths, hairdressers, everywhere. Known to everyone—a star, quite simply! With no precautions or emotions or feelings, because he always forgot in a moment where he had been, what he had said. Jokes, funny stories, but also rude remarks that might have cost him dear. Always relaxed, of course; no one would have guessed he was ill. Or only someone who'd known him a long time, who was used to his physical strength, good sense, and seriousness of old.

He needed the special immunity that only special authorities can grant, as you said. I only grasped that after the second operation, which, instead of putting right what the first had got wrong, also added difficulties of speech and hearing. Now the euphoria is suffocating him, as you know. Yesterday I watched him for nearly two hours among the Association's pensioners and patients. I tried to convince him that his name is Toma, not Tomescu, as he introduces himself here. Again and again I repeated his name, Mihai Toma; his brother's, Aurel Toma; and my own, Toma A. Toma. Useless. When the nurses finally agreed to call him Tomescu, he changed his mind. He kept stuttering, Tom, Tom—like that, American-style. Tom, always Tom, until I achieved a compromise: Tom Tomescu. I've done you justice again. The Association's home, modest though it is, provides an assurance of order, strict subordination, modesty, and apathy—yes, I know all that. But the danger of an explosion in someone like him cannot be totally discounted—I know that, too. Only a son can understand, an adopted son like me. I am in control, as you must realize. Persevering, perspicacious, I know—that is, intelligent in the things I do.

My report on the Narcissus case: another time. I'm still reeling from the Association's asylum; I can't get back into the routine of things so quickly.

DARKENED WINDOWS. THE RAIN had been falling all night. The sluggish hour. Sleepiness, bad temper. The languid floundering continued to spread. A rage leavened through postponement.

'What did I ask you, Comrade Vasilică?"

The phlegmatic Boss Gică, dark and mysterious as on his off days. A harmless-enough pig, brought up among poultry; you can't even be sure he's not a tomcat or an ugly bitch; until one giddy day when it occurs to him to appear as a wild boar, so that his skin snaps at the seams and the fire catches hold of that coarse, putrid snout full of poisons and manure.

"What did we establish once and for all, Comrade Vasilică?"

If he called her by the male diminutive Vasilică, instead of the female name Vasilica, it was bad news!

The poor woman had stopped in the middle of the room with a tray in her hand. There had been no advance warning. She had come in nice and easy with the tray and laid out a little cup and saucer for each of them. First for Mr. Teodosiu. Mr. Gică Teodosiu, the Boss. And next to it, on the same little table, a coffee for Comrade Titi, as she did every day. Then for Miss Gina at reception. Then for the professor, on the stool in front of the armchair. He had not so much as raised his bald head from those French German or whatever weeklies, not even moved those long, sprawling legs. So she had arranged everything nicely, as always. The professor had not looked up from that color magazine, but he had slowly put his hand in his trouser pocket, taken out a banknote, stretched slightly, and slipped the ten lei baksheesh into the pocket of her blue work coat. Everything in its place. What could have got into the fat man? Mr. Teodosiu of all people! In fact, he knew her: they had been neighbors, and how her niece Steluța had helped him when Ortansa, Mr. Gică's wife, was in hot water over those medicines that had been taken in kilograms from the hospital and sold under the counter! A search, lists of persons and medicines involved: if it hadn't been for Steluța, if she hadn't spoken to the right people at the right time, Madam Ortansa and Mr. Gică wouldn't have had any servants to put cups of coffee in front of them. What hadn't she done for Mr. Teodosiu or for Comrade Titi! How much walking and standing in line and keeping secrets! Because that's how Vasilica is: she wouldn't breathe a word if you cut her into little pieces. You can't know how things stand: those people fix everything between themselves so they always come out on top. Better be blind and deaf—that'll keep you out of trouble. But then look what gets into him all of a sudden! As if he hadn't seen every morning how the professor slips her a note. You don't find anywhere such hot, thick, creamy coffee as Vasilica's. And anyway, that's what the professor's like. It was no use Mr. Teodosiu announcing in a loud voice, for everyone to hear, I'm paying for the coffee and there's an end of it, that's what Comrade Teodosiu kept repeating, but it wasn't any use. Because the professor's like that: whatever you say to him, he does what he feels like doing. That's his style, generous. He gives himself airs handing out tips, like the silk-stocking gentry, even though he's not exactly well off. How could he be? It's true that he gives her a note every day, three lei, five lei, ten lei—yes, sometimes even ten lei, as if he didn't know what he was giving. And it's true that every week she puts aside an envelope with coffee beans, for Mr. Tolea to take home. They come out of her ration, and Mr. Vancea pays her for them separately on Friday. Coffee is like gold these days, and Vasilica has a right to save something herself, because she doesn't drink coffee anymore. One or two a day—she deserves at least that much, so she can put it aside. For three years now the doctor hasn't let her drink coffee, the old stick-in-the-mud; in the early hours she can hardly crawl about, as if drunk, so it's just as well she can still sniff some of the rich people's coffee. Otherwise she wouldn't be able to move an inch.

"What time did you get here today?"

The old scarecrow hasn't given up. He's keeping her standing there, in the middle of the room with the tray in her hand, while he gives her a dressing-down. And the others? Not a word: the puppets don't hear or see a thing, don't utter a sound. That spineless flunky Titi, that real nasty piece of work, little old four eyes, as Gina says, who sees everything to do with everyone and reports it to those who keep him in his job. And the little pussy cat, snort snort, of course she purrs and rubs her whiskers; she wouldn't say a word; all that loafer wants is to be stroked on and under her fur, to find a nice hidden corner for herself where it's warm and some tomcat will take pity on her. As for the professor, he's a real loony: he can suddenly have a funny turn, throw a saucepan and frighten the life out of you. He must have connections way up top to play such dirty tricks on you when you're least expecting it. When he goes into one of his tantrums, he can do just about anything.

"It was still night when I left home. I left at four, you know, before there was even any daylight."

"I didn't ask when you left. I asked when you got to work."

Start telling Mr. Teodosiu that you, Vasilica, the rag he uses to wipe the floor, got here on time. You arrived at the time laid down by law. You, Vasilica, a rag, talking about the time fixed by law! Say it to that fleecer who'll have your guts for garters and who's just waiting for you to say it so he can scream and shout some more.

"Well, since they started work on the metro the trams haven't been running. I come all around the houses by bus. I have to change three times: I get sick of it, as I told you before."

"And you stop off for milk. There are two bottles in your bag right now. I told you to get the milk here at the corner."

"I had a row with Nuṭica, the woman in charge, and now she won't keep any for me. By the time I arrive, there's not a drop of milk left. She said she asked you for some cigarettes, some of those Kents, for a doctor of hers. She's ill and hard-up, as you know. She goes to those gynecologists all the time. Well, she's angry with me because you didn't give them to her." I've got you there, you dirty little dog. You know what women's disease I'm talking about, because you got your paws on poor Nuţica, too, didn't you? Yes, I haven't said anything before. Quiet as a mouse I've been, so that scorpion wife of yours, Ortansa, doesn't find out.

"I'm not interested in your relations with Nuţi. I don't ask much of you, Comrade Vasilică. Just a couple of perfectly simple things."

Comrade, d'you hear! As soon as you mention his piece of ass, you're comrade all of a sudden, just like at the courts.

Employee Vasilica Vasilică, known to everyone as Vili, pulled her kerchief straight. She lowered her right hand—the one with the tray—down the length of her washed-out, oversized work coat; and with her left hand she straightened her kerchief. She raised her head. A small face with curly hair. Her big, long hands dangled beside her small, bent body. Piercing eyes, a broad strong mouth with small, misshapen, bleached teeth. She was staring Boss Teodosiu straight in the eyes.

"What I ask of you is quite simple, Comrade Vasilică. That at the reception, and here in my office, it should be as clean as a chemist's shop. Cleaning and coffee, that's all. It's not much, you know. Less than that, I won't accept. I'm not asking you about the other things. But I know everything, don't you worry. And I know what you talk about with our customers. To get the ones from Tulcea to send you some fish, or the ones from Oradea to find you a sheepskin coat for Nelu, because that good-for-nothing boy of yours doesn't look right if he's not dressed like Alain Delon . . . You make use of our contacts, of our name and the hotel's; I know all about it. And how you wangle some cotton from the drugstore, and why your friend Stelică at the food store sells you the best cheese when no one's seen any cheese at all for months. And what do you tell people when they ask how things are going here? You tell them everything, much too much. Lies, Comrade Vasilică. Exaggerations and prittle-prattle, Comrade Vasilică. You talk too much and you say what you shouldn't. But you know, everything gets to me in the end, and you get to me as well, I can tell you. As for the Kents, don't ever say that word again! I don't ask you how you clean the rooms, or what arrangements you make about the soap and detergent. Nor who gives you packs of Kent and for what? I don't ask because I know."

Oh ho! You're stirring up too much this time, you scumbag. This crazy weather must have really screwed you up. Your foul mouth has poisoned you, and your fat ass-licking soul has gone completely black. You wouldn't like to have to swallow it, you dainty little creep . . . Vasilica Vasilică had withdrawn, disappeared, with raging, mounting hatred pumped up with fury and perfect soundproofing so that nothing could be heard.

Corkscrew Titi had meanwhile forsaken the landscape of the liquefied window. Leaning on the wall, he straightened his metal-frame glasses. The police skunk seemed like a sarcastic Oxford don. He looked rigidly, unsmilingly, at colleague Gina, who kept doing up her work coat without ever managing to do it up. Then he went toward Old Gică, who, looking either at Comrade Titi or at the professor, was uttering: "Come, *amantissime*, let's draw up that list."

No, the professor had no inkling that those magic words had been uttered! Nor that they had been accompanied by a sly wink, the usual twitch of eye and eyebrow that always occurred when it was a question of his astral person. With his legs sprawled on the stool in front of the armchair, absent and self-important, merely deigning to take occasional sips from the excellent Vili coffee, and otherwise sheltering in the thin sheets of *Monde* or *Match* or *Nouvel Obs*, the professor did not register anything around him.

"Cancer, skin cancer, that's what it says here, comrades. A small pink mark near the eyebrow, like a rash. It must be detected while it's still in the incipient stage! Otherwise it's fatal, for five generations." The familiar voice could be heard from behind the cosmopolitan pages. "For five generations, do you hear? *Une fatalité*, do you hear, *une catastrophe.*" Titi Măndiță frowned and scratched his eyebrow with an air of boredom. Already seated on the chair next to the boss, he sipped his coffee, took a pen from under the flap on his bag, and prepared to make a list of urgent tasks before the asylum's telephones began their daily ringing.

"Yes, *amantissimie.*" The servant Titi Măndiță repeated with a mocking smile the words and smile of Boss Gică Teodosiu. There was no longer any way Tolea could ignore the coalition.

Amantissime had a mocking ring, of course. Were they perhaps signaling him that the little scene with Vasilica did not concern poor Vili alone? They knew that Tolea's reaction would be unpredictable. He might keep quiet and pretend to be busy, as if he had noticed nothing, or he might start the act of wounded vanity. Or quite simply deliver the most peculiar speech, with no apparent connection to his surroundings. "How would those poor wretches have greeted the liberators of the camps at Dachau, Maidanek, or Auschwitz? Like gods! But after that how did they look at them? As at mentally retarded animals. What do they know? Only we know what life is: pain and suffering! Beaten, spat upon, burned. Forced to eat our excrement, to dig our own graves, to abandon our parents for a crust of bread. To betray a friend for a smile from the butchers, to dance in front of the murderers, to drag ourselves along on all fours. What do these happy, normal, frank people know about anything? They're not serious; they're too free, too available. Calamity, misery, fear—those are serious, very serious! That is, boring. Freedom appears light-minded, infantile. Something for fools and kids, for clowns, for people who like to loaf around."

Would he suddenly bang out that aria for the comrades at the hotel? Very appropriate for the audience. For it had learned the strategies of patience, the misery and fear and suspicion, the torpor of depraved boredom. Poisoned, cannibalistic boredom, the boredom of submissiveness and betrayal and torpor, even the boredom of fear, yes, yes. "Have you ever seen a dictator talking to children? Uneasy, imbecilic. As if he's talking to soldiers or a heavenly tribunal. Serious phrases delivered with hatchet cuts. A lonely and serious man—absolutely serious! Freedom seems a joke to him. A kind of hooliganism, a cunning trick directed against him, the poor prisoner. So frivolity in a dictatorship, frivolity is no longer what it was. It becomes provocation, regeneration. Humor and a necessary insensitivity. The miming of liberty, yes, because mime also—Yes, yes, when there's nothing left, then mime—"

Petty suspicion, petty backbiting, petty deception. Petty acts of treachery committed by petty, shriveled, crushed souls? Boredom, boredom! The specter haunting and devouring the world! What gloomy people. The boredom, *frater, dulcissime, amantissime.*

Talking in his sleep, or so it seemed. And he didn't care. Anatol Dominic Vancea let loose his tirades as if he were debating with former colleagues at the faculty. As if he did not know he was at the Hotel Tranzit reception, where the Gică-Vasilică puppet sequence had just concluded.

And then you ask yourself, for the umpteenth time: Who is holding baby Dominic and making sure he doesn't fall? Dismissed as a teacher on far from trivial grounds, given shelter here at the Tranzit —at least if he had his head on his shoulders, if he kept his trap shut, if he showed some zeal in his work. Like hell! All he's concerned about is to show how great he is. To show the dunces how brilliant and liberated you can be in a kennel, because this isn't the fifties anymore. We've been through another thirty years' war; we've got used to our daily morass, our daily bread. He had heard only too well the dialogue between Teodosiu and Comrade Vasilică. He had picked up the irony with which the holy words had been repeated. *Amantissime! Amantissime!* Mr. Gică Teodosiu, do you hear? Is "Mr." Gică Teodosiu taking over your formulations?! *Frater. Dulcissime. Amantissime.* Simple mockery? An allusion to his suspect morals? Oh, not just suspect! Shameful guilt—the immoral professor removed from teaching? He didn't care. Receptionist Tolea Voinov did not even hear the poisoned warnings.

The crank was raving away. It was again the year 1000. The Apocalypse. *Saeculum obscurum.* Now about Tacitus, now about Hitler, now about the early Christians, now about the extraordinary Otto III, "Greek by birth, Roman by empire." And what a mentor that visionary emperor had! "The fantastic Gerbert! He dreamed of world empire and absolute renunciation of the world."

They listened, didn't listen: what did it matter anymore? The invisible bug was working, of course. It transmitted clear as a bell: "The divine Gerbert anticipated the sublime. The crowd is controlled not only by force, and not just by intelligence. The depths of human nature yearn for something else as well."

"Come, let's draw up the list, *amantissime*," Uncle Gică Teodosiu had said, and it was Wednesday and rain was falling. Comrades Măndiță and Teodosiu were actually bent like good managers over the list of priorities. The Year of Disgrace nineteen hundred and eighty and—days crammed with the stumblings of the century and of the honorable clientele: you must set the plan of battle in good time. Otherwise you'll lose precisely where the victory cannot tolerate being postponed. Their eyes were sparkling. There was arrogance, not just hunger to succeed, in the eyes of the skilled finaglers.

"Give Vlăduț a ring, *amantissime*. His daughter—the one with the furs—was trying to get hold of you yesterday." And it was April, eleven o'clock, optimal biorhythm, a superb Friday morning, already Friday, in the mad chase of the calendar and of words spoken. So Uncle Gică Teodosiu picked up without delay the call passed on by Comrade Titi. He immediately rang Liliana, daughter of Comrade Vlăduț, at the special depot. Comrade Vlăduț, head of the special service, was the brother-in-law of Smaranda, director of the shop for special persons, with whom Ortansa Teodosiu, matron at the special hospital, was on very close terms. The code was certainly working well. They fixed up exactly when and how she should come, what she should bring, how much where what. They had the force of words pared down to essentials. Nouns and verbs, clear precise orders, hitting the nail on the head time after time.

A confused moment of senile siesta, when Comrade Corkscrew Titi felt like undoing his collar and belt, throwing out a line himself, taciturn though he was, and catching the buffoon so that he breathes all his fibs out through the nose.

"What are you saying, *amantissime?* That that Hitler of yours was a genius? That the spark of madness, as you put it, made everyone lose their head? You were telling us about the invasion of Poland . . ."

A crude provocation! Fawning, of course. So that the professor will issue a refined curse and suddenly switch on the transistor lying on Gina's table, full volume, superdecibels, Rock Rock again. Or go and . . . excuse me, naturally announcing his important toilet operation . . . and afterward return relieved and fondly, as it were, tell languid Gina of the diagnosis linked to the smarting pain that troubled him just now as he was dealing with his urgent need, the lesser of the two. "Doctors, do you hear, just hand me over to the cretins. You stuff a hundred lei in their mouth and a carton of Kents between their breasts and ask them to do the bullshit tests on you. They're a bad lot. Businessmen, every last one, germ-carrying flies. A friend of mine is a doctor. He plays the fool, the saint; deals in big words, ergotherapy, I don't know exactly what his conjuring trick is called. He doesn't take money, not even presents, but Sluggish Jeny does the cleaning and cooking, and Old Syphil Bazil, with his child's heart of gold, plays the lackey of the British crown. The gentleman lets the patients wait on him, because it does them good. Tests, do you hear! Analysis and synthesis: his brain in curlers and his stethoscope on the client's pouch. Their analyses: Dialectical materialism. Clean materialism, dirty dialectics, as Father Marx used to say."

But no—wait. Outside, the sun is shining: we're only in April, maybe the thirteenth, or maybe the twenty-third, the day that reminds him of a girl and a school and a bicycle. So, no irritation, none at all. The multilingual receptionist is in a mood to answer questions politely, however impolite they may be.

"If it makes you happy, Corkscrew, I can repeat. The century is iron because of its baneful severity, lead because of the prevalence of evil, and dark because of the lack of wise men. So, the year 1000. The Apocalypse. So, Hitler. The twilight of the world. The end? For the crowd. It is not in man's power to give a date to the end of the world. The Church itself will recognize that, if it maintains the mystery of the divinity. And politics, well, let's recapitulate."

When he called him Corkscrew—which he did all the time—Comrade Măndiţă became red with anger. Was he, Comrade Titi, who wouldn't put a drop of alcohol on his old ulcer, supposed to put up with that sort of thing?

"I can repeat, *dulcissime*. For you, Corkscrew, I'll repeat anytime, anyplace."

The professor looked up from the screen, adjusted his dark-red silk scarf beneath the raised collar of his black shirt, lunged gracefully beside carnation-pink Gina, caressed her briefly on her cheek and little double chin, and exited behind the screen on which the English word RECEPTION was written in gold letters. Not to take a bow in front of the audience, as one might have expected, but to sit on the armchair by the window.

He perched both legs American-style on the little round table, then lifted his palms upward as preachers do—yes, that's what they are—in my black suit of an apolitical wage earner, my Roman consul's head, bald and steadfast, exiled among a bunch of ruffians. Okay, at your service: our supervisor, our customer, our master.

"As you know, distinguished colleagues, in 1934 a non-aggression treaty was signed between Germany and Poland for a period of ten years. Thirty-five million citizens cannot be denied access to the sea; let our two countries live together, said the dictator. In January '39 the Führer brazenly announced that German-Polish friendship was a factor helping to relax political life in Europe. On August 28 of the same year he was already screaming to the British ambassador: I'll wipe out Poland. Do you really want us to recapitulate, *dulcissime* semi-scholar, does it really interest you?"

Mr. Vancea did not turn around in the direction of Corkscrew, to whom the words were addressed, but spoke just like that, in general. He needed a medium, as it were. So now and then he looked into the sparkling green black eyes of Gina the witch.

"Goo-ood, so you find tyrants interesting—that is, mentally re-tarded children, irrational and inspired, with their paradoxical logic of loners? Goo-ood. The British ambassador had just a few seconds to reply. He asked: Are you prepared to hold talks with the Poles, to discuss a population transfer? How did the visionary answer? With a question, of course. Would Great Britain be prepared immediately, as an assurance of its good intentions, to donate a few colonies to Germany?"

Boss Gică was grinning at the door, with his legs wide apart. Sir Corkscrew was staring at the ceiling. Lewd Gina kept fastening unfastening her work coat.

The buffoon had suddenly stood up. He was bored, no longer in a mood to recite Henderson's words!

He was just no longer in the mood—as simple as that. A suddenly aged harlequin, in his black workclothes. A tired, wrinkled mask. And when you think that the earth had not completed so much as one turn on its axis. The sky, a little green Seiko-branded ellipse, showed 1:24:14. Not even a quarter of an hour had passed! One o'clock and twenty-four minutes and fourteen seconds that have gone, flown away, 15, 16, 17, 18, the hypnotist pronounced the finale: "That's all, *dulcissime.*" And he bowed mockingly before the au-dience: "Bye-bye! I can't find the words." He had not even taken his hunting bag from the peg. He couldn't care less about the eight-hour working day for which the workers of the world had struggled so hard. He waved his arms about one last time, in thanks for the ovations: "Pa, pa, bye, *ciao, amantissime.*" They were used to it, of course. He irritated them, entertained, humiliated, provoked, and infuriated them. They put up with him because, without understanding why, they felt he was tolerated by greater ones than they.

So the Knight of Assland has been removed from his teaching post, that he will not pollute our pure young people full of constructive enthusiasm. About to be flung in jail but—no one knows how—saved at the last moment and even brought back to the capital, would you believe it! Recruited, probably. Recruited, certainly, for delicate assignments, like all his ilk; any illiterate old woman in our multilaterally watched society knows all about that. But the monster displays an insolence beyond anyone's ken! As if his task was none of the rabble's business, as if it had been assigned to him by a grade higher than that of his colleagues, as if the banal listen-and-report network in which they were all involved did not even concern him.

It really drove them wild, but also intimidated them. Suspicion, combined with mystery, dulled their reactions. They would have liked to kick him far away. His madness was a trap, they were sure, and they never knew how bemused or skeptical they should appear. He spoke of dictators as if it were the most natural thing in the world, then philosophized about mediocrity, delusion, fanaticism, and—quite out of the blue—he kept coming back to—Argentina. The family horoscope, of course. He talked heedlessly of his brother who had run away to Buenos Aires, become rich and senile, but also of the troublesome political similarities with that distant land. Always looking disgusted, spitting out words that came from somewhere right up at the top, where poor mortals are not allowed to tread.

A long time after the World Cup in Argentina, old Gică had

bitten hard on the bait. "You say they come from Spanish men and Indian—that is, native—women. But what the hell! They look just like us. I've been watching TV closely. They've got our faces."

"Well, they're our Latin cousins, *amantissime*," Tolea began, without lifting his bald head from the accounts book, as if he had spent the whole day doing nothing but bringing the hotel's books up-to-date. But the stream of words, long since prepared, had already begun. "The conquistadors procreated with native women. Yes, the greed for time and space was paid for in women's bellies. The loner who has no respect for anything. The native prostitute, courtesan, perhaps even mistress. In Latin America the brothel remained a durable, classicized institution."

The eminent professor had not raised his thin beard from the accounts; his superior Gică's eyes were bulging, as at the sight of a bear. "The white man introduced depravity and cruelty. Spanish wives lived under the same roof with mestiza mistresses, legitimate children with bastards. The result? Feeling cheated and degraded, the mestizo does not know pity. He considers love an abasement, a weakness. Brothels, old Gică, are the traditional institutions of solitude! Don Estrada out on his pampa . . . But I've told you what the old man wrote about the tango, the dance from the waist down"— oho, he was speaking as in a book, m'sieur.

Old Gică was smiling: he was wasn't in the mood; he rather liked the game. He even jumped ahead of the buffoon, in order to provoke him. "So, you were saying that Carnival is the celebration of despondency. Desperate glee, you said. The need for glee is their sickness, and glee is the mask of despondency. Isn't that what you said? Hostile glee, mixed with hatred." Old Gică did not wait for an answer: he forged ahead, not even giving Tolea time to breathe. "It can be seen in politics and in sport, you said. Farces—with all those dictators and football players and coups d'état. It's a theatrical nation, old Argentina—Martínez don Estrada. The mask of impotence, as you put it. Jokes, first-class jokes that do the rounds for years and are never forgotten. Joking hides sadness at not having achieved what you wanted. Isn't that what you said? But what about sport? What's the connection between sport and politics?"

Mr. Vancea did not heed the question, as if it had gone in one ear and out the other. He did not break off what was supposedly keeping him busy, whether it was pretending to write in the accounts book or arranging the room keys on the board or reading the paper or picking his nose. He went on imperturbably, but the words suddenly began to flow. "A dark, old world, over which something else is constantly being sown. The cross between white and Indian is blurred; it has been drifting like that for hundreds of years. Rude, surly, hard to say—like lumpens. Braggarts! A braggart has an innate sense of theater."

He was describing a braggart—hard to believe one's ears! He, Tolea Anatolea Dominicus, was talking of braggarts! As in a doctoral thesis he was describing what a braggart is like, enough to frighten you out of your wits! The listener's suddenly dilated eyes did not intimidate him, of course. "Yes, an innate sense of theater, carnival, circus, despondency. Politicians and the army live in the same world. And football, of course. A life of perpetual waiting, *amantissime*. When you spend all your time waiting, improvisation looks like salvation."

Weeks, months, until the subject was exhausted, until old Gică had had more than he could take and no longer asked any questions, until Firecracker Tolea himself had completely forgotten the serial. But no, when no one was expecting it—flash, bang! Professor Vancea insisted on offering a conclusion. One morning the collective was absorbed in the happy new theme: Bulgarian slippers, for which the whole city had been lining up for hours on end with the next winter in mind. Gina had managed to get five pairs, for her sister and mother and brother-in-law and little nephew. Very good, warm, fur-lined, they would perform miracles in next winter's freeze. No way, argued Corkscrew, their stink's enough to knock you out! Anatol Dominic Vancea Voinov seemed to be following closely the academic dispute, but no one knew whether he had it in mind when he spoke up, as if continuing an older thought suddenly come back to life.

"Improvisation operates as salvation, as I said. More than a diversion—as salvation. Hmm, slippers, yes. Improvisation—like the Argentinians. Uniforms, stripes, circus. As I was saying, they're impulsive and shrewd; they catch on quickly. Weak and garrulous. Foolish pride, solemnity, demagogy, but also artful manliness. Your football, Gică, old man, your improvisation is just right to discharge the load."

Old Gică did not react; the others kept silent, surprised at what they had just heard.

"By the way, have you seen that wrinkle of the eyes? That winking. I mean the scar. A little mark, by the eyebrow. Did you recognize your mark, old Gică? Have you ever touched that almost invisible mark with your finger?"

But Gică, left speechless, did not have time to pull himself together; the words scampered off in another direction. The speaker was becoming extremely worked up. "Where is Vasilica? I've been trying to get hold of her for three days. I mean, not her exactly, but my bag of coffee. Maybe the baksheesh no longer interests her. Doesn't she line her bottom anymore with twenty-five-lei notes? Has she decided to show it bare in front of the Holy Virgin? While I'm stuck without any coffee. Is the lazy layabout suddenly afraid of being reported? Mmm, stealing also has its risks and its code of practice. It calls for respect and a certain seriousness. Can you still believe in people's word, in honor among thieves. The world's heading for the brink, that must be it. God, where can that parasite have got to?"

The professor really would not let his audience go. When he saw their attention flagging, he'd come up with another round of abuse to liven them up. Humiliating her like that, poor Vasilica. Not even

Comrade Gică Teodosiu had let loose so shamelessly. They all knew and all pretended they didn't notice the little business like so many others. After all, Vasilica was a human being, too, and had to wangle her way in life. Ill at ease, she would take the provocatively large baksheesh that the scatterbrain tossed to her in sight of everybody. Vasilica took her coffee ration, a few teaspoons a day, from the communal bag, even though she was not among those who drank coffee. In this way she collected the weekly bagful for Tolea, who paid her for it separately. But to say it openly, just like that?! To throw the slops around, so that at least you see their mugs shaken by the poseur's nerve. Just take him by the nose and spin him on his heels until he can't take any more. He's got someone protecting him up there—otherwise he couldn't possibly . . . So many bad marks in his file and so much impudence, always shooting his mouth off. And the bullet never hits him: he can gulp down some poison and then go straight off to dance the Charleston. Best keep out of his way; spit over your shoulder to keep the devil away.

If only poor Vasilica hadn't passed by reception at that very moment! The audience froze with expectation. You've found what you were looking for! Here she is, carried on the Old Serpent's invisible black wire; here she is, opening the door.

"Dear madam, you forgot to give me my bag on Wednesday. I'm right out of fuel! Energy crisis! So, about turn, bring it here! Make up your little bag." Little baggie, little baggie, who are you leaving me to? the odd fish begins to hum. And suddenly you see how different he is: he's forgotten everything, he's gallant and polite, as if he's really lost his marbles.

He jumps fresh from the springboard and lands in front of the fortune-teller. The beauty is hiding the cowrie between her breasts, warming it up as the gypsy wanderers taught her to.

"So, sweetheart, you live at Bulibaşa Square, is that right?"

The odalisque is not angry at the playful allusion to the legendary gypsy captain. The honor of the ancient tribe has taught her never to be angry; queens cannot be offended. She lifts her black locks from the accounts and offers her colleague at the Tranzit reception a faint, archaic smile. Red lips, enamel keyboard, perfect, snow-white. Her slender hand slides down the crease in the middle of her work coat. Long delicate fingers, small fragile bones, deep eyes, night without end. Slim bird, torrid crease. No, she had no reason to feel ashamed. The tribe could be proud of how she raised her shiny copper neck, of how the nocturnal leaves fluttered.

"Will you pay me a visit, then, *dulcissime?*"

"There's a special school around there. You know it, don't you?"

"Maybe. I don't pay much attention to schools."

"Between the blocks of flats. It runs down from the crossroads to a kind of square. An unpaved road, still a building site, they told me. A big supermarket, a soda-bottling center. Then on the right, as far as the electricity transformer. From there a tree-lined drive, with the school at the end."

"Well, I see you know it. A big supermarket that's shut all the time. Then the soda-bottling center. You'll see it straightaway. The line always stretches to the corner of the street. Then you cross over and take the first on the left, down to the end of the blocks. The cranes can still be seen. Piles of bricks, concrete casing. You pass through the mud until you come to the next-to-last block, with four floors. You can't miss it. The balconies are full of flowers. They've even painted flowers on the façade, because it's pockmarked where the plaster's fallen off. My wanderers have always loved flowers. That's where I live, on the second floor. No need to ask. There's a whole lot of them in front of the block. They'll ask you who you're looking for. They'll escort you to the door with a show of pomp. Or, if it's one of their good days, they'll shout up from the entrance: 'Heh, Gino! Ginooo, come to the window! Your prince has come.' You won't lose your way, don't worry."

Mr. Vancea, the great jester, did not understand the joke. He wanted to have a serious conversation; he needed some advice.

"You know, out there by the school. In one of those older blocks. It's a friend. Or no, not a friend. An acquaintance, an old acquaintance of my brother's." The professor leaned for days on end toward gaudy Gina's ear of jade. She came from an old community, with long experience of adaptation. You could get some useful advice from her, no? And indeed, his colleague did not seem surprised at the improbable change in the buffoon; she wasn't surprised at anything. She immediately accepted the new role in which he placed her, as confidante giving advice in a murky way-out story. They suddenly began to seem like a couple in a shady sect, whispering and murmuring to each other all day long, quite delightful . . . *dulcissima*, long blue eel-like fingers streaming around the button on her closed open work coat, and the *frater* pedagogue constantly pulling new pieces of magic paper from his pocket, which he has brought to be deciphered.

"Retarded development of the psyche. Reduced and superficial criteria of judgment. The language of mime and gesture sets up walls. The defects of the language accentuate inflexibility and negative manifestations—envy, jealousy, rigid behavior. However, when grouped together in an organization with strict and simple rules, the disabled may display excellent qualities of subordination."

Slippery Gina was sitting open-mouthed, thoughtlessly repeating the words she heard. As if she were preparing a play or an expedition into a jungle inhabited by Martians. "The instruction must respect some elementary rules of communication. They should be addressed in such a way that, without any reduction or decrease in the speed of delivery, they can hear at a distance of .5–1.5 meters, and the speaker's position should be well lit. The speaker's mouth should be lower than the hearer's eyes; he should never have a cigarette in his mouth or be chewing a sweet. The speaker is not permitted to wear sunglasses or to turn his head while engaged in dialogue. He should use simple, repetitive sentences, should not display impatience, but should be persevering and remain in good humor. The greatest difficulty is presented by the verb." Gina returned several times to some rather obscure passages, and then they would go over the stage directions together. They did not see that the ears of the surrounding collective had grown larger in trying to grasp the code of their bizarre intimacy, nor did they notice how Corkscrew excitedly raised and lowered his eyebrows, or how Uncle Gică's eyes kept bulging as if he had seen a ghost. "Tactile memory. The hallucinatory gratification of certain needs through dream. Dream, being both the road to the unconscious and the expression of the unconscious, may be used as a force of induction—to consolidate the group and direct it toward greater efficiency; that is, toward respect for secrecy, belief in the goal, execution of orders, and solidarity in action."

Was this instruction in parapsychology? *Frater* Vancea and *dulcissima* Chick were apparently preparing for cosmic or subterranean encounters invisible to the uninitiated, by learning the rules of cooperation in some organization of the future. Mr. Vancea did not seem too wary of the dangers, although there were dangers all around. He had no time for those who gathered together cowering, so that their thoughts could not somehow be read before events were ready to be set in motion, nor for those whose membership could be read on their face or their wallet. Provocations, nonchalance, and insolent behavior proved to have a protective dimension, as it were, after you had achieved the status of a scatterbrain capable of the wildest eccentricities, of which the wildest of all was precisely the peculiar status of a tolerated person. Tolerated by shadowy forces—that was what he had gradually made those around believe him to be.

So that one more bit of tomfoolery hardly counted any longer. They knew that *Frater* Dominic could not stand being bored; he hated nothing more. Therefore, Gina did not dare express surprise that her colleague had suddenly decided to look for a former neighbor or colleague or a friend of his brother in Argentina; nor that he told her in excessive detail about Gafton or Marga, when the whole dark story that had seized his passionate interest was not exactly of the kind that you confide to a colleague at work.

To a colleague, to some colleagues.

Tolea had chattered away in front of both Gică and Corkscrew about his correspondence with the family in Argentina and all the rest. In the end, it might be asked whether the risky display of things best kept from public view was not part of the same capricious strategy of disclosing precisely the most troublesome facts in order to place a question mark over them. To reveal and emphasize them in an offhand manner came to look suspicious, incredible, unreal. Was that perhaps what the incautious Tolea, the scatterbrained Tolea, was basing himself on? To insist on recovering through "the language of mime and gesture," from a mute photograph, an old and complicated happening about which both Gafton and Marga could have recounted something much more coherent, probably? To appear convinced of Dulcissima's capabilities as she listens to you? A kind of mystical kid sister, prepared to use the metempsychosis of her nomadic ancestors to help you in unraveling the sorcery of the disabled? As if, anyway, you wouldn't find your way alone to the door with the fugitive's wonders—a fugitive hidden in the gypsy part of town, to the right of the supermarket, after the soda-bottling center, in the vague topography of fiction, as in the cowrie hidden between a colleague's breasts at the Tranzit observation post. So you can't tell anymore what is invented truth and what is plausible falsehood in the real world just a step away?! Shadows, magnetic accident, nervous deviation, jumbled codes, borealis illusion. He had disappeared, quite simply! The fakir had suddenly vanished, with questions and answers and everything. After so many tender introductory sessions on the subject of disabilities, the suspect had vanished. Sick, do you hear! Professor Vancea sick?! As if the Prince of Darkness were to catch a cold—the poor thing!—and snuggle into bed wrapped in burning leaves of leprous hemp, so that he, the orphan boy, can also warm himself up. Drinking from a pail of prescribed beladonna tea and bone filings, and tossing a blood-red aspirin into each mouthful.

When no one was expecting it, he disappeared! Sick, medical leave, fancy that. But he reappeared after a few days: purified, pale, rose-colored. Dressed in white, would you believe it! On workdays he never wore anything but black, like a gravedigger or a night-soil collector. But he made his next entrance all in white! Penitent, festive, so everyone could see that although he was paler, as befitted his role, there was actually nothing at all wrong with him. Snow-white, purity itself, with his same old smile: slanting, sinuous.

His partner held out her delicate hands to the master. Her face glowed with the frail, wild beauty of a loose adolescent. She kept closing opening her work coat, smiling conspiratorally, showing white piano keys, white fangs. Her lips moistened, soft and pink. She looked coyly at the master juggler, but with a predator's gleam. Lewd, maternal gentleness.

The skunk didn't even see her! With a single movement he flung his bag onto the peg. He did not notice anyone, remember anything; he couldn't care less.

But when he passed behind the desk on which RECEPTION was written in large golden letters, Monsieur Anatol Dominic Vancea Voinov accidentally touched his colleague's electric elbow.

So Gina could be patient no longer.

"Well, what was it like? Come on, tell me. Have you been there? Did you go?"

The professor opened his eyes wide, not understanding whom and what she was talking about. Not about himself, obviously. The poor man did not understand the confused state of the office worker who was his colleague.

"Piss off!"

The whistling of the words coiled the greenish air and seemed to extend into a long white hand. From the silken sleeve a shiny white bag dropped onto the red desk.

Long fingers of polished ebony took from the paper bag a long, parallelepipedic, pink sweet. Then another—coffee-colored, cylindrical, shiny. Sweets, sugar candy!

A brief snigger could be heard. Gina began furiously to crunch the poisons.

COMRADE OREST,

I approached him at last. It seems Chatterbox does not want to talk to me. He answers politely and tries to get away as fast as he can. Narcissus? I know that for him, too, days and nights are divided into hours for eating and shitting and sperm, films, sleep, clinic. That's all, he's not a Martian. The key aspect remains the economy, I know. Precisely here people forget the great Marxist discovery: being determines consciousness, not the opposite. The capitalists have learned to use the weapon well. That's the real question, the central point; that's where the stethoscope should be placed, I know. It's not like thirty years ago! What matters isn't what you think but what you eat and how you pay for it. Since we're all state property, it's easy to find the answer. Economic studies also become political and psychological, I know that. The great human dilemmas? In a place without paper, even toilet paper? Do you remember what I requested for our correspondence? Durable, good-quality paper, that's what I asked for! Acid-free paper, acid-free, that's what I wanted. You gaped in astonishment. You couldn't believe I wasn't afraid of paper that lasts; that is, of my own actions. Then you understood what kind of correspondent you were dealing with, I know that. No whining, complaints, and retractions, as with so many others . . . Forgive me: I've been rather drifting from the subject. It's my bad mood after meeting one of those people who like to put on airs. Their mysteries aren't worth a penny, believe me. I know that: they're state property, too. I've also got other reasons, it's true. Uncle hasn't received any medicine for two weeks. He's on the point of exploding, I know. The only hope is for you to step in, as usual. Otherwise no one will do their duty, I know that.

EVERY WEDNESDAY TOLEA SET aside an hour for his telephonic endeavors. Afternoon, evening, morning, lunchtime, however it came: the operation had to be completed, without fail. The dial would turn sixty, ninety, a hundred times, according to whether Tolea was in a hurry or idling and soaked, like a frog after a heart attack, or a chirpy goldfinch hopping and skipping all the time.

His eyes on the face of the watch: one o'clock precisely! Not a second more. No one answered, but Tolea did not give up. The address was the only one possible, taken from the Exemplary Association and then checked in the telephone directory. The name was the only one possible; so, therefore, was the number. What happens if the perfect disabled person, concentrating hard, disciplined, submissive as the new man is supposed to be, nevertheless cannot hear or speak, as the statutes envisage? Well, maybe there's a wife, sister, maid, son nearby who can answer. No one answered. If the Benefactor, the Great Cardsharper, doesn't wish it to be so, there's nothing to be done: you can't force the wheel of fortune. But you can: yes, you can if you persevere. Even the Invisible One gets bored and gives way in the end; after all, He's built in our image and likeness, as it is written in the Book of our identity books. And as for the other, the Evil One, the partner with whom he shares the game, His Majesty the Prince of Sin, twin and bastard, well, he also resembles our wretched human shape. So again and again, a thousand times over, shall we force our luck, our bad luck? Yes, Octavian Cuşa: he will deliver the truth; he's the right witness for the complex crime. Except he can't speak and can't be found. Not even found.

So he dialed the miracle number.

Wednesday lunchtime, evening, night, morning: let's bewilder the adversary. Still at it in the amnesiac hours, lazily curled up, when the wind is whistling unheard through confused spaces and the clockmakers' lids are bursting and the cardiac arrests are multiplying.

It was in such a time hole that Mr. Dominic suddenly had Inspiration. If I've asked Information a thousand times and been told that the phone is not out of order, or disconnected, abolished, or recoded, it simply means there's no reply. So no one's at home. So let's go there, to the scene itself. If there's still no one, maybe the door will be opened by no one . . .

The decision had been made: Wednesday telephone, Friday visit. Ah, the number of things to do suddenly shot up, the week kept shrinking and shrinking. Some still speak out of boredom. The television goggle box, the patriotic radio, the nonexistent bars, the forbidden poker games, forgotten brothels, secondhand books, dead reflexes, played-out chatter—but initiative? Personal initiative? Some initiative is also necessary, dear disabled persons, colleagues of the underworld! Bored? What do you mean, you're bored?!

Therefore Wednesday on the phone, Friday on the spot: the expedition to Istria, as that street on the edge of purgatory is probably called. From the crossroads down to the supermarket, then right as far as the school of the new man, then somewhere else, to confuse the tail.

Mr. Dominic is standing at the Rond stop and waiting for a tram. The tram does not come: the passenger waits and waits and waits. The tram comes, jam-packed, no room for a fly. Let's wait for another, wait until the eyes blanch in your head. A tram comes: the passenger manages to hang on to the slippery steps, moves up one at the next stop, the future is close at hand, another step, one more, here's paradise, you're already in front of the door, you feel the shoulder and elbow and knee and gasping breath of the man next to you, that's it, connecting elbow to elbow, shoulder to shoulder. Goo-ood, so off at Mihai Bravul, change direction. This time the tram appears after just an hour's wait and it's empty—a miracle, utopia finally made real. Mr. Dominic punches his ticket. One ticket, two journeys: saving paper. Savings, savings, we need paper for posters newspapers instructions memos statutes, the codes of the Exemplary Association.

From the stop he catches a bus to the bread factory. Then the traveler walks back a hundred or so meters, as it is written on the note in his hand, and comes to the Scampolo store, which is shut for stock-taking. He chooses the little street on the right, as far as the old gray block of flats, goes up to the second floor, gropes around for the switch. He presses it and a dim bulb lights up; yes, now he can see where he's treading. It's only one step to apartment 8.

He presses the bell, hears it ringing on the other side of the door. Long, long, long, short, long. Nothing, no one, not a trace. Again, long long long short long. Silence, emptiness. He waits, waits patiently for no one to appear, at the door, with the smile of Old Nick. No movement. One step back, he again presses the light switch. The filament starts glowing and he can see the stairs to the street. He feels his way carefully down. There's the street, the Scampolo store, the bus stop, the bus, the tram stop, the tram, again the street, again the stop, again the tram. Adventures, everyday expeditions. Enough to touch reality at the edges for everything to expand, to slide, to dissolve—an imposing void, gray, gray, marshy, with huge purulent gums. With Friday a failure, there remained the following Wednesday. An hour by the telephone, the prescribed time for the wager. He dialed halfheartedly, once, ten times, eighty times.

Even if the Supreme Being remains invisible, indivisible, blind deaf mute, he's still a man. Otherwise how could he manage?! If you catch him at the right moment, when he's really fed up with things or full of pity or disgust—then, the miracle! The miracle happens: you get through. Click, sparks, an answer at the other end. Self-willed, with sneers and grimaces, once, three times, sixty times. Nothing. The number kept refusing to answer. On Wednesday it is raining. A tree branch outside the window, a wet stick. Taking bites from an apple. Holding the apple in our left hand, turning the dial of fortune with our right. Casting out the hook. Maybe we'll catch reality, maybe we'll latch on to reality and become real. A swoon— that's all reality is. We cling on with our final effort, we beatify chance: "but but, maybe maybe." Nothing lasts, absolutely nothing. The receiver left nearby, on the table. With his right hand he dials the number, the deaf-mute code. In his left he is holding an apple. The thirty-ninth spinning of the dial. It rings: the bell of purgatory rings shrilly, perforating the super-imposed walls of greenish glass, ever new glassy barriers on which huge clusters of rotten matter and phosphorus are growing. No one ever wants to interrupt their sleep, their hibernation. No one wants to recognize his own name or voice; no one wants to stir the thick swamp of apathy that swallows up sound and motion and feeling—and feeling, too, thank God!

Chance had well and truly shut itself up, postponed everything; it was playing at rain, at the apple of sin, what's been gained? It's all been a waste of time. His teeth grind on the downy vegetable flesh; his eyes are looking up, up, to the opaque ceiling. It is raining on Friday, too, in bucketfuls. Receptionist Vancea leaves the hotel under an enormous black umbrella. The city is wet, grown smaller. A rusty, murky rumbling, dragged through the streets by the long, cold tram carcasses. Life—bodies linked together in one huge, thick, knotted body. At each stop more fragments break off, a different assemblage sticks together. Between the elbow of the man on his right and the kerchief of the woman in front, a telescopic slit opens up in which a popular icon of the Madonna is swaying to the vehicle's drunken rhythm. The Vancea retina retains the face of white porcelain, the wounded look, the long eyelashes, the fluttering of black butterflies. He would like to move so that he can look at her, to make the image whole, to see her arms and bust and neck, but all he is offered is this iridescent medallion as in a hallucination. Forgetting his stop, he allows himself to be squashed, carried here and there, annihilated in the great communal body from which he awakens at some point when he is flung dizzy into the street. He recovers his senses and looks for the face of the teenage girl. All he sees are crumpled hats, torn bags, clusters of buttons scattered on the pavement. Why am I avoiding prison, why don't I have the courage to be locked up, why don't we have the courage, all of us, suddenly to fill the prisons? Overpopulation of the prisons. Overpopulation, yes, mumbled the receptionist as he looked at the tired tireless anthill. Let the moment come, another moment, before the giant black heel of deaf-mute Gulliver suddenly crushes the mass of vibrant nothings.

His steps start up with difficulty, uncoordinated. He gets on a bus, a tram, another tram, another bus. He arrives before a decaying gray block of flats, a dark staircase, a black door. And then back again: the hazy, languorous journey. From time to time a shudder. He wakes up, looks at his watch, at the confirmation it gives. He finds again, Friday, the hour which exists and races along and shatters on the uncaring display screen. Why don't we overpopulate the prisons one fine day, why are we so wary, overwary, so overwary? mumbles schoolboy Vancea, until he suddenly remembers the sentence he has been searching for: "When you spend all your time waiting, improvisation looks like salvation." All your time waiting, waiting, improvisation, salvation. Improvisation will save me, save me, postponement, postponement, why don't we all fill, all at once, salvation, salvation, mumbled teenage Tolea, tottering on the bicycle of bygone adolescence, when he repeated, still in ignorance, "Improvisation, salvation, salvation," with that modest and secular gratitude which the years have scattered to the four horizons of nothingness.

Still alive, however, still alive beneath the torrid spring sun, in the foul-smelling dust of the city's outskirts. The fair is still not over: the mad action is continuing and taking him in. Look, he has found some precise and stupid thing to keep him busy, something crazy that belongs to him—fixed hours and days, repeatable, but his alone.

Again Wednesday, lying in wait in the earpiece of the receiver.

Again Friday, on the spot, ghost-hunting. He would like to increase the frequency of this futile behavior: more hours, more days, all hours, all days.

But it is Thursday. That's what is shown on the calendar, on the watch display. This suspect sun is called Thursday. Still a century to go until Friday.

Anatol Dominic Vancea Voinov can wait no longer. He needs a provocation, a neurotic subterfuge. Now, best now, in this burned and narrow cone called Thursday. Hurrying and harassed, he jumbles twists loads the dice. He cheats feverishly, blindly, in a trance. The mystique of the ridiculous will permit this new artifice! Only the slightest departure from the beaten track is necessary. Look, the face of the dice has accepted the move. It's going to be Friday instead of Thursday.

Today is Friday and tomorrow is the same, Friday. We are allowed to progress in futility. Thursday, then. A lunchtime seething with heat and neglect.

COMRADE OREST,

You are right: Madam Mushroom knows more than she lets on. Each time Virgin Veturia plays the same innocent act. But after she opens the door a little to the family toilet, she soon livens up. Dirt acts as a stimulant, I know that. She's not doing anyone any harm, and she may even be doing herself some good, as I keep telling her. Gossip, the national art of conversation, is a popular exercise in intelligence and style. It keeps the mind alert, I know. What are the pieces of information that so much fuss is being made about? A gossipy letter, that's all. Little folkloric studies about workplace and family relations, about the economic troubles and sexual preferences and tensions among individuals and groups. Suppressed ferment, I know. Petty envies, fears, pleasures—sordid stuff. But our good-natured, gossipy nation doesn't concern itself with plots! The proof: no one has been arrested. Nowadays you're not arrested for listening to foreign radio stations, as everyone does, or for drinking coffee bought from speculators, or for making jokes about the vigilant ear of the nation, or for secretly bonking the woman next door. Besides, the real history of our epoch is not to be found in the whining of some schizo Narcissus or his conceited admirers. Time-resistant paper should be reserved for the time-resistant archives. It's there that the popular odyssey of our times will be rediscovered. The plebs have healthy instincts, common sense, modesty, I know. But to return to Madam Mushroom's gossiping. Her Arab students don't talk about politics, she insists. They're more interested in love, which is easily available if they've got hard currency, or even cigarettes, cosmetics, or foreign drinks. Some of them even seem to pass their exams like that. She says she's never once received or distributed porn videos from the foreign students she's in contact with.

In fact, she's never even heard of such videos existing. That's hard to believe, given that the whole of Bucharest knows of the network originating at the foreign students' hostels. But what about those senile studies of her husband's? Madam Mushroom made a weary gesture with her plump hand. That is, it's of no importance. Childish manias, quite harmless. She gradually came to life and served me cigarettes, whiskey, chocolate. She's pretty well lost her head, I know. And do you know what the little old lady mumbled at the end? "Don't tell anyone what we've been talking about, young man." Her parting words! Can you imagine! Our fellow creatures still have a sense of humor, I know. Humor, and not a clue about anything else.

P.S. I asked her to meet me again, after two days. On neutral ground this time. In one of those nominal apartments, where the family's not at home in the morning and doesn't have an idea about anything. Everything's so peaceful, so ordinary—enough to scare you stiff. There had been too little time since the previous meeting and she wasn't used to the place. If she still doesn't want to tell us anything about Allah's circumcised sons, at least I can try to find something out about our own circumcised minority. What is the synagogue saying about the burning of the apartment, the attack on the tenant, and the madwoman's dogs and cats? Panic, pogrom—is that what the curly sidelocks are shouting? Madam Sourpuss is ready to faint, no less. I insisted. What SOS messages are the traveling salesmen sending abroad? Are they shouting that they're in danger and must be saved? The poor old lady doesn't know a thing; she never sees anyone. That was too much. I lost my cool. But what about Moshe, I mean Comrade Gafton, her hubby? And their tenant, the bisexual language professor, old Chatterbox baptized Vancea? What is he, in fact? She got completely confused, even lost her voice. I pushed harder on the pedal. Don't tell me that even Marga . . . Dr. Marga is also some kind of Margulis or Maimonides? I can't believe that even he should . . . And how many more of them are there, eh? Why are their names Romanianized, madam, why? Why don't they pull their little prick *out so we can see what's what, I asked her as she threw a fainting fit. Come now, Comrade Toma, what are you saying, Comrade Toma? Well, as you know, in our country sexual matters are so . . . so . . . We're not talking about sexual matters, madam, don't play the fool. We know all about the itching in the pants and under the skirts of the fatherland, but that's not the point. Why do they conceal themselves? —that's what I'm asking. And surely you must know, being on the spot like that. Well, Comrade Toma . . . Marcel says that assimilation . . . They weren't accepted like that either . . . but now, now . . . Marcel says—do you know what Marcel says? Well, what does that half-wit Marcel say? I asked mentally. Marcel says that nowadays we've all become Jews, we're all oppre— Oppressed, the little pygmy meant to say, but she put her hand over her sinful mouth. Well, not quite all of us are Jews, as your comrade husband thinks, I replied at once. And even if we were, we're not yids. Or gypsies, or those wild Hungarian cowboys. At that, the old pie went whoosh. Whoosh—all the air went out of her. She'd seen the devil—in an ace of fainting good and proper. She didn't say another word, just looked at her twisted shoes wet from the rain. She was no longer breathing, I know. To get scared—that's all they can expect if they forget their place! One of these little fires can have quite an effect. After all, the masses have healthy instincts, common sense, I know that.*

DOMINIC WAS NOT DR. Marga's patient. No, he wasn't. There would have had to be indecent consultations for which neither seemed prepared. Dr. Marga probably still saw in the muddled over-fifty the same shy adolescent of yesteryear, the brother of his former friend Mircea Claudiu.

The problems with which Professor Anatol Dominic Vancea Voinov appeared one morning at Marga's consulting room, trying to explain the reasons for his dismissal and the implications of the trial he had been forced to undergo, had aroused the doctor's compassion and goodwill. He was ready to help the outcast escape his troubles; that is, move from the provinces to Bucharest and find a job and a room, rather than to investigate and amplify his confessions or to suggest treatment for something that was not clearly an illness. He never alluded to those unpleasant events. But of course he registered everything, the kindhearted psychiatrist, mother of wounded souls, humanist debauchee. The professionals of ruin do not need many words before they recognize a client. They look out the window, admire the landscape, light their pipe with an air of preoccupation, but also catch the nuances that give the game away. Attentive to intonation and the order disorder of the words, peeping to see what you're doing with your hands and eyebrows, whether you have shaved carelessly or for some reason are wearing a foppish red scarf.

No, Herr Doktor did not mention the scandal of his dismissal from his teaching post, nor that that was in fact why they had surprisingly met again. He did not want to appear tactless, probably; or that people should think he totted up his good deeds.

In the rear of the confessional, however, the professional was watching, registering, connecting. He did not manage to shake off the pressure of the secret consultation, hidden in the most banal dialogue of the doctor's routine police activity. Nor did he say a word about the accident from teenage years, although in his mind's eye he certainly often saw again the schoolboy's bicycle suddenly hitting the shapeless, greenish, shadowy old crock of a woman, the curse of all the hours that followed in the history of the Vancea family. Nor did he sound him out about the episode of Marcu Vancea's death. He did not ask when how where Dida met her end, or about his former colleague Mircea Claudiu and his icy German wife in heat. No, Dr. Marga, with his heart of gold, Lacrima Christi, respected the discretion required by his Hippocratic oath, *dulcissime*. A *dulcissime frater*, Señor Marga! Served by piss artist Bazil dressed in livery, fed by Lady Jeny with her alms, cats, and many layers of playacting, and occasionally entertained—no?—by Tolea the clown, as the therapy recommended: Let's look after the clothing, belly, and good humor of our good old doctor, his delicate soul and delicate stomach and delicate purse. All he had asked about, delicately, was Sonia. When he found himself in front of the door with an airy gentleman who introduced himself as Vancea and claimed to be the youngest son of Marcu Vancea, philosopher turned wine stockist, and the strange Dida Voinov, Dr. Marga had asked about Sonia. Only then, at the first visit. Whether she was really married to that massive, quarrelsome prophet. Dominic had remained silent, thereby confirming it. So, married to that Matus—as if he actually knew everything. Years of life under canvas, in the desert, where Sonia had given birth to her first daughter and Matus had been injured by a shell splinter. Aha, so they played at being settlers, the doctor had mumbled, avoiding his guest's searching gaze. Yes, yes, I've heard they lived like real pioneers, in a tent, under blazing heat and wind and bullets—and he smiled, delicately. She may well still be beautiful, he mumbled. She shook us all up in those days, he added, just as the fifty-something teenager was preparing to ask about that

Octavian. Marga sensed the danger, of course. So he took him by the shoulders and led him into the house and plied him with questions about the high-school scandal, the trial and expulsion, and then never touched again, unless forced to do so, on the theme of the moral and political trial that he was at pains to avoid. But not as a doctor, oh no. As a friend, do you hear, as a friend! It was also as a friend that he now wanted to push Irina down his throat! Not as a doctor—as a telltale friend, do you hear?!

Recently he had been talking to him about nothing other than Irina. What miracle was the humanist expecting, what was the *lieber Freund* Freud hoping for? To hear what? Why he no longer wants Irina, or why he no longer wants to want her? Or what? Has everyone always felt the same, since long ago, while knowing they are no longer alien— Is the alien within us nevertheless forced to admit that it is alien, to its own body, not just to its aged soul and cloddish mind? Horror of one's own body? Yes, clever Marga would be capable of such a clever question.

Is it that secret shyness we had as adolescents and find again in the proximity of adolescents, Herr Doktor? A potentiality, Doctor, a trembling? Illicit camaraderie, which creates its own cruelties but does not lose that hazy, intense chord, that musical giddiness of April, when spring drugs inject fire into our weary blood. Still young, ye gods! As if we didn't know about the filthy hag we were bound to hit, as if we were still capable of keeping the handlebars straight. As if the lie promise illusion—what melodramas call the cavalcade of youth— could face the sun and moon, as if, as if . . . the monster Orest didn't exist, or the Tranzit brothel or the masks of dark remembrance. We don't care, Doctor: here's a big spit on all your rules and routine! Suffering exults more simply and more complexly than in your treatises on therapy, than in your vaccinated soul, *Frater* Horatius. Is it the magic of the illicit, in this dwarfish world suffocated by hunters lying in wait for their prey? Simpler and more complex than so much else, really.

The moment had come at last. Dominic had suddenly decided to have a real talk with the friend of his father and brother, who claimed to be his friend as well.

He would appear, hurried and resolute, in front of the room of mystification.

Anatol Dominic Vancea Voinov no longer had the patience to wait until evening to visit Counselor Marga's home. He would go to the hospital, to the popular consulting room, where History daily writes its sarcastic reports. He would finally clear up the parentheses . . . The accident, the hospitalization of the old woman hit by the schoolboy cyclist, the death of Marcu Vancea, the Association of Exemplary Deaf-Mutes of the Future, the new man Cuşa, the Ghost of Hobgoblin Photographer Octavian Cuşa. The morality scandal concerning high-school teacher Vancea Voinov. The police informers who worked at the hotel alongside receptionist Vancea Voinov. Veturia and Marcel, neighbors of wanderer Vancea Voinov. Everything, absolutely everything, until the doctor finally divulges the recipe for survival in the throng that races and sighs and eats its fellows and spies on its fellows and buries its fellows and multiplies, keeps multiplying, and multiplies its ever more cunning reflexes of survival. Yes, he was ready, he had decided. Quick, quick, straight to the consulting room, to the hospital.

"Has something happened? What's up?"

"Well . . . nothing."

"That is?"

The doctor would take off his glasses and pass his hand over his forehead, over his eyes. He would open his right, healthy eye; he would close his left, glass eye. Tired, too tired, he would replace his glasses and again pass his hand over his forehead. He would make a sign to his assistant, the policewoman Ortansa Teodosiu, wife of Boss Gică, for her to leave the room.

"Do you want to be admitted, perhaps? A certificate, a prescription . . ."

"Cut the certificate crap! What are you talking about? I've come just like that. To greet spring in its magnificent headquarters at Bedlam."

Dominic would put his fine hands on the table, near Dr. Marga's plump hands with nails trimmed at a manicurist's salon. Preparations . . . pah! You come here thinking of confessing! And you lose all interest, if you ever had any, as soon as you cross the threshold. And with what determination he had come! That's it, all you can do is turn your hands palm up and think long and hard about the intricate lines of fate.

"I've come just like that, to look at your eyebrows. To find out the hidden sign, the code. That invisible scar at the end of your eyebrow."

The doctor would not respond to the provocation; he still would not understand what it was about. A joke, an idiotic joke, some other mad stunt of the madman. But he would be sufficiently nervous to move his plump hands under the table, onto the lap of his smock coat.

"I dreamed of a letter."

"What letter?"

"The bachelor's letter. The dear boy's. The blockhead, you know. Because he must have written it, m'sieur, it must have been him, whatever his name is. Octavian, phantom Octavian. I opened it out of curiosity, under a streetlamp. Sender unknown. But it was the bachelor's letter, I swear. Addressee: Father. Who afterward—you know."

The doctor smiling, tired out. He would take a handkerchief from his pocket, forget about the handkerchief, say that he's exhausted. But he would not want to say any more, he had no way of avoiding the subject, he knew how persistent a madman can be. They would look for a long time into each other's eyes, searching for a solution. The solution: to accept the chattering, to see the mad prank through to the end.

"Dead or alive, let's bring the bachelor in. That's what the gentleman in Buenos Aires wants. That is his wish. Crime, culprits, revenge! That's the play in full, the whole of it. But I'd go even further and say: I'm afraid. I'm afraid of the truth: I'm as scared of betrayal as of the truth, and vice versa."

"What truth?"

"The one I smelled long ago and all the time . . ."

"I don't understand."

"Well, my dear sir, let's put our cards on the table."

"Go to it, my boy. Well?"

"Well?"

"What letter? What bachelor?"

"The chatterlogue. The nihilist. The bachelor. The dear boy. The stutterer, 'Coz he was head over heels in love. And he felt he was losing her. 'Coz that missionary had come and taken her away. And then bang!—the last attempt. A forgery. A mere forger. He copied not only those slogans but their writing as well, their illiterate writing. All those green, worm-eaten slogans around the hooked cross. So *courage*, yes. An anonymous letter, but we all sign. He had signed, illegibly, and put that head in three parts above it."

"What head? What three parts?"

"The three-headed emblem. The cross wasn't enough, so there also had to be the three-headed emblem. That's what gave him away. But Father didn't tell anyone. He was afraid: everything had started to get too dark all around him. Beneath an appearance of calm, yes. There seemed to be a lull, a glimmer of hope—and that's just when you forget to defend yourself. And that's what Father was scared of—the apparent calm. Under which the old old danger was bubbling up: you know what I mean. Where there's no morality, not even corruption can succeed in solving problems. A society without principles: it just shouts that it has some while it is chopping off your rocker. The danger could come from anywhere. In madness not even corruption helps any longer. In vain did Father become a wine dealer. That's what he was counting on, as a philosopher. On weakness and vice and corruption. The stuttering and vengeful man in love. Only he had heard Father talking about Macrobius, Giordano, the three-headed emblem. Because Father was a philosopher, mad about things like that—as you know."

"Come on, you're joking."

"I'm sorry: this is called dreaming, not joking. What am I? A child?"

"Okay, okay! Do you want to say something to me? Go ahead. Do you want to tell me something, after all, Tolea? I get the feeling that— Otherwise we should go. It's late."

The doctor would adjust his clothes and glasses.

"I don't know what you want, Tolea. I'm going home now. I'm off . . . You're having a bad day, Tolea. That's the problem with you: you're always having bad days. Insistence, insistence, your bad days, your defect, believe me."

"The dear boy's capable of tackling any subject, eh? Listen, the dear boy is capable of tackling any subject, isn't he? On the evening of the quarrel, Father had received the letter and understood the danger. You've met my people. But only I know about the threatening letter. Only I and Father, do you understand? Sounds plausible, no? Do you admit it sounds plausible, my dear sir? Come on, admit it. If you love me, if you really care about me, potbellied sir, then admit it. Let's say there was an emblem above the text or above the signature. On the envelope, too."

"And so what? What are you getting at? You're making things up—and not even with any purpose."

Too late. In vain would the doctor rue his words, or turn from the door to comfort the madman. Mr. Tolea would quite simply no longer feel like talking. And if he didn't feel like it, that was all there was to it! He was dead beat.

So, failure—yet another one. Just when we were at last on the point of finding Comrade Octavian, the exemplary photographer of the Exemplary Association; when we were finally prepared to test the charity of the charitable doctor, tell him that it's no good trying to slip life-giving Irina into our bed, to recondition us so that we, too, are in tune with the world. Just when we were able to offer an original hypothesis about the past that has not yet passed. Just then, the battery ran out. Look, the wish to astound the doctor has quite simply vanished! It's vanished and there's nothing to be done about it.

Vacant eyes, moist limbs—the battery is flat. That's the problem with us, Anatol Dominic Vancea Voinov, also called Tolea: we have our bad days, that's all.

Vacant eyes, flat battery: any desire for fun and games and entertaining diversions was swept away. The hour of the wolf had come, the gray hour when aggression is imminent. Night was already advancing on all sides, with its invisible army of lepers. Soon he would feel the epileptic shudder of an encirclement from which there was no escape. The walls would sigh again, demented, shaking under the bolts from a poisoned sky; the roof would dance again, vibrating under the nocturnal bombardment; the windows would clank with the intoxication of terror.

Trauma coming from the ground, an earthquake like the one three years before, on that clear spring night when the crust suddenly began to crack and to throw up the pestilential burden of the morass. Just yesterday—three years ago, like three hundred years ago or three nights ago or never, like now. A cool, cloudless evening— like now. Freshness and peace. Tolea went to the window and looked at the street. An empty, clean street on which a young man was slowly limping behind a long-haired Afghan hound. A solemn, aristocratic, golden dog. The silent street in perfect repose, the perfectly absent dog, the lame young man in a thick black wool cape hanging down almost to his shoes.

He turned back inside the room and looked again at the library.

A high wall completely full of book-bearing shelves. The old lawyer, once a friend of philosopher–wine dealer Marcu Vancea, had asked him to pay a visit to inspect his library. Having recently been left a widower, the pensioner wanted to sell off his collection of books. He had thought of Tolea, whom he knew to have been an avid reader as a young man, at the time when he himself had been a lawyer in that wretched trial over the bicycle accident.

An impressive library indeed. Old books in valuable leather bindings, a whole series of French classics, but also famous German and English titles, and, oh yes, a first edition of the Bible in Slavonic. What a miracle that it had not been confiscated in the years of Stalinist hysteria, when he could have landed in big trouble. Tolea advised him to contact Marga. Perhaps a connoisseur of rare objects, but also a possible link to the medical caste where there were still people with money and, who knows? even with soft spots for culture. The lawyer made a gesture of annoyance at the mention of the name. Obviously he knew Marga: they had played poker together for many years. No, he didn't like the one-eyed doctor's cautious style of playing. "Only one eye for so many books—just imagine," muttered the old man, perky with spite. "Not even two young eyes would give you the strength for such wonders." Tolea did not give up and insisted that Marga was a real possibility, if not to buy it himself, then at least to find someone who would. But the old man suddenly remembered the pills he was supposed to take every evening and hurried toward the kitchen to make some tea. "I'll make some for you, too. A special tea. It's a superb Indian tea—really quite special. It works wonders. Sometimes uncomfortable wonders, believe me," the bibliophile mumbled as he withdrew to the kitchen. While Tolea waited for him to return, he looked at the extra-high walls brimming with exotic golden spines. Then he turned again to the window. The pair was slowly moving into the distance. The noble dog, with its tapering head and its learned locks waving in the breeze of the spring night.

And one step behind, its black-mantled companion limped rhythmically along.

The image suddenly shattered. The window shook, thunder hit the walls, everything began to tremble. Tolea jumped sideways in the direction of the door—crash! tray and cups falling to the ground in the kitchen, whoooom! the whole wall with the books tumbling down in a flash, explosion one step away, a miraculous escape, whoooom! one step, one second, the windows clanking and walls tottering, table chair television. The old man was already here, pale, shivering, spasmodically pulling him by the jacket with his bony arms: "Out, out, earthquake." Already in the shaking front doorway, the walls floor windows people, yes, they had all gone to the doors: shouts, screams, and sobs—with the shell cracking and crumbling, they held on to the door frame, hurled from one side to the other, "like in 1940, an earthquake," the old man was babbling, and they were lying on the ground and there was no end to it. "Under the door beam, must get under the beam"—the little old man was holding on to the panel of the crackling door; the beams were going crack bang, the floors, the pillars, no end to the swaying, the jabbing. The shell was cracking and tumbling down, this is the long dismal end, hit from one corner to another, frantic dizziness, rocking rocking, no end to it, long long dismal macabre never-ending minutes. Neverending, never, no, not yet, no, finished, looks like it's over. "Quick, quick, to the stairs," murmured the old man. "Wait, let me get my coat, I must just get my coat," and they grabbed their overcoats and went running running down the stairs strewn with debris and bricks and clothes, to the street, salvation, springing, stirring, stairs, street, yes, in the street, saved, Our Saviour, supreme, saved by Our Saviour supreme, thanks be to Him. Crumpled clothes, deathly pale but alert faces, the street full of victims stamping from cold and excitement, and streets full of rubble and hubble-bubble, columns of bodies and the buzzing of hurried voices, all hurrying here and there without quite knowing where, a kind of mass breakout, as if the disaster had also meant liberation, because it was not possible to return to the shattered cages, now forced at last to rediscover one another, no longer having any shelter, lacking the protection but also the limits of walls, nomadic and free, in the unknown night given back to us. "This is where that little dynamo of a poetess used to live," said the old man as he pointed to a tall building in ruins. "I was a colleague at the bar with her father. And look at this—it was the perfumery. Now it's gone, turned into dust."

They left Sfîntul Ion Nou and went to the university, squashed between waves of people thronging the pavement, beneath flurries of dust raised by the wind from the craters of collapsed buildings. The pensioner stopped in front of the Hotel Ambassador. "There's no point. I can't go on. This general hysteria isn't doing me any good at all." And the crowd really was on the boil, its gestures and voices irrepressibly accelerating and expanding. The city seemed to be on the eve of a great siege, disturbed still more by the insurrection of its shelterless inhabitants than by the catastrophe that had just struck it. "No, there's no point; it's really bad for me. I'd do better to go and look for my sister. At Drumul Taberei, that's where she lives." Tolea tried to talk him out of it: it's late, the buses aren't running, thieves flood the streets at times like this. But the old man did not give way. He was determined to see what had happened to his sister, because it was quite likely that every one of those socialist-constructed blocks in the new parts of town had come crashing down. "It's a terrible earthquake, you know. Stronger than the one in '40. It lasted longer, too. It's ghastly, really ghastly." So Tolea went toward Drumul Taberei together with the man who had been his defense lawyer at the trial of his youth.

It was a long way, an hour and a half or so, along unfamiliar streets bustling with a motley and noisy crowd at the peak of over-excitement. The situation did not grow calmer as they moved away from the center. A kind of explosive sleepwalking hypnotized the poor tenants who had been driven from their damaged cells, traumatized by unpredictability and death. Authority had also suddenly disappeared. People were obviously overjoyed that no one was telling them what to do, but they were also stunned, like so many orphans, at not being able to regain their sense of the moment—the only reality, the reborn present at once volatile and voracious, which had to be seized quickly they knew not how, with claws mouth eyes mind, bitten salivated eaten swallowed digested eliminated, get out into the wasteland, that's all, a moment, an earthquake, we have no right to waste the moment, because soon the sellers and the customs men will be back. "Listen, what are they saying?" murmured the bibliophile, pricking up his ears. "That it hasn't been broadcast. They still haven't reported the earthquake on the radio. You see, they already sense the lack of authority. They really should be told what's happened, and what they have to do." The old man from yesteryear seemed completely calm and detached, merely adjusting his gold-rimmed spectacles from time to time and giving a pull on his hood, a kind of cone-shaped woolen black stocking. He was breathing with difficulty, it's true, and his back was bent. But he bore up to the long trek, and despite the shock never lost his good cheer. "Just think: two hours gone by and they still haven't got the courage to say in public that something has happened beyond their control. Something unavoidable, unpredictable, which challenges their power. The surprises of our Mother Nature! And it does still exist—just think—it's still capable of springing surprises. The poor officials are suffering from shock. They're all paralytic, believe you me." A sign that he was in a special state, however, was that he kept sneezing. Every few minutes he buried his head in the fur lapel of his grand old moth-eaten overcoat. He took from the lapel a large white handkerchief, a kind of napkin, which he then carefully refolded and put back in its place, although it was evident that he would need it again all too soon. "And on top of it all, their boss is out of the country in Africa—just now! I'm telling you, they don't know how to break the news. They don't even know how to tell him. Bad news will make him upset—that's obvious. I don't envy them, the poor things—they must be scared stiff." The old man's voice could be heard faintly beneath the material.

"Now is the hour. The great chance for the conspiracy. The act of treason. Time for the lower ranks to take the wheel. A perfect moment, believe me. But they won't do it. That's how they've been selected," the old lawyer continued, rolling his r's in the interwar manner with all the ease of youth. "From tomorrow there'll be a new strategy—you'll see. Visit to such-and-such a hospital, invaluable suggestions, big rallies, chats with people saved from under the rubble, parental care of the nation's parents. Hold tight: from tomorrow the old jabberer will be at it again." But they were now in front of the block they had been looking for. And it had not collapsed; in fact, it looked quite solid. They went up the dark staircase, stumbling over pieces of mortar and scrap iron. From time to time Tolea lit a match: voices could be heard from all the apartments, where people were still frightened and had not gone to bed. They eventually reached the top floor, the tenth, where the pianist had just clambered up. A small, elegant apartment. Some six or seven people were praying around a candle, with complete presence of mind, while the radio was broadcasting, in French, news about the Bucharest earthquake. No, the national radio had still made no announcement, but foreign stations were confirming that what they had all experienced a few hours ago really had happened. Seismic monitors had registered many degrees on the Richter scale. He remained in the doorway, declining the invitation of the porcelain figure Paulina, the pianist, to remain with them. "You know what they say: there will now be a number of smaller shocks. It's best if we stay together." Yes, he himself felt the shudder: a kind of strange induction of the danger was floating in the air; an obsessive headache had taken hold of the thoughts and the body in which that cosmic trepidation had burrowed so deeply, the traumatic cough of sick Earth shaking the Chinese walls of the illusory little refuges. He looked at the pensioners from the door; it was as if he had seen again his long-departed parents and uncles and aunts. He did not feel much like being alone, it was true; he was even trembling. The shaking of the walls and the ground had entered inside him. But no, he was not tempted to join these old people asking for God's mercy, nor did he want to stay under any kind of roof. He would sooner be out roaming the city's nocturnal wilderness. They were concentrating so hard, both on themselves and on the voice of the distant announcer, that they evidently did not notice when he quietly shut the door behind him.

He gripped the banister with his right hand. The thick heel of his shoe faltered on the first step below. An ordinary step, yes, as on the way up. He looked for the matches that he always carried with him; their ancestral fire had proved the only salvation during the energy crisis. The first stick did not light, of course. He tried another two until he succeeded. By the little phosphorus flame he looked at the abyss of the stairwell. Yes, it was normal enough, as on the way up. Without striking any more matches, he groped his way down, step by step. It was quiet: the voices had grown fainter—just a low indistinct sound from time to time. Ninth floor, eighth, seventh, fifth. At the fifth a door opened somewhere. The darkness was total, yet he did feel a door opening. He stopped. "Is there anyone on the stairs?" a woman asked. He hesitated before replying. "Yes, I'm just on my way down." Pause. Tiny particles of magnetic obscurity carried her voice back, deep and slow. "You don't have a match, by any chance?" The black, impenetrable texture of darkness, the imperceptible pulsation of darkness—perhaps also of the walls, of his knees. He clenched the cold rail with his fingers, trying to catch the hushed voice again. Deep, young, clear—a burning jet. "Yes, I do," he replied. Still night, about to resume the quaking. "Yes, I've got some matches," he repeated. Still, frozen lava about to explode. "The apartment on the right. The first by the stairs. To the right." A deep voice filling the darkness with its perfumes. He took a step back. The match did not light. Another one. He turned, with the tiny flame in front of his eyes, toward the first door on the right. He was beginning to see: the clear white oval of her face, huge watery eyes, and especially her red hair, short wiry red, burning. A thick dressing down like a bathrobe, and a snow-white shoulder. The match went out, but he was already at the door. She touched his hand, her fingers linking together with his. He was pulled inside. "There's a draft on the stairs. Matches keep going out." Yes, there was a draft on the stairs. Impossible to keep a flame alight. A clear deep voice, thin strong bony fingers, short wiry red hair, burning. He made to light another match. "No, not here. I'll get a candle first," and she pulled him after her, through the narrow hall to the living room, and then unclenched her fingers. She went, probably, into another room to look for candles. "No, I can't find any. Please light a match." The match flared up, but then went out at once. He struck another, which did not light. Finally a mini-flame was cutting through a little zone of semi-darkness. They looked at each other—smiling, one might have said. Pale, excited. Yes, she was slim and tall. Her dressing gown fluttered briefly over her black-stockinged legs. He saw again the pale, stretched oval and the huge eyes and boyish haircut. The match went out, burning his fingers. He made to light another, but her cool smooth palm covered his hand. Again their fingers locked together, phalanxes tightly pressed, and then opened again in search of buttons and zipper. His scarf, coat, belt, pullover, shirt flew off. Her lips remained glues to his, not moving, not kissing. Smooth vibrant lips, young slow breathing, erect nipples. Cold smooth breasts and a long, powerful, impatient tongue. His coat, trousers, and pullover fell quickly, then the rest, quickly, quickly.

Her hands felt him feverishly. Her voice was calm, but her body was trembling, in panic, fingers hurriedly sliding over the stranger's body—chest, hips, lower down. She was tall and young and naked, glued to the stranger's foreign body. Thrilled, eager to find confirmation, union. A brief shudder passed through her throbbing body when she took and sheltered the frail, stunted babe in the palm of her hand. Only then did she kiss the man's mouth, heavily, without passion, in a kind of pact of urgency. She held the python in her skilled, protective hands, as in a resuscitation tube. She held it very tight, and she, too, was tense. It existed, they still existed, after everything. "Tudor, Tudor," the lamentation began. As if her youthful murmur were sucking in all the air from the room. Not a flicker could be heard anymore, not a movement, just the prisoner's breathing. Her fingers became more and more silky, velvety, in the smooth ritual. "Tudor, Tudor," the unknown woman repeated tenderly. "Tudor," she urged on the creeping stalk. The snake, ever hotter, ever more erect in the palm of her fluid, magnetic hand. Enlivened, powerful, under the vestal's spell. "Tudor, Tudor," she spoke rhythmically, in a trance, with her palm rolled around the wonder. On her knees now, as if at prayer. "Tudor, Tudor," she groaned, with her lips glued to the obsidian head. An expanding totem, with the name of the absent one it was to replace. A substitute, of course, that was all it could be in a world of substitutes, perfectly identified with the name and role and memory it had to mime, so that no identification or differentiation would be possible, as the underworld of masks and substitutes required. Tolea was already kneeling as well: their fingers interlocked once more and opened again. The hushed darkness, frozen solid—not a vibration, not a throb, as if they were in a burial vault. Their haste injected its dizzying alcohol, speeding up their breathing and movements. Coldness and burning heat at the same time. The woman lay down on her back, but gripped his arm tightly and guided his fingers through the prickly, heated bushes onto the flower in flames. The sepals opened to receive him.

"What's her name? What's her black hole of a name?" murmured the darkness. "What's your jungle called? Your black mouth. Your gateway. Your man-eating flower. What's she called? What's the name of yours?" asked Tudor's woman from her trance. It hurt him, the waiting and the silence hurt him, the snake in the darkness hurt him, but he knew he wouldn't gain access until he handed over the coupling name. "Irina," whispered the wanderer in defeat, barely heard. The walls seemed to shake, or not quite, carefully, dangerously, and the floor as well. A slight warning clank of the windows, or so it seemed. The walls and floorboards and ceiling were slowly vibrating, slowly but tangibly. "Irina," repeated the priestess as she took him in. "Irina," sighed the woman. "That's my name, exactly. Exactly my name," whispered the sleepwalker, happy and relaxed, as if she had suddenly been liberated. "Irina! My God —that's exactly my name," whimpered Irina, in whom Tudor was hysterically pumping the lava of the fiery night. The shell was shaking, trem-trem, trembling, earth tremor; the crater had released smells and microbes, the magma was pulsating, wounded and scattered, and the walls were swaying, swaying, the shaking ever more furious, but Irina stopped him, "No, not now," and he was again in her witch's hands and lips, rocking, calmed, reborn in her cool and salty hands, between marine, phosphorized lips. Her long legs trembled on the trembling ceiling, like the walls and windows and floor and the jet of fire in night's bottomless udder. "Oh, Irina," the orphan finally expiated, expired. "Irina, Irina," the saved clown confessed, bowing his tearful mask on her electrified breasts, moving his vanquished head down onto the cosmic abdomen, to catch the echo, the confirmation, still lower down, when his lying lips, in the ultimate act of gratitude, glued themselves to the cannibal flower.

Healed he died, fell asleep, awake, the final sleep. The airplane banked to the left, the seats vibrated, a shiver of alarm passed through the metal belly. The stewardess was there in front to serve him, naked beneath her long voile dress. The silver tray in her long hands was shaking, as was the shell of the airplane. But she bent toward him, holding out her glossy breasts with their pea-lightbulb in the middle. Huge empty eyes in which nothing at all could be read. But her lips were quivering over small, sharp teeth. She whispered something. "Here," she whispered. "It's allowed here," whispered the nymph. "Here in the air we're allowed to. They can't forbid it anymore. Here, up in the air," mur-mur murmured the strip-teaser, mur-mur, the airplane spun more and more tensely, jerkily, but the whispering persisted. "Don't be on your guard anymore. We're up here, in the air. It's possible up here"—and Tolea again felt Irina's lips on his lips, nibbling ever so finely and murmuring mur-mur, melting away. Somewhere a candle seemed to be burning; the room was floating in its dim flicker of light, somewhere. He looked at the woman, her short red hair on the carpet beside him, her lips glued to his own. Naked, white, long, slim, a narrow, pale face and big green eyes and soft lips, mur-mur, glued to his lips, mur-mur murmuring: forgive me. She stretched out her glossy breasts, the left one, the right, for him to recognize them, to kiss them. Superb delicate fruits, indeed— pale violet, strong, juicy, with a long and bitter sucking bottle.

"Forgive me, Dominic." She had fastened her mouth to the lobe of his flagging ear. "Yes, I looked in your wallet. To find out your name. Forgive me, Dominic"—and she resumed the ritual of arousing him. Still listless, worn out, the weak Dominic was in no hurry at all to recognize his name; he had no desire to replace the replacement, to play the second act, in which his role would be himself, the absent one; no, no, he did not want to wake up in his own skin—the swaying of the cupping glass would not arouse him, no, the neurosis of the earth and the walls and the somnambulist moon would not oblige him to become himself again, delivered over to nothingness. Yes, he missed Irina. Why not admit it? They would have been a couple, maybe brother and sister, better resisting the pressures of annulment that had still annuled them. Now, at least now in the cataclysmic night, when the ramshackle house of purgatory was shaking wildly and danger seemed so akin to liberation, he ought to have gone out and found her, so that after so many detours they could finally recognize themselves as a couple. "Irina and Dominic,

Irina and Dominic." The priestess cast her spell, with her hot mouth over hot torch. It grew again, very slowly, incubation, vibration, quaking, earthquake. The windows were shaking already, like the drunken walls and the floor. Her mouth, filled with saliva and bacteria and aphrodisiacs, stammered ineffable curses. He woke again in the vulva of the volcano, among voracious, moist, boiling petals, in incestuous Mother Africa. Painfully did Dominic discover the desire of the captive *sorella*, in the dark jungle, blazing and cannibalistic, tre-mor, tre-mor, whimpered Irina and the torrid swamp. A failed exercise in transference, that was all it had been. A humiliation, a powerless assumption of a name that didn't work, clearly didn't work. He woke up ejected and Irina was laughing, brazenly. "Three angels for Sarah, Abraham's wife," the brute was guffawing on all fours, bitchlike. "The ancestor, with the three angels. One for each orifice"—and the candle had gone out in the whirlwind of blasphemy, which was also one of fury and wild rebirth, look! fury and repulsion with himself, with his fellow creatures, and with the gods, the full, pagan, barbaric pleasure, yelping its triumph, challenging Cyclops, who was spying on his heart and mind and sex. Until this evening, until a few hours ago, when the earth shook with disgust at the tedium that kept fermenting hatching evacuating on his overly patient back. A rabid greyhound on his rabid bitch, shaking epileptically on her narrow back, setting on her snow-white neck and treacherous hips and red crewcut, yelping together with the immediate, illicit pleasure in revenge for so many postponements and prohibitions. The therapy of mad fury, liberation, yes, unfettered, unrestrained, callous pleasure which cures the horror of your own estranged body and estranged name and estranged soul in a world of estrangement. Dom-dom-min-min-nic, yelped roared Dominic and ri-ri-rina, yelped the rabid redhead, the beat of the wilds, dom rina, domirina, dum dom ri rina, domiri, until lights out. Then lethargic, pacified, stretching beside on top of each other and moving away from each other, emptied, weary, sated.

Only now, in the breakdown spleen of separation, did the long-ing for Irina truly return. That hysterical night, driving wild heart and mind and blood in the hazard of death and liberation, as befit-ted the still living dead, ought to have been one of rediscovery. For however brief a respite—if only for the minimum sequence between two final convulsions of the planet, if only for that—the orphans ought to have been able, finally, to take revenge for all the delays, to rediscover each other at last.

Yes, he really missed Irina, the one far away, who could have been if she had ever been—so yelped cur Dominic, lying on his back on the carpet, beside the bitch Irina, who fawningly licked his juices, skin, and hair. "Hair," the bored puppy barely articulated. "You didn't use to have red hair. Since when the red hair?" the stranger asked, scarcely breathing. "Irish, baby. I'm Irish," the stranger promptly replied. "Pure Irish stock, I swear," the Irish-woman repeated firmly, and she licked him again with her long, red, Irish tongue, until she dozed off from exhaustion, with her muzzle between her rear paws and her lips glued to the defunct Dominic, now a little finger, a shrunken, senile snake.

And so passed a century of peace and oblivion, until the windows shook again and Tolea woke up scared at the vibration of the walls, as in another earthquake.

It was only a truck or a tank or a tractor, perhaps, rattling down the street that was just then waking up. Dawn had come—the petrified cage as indifferent as ever. Nothing was moving: it was as if nothing had happened.

He got up, looked around at the strange room, looked at the window and the unfamiliar street, then dragged his scattered clothes from the carpet and put them on.

The hostess was asleep. Naked, perfect—perfect sleep. Now he saw her in reality. Broad hips, narrow waist, sturdy calves, smooth sole, slim ankle, pale elongated face, lips twisted in an evil smile, short red hair of a setter, white, overlong arms. She did not move, did not hear a thing. He took a first step. The corpse remained the same, immobile, perfect.

Her sleep was too perfect to demonstrate indifference, innocence. Did the courtesan not have something to hide; that is, some reason to be on the alert? Perhaps her haste to search the stranger's pockets, to discover his identity, address, distinctive details, had after all been only a harmless impertinence or an excess of curiosity and even friendliness, nothing else. A cosmic, total sleep, as if nothing suspicious could be discovered in the Mata Hari boudoir. All around and on the floor, books, clothes, tableware were lying in a heap as the earthquake had flung them.

He leafed through a few books on the carpet, opened drawers, paper files, albums, and cupboards to unearth the weapon of the officer in disguise or her secret identity papers. He kept turning to make sure that the nude was in the same position, anaesthetized in the same indecent, intangible slumber. He looked among brass and nylons and photographs, among towels, cosmetics, and shoes. How could the captain allow herself to sleep while a stranger was rummaging through wigs, slips, panties, and tights. Had the earthquake been so high on the Richter scale that it had confounded police regulations, granting her indefinite leave for this implausible, indefinite sleep?

No, he did not find the props of disguise, or the revolver or uniform or secret orders and reports. But he knew that the futility of the search lay in its own premises: the results did not mean anything. The lack of proofs only showed how abundant they were, and the falsified evidence was more convincing than if it had been real. No, not even her sleep, as greedy and imprudent as the loveplay had been urgent, famished, and reckless, absolved the mannequin of the suspicion of which no one these days had a right to be absolved.

He listened for a moment longer before leaving. Nothing—not a flicker. He wearily left the resuscitation balloon. He stood clinging to the door. Gray-blue dawn. The daylight had scarcely broken through: night was still sarcastically dawdling over the damaged city. Scarcely able to make out the stairs, he lit a match to guide himself down. But then he turned back to read the name on the recessed door. It was engraved on a little bronze plaque: FRANCISCA POP. The match went out and he lit another. FRANCISCA POP. BALLERINA was written clearly on the door to the trap. He read it, read it again, memorized it, read it once more. "Irina, how about that! The Red Hole. The Irish mouth! The Irish setter, huh! The Cannibal, or witch! Witch Francisca Pop d'Assisi! Irish—huh! What a con merchant!" The wanderer was still mumbling on the last stair before he went out into the street, into reality.

"Irina, how about that! Irina of Hymenland!" he said, stressing the words, refreshed by the cool of the unreal morning. "A ballerina, huh! Ballerina Mata Hari!" the pedestrian repeated to warm himself up.

After just an hour it would no longer be possible to find the green-painted staircase and that block of flats and the fir-lined drive and the name Francisca Pop—of that he was convinced. They would have scattered without trace in the dark labyrinth of the beehive, which would conscientiously begin again its static daily grind. Scattered himself, too. In a hurry to be scattered without trace as fast as possible. In the night that was being scattered, in the dawn that was freezing and scattering him.

He went forward in the gray hour, the hour when aggression is imminent.

He could already feel the epileptic shudder, the encirclement without escape.

Night, emptiness. Nearby can be heard the cranes working beneath jets of reflector light at the WHITE PALACE of the future, the headquarters of the exemplary deaf-mute circus where the Exemplary President of the Exemplary Association will sit on the throne! The street is wearily grating under the caterpillar tracks of the night's transport. The loads are marble walls, conduits, barrels of fuel oil, concrete slabs, gilded door handles, and taps for the boudoir of the generals, the exemplary watchers of the exemplary watched. The sky is being torn to pieces by the fire serpents with their soldering operations.

Clear black sky, few stars, no moon: in vain would you look in the sky for someone to talk to.

A few times he seemed to feel the obsessive shadow of someone watching him. Past midnight. The hour of nightmares, the hour of Toma.

"People are capable of anything, hunter Toma A. Toma. You might quote this banality in the reports you file in the Archives of Suspicion. The prisoners hardly have time to understand the brief trajectory that is allowed them. They can hardly evaluate the deformed specimen called man. Who better than you to know their failings and their helplessness? But Vancea? What can one think of me, the ephemerid Vancea, the ex-teacher Vancea?"

He would smile, happy with the dialogue. His knowing, conceited, artful smile.

Tolea the sleepwalker felt that he was no longer alone in his room.

"You don't interest me, Mr. Vancea, I told you. I asked you about Ianuli, about our old obsession Ianuli."

"I don't know him. I don't know Ianuli, as I've said time and time again. I never had the opportunity: I don't want to, and there's no need for it either. No, I don't know Ianuli. I don't have any opinion about him. None at all."

He had pressed his head in his hands, so he wouldn't hear the sound of himself thinking, so he could remain alone with the darkness. But after a long while he looked up again. Something very strange was shining in the dark, like a gold tooth in an invisible mouth or a bleeding scar on a ghost's temple. And silence fell, after the avalanche of unuttered words. The windows were gradually dissolving in the bluishness of dawn.

"Do you really not know Ianuli at all—not at all? Or his wife? Or his wife, who has worked with us for so . . ." And someone made a chivalrous gesture, an act of reverence in the face of the priceless memory.

"Ianuli, Ianuli. I've seen him a few times. I've caught sight of him, I mean, in the street, at the theater, I don't remember where else. But I don't know him in fact. All I know is what everyone knows: the Ianuli legend. A young bookworm fascinated by revolution who leaves his family and goes off to fight in the mountains; he's wounded, leaves his age-old Greece, and soon after the war comes here, to the gates of the Orient. He's very ill nowadays, that's what I've heard. I happened to see him a year or so ago in the street. He was pale, all skin and bones, with disheveled hair. A real ghost! No, I don't know him. But Emilia— Well, Emilia . . ."

Nonsense. Rambling words that should not have been said or even thought. Maybe our thoughts can be intercepted, maybe the technology has been developed. Does the exemplary institution already have such an invisible instrument at its disposal? We shouldn't always be asking ourselves who the devil is. You shouldn't talk nonsense. That's just what spies are looking for.

Toma was no longer there. Just as he was preparing to shout "No, I didn't mean to, I didn't want," there was already someone else in front of him.

"You—you are the devil, you are our salvation. You, adored one, cannibal, rare mountain flower, scumbag . . ."

Emilia smiled, as if she had not heard the whispering. Emilia smiled and was close by; you had only to stretch out your hand. Close, close, as he had always wished. Finally, just here, with no witnesses. A spark would be enough, and then at last revenge would be had for the sick expectation. At last he was just one step away from the unlikely moment. Should he tell her something else, anything? The thoughts are different, *dulcissima*, just listen to my crazy pulse, booming like the jungle tom-tom, the wild racing of the blood thudding in honor of the beloved!

Emilia either did not hear or heard something different: she continued to smile indulgently. "You—you are the devil! Your indifference and your happiness, both unquenchable . . . You overripe nymph, mare in heat. Perfect, like the forbidden fruit. Elemental, insatiable. As simple as light and death. You, venerated scumbag, desired by all."

The professor had bent under the weight, overwhelmed by the words unsaid. He was sweating, driven mad by the miracle of the moment that would fade and die. "Emotion—that's all I am. Raging emotion, *sorella*. Emotion is ruining me. It's driving me wild, wiping me out, *amantissima*."

And he no longer had the courage to look up. Toma, the waged spy, had disappeared, as had Irina, with her perverse adolescent headaches, and Tolea flying through the air without handlebars, and old Marga and the retired Gafton couple, and the Argentinian Mircea Claudiu with his glassy Astrid, and the subterranean Octavian Cuşa, known as Tavi, photographer of the deaf-mutes—all of them. All.

"Why are you laughing? There is no escape, is there? There's no point in making the play more complicated, is there? You're laughing at our fearful caution. Is there nothing other than the arrogance of the pleasure in which you gleam? Only the plenitude of this oblivion in which the avid harlot, Death, roars with satisfaction? The elixir of oblivion, you, your phosphorescent legs, your lips and breasts and cosmic sex, and those big, ingenuous, primordial eyes. You, *dulcissima*, the planetary whore."

The thoughts slowed down as the author curled up with fatigue. His pate still seemed to be glowing. The light slowly increased, a sick vibration, but his thoughts grew weaker, diluted, disconnected.

Emilia was seated at an austere desk, elbows resting on the glossy wood, young hair fluttering here and there. Those unforgettable angular cheeks, those eyes, ah yes, those eyes . . . He looked down, humbled by so many tottering thoughts, ashamed at the unexpected neglect, disarmed. "Are you wisdom? Without character, without restraint? Just the purity of sudden feeling? How much I longed for the meeting, the miracle, at last! The plenitude of sensation, of the joy of the moment, that's all. Nothing else: the plenitude of oblivion. But he, the dangerous Ianuli, he the failure? But what about Comrade Ianuli?"

She did not hear him: the low moaning sound did not reach her; the gods protected her from such wretched jamming. Sublime, perfect, she was deaf to such whining. Deaf; deaf as a radish!

The sleeper smiled guiltily at the feeble simile. But he was happy that it had not been heard.

Emilia went on smiling. The expression on her face seemed to be changing all the time. Subtle variations of line, imperceptible migrations of color. He had seen her so many times and heard so much about her fabulous appearance, but her voice, no, that he had never heard.

Emilia had stood up in front of the desk. Supporting herself on one elbow, she jumped up and sat with legs crossed on the desk. He recognized her: yes, it was she, wearing jeans, as young girls do, with that usual see-through blouse which seemed not to be there at all.

She looked at him, let herself be looked at. Close by, a step away, within reach. She had it in mind to speak—or so it seemed. That deep voice which people described as coming from the depths, burning the air and words.

"You're like me, sweetheart. I mean, you were, you should have been. You didn't have the strength, weren't courageous enough. You could have—you wanted to, admit it. You had no idea how much strength and how much courage you would need in that tight corner. You desired me, but not enough. Although you did often desire me passionately, like a child. Why why why didn't you persevere? Champagne, dancers' thighs, dirty jokes—you really could have been the songwriter for a cabaret! The ladies, including young ones, spoiled and pampered you. You certainly had the good looks. Both

fickle and sharp. Talent? Only I have talent. But you found something that gave an appearance of it. Songwriter at the Cabaret Levcenco! Or the Cabaret ATOMICA or the PUSSY Club. A king, a real
giant! Like me, the giantess . . ."

It did not sound like a joke. Why why why. The giantess had cut
through the air with her gigantic legs. And what if what if. Suddenly
the sleepwalker sensed the falseness, the dissonance. No, it hadn't
been the giantess's voice. A kind of dubious post-synch. Why why
why why. The movement of those delicate, devilish lips, the luster
of shiny teeth perfectly smooth like bullets. The voice: what why if.
It wasn't her voice, it couldn't be!

You were like me; you could have been. When you still had the
choice, you could have been like me, Professor. You would have
had the talent. But you couldn't. In a corner now, deformed. You're
right: you do deserve a little reward, a little inadvertence, I know. I'll
pay you back. You will have the moment, a breath of air, that's all. A
fake, at hand. Our journey is short: you deserve this little piece of
guile, a sweet mockery, oho . . ."

She must have wanted to laugh, but her giant's laughter did not
start up: it couldn't. And the voice was borrowed. It was his voice,
actually his! What a devilish swindle! It's hard to recognize your
own voice, why why why. He did see her gigantic, tender figure
coming toward him again. With a short jump she was down from
the desk and standing on her feet. Whole, whole, at last . . . With
those long legs and that rough head of hair carefully smoothed at
the temples. She joined her slim, delicate hands, as if to ask forgiveness or simply to reassure him in preparation for happiness, so he
could receive the young light of her eyes as it kept drawing nearer.

She moved toward him, but somehow the contact was lost. He
perceived her floating motion, her smiling face, but her approach
was delayed and became blurred. There would have been no point
in holding out his hands: he had felt the break, the interruption.

The shadows were reborn around him, teeming again in a viscous, rustling expectation.

It was as if a signal had been given. Was it the telephone, the doorbell, or the alarm clock? Neighbors, the postman, or the block manager? So it was back to the beginning again—the voice from the other day.

Only a step separated them, but he had lost the giantess, he knew. There's no more to be done; the day was dragging him toward her rugged haven. He recovered his senses: there was no longer any escape.

"Our collaborator," that was how Toma had presented her. He'll find her again, then. He'll find them all again: he just has to pay attention, to recognize them in time, so that he can make an approach to them.

He smiled, ready for the new meeting. Oho, the poor apprentices of reality—they deserved his naïve participation, his uncertain share.

About to open his eyes. On the lids is the infinite zephyr, the cool long hands of morning.

The buzz of routine penetrated the window. He was prepared.

The high-school teacher in that wooded town of his adolescence, pampered with springs and melancholy hills, played a star come down for a moment to flummox provincial teenagers. Colored scarves, machine-gun ripostes. Always irritated, bored, spitting out aphorisms, accompanied by a motley retinue of raw, chaotic youth. Step one, just inside the classroom: throwing the register on his desk. He would mount the chair and look out at the lazy good-for-nothings. Lip hanging down in spleen, eyes fixed in loathing. His forefinger would point to a dunce and summon him to answer a surprise question. Tense silence, enraptured, terrified audience waiting for the blow. But the professor does not have the patience: he gets bored and looks out the window. Then he suddenly stands up, writes the title of the next lesson on the blackboard—in huge letters as if for idiots—and is on his way. He does not even take the class roll with him. It stays like that, open on the desk, while the chair still retains the vibrations from the thin, swaying body, wrapped in extravagant clothing, of the clownish m'sieur professor.

But in the afternoon—oho! In the main street, in the cinema lobby, on the shaded paths leading down to the river, anywhere and everywhere is TOLEA: the focus of the teenage public. Dragging after him, higgledy-piggledy, thickheads and prize winners, bobby-soxers and even young ladies.

He growls, tells stories, ever changing his voice and adjectives: how students in the capital, exhausted with drink, are said to organize escapes from bars without paying; what happened last year, supposedly, at the jazz festival in Newport, Newpork; which is the favorite drug used by actress Merry Very; how somebody wrote a fan-tas-tic story, the last word, which begins one morning when two agents arrest, as it were, citizen ABCK, yes, Mr. K., in metaphysical and jokey Prague, *The Trial*, yes, yes, the famous, fan-tas-tic tale; and how the plane carrying diplomat Homar Hamar or Olde Eld Elsen was brought down in that moussaka Middle mystical East; and what the Pope said when it was suggested to him that he take a stand against Hitler; and what is being said about and how does it happen that and what is brewing in and what will it be like if where when—yes, that's it!

Late in the evening, at the house of his bookkeeper friend or the gambling lawyer or the drunken music teacher Schnapps or Madam Madama, listening to records, leafing through picture albums alma-nacs astrologies. The pedagogic circus number, played in class dur-ing daylight hours, diversified and contradicted itself and gathered energy through the acrobatics of afternoons stretching far into the night, until the break of another day.

Very occasionally he went out with some developing little broad. A bald, talkative page maintaining a state of alertness, pleased with the pussy cat's smile, buoyed by the breeze of long pleated skirts. For a whole season, however, he devoted himself to the major's statuary wife! He also made friends with the mustachioed artilleryman, and they would go out in a threesome as if to make official the scandalous liaison that the locals were following with envy and indignation.

In that provincial past did Anatol Dominic Vancea Voinov called Tolea figure as a kind of symbolic fixture, along with the clock on the town hall and the various picturesque characters from the town's everyday mythology? Did his removal from teaching raise or lower the bohemian's stature? Certainly, questions suddenly began to pile up. Playful old Tolea has gone a bit too far this time! His sensational removal from the didactic corps ought to have reminded those who knew him not only of what had, perhaps, been codified in many of his bizarre acts of public impudence, but also of what stood in contradiction to those acts. His attachment to his mother, for example, went so far as to seem implausible. He had cared for her like a martyr, never once complaining or even saying a word about it. Nor was he in the habit of mentioning the bizarre trades he practiced in order to spare his mother the humiliations of a harsh widowhood of poverty and depression.

A good-looking boy, always quick to reply, that was Tolea Voinov from the start! Only good to crunch between the fangs of his ravenous female colleagues at work. First at the library, where he was beset with provocative notes from female readers. Then at a record shop, next to the ones selling buttons and perfume and ladies' underwear. Then settled for a while in the photo studio of Primadonna, a former soloist, who didn't give him up and from whose sanctuary he took off with some savings, so people say, straight for academia . . . And there at the university, what a surprise! His relations with the attacking sex, for five whole years of study, became timid, evasive, apathetic. The sarcasm of his unpleasantries actually expressed a weary indifference. Then also, it seems, began the suspicions and gossip about his odd way of behaving. He avoided any intimacy, any closeness.

An incipient incompatibility, perhaps, of which he himself was not yet aware? Perhaps he did not yet know enough about himself, or that he ought to be careful with what he would discover.

How bountiful the pubescent public must have seemed to the young student and then teacher Vancea! A real compensation, a rebirth! What a tumult of weaknesses and danger and expectation, in that gray area between ages and between sexes! Between sexes, indeed, since all those boys wavering on the threshold between ages still had a certain effeminacy, a turbid potentiality, but at the same time they succeeded in curing you of the dull repugnance to which you had grown used, too early on, from women's rooms and voices and clothes and bodies. Was it their delicate obtuseness, their voracity appeased in swooning lyrical strategies and then exploding in that alloy of pagan sensuality and domestic piety? Did they all seem to herald the tedium of the property contract, the marriage contract? What prolonged relaxation, on the other hand, in the refuge of adolescence! Still capable of thrilling, taking fright, surrendering . . .

However frivolous receptionist Vancea's rambling talk may seem —a kind of trivialization of Teacher Vancea's rambling—it is enough to follow the proliferation of substitutes all around, in a world of substitutes, to realize that at least Tolea is parodying himself and not other people. Now, after he has been found out and punished and placed under watchful scrutiny, it would no longer be right to speak of frivolity; although even that term, in a world of dull, oppressive seriousness, is gaining a certain new validity. A form of liberty— however deviant—minor, of course, but still undefeated. An irritant at least. At least that! But what if this smart little fragment has simply been manipulated by the Exemplary Association? What if he has fallen into the trap it held out for him? For nothing is left to chance in our chaotic underworld.

A summer evening. Ştefan Olaru meets a former classmate. An evening that seemed to be summer, in front of a kiosk that appeared to be real, which incredibly had the words FRESH PIES written on it but was, of course, selling only substitutes. Odd-looking sandwiches: two slices of rubber calling themselves bread, which had been grilled in hell's fires and had floating between them, like a thin red cat's tongue, a shiny slippery leaf of substitute. Your old classmate from school Ştefan Olaru is nowadays replaced by a tall, severe, timeless gentleman. He immediately approaches and, in his relaxed way, overwhelms you with his clear-cut judgments. From time to time he rubs his huge palms together, as if to bring them to life. From time to time he straightens his thin spectacles, on the perfectly cut mask of the new Ştefan Olaru.

Yes, he admits it, why not why not, why not admit it, he has resigned himself to being content with success. He works hard, as an engineer, and has become indispensable there. He is frugal in what he spends, does not have any illusions, regrets the few he ever had, only gets up to the usual domestic tricks, has no great problems, as the needs of survival dictate. It is a steamy evening. The city is being burned, at the bottom of hell's cauldron. The two former classmates speak about other former classmates. So-and-so is rolling in it, can you imagine? So-and-so's a famous medical man. Yes, that's the one I mean. So-and-so committed suicide, for no real reason. Then on to former teachers at the old school.

"But what about Tolea? Have you heard anything of him?"

It is not clear who asked the question, but the answer comes from the engineer.

"Ah, it's a nasty business. Maybe you heard. If it's really true—"

"If it is—" —in other words, he wasn't just a loony but also—

"Well, that's what things are like. Yes, the Law, the State require people to act decently. The Law is conservative: it protects us from a lot of things. Of course, it also allows some ambiguity. Yes, we do have a sense of decency here! People must be kept on a leash. If you let go, then heaven help them! Look what's happening over on the other side, at our pompous rival, Freedom, Incorporated. Here we've got decency—we should never forget that. There's even enough ambiguity allowed, if you know how to discover it, to win it, to ally yourself with it.

"You see, I met him a year ago. Also like this, by accident in the street. I didn't expect the loony professor to recognize me. But, well, he knew almost everything about me: he said he respected the clear-sighted way in which I'd got on in my career, et cetera, et cetera. We exchanged telephone numbers—you know, symbolically, like people do. And then, would you believe it: he rang me! Not just once. He kept doing it all the time. Incredible! He's a changed man: sad, weary, lonely, sometimes frightened. Exaggeratedly polite, morbidly so. Mister this and Mister that: I was completely taken aback. I've got used to it by now, as if it's a poor abandoned relative who's calling me. He just talks and talks: he's lost all discretion, all pride. He doesn't shrink from complaining, he of all people. You know how puffed up he used to be. But now it's all about how poor he is, and old, and he doesn't have anyone, and he's a failure, even the most stupid wretches have fixed something up for themselves. You won't believe it, but sometimes he talks to me about his mother. Without any scruples. To me, a stranger! He curses, cries, jokes, moans and groans, confesses all sorts of things, repents like a little kid. Can you imagine a confessional tone like that in arrogant old Tolea?"

Yes, the confessional question came from the elusive engineer, the arrogant fibber. Traces, fables, concoctions. The confused outline of the masquerade.

Tolea, as a substitute? That is precisely what it turned out to be, at every step. The landmark for a certain place, its inside-out emblem, when truth and fakery switch around and assist each other, both heads and tails, faces and masks with their clownish reverse side, a laughing wound.

Look, the madman's ghost has appeared just one step away, back after so many years in the little town of his adolescence.

The train was late; the heavy reddish contours of the old granite station could only just be made out in the languor of twilight. Night was rapidly falling, as in the past, over the silent hills. The ghost put his suitcase down in the cinder yard and raised his eyes: yes, he had reached his destination. He recognized the brick façade, the metal pillars, the dirty glass roof.

Now he reached the bus stop. Fur hats, shopping bags, kerchiefs, bundles. Waiting, waiting, multiplying all the time, they huddled together around the closed kiosk where cigarettes and biscuits were sometimes sold.

After nearly an hour of waiting, the old girl finally appeared with glowing headlights. She was snorting, staggering, rattling her screws; the doors flapped about, and the wheels sniffed in their worn-out covers.

The pensioner could hardly pull along such a mass of people. She moved with difficulty down winding, slushy streets and stopped at the level crossing. The Old Lady passed the bridge and began to climb, exhausted, the poplar-lined highway. Here, at the bend just inside town, he always felt he was back home.

In his early student years and at every homecoming after that, the senile, dismembered vehicle, reeling between stately poplars, eventually reached that point in the bend where the gradient suddenly increased, signaling the town, the rediscovery. Always the same place and always different ages and the same age. Immediately after the bend there was for many years a halfway stop. The bus would brake, gasping, in front of a pretty shelter with panels of green glass. He could see two seats and heaps of rags, paper, and wire. A few passengers got off, others got on; it remained as crowded as ever and the old crock could not start again. Suddenly the irritation of a passenger clinging to the steps: "What are you doing, you fool, can't you see I'm getting on?" The fool was a stocky man, with a round pale face, in a short coat made of rough gray material. Opening his eyes wide in astonishment, he did not answer but moved to one side by the door to make room for the growler. The bodies pressed harder against each other, so that the brawler could climb aboard. "Stay like that, you idiots, don't move." The quarrel was about to start, as usual—curses and fists. But no, nothing happened: they were all too tired. But the vicious creature did not give up: he went on with his grumbling. Aggressive, arrogant, he could do with a slap or two in the face. A foot on the steps, an open overcoat, a huge suitcase in each hand, spectacular, thick, genuine-leather suitcases with dozens of colored labels, as if the tourist was coming from Monte Carlo. It was probably that which intimidated everybody into remaining silent, so they did not answer the insults. His smart coat, made of soft camel's-hair material, the color of camels. Around the dromedary's neck was fluttering a large Dior scarf, in red green and sandy check. The upstart kept spitting out abuse—at the driver, at fellow passengers, at the dirt, the smelliness and squalor, and on and on without end.

And then the phantom raised the bald head and clean-shaven face of a Roman consul. He didn't see anyone: he had no time for trifles. Sweating and furious, he had no time for trifles.

Why has he shown up just here? Where do the showy cases and jet-set clothes come from? Jerky rattletrap, rattle rattle trap trap, rattling along narrow muddy winding streets. The populace is asleep, defeated, deaf-mute. Only Her Ladyship is whistling and shouting and turning somersaults. Between his suitcases full of conjuring tricks, hanging from the trapeze bar, whirling his Parisian scarf, setting the air alight with his grumpiness and his juggling. He shakes his hands and head about: the camel's mantle flutters in the arena; the fakir does not have enough space and air and applause. He towers over the planet—he's alone as always. Ever alone, alone in the world.

COMRADE OREST,

You are right: Ortansa Teodosiu can be approached. Lively, prying, good at wangling things, she gets into every little corner, as you say. I would suggest the code name Masterkey. The fact that she lives here in the block is a big advantage. We are on friendly terms with each other, not like between manager and tenant. It would have been harder with her husband, an arrogant little upstart really full of himself. They both make illegal profits, of course, but Masterkey hasn't lost a certain modesty and decency from her original condition in society. She's clever, charitable, and crafty, I know. She's got brains and a heart, everything in fact, and she likes having them. You can see it from the way she talks about the doctor. She knows his qualities, but also his little dodges. She's attached to him in a way, but she's well aware of his darker side, I know. Ortansa represents our national characteristics: that is, the close, inseparable collaboration of good and evil, of what people call good and evil. It's an extraordinary, highly respected quality of our place in the world, our precious treasure.

Masterkey recognizes that everyone must pay their fair share, in one way or another, so as to be sure of a bed, a bite to eat, and a bit of nookie. Whoever breathes the air here has paid, or will pay, their share, as you said. Masterkey also understands that, as you said, medical files are as important as the File itself. She laughed when she accepted that. Right from the first time we met, she promised to get some imported medicine for my Uncle Mihai. It's a good sign, I know. Next Wednesday we're seeing each other again for a coffee.

THE PROFESSOR FELT THE burden of doubt, as so many times before. Moments of discouragement and loneliness when nothing made sense, and his weird occupation still less than anything else. Is the slave defined by his fear of death, the master by his will to take risks? Did fear or risk define his stubborn solitary resistance? Why can't we all go to prison simultaneously? Why do I myself avoid prison? Why don't I shout out loud my disgust?

The shades that visited him at night, and even the people he sometimes heard during the day, repeated the same petty phrases. "Mind your own business, stranger, stop interfering. You're not going to change things, otherwise they'd have changed themselves. Get lost with those annoying questions of yours. What's happening is nothing or anything, and it is not permitted to predict the future."

He got up from the rack. To go out into the street, into the spring, where the humbled crowd was still surviving. To see what effect unshackled force has on a restricted medium. He took the lift, tram, trolley. That is, he went down into the street, into paradise. With a single thought: that he would go to the theater. He looked at the dirty street, the weary faces, the listless agitation. He stopped at a kiosk and moved antlike to the end of the line for a tasteless drink and a stale sandwich. Slices substituting for bread, with a red film in the middle substituting for salami. The substitute pedestrians moved forward awkwardly and in silence, salivating as they waited for the trophy.

When the time came to stretch out his hand, someone pulled his elbow back.

"What are you doing? Eating that garbage?"

He turned around apprehensively. The stern voice belonged to a stern gentleman. Should he recognize him, or should he not?

"Were you on your way somewhere? And why are you frowning like that?"

"Well, I'm going to the theater. On the off chance. Maybe I'll find a ticket."

"Bravo! And why the frown? Which theater?"

"The National. Where else?"

"What's the play?"

"I don't know. I haven't got a ticket. Maybe I'll strike it lucky."

"What's this, old man? Going to the theater like you go to the beach? Without knowing what play, what director, or anything else about it?"

"Well, come on now! The National. That means a national play. Like at the Comédie Française, where—"

"Okay, okay, but it's no reason to be frowning like that. I won't keep you. Anyway, you've still got some time: we can walk a bit of the way together. After all, we don't see each other all that often: the thirty years' peace—ha, ha—yes, that's how long it's been. Our thirty years' war. You're talking about a lifetime!"

A pleasant surprise, Fănică. Clear-cut judgments, icy objectivity. A nervous type, though. From time to time he rubbed his large dry palms together, and he kept adjusting his spectacles. He talked about his family. His wife is not one of those who stuff their pockets and bags with baksheesh, like so many people in restaurants, law courts, and everywhere. When it comes to his son, the conversation is broken: young people are too tough these days. As for Engineer Olaru, he works an enormous amount: he's become pretty well irreplaceable. They stop at the corner of the street leading to the theater. Fănică bows briefly to a woman passing by. The professor had been staring at her already, before she came closer.

"Who's the lady?"

"Oh, someone. It's not important."

Fănică is about to resume his family history, but Tolea is not paying attention. The woman in jeans has just turned the corner and disappeared.

"Who was she?"

"Just a . . . Emilia. It's not important. Emilia, her name's Emilia Ianuli, I think."

Fănică seems ready to say more, but his interlocutor is hurrying off in the direction of the theater, really speeding up to catch the comet.

But it's no use: the magnificent woman has vanished.

The crowded pavement in front of the theater. The theatergoer makes for the box office. A doll with curly hair is chatting to a doll whose hair is tied in a loop. The theatergoer presses his head against the glass. The doll couldn't care less. The theatergoer coughs provocatively.

"What do you want?"

By the time he replies, the toy has turned her head back, as if on a spring, to the one beside her. I want you to tell me who Fănică Olaru really is, the theatergoer was on the point of stammering out. I didn't have time to confront him with his own version of things, to find out who the comrade is replacing. I was hurrying to catch up with the fairy-tale lady. I hurried off, but the opportunity was lost, a lost opportunity, mumbled the stranger, overcome.

"Did you say something?"

"Not yet. I haven't started. I'd like a ticket."

"What for?"

"Well, a lost opportunity—what else. For that."

"What opportunity? Which *that*?"

"Well, this evening's performance."

"This evening we have *A Lost Letter*."

"Exactly. *The Letter*. Yes, for this evening."

"We're sold out for this evening."

She turned back to the clockwork doll on her left and continued telling her about the little boots the Libyan living with Mariana had brought for her, which she had then sold to Kati. But they were too tight, so they found their way via a student cousin to—

"What do you mean you're sold out? It's the national play, the hallmark of the national theater! It's on every season, all the time."

"It's not on every season, I can tell you! Sometimes it's not on at all. It's not authorized, if you want to know. In fact, the rumor is that the season's ending early, precisely because of this play, so that it's not shown."

"So now we're following every little rumor, are we? The play's lasted a hundred years and it'll be with us as long as this country is, this sad jolly little country of ours. Anyone who bans this play bans the country, miss. We can't believe every little rumor, follow all these — How could it be the last one, how could it be a lost opportunity. No way! The play, I mean. It's a classic. It is a classic, after all, miss."

"That's just it! Because it's a classic, sir! The crowds flocking to see it, sir. And stop holding me up: I've got things to do. I told you: we haven't got any tickets. I'm sorry, there's nothing I can do. You're just unlucky."

The theatergoer still did not move from the window. The cashier ignored him, although she seemed ready to cut him short if he asked anything else. But the customer no longer felt like asking questions, even though he would not move away. "Unlucky, huh! A lost opportunity—unlucky! That's the national word: unlucky. Huh! We're always unlucky—no more than that. It's our character that's the problem, madam! Nothing to do with being unlucky, monkey-face."

Or better not: he didn't have the energy for a rumpus. After all, the evening had been generous enough. Comrade Fănică had saved him from indigestion, then offered him an edible version of his life story. Then Fănică had greeted the magnificent, planetary passerby. Yes, it had been a hospitable evening, in the Lord's garden of wonders.

So the former professor kept up his incursions. Whenever he felt tired and depressed, ready to drop the whole project, he went down into the hubbub of the street. Was it the immediacy, the availabilities, the fantasy of the real world? The blind alley of reality! Fermented energy, twisted and poisoned, which did not succeed in going public, in exploding—stifled before it reached the kinetic threshold. Was that also what Marcu Vancea had once believed? That nothing would happen, however much the dangers seemed to increase, however much the poverty and hatred and fears intensified—the obese, shameless, insatiable lie towering supremely over everything? Starving people and spies and guards, the gray of apathy without hope? Precisely in this somnolence of despair anything can happen to anyone, Irina said sometime or other. No one escapes the slow poison and no one escapes the blows of fate raining down on those you don't expect them to.

He saw again the street's long slim feline shape, and heard around him the wild shouts of the crowd: Whore! Mega-whore! The brief flame of the snake, lasting but a moment, in the toxins of the street.

Suddenly he felt capable of meeting the apparition again, of speaking to Mrs. Ianuli, if that really was her name. By chance he had seen her once in a bookshop. Spectacular, in green silk trousers, as at a fashion parade. Hair tied in a ponytail at the back. She was leafing through a book, next to him, in fact. He looked without seeing her. He felt her close by. A magnetic emission, impossible to avoid. He left quickly, moving away in panic. Then a century had passed. Again twilight, again languor. He opened the window, went down into the street. Hypnotic spring, giddiness, desire, indecision. He went into a café and sat down next to an aging man with a fine white beard and mustache, code name Marcel. He ordered a coffee, although he knew it wouldn't be coffee that he received.

The revolving door turned merrily. Two phosphorescent women came in laughing, as in a normal world. He took out a handkerchief and wiped his brow. Unable to restrain himself, he turned around to the table behind him. The woman in red smiled at him. His hands were trembling: the barley substitute called coffee was giving off its vapors in the cup, which was trembling in his trembling hand.

"It's painful, sir. Don't keep turning around like that. Stop looking at her."

"It's as if I knew her. But I can't hear her voice: I'd like to hear her voice. Maybe I'd recognize it."

The man next to him gave a childish sort of laugh. He passed his rough hand through his white hair, raised a glass with the dishwater called lemonade, and screwed up his nose as he sipped it.

"You know her only too well. The whole country does."

"What do you mean, the whole country?"

"Quite simple. She once said good night to us all. All of us."

"Good night? I don't understand."

"The fairy who says, Sleep tight. She's a TV announcer, for God's sake!"

"It's not true. I've never seen her on television. I know I never switch it on these days, what with all those endless speeches. But I don't remember. No, I don't think I've seen her."

"Well, she was on TV for a short time. But that was many years ago. I knew her when she worked at the radio station. Won't you stop turning around like that! The ladies are making fun of us. You're acting like a kid! Sit still. Look, I'll give you all the information, but you must behave properly. This is a select café, and this evening it's empty as well. We're making a laughingstock of ourselves."

"Okay, Comrade Gafton, I promise, I promise. I've glued my neck in place. I'm listening, go ahead."

"She's a delightful creature, there's no doubt about that. Generous, cheerful. Full of fun. Simple and sincere. Delicate, I would say. I don't see why you're smiling, I really don't."

"Too many epithets, my friend. An exaggeration, Mr. Gafton, that's why I'm smiling. With so many qualities, she isn't fun anymore. Everyone loses interest."

"Oh no, they don't. Don't you worry about that side of things. The interest is still there, I assure you."

"So why was such a joy kidnapped from our small screen?"

"As if you didn't know! The qualities I told you about are not absolutely necessary."

"But they don't do any harm either."

"Maybe they do, when it's a question of repeating all that non-sense on TV. And anyway, she wasn't the only propaganda beauty. If we've got so many beautiful women, why not share them around. You only have to look in the street, even in the misery of today."

"I'd sooner you told me how she got into television. Or radio—which is where you met her. And how she left, and why. After all, not just anyone is allowed in anywhere. You have to be proposed and accepted."

Mr. Gafton smiled and signaled the waiter to bring another glass of the hogwash called lemonade. But the waiter went to the ladies' table instead, to make up the bill.

Their departure did indeed become visible behind. The round room with mirrors seemed to grow abruptly smaller. A dull evening all of a sudden, like any other.

"Yes, it's simpler to answer simple questions," the polite gentle-man resumed, straightening the knot of his tie and drawing his chair closer. "Emilia got into radio because of her husband, probably benefiting from his prestige or his contacts. But her own qualities soon made themselves felt."

"Let's move on to when her qualities became unnecessary."

"I don't know: I wasn't working at the radio station by then. I know she went to the small screen for a while. A promotion. It was a pleasure to watch her, to hear her, even when the little she-devil read from the jabberer's speeches. The reasons why she's no longer there? I only heard later and at fourth hand, so I'm not sure. But it seems a moral pretext was involved. As you know, that's often been used in recent years. And it works."

"Do you mind if we stay on this?" ventured the curious questioner.

"I don't mind, my boy. You're probably waiting to hear from the old duffer's mouth what the public prosecutor had to say. You probably think the whole generation of mistakes, as you put it, was made up of bastards. Dreamers who were easy to manipulate—incurable schizoids. Well, listen. Emilia was a real stroke of luck for Comrade Ianuli, believe me. Despite a lot of—"

"I understand, I understand. You're a poet, Mr. Gafton."

"Is it true that paradise is flat, my boy? The image of the divinity is flat! It was only the devil who introduced a third dimension! A man like Ianuli represents something profound, just, and noble. Yes, my boy. But Emilia was precisely the missing volute, a boon if ever there was one."

Mr. Gafton was on his feet. In a white suit, with perfectly trimmed white hair and mustache, he was substituting for a distinguished epicurean, calm and skeptical in his wisdom. Just fancy! Marcel the substitute. Incredible! "Let's be going. It's late. Madam Veturia can't bear me leaving her alone for so long."

They got in each other's way in the revolving door. Gafton took a step back and put his big pale hand on the lost man's shoulder.

"Emilia is a gift of nature, my boy. A nature which rejects artifice. The word you hear all around you is: if. If it was possible, I'd do it. If I'd spoken up, if I'd dared. When we escape from this original quarantine, everyone will claim to have been a victim and denounce everyone else, just like now. And they'll fight for the new padded seats, the new gold braid. And they'll lie and cheat, my boy, just like now! They'll lie in freedom, as in today's captivity. Whereas Emilia dared to—"

"Just a moment," cried the novice. "Did you say captivity? You, Comrade Gafton? Captivity? Do you dare say things like that? Let me see your eyebrow! Quick, quick, let me see your scar," and he fell upon Gafton and dragged him to the first lamppost. It gave no light, of course. It was evening and the streets lay in darkness. Only the tramping of guards could be heard. The stench of uncleared garbage rose over the city, in the soft and loathsome darkness.

"Joy deserves all the honors, Professor! When I was young and was fighting for paradise, they locked me up in a real prison. In captivity I despised those who looked too much at a flower, or at the starry sky or freshly fallen snow. That all seemed a subterfuge to me, a frivolity. But now I'm getting close to the day of reckoning."

He stopped, ashamed of the rhetorical excess. Then they walked together, on their common way home, through Cişmigiu Park, through the Park of Liberty, Pache Park, as far as their building with its lighted windows. In that long detour they did not speak about anything but the performance at the National, the clumsy improvisation, and the half-witted seriousness thrust upon Caragiale's famous comedy. Nor did they refer anymore to the beautiful woman in the café. Tolea had forgotten her, for a while.

And at some point he remembered her. One evening when spring looked like autumn and when the fire serpent—the hallucination, the desire without name or object—was again writhing in the shadows of the window. Besides, he also saw her among the flurried pedestrians, in the rout and the tide of daytime aphrodisiacs. She was coming down the steps from the university. White fluffy cape. Huge, slender, with black, heavy, shiny hair the star of stars of the silent film. Incredibly she decided to wait at the trolleybus stop! The people there gawked at the rare apparition, forgetting all about the vehicle.

Receptionist Vancea followed the sequence from a distance. The wind coiled in hot blasts, the dampness grew thicker and thicker: everything was floating in a cold mist that soaked bones and thoughts. A short stocky man with a shopping bag overflowing in each hand moved closer to the star. They exchanged some words, like two neighbors, or like the mistress of the house with a servant from her parents' estate. The swarthy man kept trying to free one arm so as to bow and kiss the princess's hand. Suddenly she drew herself up over the whole of the surrounding gallery, higher and higher on her high-heeled boots. From her cape rose a long golden shaft, a long thin sleeve in gilded wool, like the metal embroidery worn at feasts in the Middle Ages. She waved excitedly at an approaching taxi. She gave a shudder of joy, cheered by the good fortune that was braking perfectly, right at the red beak of her little boot. Only then did she notice the agitation of the poor wretch who kept moving his bags and bowing to her, a changed man. She smiled, tapped him gently on the shoulder to calm him, and stroked his damp round head. She carefully inserted her long body into the chassis, just a last wee bit of cape, then the door went bang and the engine revved up. Receptionist Anatol Dominic Vancea made bold to approach the witness of the miracle.

"What are you doing here, Mr. Teodosiu? You and trolleybuses? What disaster could have—"

"It's no joke, I can tell you. If even someone like me can't get hold of some gas, then it's gone beyond a joke. We had an arrangement, clear and stable. A driver at the hospital where Ortansa, my wife, works. I paid and he kept me supplied: perfectly straightforward. But now he's got a nerve, I'm telling you, he wants goods instead. Goods, do you hear! He's lost interest in money and wants the value in goods! Cheese, coffee, meat: that's what he wants. Because he's simply got to turn the money into cheese or wine, you know what it's like. Well, it was too much for me. Such nerve! Am I supposed to line up for days on end, or find contacts with butter or paper for wiping your ass or cotton for women, because Mr. Costică simply doesn't have the time?! That was the last straw! So here I am, standing in the sleet. Waiting for the camel on wheels to arrive."

"There's something to be said for that, though, Mr. Gică. You get to meet people, you see more of the world."

"It's no joking matter, believe you me. What troubled times! When even someone like me can't get what's necessary."

"But you also have pleasant moments. That goddaughter of yours, for example, looked really superb. Or was it your god-mother?"

"What goddaughter? What are you talking about?"

"Well, the lady. You looked pretty glad to see her, like a godfather with his goddaughter. Or maybe she was the director's wife."

"Who? Mrs. Emilia—Mila? She's in a different category, sir! Mrs. Mila is the wonder of the earth. A real princess, I'm telling you. Not like those who just smell of the stable if you take away their ointments and rags. The lady is a real jewel. And she's the Lord's bread. It never happens that she'll refuse if you ask her for something. She'll help anyone. Because Mrs. Mila has her contacts, all right. There's no comparison."

"So you're not related?"

"Leave off! I told you, cut the wisecracks. I know her from the time she worked in that tourism business, with groups of foreigners."

"Ah, so it's from work."

"Mrs. Mila got on only with me, worked only with me. The rest don't even know her. None of them. Not even Corkscrew, not even you. I was the only one she trusted, because I know how to hold my tongue. You know what it's like, one man or another used to come."

"What do you mean: one or another?"

"Aha, that's a professional secret. First-class woman, hard currency. Need I say more!"

"Really? Just like that?"

"No, it's not what people think. Mrs. Mila wouldn't go with a man just like that, just to get things from the dollar shop, whether she fancies him or not. But for her to fancy one, that's it. She did it only occasionally, I can tell you, and in great secrecy. But she has a heart of gold, as I was saying. A real soul, a countess! She's not stingy when you ask her for something: medicine, some clothing, a toy for your kid, anything. Because she gets around, wow, she's always off somewhere."

"How does she get around, as you put it? Where does she go off to?"

"To the big wide world, that's where. The wide world that's not for dumbos. Do you think everyone stays cooped up here, that no one gets out? Well, there are exceptions, I can tell you! There are also special interests. The world has shrunk only for some. Lots of things aren't for the likes of us, you know. The earth goes round, it doesn't stand still, even if we don't see it moving."

But the trolley cut short the lecture in philosophy. Suddenly prevented from offering other professional secrets, colleague Teodosiu Gică, known as Poxy, a.k.a. the Boss, made admirable use of his elbows and bags to force a way through the hysterical mass of people, to be first in the ark of salvation. Receptionist Anatol Dominic Vancea Voinov found himself alone once more, guilty at how depressed he felt and at how distrustful he was in the presence of his daytime and nighttime interlocutors.

But the woman reappeared in his nocturnal reveries, laughing, crying, neighing, rehabilitating the therapy of the heart's desire, parodying pleasure as the grimace of liberty. And did Sleepwalker Tolea let himself be seduced!

Cool, lucid night. The absent dead, like the living; situated in eternity, from where everything could be seen perfectly, as if nothing could be seen. The woman reappeared, scrupulously, invented herself anew, at once immediate and fictitious. Sometimes he even saw her in the illegible daytime sky, the torrid blindness of the crowd. Attracted, intimidated. At once a longing for abandon and an immense fear. Death—yes, that was probably what she was, the beautiful and insatiable one. Tender, ravenous, hospitable, enveloping you in desire and faintness and panic: Death. The mask of indifference and joy, the voracious glitter, the frenzy, the extreme intensity.

Nor was she an abstraction. She had a name, an address, a telephone: she could be reached. But the sleepwalker did not have the courage. He just tried to forget the vortex of imponderables, and then to escape again into the confused murmur of the street. Despotic spring had made the prisoners hysterical. The heart of the ants had grown enormous, roaring like a compressor. Giddy intoxication, through stinking parks full of garbage and policemen, in the dark of lifeless boulevards, in the crowd standing in front of empty stores or trolley stops overcrowded with passengers, in the intense heat, and in the capricious rains of the underground. He came back exhausted from these sleepwalking adventures, but would go out again to rediscover the excess tiredness that cured him of despair. Back in the street, he found the tumult again. Chimerical series, accelerated emissions of magnesium, a pink smoky fog perforated by the tingling of aerials.

It was a strange twilight: spring was winter and he was in front of the Atheneum. The woman was on the other side of the road, coming from the Palace. He had seen her in the distance as she approached. She was wearing high boots, far above the knee, which gripped like funnels her brown velvet trousers. Her body seemed frail inside her large red fox-fur jacket. She crossed the street and walked up the drive. Her face had a gleaming pallor, eyes shining provocatively beneath a perfect forehead and hair carefully brushed around her temples. She moved among the groups of music lovers waiting to go into the concert. She responded to greetings with a youthful wave of her arm and hurried off toward the entrance. There she stopped for a few moments in front of a man who seemed to have called out to her. A merry conversation: her lively, luminous, unforgettable laughter rang out. The man could not be seen. Facing away, much shorter than the woman, he stood on tiptoe to kiss her hand as they parted. And as he turned after her, his face became visible—the spitting image of Pushkin! Long side-whiskers, thin beard. "Oho, it's you, Doctor! I thought you liked your music at home, not in public."

"Today's the exception. A special case."

"And the lady? Is she a patient?"

"No, no. No. I've known her a long time. The wife of a colleague."

"What kind of a colleague is that? Combatants call each other comrade, not colleague. And I didn't even know you were an ex-combatant."

"I'm not. The lady was once married to the famous head of a clinic. I spent some time working under him: he was my professor."

"She still looks young, the professor's ex-wife. Now she's married to an ex-combatant."

"Yes, yes. There was a scandalous age difference. She was younger than his daughter from another marriage. If the old man's still alive, he must certainly be missing her. And if he's reached heaven, then I'm sure he's still missing her. He'll be bored without her. She was a wonder, a breath of life. A ray of sunshine."

"Who? The Great Whore from the Bible? You know that's what they call her."

Dr. Marga refused to smile. The face shaded by its romantic beard remained unmoved.

"What nonsense! You just chatter away. The sources of joy are few and far between in this life, my friend. They must be cherished, you know. True happiness is an intangible force; and the lady warms the cockles of your heart. Don't listen to the mob—it's just stupid gossip you'll hear from them."

"But yes, I do listen. Do you know Toma? Manager Toma A. Toma?"

"Which Toma? The saint, or the other one, the doubter?"

"I'm not joking, Doctor. Toma, the exemplary deaf-mute! Who sees and hears and finds out everything, but only tells when and whom he's supposed to. A very precise man, with a lot of experience and practical sense. He doesn't give two monkeys about our fellow citizens; he doesn't think substitutes are dangerous. But he keeps an eye on anyone who—or who might—or who—"

"Come on, quit the fooling. Let's go into the concert."

"Toma has no faith at all in our fellow creatures. He doesn't think their improvisations are dangerous. Toma the professional could be mistaken, though. After all, he's an expert in the real world. And well, this Lady of Delights is a substitute, too. That's all she is, you know, Doctor."

"She's no substitute! I saw her not long ago: she came to see me at the hospital and—"

"So she's a patient, after all."

"No way. She's a cure, not an illness."

"Death, Doctor, that's what she is! The Great Whore of the Apocalypse. The unclouded happiness, contented indifference, and superb vitality of death."

"That's enough of the metaphors, kid. She came to the hospital about a patient."

"Ah, it must be her exemplary new husband, the ex-combatant. A gala patient. They've screwed him up good and proper, Doctor. His exemplary comrades have put death next to him in bed to finish him off. As I said, it's only in exceptions like him that Toma sees any danger. The Exemplary Association knows how to manipulate the happiness and delights and temptations that will wipe him out. It's possible that Toma thinks even I am dangerous, like the dreamer caught under the skirts of the Great Whore."

"Cut the crap, for God's sake. I don't know the lady's husband, and I'm not interested in him. I've heard something about the Ianuli legend, but I don't find it interesting. I deal with reality, you know. The most burning reality. That's my profession."

"Well, our neighbor Toma also deals with reality. He's an expert in reality, as I was saying."

"You're raving away, kid, and I'm missing the concert. The fact is, the lady came to visit a young student, a distinguished student. A splendid boy. And she asked about him with an infinite, angelic tenderness."

Becoming irritated, Dr. Anton Marga undid the collar of his starched shirt. He was wearing a light summer suit, the color of forget-me-nots. A light summer suit, although the person talking to him thought it was a sluggish winter evening. In his right hand the doctor was holding a short rubber stick, the case of an umbrella. Now and then, using a fine white handkerchief, he wiped his face, which had been perspiring from the intense spring heat, and also his spectacles, forehead, and beard. "I had a chat with the student when he returned. He confirmed the extraordinary devotion and happiness that Mila represents for him. It must have been love—or sex, as they say nowadays—I don't care. A sentimental education, you know what I mean. And not only of the body, you can be sure. A therapy in which the concentration is so intense it brackets evil out."

"Well, why don't you hire her, Doctor? You can even make a scientific report: the priceless idea will bring you fame and immortality. Bring her on board at the hospital! Madam Death, with her superbly gleaming mask, her charitable soul and therapeutic body. The vestal providing an initiation in futility. Land! Land! cry the mariners. Women! The shore woman who gets us used to land again. The first and last truth. Earth we were, to the earth's belly we return."

"That's right, kid. Lilith, Adam's first woman, was only earth, like him. She's known for a single action. She seduced two angels, found out the code word from them, opened the gates of heaven, and flew off. She deserted Adam. Only afterward was there Eve, his wife. The earth woman cannot be held fast by anything or anyone; she takes flight. Paradoxically she takes flight and arrives back in heaven."

"How nice! Is the worldly old rationalist Marga really a believer? We all wear masks, we're all substitutes. Are you a believer, Doctor? "No, I'm just mad about reading. It gets me closer to heaven, to my patients. You see, I could have listened to this evening's music at home, as you said. But I wanted to be in a hall, among people. It's not church, and the Bach organist isn't a priest. But still—"

"I'm sorry. I didn't think you were in a lyrical mood. I'd have kept clear of the ribaldry."

"Ribaldry? My God is an atheist and he likes provocations, alternatives, improvisations, as you put it. And jokes, of course. He's like us. He did make us in his likeness, didn't he? So I'm on the side of that woman you find so intriguing."

"Death! Lies, jokes, accommodations. Indifference, the improvisations of survival. In other words, Death, Death."

"Mmm, I'm with the nameless ones who survive. Fickle and skeptical jesters are not my enemies."

"But they don't have a right to testify at a trial! That's the point! Your nice guys forfeit their capacity to act as witnesses. That's what's written in the Koran. Jesters like that lose their capacity to bear witness at trials. That's what it says, Doctor, that's what it says in the book."

"Okay, I'll have another look at it. Books aren't perfect, and readers aren't either. If that's what it says, I'll ask for an erratum slip to be inserted. A little humor wouldn't spoil the Holy Koran, believe me. As for truth, it can't do without deception. The two stay married together, have adulterous affairs with each other, and do not part even in divorce. They're always in contact, inseparable. You're too morose, my little professor, really you are. The concert would do you good, believe me. Go into Bach's chapel and learn some peace of mind."

The doctor was really hurrying by now: he ran up the stairs and disappeared under the twilight arches.

Morose. Huh! Mr. Fănică Olaru and tonic Toni Marga proclaiming peace of mind. "Listen to me," Marga had shouted in farewell, turning back from the top step of the Atheneum. "Once they're said, lies take their revenge. They come true. They become reality, and that's the ultimate truth."

Reality is not the ultimate truth, Doctor, murmured the patient, now sitting on one of the benches opposite the Atheneum. The conjuncture called reality can be negated, and waiting is not necessarily a lie, or an illusion, nor is resistance or truth a lie, or— After a long time he tightened the thick collar of his coat. Again he was far away, in winter, a stranger in winter, stuck in a long, implausible winter.

NO ONE ANSWERED. HE had checked the address, the name, the telephone number: everything was correct, but no one answered. It's working but not answering. So let's go there, to the scene itself, to the house. If there's still no one, then just maybe that no one will answer the door.

The week becomes dynamic: Wednesday on duty by the phone, Friday on the spot. Something will happen in the end, even if it is nothing that happens.

He waits at the Rond stop for tram number 23. The tram doesn't come. The passenger waits, the tram comes, completely full; he waits for the next one, also full. The passenger clutches the bar at the doorway into the tram: he feels the shoulders, the sweat, the weariness of his fellow creatures, the real connection. At Mihai Bravul he takes another tram, number 5. Empty car. Mr. Dominic punches his ticket, folding it as the regulations require. A return ticket. But when he gets off, he carelessly throws it away. He crosses the street and catches the bus to the bread factory.

He gets off the bus, walks back about a hundred meters, arrives in front of the Scampolo store. The store is closed, for stock-taking. He turns into the little street to the right, as far as the old gray block of flats. He goes up to the second floor, gropes for the light switch, presses it. Somewhere a filament lights up. It's only one more step to apartment 8.

He presses the button and the bell rings. The sound rushes into the apartment behind the door. Nothing. Once more. He waits: no movement. He rings again. One step back. He presses the light switch, the filament comes on, a dim light, hardly enough to see the stairs, the metal rail covered with green plastic dirty from so many hands and worn away by the years. He feels his way cautiously, walks down the stairs, finds again the little street, the Scampolo store, the bus stop, the bus, the tram stop, the tram, the return from the adventure.

With Friday a failure, there remains the following Wednesday. One hour bent over the dial that forms the roulette wheel of life, which he keeps turning, once, nine times, sixty times. Nothing. The number denies him dialogue.

Reality is a faint, a showing off, crumbs, a dandelion, a faint, that's all. He dials with his right hand, holds an apple in his left. No one answers.

On Friday it is raining, in bucketfuls. Bus, tram, another tram, another bus. The gray pockmarked block. The dark door, the bell, and then back to the reality called Friday, which still exists, still houses him. Wednesday at the receiver's silent mouth, Friday at the rebus scene. Again Wednesday, again Friday, swinging backward and forward in sleep. He no longer has patience; he demands to take the offensive. There's still a century to go until Friday. Impossible to wait any longer: the faint called reality must be conquered, come what may. Anatol Dominic Vancea Voinov shakes the dice differently; he cheats. The slightest departure from the beaten track and, look, Friday appears instead of Thursday. Thursday rebaptized Friday. Today is Friday and tomorrow's the same, Friday, doubling the ace, doubling his bad luck, doubling the uncertainty.

Waiting for the bus had driven him wild. Ever waiting, ever studying his fellow citizens' footwear. He looked up: Gostat. State Stores. Vegetables, chickens, eggs—they ought to be in the Gostat hall, where there's nothing but jars of pickles. But marvels do also appear, with their tails streaming behind. Look, here's one. Some more time passed, some more thoughts passed through the observer's pate as he studied some more pairs of nearby shoes. He looked up at the people across the street, fallen in line before the store. GOSTAT. GOSTAT. Eyes gazing into space, somewhere across the street. He kept staring at the substitute-leather shoes, at the line across the street, at the substitutes jostling each other for—for what? They ended up driving him crazy. Again he looked at the line of people, the door of the GOSTAT store, then the wheelchair. He had seen the cripple's wheelchair, and his mind went spinning with the wheels as he moved it off. Aimlessly, with a clear aim, he no longer saw anything, he saw everything: he crossed the street. No one was there, only Robot Windwhistle, blind, deaf, perfect, a screw loose, faultless mechanism, great speed, perfect working order, the fiery meteor was coming. Just a step away from the line he turned sharply and headed for the back. No one paid him any attention. The wheelchair had already started. Excuse me, would you mind, could you let me through. People made room. The gentleman was turning the wheels with great care: wheee whooo . . . something somehow . . . Hardly had the cripple's whimpering become audible when the vehicle was already inside the hall, steered with great dignity by the elegant gentleman in white. Shiny red scarf around his neck, bald head, cosmopolitan self-assurance. The spectators shyly moved aside to make room for the distinguished samaritan and his sick relative. The pair had arrived in front of the counter. Four packages, ordered the intruder. The assistant did not even look at him. The bags had already flown off to the scales—"109 lei" was heard. Four chickens, 109 lei, was the judgment pronounced. The gentleman held out 110 lei, refused the change with a gesture of disgust, gripped the bar of the wheelchair again, and turned it around and around. Wheee, whooo, whined the cripple. They were back at the door. The packages with the headless chickens lay on the sick man's knees. A shudder passed down the customers' side. The voice of the crowd converged in the croak of one pensioner, who was hopping with fury: You shameless rogue, taking advantage of this poor wretch! You good-for-nothing, spitting in the face of the hundreds of people waiting their turn! You little drip! You dirty little swine!

Too late. The wheelchair had left the hall and crossed the pavement, with the glorious packages on the cripple's lap.

Huge eyes, about to start crying. With two fingers the conjurer lifts two packages. He makes a present of two to his friend and then walks off, holding aloft in two fingers the cone-shaped bags in which the headless chickens are swinging. What the hell do I do with the booty now? All I wanted was the adventure, the challenge, the victory. Now I'll have to carry the corpses to the photographer. What else can I do? Maybe the disabled photographer will remember the crime, maybe the ghost will grant me an audience.

He heard the murmur of the crowd behind him, ever fainter. He would have liked to go back and repeat the act of impertinence, to humiliate them even more, to arouse them, to tear them from the torpor of hours spent nicely waiting for their wretched portion of survival, the trophy of deaf-mute submission. I am absent, gentlemen, I would have shouted at them. Among you and yet far away, reinventing the nightmare of long ago in order to forget the one of today. To escape from boredom, gentlemen, to escape the hysteria of spring which humiliates and lashes us and makes us hysterical. I accept the provocation, I accept myself, that's all. That's all I am: I am this day I've called Friday. I'm bored, gentlemen, that's all there is to it. The bags were waltzing, the hunter's kill was waltzing. Burned air, two rustling plastic bags, two model corpses from the freezer of the everyday butcher. We're together, look, all three of us, in the day's great bag, facing the tram lines, ready to throw ourselves down and stop the fair. One moment, one raw, morbid fraction, one enormous, sublime chance to take control again, to bring the parody to a close. We cross the road at the traffic lights: the light blinds us, we cross carefully under the punishment of the pitiless sun, the raging sun of our boredom. Here is the flower shop. Here is the Scampolo store, closed for stock-taking. In front of the window, an old woman is straining to read the objects, the publicity. She hangs wearily, like a chicken in a gray, creased bag. She's withered and bent, carefully wrapped in the standard bag.

We collect the bags, slowly swing the corpse in the pink fermented air of the poisoned day. The danger is lying in wait. The unseen claw is nearby, ready to get you in its clutches, but it has already veered off toward the others. The black wings have passed, we are still alive, more than this is not permitted us, nor do we wish for anything more. We just move ahead unconsciously as if standing still. Here is a cube, a house, a concrete step, a light switch, a filament, a bell; it's Friday, like tomorrow, like a hundred years ago, another century, as if we never existed.

The door shyly opens a little. And behold, it opens wide.

In the frame, a woman. Watery eyes, hair gathered up at the back, dumpy body tilting to the left, small fleshy hands.

"Mrs.—Mrs.—" stammered the stranger.

"I beg your pardon."

"Oh, I'm sorry. I, er . . . The Cuşa family lives here, doesn't it? You are Mrs. Cuşa, am I right?"

"No, you're not. Mrs. Cuşa isn't at home. I'm a friend of Tori. Of Mrs. Cuşa, I mean. I am—"

She uttered her name, but the air immediately scattered it beyond Tolea's grasp.

"Aha. Well, actually I'd like to see Octavian. Tavi Cuşa."

He managed to get a quarter of a step inside. The woman took fright, but she did not have the strength to stop him. Yes, the stranger was already well inside when he met the dark fixed eyes of a dog crouching by the hallstand.

"I'm an old friend of Mr. Octavian Cuşa; of Tavi. I'd very much like to see him. I've been looking everywhere . . ."

The woman had a gentle but cautious look in her eyes. She was dressed in a kind of blue work coat, like that of a laboratory assistant or housemaid or doctor: it could have been anyone's.

Tolea sat down on a little stool he had already brought into the hall from the kitchen.

"You know, madam, just now they were giving out oranges. I didn't need any, in fact. But I saw the long line, with hundreds of wretched-looking men and women, and I thought, Let's get some, too."

He was looking at the two bags with headless chickens that he had put down by the stool.

"Since this is where I've landed, I may as well get some, too. Oranges, as it happens . . ." —and he pointed to the bags with chickens lying by his cream-colored, porous shoes. The woman remained silent. Dilated eyes, gripping the door handle.

"So I joined the line. It must have been some twenty years ago. I had joined the line: it was in Lisbon or Salonica, I don't remember anymore. I was—um, how old?—twenty, thirty, I don't remember. So Siena or Salonica or Seville, I don't remember. I didn't need any, but I joined the line for oranges, just like that. In front of me a lovely young woman was lost in her fiancé's eyes. We were moving forward very slowly. At a certain moment a woman in front of us detached herself from the line. Elegant, with hair neatly done, a fine Oriental profile. Well then, when I was skiing a week ago in Switzerland, I also joined a line to go down the run. I'm not all that keen on fruit, but you know how it is: I follow the lead of others. I'm easily influenced: as soon as I see a line I join in as well. So, as I was saying, a fine elegant lady who's made up her mind to protest. Won't you come with me? she asked the young fiancé, who didn't say a word in reply. The woman was right: something had to be done or we probably wouldn't get anything. The boxes were nearly empty. The young fiancé smiled mockingly. Why did she pick me as the most representing, he whispered nervously to his fiancée. The girl looked up into his big eyes in total admiration. Most representative, she gently corrected him. Total admiration. But she still corrected him, the sweet thing. So there we were, inching forward, just. The line behind us had kept growing, and now the rumpus was beginning."

The woman fearfully leaned on the kitchen door. Holding the handle. Speechless, completely melted away.

"As I said, madam, we were just inching forward. I was a child, that's what I'm like. Maybe I was fifteen, twenty-five, thirty-five, but no more, certainly no more than thirty-five. A fat saleswoman appeared and took a box of oranges for the staff of the shop. A commotion started up. Then a saleswoman appeared from across the street, from the electrical shop over there, and also took a bagful just as a customer was asking for fifteen kilograms to be weighed out for him. Do you hear? Fifteen kilos! That triggered the explosion: the shop manageress appeared and there was one hell of a row. So the inching forward resumed. People were yelling, Don't give anyone more than two kilos in future, so there'll be enough to go around. The saleswomen, all very nice and obliging, calmly got on with their job. Everyone got what they asked for up to six kilos. That was the manageress's decision. There was also a drunk there. Good job it's warm, muttered the drunk. Because you know what it's been like the last few years, madam. We only have to hear the word winter and we shudder with fright. It's as if we were living in caves, madam: hard winter months with no heating, no hot water. A nightmare, as you know. The drunk was right: a good job we were inside there, you know, at the Corfu café. We were inside and it was warm, we didn't feel the winter, the drunk was right. So forward, inch by inch. Lovely, jolly girls weighing at the scales."

The woman was still holding the door handle. Tolea had settled down comfortably on the stool. The black dingo dog had stretched out his neck a long way, so that his head touched the tip of Tolea's yellow shoe.

"Tavi. Easy, boy!"

Tavi withdrew his black snout from the yellow snout, but he remained alert and on guard. Auntie Venera had a pleasant, very pleasant voice. I hadn't even noticed, or else I'd forgotten. Yes, quite simply Tolea had forgotten, had started speaking, he didn't notice. Venera did indeed have a pleasant timbre to her voice. Not fragrant, no, you wouldn't say that. He had baptized her Venera. From the first moment, before hearing the name he could not make out. So it was Venera that came to him, in a sudden flight of fancy.

"May I continue, then, madam. You see, I have the memory of a hippopotamus. So with that holiday trip of mine to Cordoba, or whatever it's called. I always change the place I go to for a rest; I crave novelty, always look for new things to happen. I haven't got the patience to stay put somewhere, as the Association, the A-sso-si-ay-shun, requires of us. Yes, it doesn't even let us move house from one place to another, or even to travel around in other parts."

"Tavi. Quiet, boy."

Tavi withdrew his long red tongue from the yellow top of the shoe. But he remained alert, vigilant. Eyes like red-hot coals. Venera was holding the door handle: she seemed calm and had a pleasant voice.

"So I finally got to the scales. The sweet girl with chestnut hair asked me how much. Four kilograms, I said. She started putting them in my bag. What do I need four kilos for? No idea. But that's what I'm like, easily influenced. Goo-ood. People were muttering behind me; the rumpus had flared up again. As I was saying, madam, the girl had already weighed out my bagful. Goo-ood. But then I got involved, I said something myself. I put my own oar in. Everyone is right. That's what I said: Everyone is right. Those girls aren't to blame if they give out two kilos or six or nine. It doesn't matter, because it will still come to an end. And it's not their fault: it's someone else's, and I know whose. The only one who's not right is the big guy himself, the Great Associate. Everyone else is in the clear. Everyone is right. The only one who isn't is you know who. What did I get involved for? And I didn't even need the oranges. I ask you: what would I have needed them for?"

Tolea again pointed to the two bags with headless chickens. He unknotted the dark-red scarf around his neck. A tired toreador.

Madam Venera, holding the door handle in fear, had become downhearted, bewildered, drained of energy.

"Just look at me, chattering away like this. In fact, dear lady, I came to see my friend Cuşa. Tavi Cuşa, I mean. There's something I need to discuss with him."

The dog started, didn't start. Impossible to say. But the little old woman released her grip on the door handle and wiped her sweaty palms on the hem of her blue work coat.

"I told you, Mr. and Mrs. Cuşa are not at home. I just call around here three times a week, to keep an eye on the house. They left Tavi for me to look after. There's been some trouble with my own apartment and I don't like to stay home. Since spring and all this madness, I've been staying here. I'm hiding here until they come back. During the day at least."

Her voice was calm, warm, fragrant, and Venera ran her plump hand over the shiny neck of watchdog Tavi.

She was now looking in a more relaxed way at the talkative and polite guest: she had no reason to be afraid of him, no, the fear had passed. He seemed a courteous and likable person, even if rather odd with those topsy-turvy and excessively long stories of his.

Likable, however, and Venera eventually opened wide the dining-room door as a token of goodwill.

Being a well-mannered boy, Tolea accepted the invitation, went in, and sat down.

He came back on Tuesday, came back on Thursday. The calendar was turned upside down: Wednesday and Friday disappeared, and Tuesday-Thursday-Saturday came to power. He stayed as long as he could, until Venera had to return home, to the apartment in which recent memories appeared to terrorize her.

He accompanied her to the taxi, where they parted with some difficulty. Venera came, went, and came again by taxi to the Cuşa family home, three times a week. It would have been hard with Tavi on trams and trolleybuses.

The dog Tavi remained fierce and silent. He showed neither aversion nor cordiality in relation to the new visitor.

About the other Tavi they discussed at length.

"You know, my dear lady, the story goes back a long way. I was a schoolboy then. Mr. Cuşa was a friend of my brother's. Also of my sister's, in fact. As far as I remember, Mr. Cuşa was then—how shall I put it?—without any defects. Normal, I mean."

"Yes, yes, I understand," said the velvety voice of Mrs. Venera.

She had just put the tray and coffees on the round dining-room table. Professor Anatol Dominic Vancea Voinov had made an intelligent calculation, from the very first moment. These days you can hardly trust anyone. Even old friends are not likely to be the same as they used to be. If they've survived, it means that something's wrong somewhere, so you can never know who when whether and how much: general distrust. Normality depends on adaptation, therefore also on adaptation to the abnormal. So the inverted criteria actually rule out any clarification. The Hotel Tranzit receptionist had therefore proceeded in the perfect manner. If you can never trust anyone, anyway, then it's best if all the doors are open at the beginning, as among people who have known one another since the world began. On this hospitable table with its steaming coffee, there is also room for our impenetrable soul, for our codified, burlesque life story.

"Lots of terrible things happened then. Our family went through difficult trials. Then my brother left for Argentina. My sister, too, left around the end of the war, and also for distant lands, since she had fallen in love with a missionary full of great promises. I stayed with Mother, which wasn't easy. I heard no more of Mr. Tavi for a long time. But I know he had a shock as well in that period. I heard then that—"

"Yes, yes, I understand" came the encouraging words from Venera, who was arranging some little cakes on the table.

"Now my sister-in-law, the German, has written to me. She also sent me some money. They used to send other things as well, from time to time. Especially at holiday time: clothes, delicacies to eat, various trifles. She says my brother has gone potty. I mean senile.

Or not quite: she doesn't put it like that. Immobile. Maybe concussion. God knows. His mind is drifting into nostalgia. That's what she says."

Mrs. Venera had shuddered, as if with irritation. But she eventually sat down opposite the narrator, to listen to what he was saying.

"Yes, yes, I understand. Help yourself."

Mr. Vancea was sitting relaxed in the armchair. He loosened the scarf at his neck and undid another button on the collar of his black shirt. He had come straight from work and was feeling rather hot.

He sipped at the sweet strong coffee. Another sip. He had lifted the tiny cup from the tiny golden plate. Another long sip, and that was it, no more coffee.

"Shall I pour you another drop, Mr.—?"

"Vancea. Anatol Vancea."

Venera stood up, took the coffeepot from its place on the sideboard, and poured into the little cup.

"Anatol Vancea Voinov. My mother's maiden name was Voinov, and she didn't give it up, precisely because it had become suspect. They were a stubborn couple, clinging to their dignity—or so they thought."

Venera also sipped her coffee. Tolea looked at her with friendly curiosity: it was difficult to refrain from asking whether she was not by any chance the sister of lame Veturia.

"You probably know Mr. Gafton."

Venera did not answer, but took another leisurely sip. "The Gafton family. I'm a lodger with them—sort of. I mean, it's not their apartment, but they took me in. They had a free room and offered it to me when I had to move to Bucharest. I haven't told you yet, madam, but I was a schoolteacher until a few years ago. I taught foreign languages, especially Russian. I already knew some from my mother, and after the war it was easier for me to study Russian. But after that dirty trick—Excuse me, I haven't had a chance to tell you about it. They pinned some stupid little things on me, out there in the provinces. Actually some well-staged exaggerations, in connection with my delicate relations—extremely delicate, I can tell you—with some teenage boys. Among whom I include myself, of course. They can sense it, the little devils; yes, our treacherous and wonderful little brothers can sense it. They can sense it, my splendid little good-for-nothings, yes, yes, they and I can sense it. So I couldn't return to teaching. I was suspended. I also left town, of course: the provinces can't tolerate rebels, you understand. The Gaftons, Mr. Matei and Mrs. Veturia, were very understanding, very welcoming."

The hostess did not blink. She slowly sipped her coffee while looking at her guest.

"Now I work at a hotel in the center. At the Hotel Tranzit reception."

There was a short long silence. The large bunch of red carnations brought by the professor shot up from the shell vase on the sideboard.

"So, at the Hotel Tranzit—"

The same long short silence went meandering on.

"Ah, please don't get the idea—I know what's said about people who work in hotels, in tourism. No, I haven't given way there, believe me. I don't like informers, you know. I've got other vices, but not that one."

"Yes, yes, I understand," murmured Venera.

"As I said, it was force of circumstance that brought me back to Bucharest. I got this pathetic job thanks to Gafton and the doctor, my friend the doctor. Solid people trained in the old style; maybe Tavi has spoken to you about them."

Venera remained silent. Her small palm was stroking Tavi's shiny back, stretched out beside her mauve slippers of tufted velvet. The dog did not stir when he heard the name that he shared with his absent master. He followed the chatterer's confessions with perfect skepticism.

"Yes, he's a beautiful dog. I don't know if you know Veta—Veta Apostolescu, the scientific worker at the dogs' clinic."

The woman did not speak. She smiled, taken aback by the filial way in which the restless professor was looking at her, with a gentle incitement.

"Everyone, including the Association, speaks in the highest terms of Mrs. Apostolescu. She also looks after their dogs: she's a member of the Association. An associate of the Association, as my friend Iopo, Daddy, put it. Maybe you know him. Haven't you ever had any trouble with Tavi? Nowadays dogs also pose a lot of problems. When there's no food or housing or medicine for humans, man's best friend also suffers. And the laws—well, as you know, my dear lady, when the laws are made tougher for humans, dogs don't do too well out of it either. You've probably heard the latest rumors that dogs are going to be cleared out of blocks of flats. So that working people can rest in peace and quiet, without being disturbed. And then there's the pollution, the stress, the general decline of morals. That all affects our canine friends as well. And human wickedness, of course. And the general distrust and the cowardice and treachery and terror—all of it. But Tavi is pretty sturdy, no?"

"Yes, yes," repeated Venera like an automaton.

"At our hotel, the Tranzit, we have a colleague, Vasilica, who's a delightful woman. Generous, altruistic, religious. Well, we rather spoil Vili. She's terribly fond of any old cur. I mean, any creature at all. Cats, rabbits, frogs, chickens, canaries, mice, anything."

Colleague Vancea smiled at the memory of colleague Vili, and was about to ask the hostess whether she was not by any chance the sister of Vasilica Vasilică. But it would have been out of place, an indiscretion, and he gave up the idea of satisfying his curiosity.

"So, at the Hotel Tranzit. A receptionist—what's there to be done? If it hadn't been for Dr. Marga I wouldn't even have found this job.

Nowadays the only people who can help you are the ones who work with the public and have contacts. Doctors, drivers, hairdressers, sellers of vegetables, meat, shoes, or petrol, and middlemen of every kind. Dr. Marga's a real gentleman! Gafton, Marga, Tavi—they're people from a different age, when my brother was also with them. Tavi has probably told you—"

The dog did not start, the hostess even less.

Then Tuesday of the following week. Tolea arrived dripping with perspiration, crumpled up, in really bad shape. He was late: the traffic had been brought to a standstill for several hours because the presidential convoy was due to take the Great Associate, the Jabberer, to or from the airport. He had only just managed to come in a roundabout way by taxi.

"Yes, yes, I understand," maternal Venera calmed him.

As the initial interest waned, Tolea's visits became ever more frequent and protracted. By now he was coming not only on Tuesday and Thursday but also on Saturday, and would have come every day if Venera had lived in the Cuşas' house.

Virtuous Venera seemed overwhelmed and discomfited by the recollection of the past, and so the professor changed the subject. He began to supply details of everything that had happened on the days when they had not seen each other. He gave a lively account of the merry and guilty pranks at the Hotel Tranzit, explained how neighbor Gafton divided up the maintenance and lighting costs of the apartment, described Chick Gina and her dangerous temperament, reported the latest jokes about the Jabberer and his sovereign wife, and launched into shrewd remarks on the exponential rate at which rumors, jokes, and gossip spread through a country. Unofficial information, he said, can penetrate at an astounding exponential speed; it's like with an earthquake, where the difference between 2 and 3 degrees on the Richter scale is less than that between 7.2 and 7.3 degrees. A fatal nuclear reaction, shock waves, and so on, explained the professor.

"Yes, yes, I understand," the hostess agreed in a tone of resignation, now adjusting the tablecloth, now moving the vase with the customary flowers brought by the amiable professor. Tolea was already describing the mechanism of raising taxes through various fines—for traffic offenses, the leaving of rubbish outside the house, or the disturbance of public order—and then he moved straight on to the impossibility of an ecological movement in a country such as ours, to the virtues of space weapons, the manipulation of terrorism, manipulation in general, terrorism, and terror in general.

"Yes, yes," repeated the chorus with the same vibrant, fragrant, celestial cello voice. The atmosphere was fermenting, rather, or languishing. Maybe the hostess would have preferred tacit forms of communication, without all those words that complicated a chaste, domestic familiarity. Tiredness, boredom—you wonder at so much verbal fireworks. But Tolea further intensified the display: surely he will elicit the surprise interjection, a fresh impulse.

"Yes, yes, I understand," the placid woman agreed without conviction. The slob! the aggressor-receptionist thought hysterically, exasperated by the pleasant cello voice that was nothing other than the rhythmic expiration of the slob before him.

"Yes, yes, I understand," Venera uttered again.

They drank tea served with modest sandwiches, occasionally a little glass of plum brandy, or leisurely sips of surrogate coffee made from barley or bran, who knows. Or they would switch on television to watch the Jabberer thundering away about the happiness of the model people and threatening the enemies of the model people. Then Tolea resumed the monologue of adventures, parables, proverbs—even a hippopotamus would have burst from it all. He felt that he would soon give it up; he had already decided to give it up.

And yet he continued with the glib peroration, no longer expecting agreement except from the gloomy Tavi. It was the dog he addressed, in fact, with ever greater irritability and impatience.

He spoke looking only into the eyes of the slave protector coiled up at Venera's feet. Tavi listened calmly, without reaction, to the constant flow of novelties, skeptically following the cement mixer as it turned out little nothings.

Perhaps it was just the silent skepticism of this witness which knocked the excited intruder off balance. He still continued to hold forth, tirelessly gesticulating and pumping out the words, but the visible boredom on the face of the lucid canine censor made him feel depressed, made him feel that he would definitely give it up soon.

Tomorrow will be the end of it! No, tomorrow is Friday, our rest day. The day after tomorrow, Saturday, the holy day—liberation. That's it: all over on Saturday!

Saturday morning was floating in a fine mist, a gauze cloth in front of the sun. The infantilized city pampering itself, taking its time.

The professor appeared at nine o'clock, an unusual time for him. It meant he had woken up early. He was completely in white— which meant he had the day off. Perfectly shaven, as always. In his arms a huge bunch of red flowers, like a funeral wreath.

The hostess thanked him with a brief tilt of her looped hair. She took the wreath from her morning interlocutor and rested it against the hallstand, waiting for Mr. Vancea to take the bag off his shoulder as usual and hang it on the peg in front of the mirror.

The professor stood still for a moment, looking at Tavi's stern eyes in the mirror. He smiled, gave a sketchy greeting to the hound, took the bag from his shoulder, but then changed his mind. He did not hang it up; he took it with him into the dining room.

"A wonderful day, my dear lady. What clearness, what softness, what hesitation! I couldn't get enough of lingering in the streets, going from stop to stop. Spring drives us wild; it drives us prisoners mad."

The tray and coffees were already there on the table. A surprise indeed. Normally Mrs. Venera started preparing things only when they were well into their conversation. Tavi was already at the feet of her chair. Venera looked splendid: the day was young, quite perfect.

"*Amantissime frater*, I'd have said to him. That's what I'd have said to the young man who was looking at me too assiduously."

It was obvious. Tolea had prepared a completely new tactic, a novel provocation, before withdrawing from the field of battle.

"Yesterday evening I was walking alone in Carol Park. Suddenly a splendid young man! He looked like an artist. I felt him watching me for some time, as if he had followed me."

The lady made a vague gesture of boredom. But the professor, though put out, refused to register it.

"Of course I didn't shield myself. He had magnificent, blazing eyes. *Amantissime frater*—I was getting ready to call out the well-known hypnotic words, as if they were a curse. To provoke him, to scare him, to see what he'd do."

The lady impatiently repeated the gesture of disgust. The professor did not have time to dodge it: he was dumbfounded.

"Mr. Vancea, it seems you had a beautiful sister. You don't write to each other often, I know; you have gone your different ways. The family was opposed to the marriage, I know. And she still went off with that fanatic, I know. She has two daughters who have had other daughters. She's a grandmother. I know all that, but it's not the point."

The professor had still not managed to regain his composure. Stiff, his mouth open, he was gripping between his feet the bag that had fallen beside the chair.

Venera was pale.

"Yes, the cats returned, in flames. Last night my burned cats came back to see me. The windows were burning, and my hair and—"

Venera was pale: she had wiped her brow with her hand; her hand was trembling. But she recovered, and the words and the expression on her face returned.

"Maybe you've been told or you remember—Sonia, the black cat who set the holy desert on fire. Tavi was in love with Sonia, your sister."

Tavi started, majestically raising his head. But the maternal hand had already dropped in time onto his powerful, shining muzzle.

"He suffered because of her. She shook him up. She bit him— let's not mince our words. He never got over it. He was an extremely sensitive young man, remember that, a quite special young man! Tavi wasn't always what he later made every effort to appear, indeed to become—"

Tavi again lifted his dark eyes. But the guardian hand promptly calmed him.

"I admit, he also made some unfortunate gestures. He didn't do them simply out of spite, though, not in a mad rage, you know. It's simply that one move had taken away every chance he had. That Matus was certainly intelligent and lively, but such qualities weren't enough for the fairy-tale princess, that's what stupid Tavi thought."

"Yes, yes, I understand," the professor finally mumbled in a thick voice.

Mrs. Venera had pushed the tray toward the professor. Tolea automatically picked up the little cup and, with his head still reeling, bent over and sipped it. Venera in turn, having pulled back the tray, raised the little cobalt cup, sipped from it, and put it back on its saucer. Still pale, still voluble, as if spitting out the words nineteen to the dozen.

"I'm sorry you haven't been able to meet the little tomcat. There are still signs—a kind of emotion, something uncertain."

The professor tensely waited for her to continue, but Tavi let out a huge smothered bark that seemed on the point of shaking the house. What force the black dingo had gathered in captivity! The lady pulled her hand away from his strong, cold neck. She held it in the air for a moment, then brought its edge down on him in a brief slap. Tavi groaned as he looked in her eyes. He repeated the dull, sinister roar. The edge of her hand struck him again, quickly, three times. Calmer now, he stretched out on the floor, with his head on the guest's bag.

"Your people still don't seem to have given up on love. Even after all that suffering, even though others think you're very clever. It's not a sign of great intelligence, I have to say. Do you still want to be loved? Even though you've seen how much hatred you arouse? Did ancestors sing in praise of your life? Did they keep telling you that nothing is more important than life, that a creature's life is the highest value? How could you not become hysterical if life, so short and full of misery, is all we have? At least if they'd promised you something else, a life hereafter—nirvana, or what the devil!"

Venera had become heated—more confessions could be expected. Detective A.D.V.V. had not erred in suddenly appearing on Saturday morning at the site of the investigation, where, look, he had actually been expected. Not only with coffee and sweetmeats but also with significant testimony. Oh yes, finally!

"Do you think Tavi is a criminal? I won't contradict you. I don't know and don't want— I don't exactly know what he did and what he's doing now. I know he married my disabled friend and takes exemplary care of her. My friend Tori. Maybe I told you before. Something terrible that happened in the period that interests you left her a deaf-mute, also rather—how shall I put it?—well, rather sensitive, let's say. As you know, the world can no longer be what it was. And it isn't."

Mr. Vancea was looking straight into the eyes of Mrs. Venera, who was looking straight into the detective's eyes.

"The version of that moment—who can say now? There would have to be more indifference. That's what your people don't have— indifference. It's a real force, I promise you. There's a real force behind indifference. Tavi understood that, I'm sure. Even then."

The hostess's eyes seemed to have lost their sparkle, and her words were becoming faster and faster.

"That moment you are investigating so stubbornly after forty years. Who knows, who—? Let's take a closer look at the next act in the play. Today we've come to defend ourselves from people as you would defend yourself from dogs. Or rather, to defend ourselves from people with the help of dogs," Tavi's mother corrected herself, giving him a mean side glance.

"If I see you're afraid, I bite. If I sense you're weak, I jump on you. I smash your doors, windows, and house, I set fire to you. I send burning corpses to visit you at night. The exceptions? What are the exceptions? Those buddies of yours? The philanthropic doctor? The housekeeper, laundress, and chauffeur—patients happy at the gods' benevolence! Psychotherapy, ergo-psychiatry, ergonomics, whatever the hell it's called. Or Bambino Gafton, hypnotized by grand ideals? A journalist, do you hear, a journalist in this day and age! And he even changed his name to Gafton, his wife's name. To show what? What exactly? That things have moved on? That we no longer make distinctions, no longer take revenge on old legionaries, is that it? But he knew that was a lie. He knew it, the fool. Or did he? Tell him that chosen fools are more stupid than ordinary fools. They are the fools' chosen ones, tell him that!"

Poor Venera was about to have an attack, just now when she had testified that she knew about Mauriciu Gafton and Dr. Marga and the wretched detective A.D.V.V., no less.

But she pulled herself together, the dear old thing. The performance was not over yet.

"You see, Mr. Vancea, the frail, sick Tavi. The sly, devious Tavi . . ."

The dog did not move: he had withdrawn into a superior sleepiness.

The air itself had frozen solid: there no longer seemed to be time to think of what placid Venera was suddenly pouring forth.

"Yes, yes, the hypocritical Tavi, the monstrous Tavi! He kept wandering around, hid himself in a blind alley."

She tried to laugh, mockingly, but all she could get out were some short sounds, a nasty bark of a cough.

"Yes, yes, I understand," the professor tried to stammer, but Venera cut short any interruption with a wave of her hand.

"I know Tavi. I do know him, Professor! My friend—who's like a half sister, you might say—is a person of great quality, but well, she's an invalid all the same. These last few years I've been the only whole person among them, or beside them—beside him—who always guarded against somehow becoming a victim."

"Yes, yes, I understand," the professor tried to repeat, but again without success.

"You should—you'd be able to understand the romantic delirium, the raw, bloated suffering. You were a good-looking boy, happy and transparent, isn't that so? Everything was perfect, no? Until that bicycle accident."

The professor groaned with surprise at the blow beneath the belt. But he recovered with lightning speed, suddenly brimming with excessive vitality. He put his feet up American-style on the armchair to his left, but Mrs. Venera did not notice.

"That bicycle turned everything upside down, didn't it?"

"Yes, yes, I understand." The professor's voice could be heard plainly as he merrily dangled his legs above the chair.

The professor-detective was carelessly swinging his legs about. Now he was pale, too. And Tavi had found a comfortable position by the window, looking into the invisible distance. Venera paid him no attention: she seemed alone—alone with her absent partner.

"They've gone away, Tavi and Tori. Taube, who's known as Tori. They've gone to her relatives in Bavaria. Or maybe that's not where he is, the dog. Maybe he went out of the blue to look for the lover of his youth! But I hope they've gone where they said—to relatives, I mean. Theirs, not mine. No, by no means to mine. I've only got myself, for madmen to hound me, and tie me up and set fire to me and my house, my belongings, my dogs and cats, everything I hold dear. What chaos—you can imagine! Complete chaos! The dolts, the crazies, the deaf-mutes. They took me for someone else. In fact,

I'm not entirely alone. As you see, I look after Tavi: they were generous enough to leave Tavi for me to look after. I feel attached to Tavi—what can I do? Since my apartment was wrecked, since the fire and the sleepless nights, I've been here for most of the time, with Tavi."

Tavi did not stir, although his mistress had held out her hand to stroke him. It was an absentminded gesture in the air. For Tavi was already by the window, and all the lady really wanted was to gain a pause, to recover her breath, before the big final scene.

It seemed as if she had decided not to interrupt herself anymore, and not to let herself be interrupted, until she had cleared the whole burden from her chest.

"Mr. Vancea, let me tell you about disaster. About the soul full of mist and dark holes, where snakes hiss around and ravens roam loose. Poison on top of poison, knot over knot, fungus growing out of fungus. No way out, believe me—only fakes. Exits which are really other entrances. A turning on the spot inside, that's all. Let me tell you about Tavi: he's all that interests me. Have you really thought about Tavi? About those he lives among, about the cripples we have all become? Tell me, have you thought about that? Has he just hidden among them or actually accepted their code? It would be a good hiding place, wouldn't it? Suspicion and informing, our daily bread—there are novel codes in this milieu, no? The sickly, crippled underground that keeps swelling and cannot find a way out, or even an air hole. It just goes on fermenting, and very occasionally a tortured stammering comes out. An extreme model? An outer limit of what we have all become, in fact? Nothing that is real is absolute: everything is full of holes, displacements, blotches. We are forced to use our imagination in order to understand, isn't that right?

"I was passionately interested in mathematics, Professor. A real passion, honestly. *Reductio ad absurdum!* The artificial means that will make the insoluble equation more accessible to our tricks and dodges. But still a reduction, we shouldn't forget it; an artificial means, no more. These model cripples involve a formidable compression—that's all. If a tiny little incision were allowed, something quite unique would gush out. Pus and flames and the aurora borealis! Genius, crime, madness, blinding hell, impossible to imagine. If only we could somehow reach the miraculous moment of liberation! If only we could reach the truth, you'd see what would spring from each one of us, you'd soon see. Something implacable and unique. Or maybe just a morbid stammer? A sick stammer would frighten us no less, I assure you.

"The genius has found the solution! He's found the subterfuge, the dearie, the vile old dog! Huge potential that could even re-create the world! Just think—think of him and us all. And of the poor amputees, who represent us so well. What reaches us from them are just rare signs of urgency. They can drive us out of our mind, Professor. Even our minds can wake up to life—even our minds wearied by so much sleep, so much coding and deviousness and restriction. This envenomed restriction, this idle, ongoing compression, treacherous and going on and on."

The long lecture could have been made much longer, suggested the mathematician's calm and inexpressive face. But she had raised both hands in a gesture of helplessness. Pleading tiredness, she announced that she was calling it off, as if what remained unsaid was actually much more important, but there was no point, she was giving up in resignation. Pause. Silence.

The watch on the professor's wrist was evenly rippling along. Vancea made a quick movement of his leg and looked at the electronic display. 1:00:2, 1:00:3, 1:00:5.

"Ah, let me give you something to eat. How the time has flown. I made some lunch. Let me go and heat it up."

Behold, the domestic servant was reborn. After a moment we shall rub our eyes; it'll be as if we have never heard the fine-spun dissertation. It was only a vision: we are in front of the same silent housewife as always. We can only gaze endlessly upon the pale, drooping vegetable who dozes before us.

A long long pause. The professor had several times repeated the gesture of refusal: he had no wish to eat. But the woman did not see it, and in fact she was not intending to get up and bring lunch as she had announced.

When her voice returned, it was no more than a whisper—a whisper shyly resumed, again and again. The professor did not understand what she was saying, nor did he stir at all. Mrs. Venera made a final effort and raised her voice. "Let me show you his work. I've decided to show it to you."

Supporting herself on the sideboard where the tray and coffee cups had remained, she took a few reeling steps. She seemed to stagger dizzily, limping, shaking with emotion, or whatever it was. For a few moments she circled aimlessly around the armchair.

"Come, let me show you his work. Come on."

The voice had recovered its vibrancy, its heat. Tottering to her left, she advanced cautiously toward the door at the back of the dining room. They passed through a short, bare vestibule, where the guide opened another door.

"This is where they sleep."

A white room, with a double bed. A thick woolen blanket, also white. A white bedside table on both left and right. By the window a little round white table. A white stool. On the wall a round mirror in a white frame.

They were already in front of the other door.

"This is Tavi's darkroom. We won't go in. It's a simple room. Cameras, films, canisters."

She was holding the handle of the door, which had a glass square covered in black cloth. She moved away and stopped at the end of the vestibule. She opened the door on the right.

"This is Tavi's study."

A desk, a chair, a worn sofa. Shelves filled to the ceiling with thick files in every color.

"People say he's got rich. Not a bit of it. This is all he's got: a reasonable apartment. A place of refuge, that's all. His fortune is here, in this room. This is where he's collected his work. And it's some work, as you'll see. He took a copy of it with him. God knows how, but he managed to take a copy with him. He must have found someone's wallet to line for that. To show a copy to his relatives. How about that! His wife's relatives! Victims given shelter in the land of the butcher, what do you say?! Do you like your relatives, eh? Well, he's gone to his wife's relatives, that's what the dumbo said. Just so long as his mind doesn't wander too much . . . in search of his lover, to impress her with the tragedy of his life and with the gloom of his work! Stupid, crazy—that he isn't. Did he perhaps take a copy for the scandal merchants? For the Freedom Circus? So it would make him famous, make him a hero? Our dumbo a dissident, a martyr? Paid handsomely—until the furor passed? To be bled white of confessions and be taught some of their tricks and dodges and striptease and idiotic arrogance? I just hope the cranky old dunce hasn't gone completely senile. Did Old Nick warn him that the day of reckoning is close at hand, that he's got to get a move on! The hypocrite, the scorpion, the poor innocent! My dotty turtle-dove, the jackal. The dirty dog didn't want to tell the truth: who knows where he's gone off to with Goddess Silentium? Who knows where the turtledoves have got to? To the Sleeping Forest, the Black Forest, the Silver Forest of Money, the poor things."

The professor started, with his eyes bulging. Disgust and bitterness continued to ooze from the fragrant voice of gentle Mrs. Venera. The professor had remained on the threshold of the sanctuary. Detective Vancea kept his hand on the strap of his plastic bag: he did not have the courage to violate the sanctuary.

"Come in, Mr. Vancea, come in. It's worth whiling away a few hours with a stranger's work. The werewolf—a man with a soul, you'll discover for yourself. You'll see what truth's precision and surprises mean. The very depths of futility, that's what you'll see. And without any words. An epic, Mr. Vancea! Homer—you'll see! Homer without words, without the help of words. Come in, come in. It's worth it, believe me."

"Yes, yes, I understand . . ."

Mr. Vancea looked at the shelves, at the desk. He sat on the edge of the sofa.

Mrs. Venera watched him sternly, waited a few moments, and then left the room. The professor was alone with the treasure. At five o'clock Mrs. Venera brought him tea and sandwiches.

"Maybe you'd like the lunch I made. You must be starving."

"Yes, no, I understand," he whimpered confusedly.

At seven o'clock the hostess timidly knocked on the door again and suggested a snack.

"No, absolutely not. But maybe you want to leave, to go home. I've more or less finished. We can leave if you like."

"Oh, don't worry about it: I can also sleep here. I see these files interest you."

She looked at him with an ironic, condescending smile, then at the untouched sandwich tray and the cup of tea. She went out again.

At eleven o'clock in the evening Professor Vancea came out of the room, with his bag over his shoulder.

"We'll get a taxi, my dear lady. It's late. I'll see you home."

Mrs. Venera was reading a French book. An old, thick cover, with a title in slanting letters that was hard to make out. A teacher of French—or mathematics—who knows. It was a long time before she raised her eyes from the book.

She stared hard into his eyes. Then she looked suspiciously at the bag on the professor's shoulder.

"We could get a taxi. I'll see you home and then go home myself. It's late."

"You can leave, Professor, don't worry. I'll stay and sleep here."

Vancea bowed as he went out. As he was putting his foot on the first step of the staircase, he heard a roaring sound behind the door, then another. After a few moments of silence, again a crescendo. Smothered barks, like a deep-seated cough. The growling of sullen Tavi did not cease, but it remained at the same reduced level. A hoarse, choking, smoldering fury.

Should he go back or shouldn't he? Who knows what's happening between the bizarre couple.

He gave up the idea of any further initiative and quickly went down into the street. On Sunday he stayed shut up indoors. He unplugged the telephone and did not answer when Mr. Gafton timidly knocked on the door, probably concerned that he had not heard his neighbor moving about.

Tolea lay in bed, thinking. More furious than delighted at the memory of the photo file with which Mrs. Venera had honored him.

MORNING, AFTERNOON, SHUT UP indoors. An ever so long, ever so wide, never-ending Sunday. Timeless time, outside time.

A deaf-mute Sunday: he did not answer the telephone, nor did he hear when his neighbor, Gafton, knocked timidly on the door, once and then once more. Tolea lay in bed, thinking. He was furious. He kept remembering the Saturday trap. The portfolio with the Cuşa photographs had not offered the long-awaited key. It infuriated him, the portfolio infuriated him, although he did not quite know why. Had he really discovered nothing? Had he discovered too much, without discovering anything?

History, indeed. The succession of several decades. Streets, images, buildings followed you for a long time. The Red Army entering Bucharest in 1944. Decoration of the King with the Soviet Union's great Victory decoration. The King's forced abdication. Uniforms, officialdom, the atmosphere of the times. Eyes of a child huddled on a park bench, in summertime. The military parade. Scene from one trial or another and from such and such a funeral. The first collective farm, pictures of the peasants, pictures of the Party activists, pictures of the militiamen. The famous writer being received into the academy, the new academician's sumptuous villa, the academician speaking at the Party Congress. The factory yard. The apartment of the landowner, a well-known collector of paintings, just after his arrest.

The story of some families. The child pianist, the stern father beside the obese mother wearing spectacles. The little girl and boy at school, the boat trip, the girl's funeral, the festival concert . . .

"Five thousand photos, Mr. Vancea! A real epic!" Venera had announced triumphantly.

The tailor and his family, the two officer brothers. The ballerina with mother and cats. The Party meeting of deaf-mutes, the wedding of deaf-mutes, the volleyball match of deaf-mutes. Pictures, hands, clothes, anger, laughter, tears of the deaf-mutes. Groups marching past, knitting groups, weight-lifting groups, the revelry and drunkenness and prayers of the deaf-mutes.

Yes, the power of the images really did linger. The professor looked, spellbound, without daring to open it, at the thick, narrow notebook that he had removed from the first portfolio, the one marked BEGINNING. Electrified, he had bent over that green file with youthful photographs: Tavi as schoolboy, Tavi as clerk, Marga, Gafton, Sonia, Claudiu. Officers, barracks, racist posters. Gendarmes squeezing deportees into cattle trucks on a rainy autumn morning. Again Matus, Claudiu, and Tolea. Yes, Tolea on that damned bicycle, Dida and Marcu Vancea at the trial, the Vancea home on a Saturday evening, at the dinner table. The photographs confused him so much that he nearly fainted. Possessed with the energy of a kleptomaniac, he had snatched up the notebook lying hidden among the images of the past. He had slipped it into his case, in a trance. He had had time to leaf hurriedly through it, in trepidation, and had seen that it referred to a quite different period, but it no longer mattered. He still wanted to have it. Back home, he threw it on the table and did not glance at it again. Even now it was in the same place. It bothered him, but he was not at all curious to look at those hasty notations, coded and illegible, from which not much sense could be made. Enigmas. Should he spend his time solving enigmas?

The professor was irritated; he could not shake off the traces of that bizarre Saturday adventure. Venera's trap: what a fool she made of me, the bitch, treating me like a brat! So that I should discover nothing? But what if I've already found out more than I should, about myself, about them? Enigmas, do you hear? Mere nonsense. Nothing interests her except the master's great secret, his incomparable work, the revenge it helped to give posterity. Documents, archives, a copyist's revenge, that's all; memory exercises, dear lady, that's all. The nun-mathematician, the spook's Frenchified housekeeper, the well-wishing psychiatrist! And the stepfriend Tori-Taube. The perfect alibi as friend, as friend's wife. Substitutes, masks, disguises, underground gallery, illnesses and diseased souls, encoding of yesterday's tale that is going to become tomorrow's.

It infuriated him, in fact. Listen, Theresienstadt, do you hear!

The Saturday gone by, scattered to the winds, infuriated him. The Saturday to which he could no longer return, the irreversible time, with the venereal phantom and all. But he will pick it all up again, yes he will. He will recapture that day. He will remember, reinvent, revive. He will take possession of the lost Saturday.

A misty, gentle morning. An infantilized city pampering itself, taking its time. Yes, he recalled the memorable Saturday. He had scarcely been able to make his way through buses and trams with the huge bunch of red flowers in one hand and his bag on the other shoulder.

With both hands full, he had only just been able to press the bell for apartment 8. The door had opened at once. It was an unexpected day, Saturday, and an unexpected hour for visits to the Cuşa apartment: nine o'clock in the morning. But the door opened at once, as if behind it the occupant had been lying in wait for him.

In the door was a completely new person. Aunt Venera the same and different. Incredible! A middle-aged woman, elegant and—why not?—somehow made to look younger by a new face. A fight to claim it was going on between a weird concentration and a festive, strident look. Her shiny bun of black hair contrasting with the ultra-white face, the lipstick-red mouth, the sunken eyes, the painted lashes, what else . . . A fine sandy dress held in a dark-green belt, the color of her eyes.

The detective had been rooted to the spot. The woman smiled and with a delicate movement took the garland from his plebeian arms. "A mad, tender day, dear lady," the clumsy man managed to blurt out. "Lurching here and there till you're dizzy—enough to drive you mad. This lawless spring will send us off our heads. Have you noticed the power it has to set us captives free? We'll go crazy, I tell you, Mrs. Venera. Yesterday evening I was walking in the park, and suddenly, a splendid young man, a magnificent flame. *Amantissime, frater*, I was preparing to swear at him."

The woman made a gesture of vexation—a gesture of disgust, which she repeated without giving him time to be surprised.

"You should know that my name is not Venera, as you keep saying. It is Tereza. I told you that the moment you appeared here in the door with that wretched bag of blue headless chickens, which you claimed were oranges. I told you my name and repeated it, but you didn't pay attention, although you seem attentive to everything. You aren't, in fact. You never could be; you're not indifferent enough. If you're not indifferent, you can't be attentive. Your people are considered very clever, Mr. Vancea. Maybe that also accounts for the frustrations, the hatred. But you lack the indifference of mind. It's not a sign of great intelligence, believe me. It's no big deal to keep running around with your tongue hanging out for love. After all that's happened to you, to still have your tongue hanging out, for love. It's not a sign of being clever."

He did not manage to be surprised, to answer, to make this and that gesture, to put out his tongue, to prove his indifference to her. The woman, it seemed, had some urgent things to communicate and could not waste any more time.

"No. I don't want you to misunderstand me. There are plenty around who could love you people. Dida Voinov, a pure Russian, went in for a pretty fortunate misalliance, let's admit it. Even your friends, I accept, are choice people. No, I don't dispute their choice qualities." The painted lips made up a smile, oh, yes. "Even my friend Tori—I can't deny her qualities. Nor her defects, the poor thing, of course not her defects. But we should be clear about the mistreatment of the old woman and the cats. The wrecked apartment, police apathy, the fire—you know what they've written in the papers. A pyre, no less, a pogrom. That old woman wasn't all that old, as you can see. I live on the outskirts, on the other side of Bucharest. On the edge of Dudeşti, where the synagogue poor once used to live. There's no trace left of the old picturesque parts, I can assure you. The old wanderers have vanished into thin air. Nowadays the area is made up of identical blocs and identical residents. I've landed there without wanting to, you understand. First they nationalized my villa and allowed me to stay on in just one room; the rest they offered to model parvenus of the model society. But in the end they pulled down the villa itself. They want identical blocks everywhere, model stables for the model herd. They rehoused me in Dudeşti. And there—I can't help it—I began to attract attention, without wanting to. They felt I was different. They took me for a foreigner, they considered me a foreigner. It isn't what you are that matters but how you're seen. They shouted Theresienstadt after me, I was told. That's what they shouted: Theresienstadt!" Mr. Vancea looked straight in the woman's eyes, and she looked straight in the detective's eyes.

"Yes, yes, I understand," the youngster tried to stutter.

"So, that pogrom is a mix-up, Professor. But I'm not complaining. On the contrary, I'm proud, you know."

"Yes, yes, I understand," the indifferent who was not indifferent enough had tried to stammer out.

"Proud and happy. In the end the barbarians haven't been able to make us all the same, as they wanted. They haven't managed to sweep away the differences, as they promised. *You* understand, I think. I assume you understand. I don't complain about what's happened. What's happened proves something important and durable. They haven't been able to make us all the same! No, Professor, really they haven't. The proof was brutal and unfortunate, I grant you that. But it was still proof, you have to admit."

Mrs. Venera had been reborn, he had to admit. Her eyes were youthful again, like her movements and her appearance. A true rebirth, no less. The poor woman had been on the brink of an attack, but she had recovered immediately, the dear thing: the performance had not finished, Holy Saturday was not over yet.

"What I'm saying is that *you* understand. You've been making all kinds of allusions. Your trial, your removal from teaching, the distrust, the marginalization. Frame-up or not, a mix-up as in my case or not at all a mix-up. Well, it's not what interests me. The main thing is that they didn't want you to be what you are, or to discover what you are, or to understand what you are. Or to assert what you are, not to mention that—Their humanism! Leveling. That's all it is. Demagogy and equality. Some more equal than others, as we know. Well, no, we are different, my sweet, and that's how we'll remain. But the crazy guys mistook me for an alien. For an alien! Those heated, nervy types wanted to burn me as a foreigner. Do you understand, my sweet?"

She pursed her lips in a kiss as she said the word "sweet," and her eyes were big and on fire, triumphant, ready for who knows what fresh and incontrovertible proofs. The detective cowered over the chair, over the bag he was holding in his arms.

"You see what I mean, Mr. Vancea, frail Tavi, sick, cunning, devious Tavi."

The dog Tavi was motionless, sunk in a patrician slumber, but the new Venera Tereza did not become calmer, not at all. A new offensive seemed quite imminent. Her voice weakened, however, and became a sighing whisper.

"Since my apartment was wrecked, since that horror, that pogrom, I've been staying here more, with Tavi."

Tavi did not start, although his mistress held out her hand to stroke him. A pointless gesture, as Tavi was sleeping right over by the window, but Tereza had probably wanted to get her breath back.

"There will be a need for heroes, you said. Substitute heroes, you said. One day, when the lid is taken off the cauldron in which we have all been boiling, the stench will be unbearable. Worms and pus and mold will break in from all sides. Everyone will hide from himself and from others. New masks, new substitutes, new heroes. Only we won't be the heroes. Not us poor wretches, or our wretched neighbors. New heroes will be invented. Mr. Cuşa, let us say! A perfect substitute, believe me. The photographer of our rusty, leaky, stinking cauldron, but also of the ghosts you keep chasing after, my sweet. Let's not forget it; let's not forget this halo. Forgive me, you're an adolescent in crisis, intelligent and sensitive; I don't wish to upset you. Come and let me show you his work. So you can see what the duffer has been hatching up. My batty turtledove, my vile cur, my deserter. Come, let me show you the epic. Homer, as you'll see, Homer."

The extraordinary heat of her voice simply muddled your brains. The detective had advanced cautiously through the vestibule to the end. Tereza had opened the door on the right.

"This is Tavi's study."

Shelves up to the ceiling filled with thick files in every color.

"Come in, come in, Mr. Vancea. While away a few hours with the prints of this substitute. The werewolf! You will see truth's memory and surprises. The very depths, that's what you'll see. Homer without words. Come in: it's worth it, believe me."

He had been alone with the treasure for several hours. At five the hostess brought him tea and a few slices of bread smeared with a suspicious-looking plum jam. The door had remained ajar. At some point he could hear a bizarre stammering. He pricked up his ears. The whispers started up again, hard to make out. A muffled sound like a spell.

He went out of the room, tiptoed through the vestibule, crouched forward. The door to the dining room was ajar: the words were being spoken again, and he gradually began to understand them.

"Free? Freer? Are we freer? Freer than we imagine? Freer than we think, you fool? Freer than we think. Answer, you cur, answer, my sweet."

She spoke slowly, stopping after each word. A kind of splashing of the tongue could also be heard, a sipping or splashing. Tolea nervously moved forward another quarter of a step. A strip of mirror could now be seen through the crack in the door. Venera's red lips pursed on the streak of a glass.

"Tell me: come on, you vile tyke. Does it seem so to us? Does it seem that they know everything? Yes, we've been trained to think they know everything. Trained not to move, because it's impossible. Tell me, tell me, you know everything, my little Tavi-wavi."

She took another sip: the glass disappeared. Now her plump hand was stroking his left cheek, up and down. Her head was bent low over the table, and the whispering became faster and more animated.

"Like hell you know, you brainless dolt! Like hell. You don't know a thing. Neither you nor your wife. The immaculate one! The victim! Just an alibi. Tavi with his immaculate alibi. Little doggie Tavi, yes, yes. The future. My future dog-face. Little Tavi. Scared of present, past, and future. The monster. Trained. So we're not able to because—"

Light as a feather, the detective slipped back to the room and shut the door behind him. At some point Tereza knocked timidly on the door. She was lively again, normal and alert. The bitch had well and truly come back to life. With each hour she seemed to become again what she had never been. Lips continually vibrating, eyes large and painted, rejuvenated.

"How about a snack? You must be starving," and she smiled.

"No, absolutely not. But if you want to go home, we can leave anytime. I've finished, in fact."

"Don't worry. I can also sleep here. There's no problem. I see these files interest you. You find them interesting."

A protective, passive smile. She looked at her guest's untouched sandwich and the cup of tea and went out.

It was late when Tolea came out of the room. He bowed to the hostess, without even looking at her, and suddenly found himself at the staircase. As he was about to put his foot on the first step, he heard that roaring, that hoarse, smothered bark. But no, he did not turn back. In three bounds he was in the street, quickening his pace and not looking back for a moment at the Saturday which had disappeared, with its dogs Tavi and Tereza. He started and tensed up. Then a jump, a leap, right into the belly of the idle, obese Sunday. To lie there wilted, without hearing the least little thing. To put himself at the mercy of absence. At some point perhaps a spark will flash from the torpor. A new idea, a fresh trick. No, it's not the end, my dear lady! We won't give in, Frau Theresienstadt! Not at all: it is only a passing defeat. We won't allow ourselves to be replaced just like that. No, we'll start the idyll again, dear lady. Very soon. Yesterday's story will become tomorrow's. Very soon.

Yes, the siege had to be resumed; he would find the strength. More ingenious, more persistent, more demented, he would find the strength. Dear, sweet little lady, look what happened to me yesterday on the train to Barcelona. A freezing cold night. Dirty, unheated train as in our country, a refrigerated wagon. I don't know if you've ever been through such situations, when we become wild beasts capable of anything. Well, in that wretched train stinking of toilets, I was sitting hunched up like some animal when suddenly I saw approaching—guess who? Or a year ago in Marrakesh, at an extra deluxe hotel with extra costly comforts, the same lean for-eigner leading a trained rat on a leash. A rat dressed by the most expensive London tailor, perfectly styled and trained, ready to at-tack. There, in that miraculous twilight— Or a week ago in Copen-hagen, at the Hotel Copenhagen, in that enormous line. Huddled, weary, frightened people, as in our country, an enormous line for some wretched little sweets. I go up to a young woman, a student, who was at the end of the line; I ask her what it is about. And what do you think, she asks for proof of my identity. Proof of my identity! To unbutton my trousers, is that what the nasty piece of work wanted? For me to show her my identity? Imagine the outrage, madam, the sex offense. That's the younger generation for you. To show her my—imagine, I was rooted to the spot. Like the war years, really! Like in Budapest—the Hungarian Fascist platoon, made up only of deaf-mutes, would stop men in the street and force them to drop their trousers and show whether or not their identity pointed toward the crematorium.

Ah, Madam Venerica won't be able to take stories like that! And if she does, we'll renew the assault. Oh dear, my respected lady, my beloved oracle, look what happened to me on Wednesday in the Place de la Concorde, just as I was returning from the demonstration of comrade veterans. Yes, I was still under the impression of our Great Jabberer and his never-ending speech. All of a sudden, what do you think, I hear from every megaphone the announcement: To all those with the mark in the corner of their eyebrow. Then the correction: To people from the special intelligence and monitoring services. So the poor things won't be allowed to wink anymore! What injustice, what violation, what terror! As you so rightly said, we must be what we are . . . Different, you said, yes, yes. A real scandal! Well, my precious lady friend, you won't believe it, but I suddenly thought of Tavi, the dog, his colleagues from the Association. Are they without the privilege of this caste sign, without the wrinkle by the eyebrow? That's what I want to ask. Is the burden not perhaps even crueler? The seriousness, I mean, the deaf-mute discipline. Our byzantine tricks, our happy leper hospital are more human, no? Victim? What victim? Arson attacks against the apartment where you shelter dissident dogs and cats? How could they think you were a foreigner? A chosen foreigner from the chosen people? What victim, my little puppet, what victim, what crematoria? What attack, old woman? Mere entertainment, that's all. Murderous boredom, just boredom. What's there to be done, *meine Liebe*. Boredom, that's what it is. Nothing else, believe me. Just yesterday I was talking to the Japanese ambassador about indifference. We were next to each other at the roulette table in Monte Carlo when I repeated to him—

Eh, Madonna Venerica will give way, she won't stand up to the avalanche. She'll want to escape, to hear no more; she'll give way and throw it all out. She'll quit the silence and the learned dissertations and the collection of photographs. She'll put her finger on the wound—Madam Tereza, at last! She'll betray, yes, yes, she won't be able to control her fury at the werewolf who ran off with his chosen cripple, in the legend, in the fairy tale. She'll reveal all the stratagems, every last one. Anatol Dominic Vancea Voinov struggled hard enough not to rush off on Sunday to the house of the Tavi phantom, or to telephone all day on Monday. But on Tuesday he again set out on the magnetic route. Mr. Dominic is standing in his black work clothes at the Rond tram stop, supporting himself on his black umbrella. Tram 23 arrives: he gets on, finds a seat, and sits down. He sees no one: the car is empty, no one sees anyone. Everyone stewing in his own juice, fuddled, sleepy, enervated by boredom. No one could say, dear lady, that they saw the character. All the same, someone has to make the effort to rise from the dead, to have a good time, to liven the film up! So I got on the stinking ship at Rond. Crowded as always: no room inside. And well, in front of me is—a real gentleman. The elongated figure of a South American. Tavi all over. I gripped the rail by the steps and caught sight of him from time to time, in fragments, through the bags and arms and heads of the other passengers. Then I get off and catch the bus. I wait nicely and—can you believe it?—get on the near-empty bus and am about to sit down—imagine, there were free seats—I punch my ticket and am about to sit down, no one sees anyone, and well, in front of me is the purebred canine profile. Maybe he was waiting for the bus, too, at the Izvor stop and I didn't notice him. What do you think he was doing, this distinguished exemplar of my past and yours? The same as in the tram, believe it or not. The other passengers didn't notice. They are tired, worn out with boredom, fear, and the daily ruses of survival. If they can find somewhere to sit, they no longer care about anything—deaf blind mute, let the deluge come. A place to sit down, that's the trophy they covet, believe me. So we were passing the abattoir, with that cloud of stinking air, and everyone was pulling their collar tight, not that they could have cared less about the dogs and cats and other dissidents dying at that very moment in the crematoria. They buried their head in a handkerchief, coughed, and sneezed, but they couldn't have cared less. So then, that remarkable gentleman, with his perfectly upright posture, his fine elongated features, fanatical eyes not far apart, a nose spread out as on a duck. What do you think that luxury model was doing? Well, he was picking his nose! Can you imagine? He had been doing the same in the tram, caught up in the delicate operation. It's not clear whether he got off with me or carried on farther. I didn't have the strength to turn around and find him once more behind me. A sleek, glossy, thoroughbred greyhound, calmly picking his nose, but watching me. I stopped close to the Scampolo store, the one that's always shut for stock-taking, you must know it. I looked in the window and—

Near his journey's end, Mr. Dominic did indeed stop in front of the Scampolo store.

A surprise: the shop was open. Near the door a stocky flushed saleswoman was ruling her domain, with a long cigarette in her mouth. Mr. Dominic stayed in front of the window for a long time, feverishly looking at his watch. No, it wasn't too early. Mrs. Venera would doubtless already be waiting for him. He excitedly fondled the old volume of Voltaire—a first edition—in his bag. He had decided against the routine flowers, believing that the rare tome would have a greater effect. But he could not make up his mind to set off: he looked now at the dust-covered window, now at the young South

American woman with eyes far apart, broad nose, and thick, painted lips who was nonchalantly puffing and blowing in the crematorium's thick black smoke.

So, dear lady, I was looking in the window to see who was following me. I had stopped in front of the Scampolo store, the one always closed for stock-taking. I kept staring in the window, as in a mirror, to see if anyone following me would appear; we all have that survival reflex, as you know, and with good reason. Who knows, maybe the emotion of Saturday evening was still having its effect on me. I was already on the stairs when I heard the yelping. That hoarse, smoldering bark, full of smothered abuse. I was about to turn back—maybe you needed help—about to defend you. Although you manage quite admirably, as I've seen; you know the model inside out. Nor is it surprising, after all that time you've lived together—you must be, as our friend Voltaire used to say, and in fact I've brought you a volume by that monster of intelligence, but that's not what I wanted to say. As I was coming up the stairs again to your apartment, I was wondering how to dispel your mistrust. No, there's no point in your protesting: why should we hide behind polite phrases? I'm frank to the point of imprudence, as you've been able to observe. Only with people who really interest me. That's how I decided to be with you, right from the first moment. It's strange: my frankness didn't unblock you. These days, in fact, frankness arouses people's suspicion. *The age of suspicion*, as Madame Sarraute said. I think you know her: she's an elderly and perfectly honorable woman from an old nomadic family. She knows what she's talking about. But she had no way of foreseeing the dimensions. I mean, she didn't know that for us the formula is reality, our daily bread. That's what I wanted to say. I hope that in our case, too, it's only a question of this general suspicion which has got into our blood, understandably enough. It's part of our metabolism. Why hide it? In other words, I hope it's not a question of me personally, of some misinformation about me. When all is said and done, you know enough about me and my family, the philanthropic Marga, Sonia, the inhibited utopian Gafton. I don't think you could be swayed by malicious gossip or foul mouths into giving me any less than my due. Nor would you be influenced by cheap slander, I hope. I know what's said about people like me. That new recruit knew what she was doing when she asked me to prove my identity, to unbutton my trousers. I know what the talk is about people like me. Instead of being in an asylum or prison, or in a crematorium, here they are working in a hotel, making contacts with foreigners. Still today, when it's forbidden to speak to a foreigner in the street, even if he asks you the time of day! That means I'm not allowed to talk to myself. Just imagine! But with you—because I no longer have anyone at all. I've decided to speak to you about that disgusting trial which cleared me out of teaching.

Or about the therapist Marga, who wants to cure me, do you hear? Without knowing that I don't suffer from any illness. Because little Dr. Goody-Goody doesn't know me at all, he just wants to get me between the legs of melancholy Irina, that's what he wants. No doubt he knows about some things. But you burn there as at the heart of a volcano: you can no longer get out; the lava pulls you deeper and deeper. Excuse my language, dear lady, I know what I'm saying. They all drag you down into the bottomless pit, and you like it and you can no longer escape, *in saecula saeculorum* you can't escape. You know it, surely you know the fabulous grotto of Hymenland, that magnificent abyss of reintegration.

I want to speak to you about that disgusting trial, from which Goody-Goody Marga saved me, I have to admit. I feel dutybound to tell you about that dirty frame-up. You are too precious for me: I cannot give up these hours of rare communication and communion. Everything you permitted me on Saturday seemed like a grand prologue, but it might also be a confused finale, a sudden stopping short. I couldn't bear it to be an *adio*. I'll tell you about the darkest region of love, for which we run around with our tongue out, as you so well put it, my dear little Venera of Theresienstadt.

You see, my dear friend, frankness arouses suspicion. But if you go where you have never had the courage to go, it's impossible that you won't break down the reticence. Where the vulnerability is absolute, the truth is simple and childlike and tender and unadorned.

I'm talking about a unique moment, a unique risk, after which we remain troubled and burdened, as I well know. I may throw the burden down the drain at some point, or I may feed it with the bafflement of a soul wounded forever, or I may use it sometime as an abject weapon, but there can no longer be suspicion, no, suspicion there can no longer be.

Truly free communication. Naïve, godly, without defenses, full and pure, my dear puppy. Only then do we become capable of understanding the souls of our friends, of our friends' friends, however strange they may be. We will then be able to speak, for the first time frankly, about the absent ghost who has left his mark on us both. Those were the anxieties I had as I climbed the stairs, my dear friend, step by step toward this special place of refuge.

Mr. Dominic slowly counted the steps. He reached the second floor, the light switch. The filament flickered and immediately went out, but the bell was working. Mrs. Venera moved with difficulty this time, no doubt busy in the kitchen or reading a book or attending to the hygiene of watchdog Tavi. Teenager Dominic took the liberty of ringing again. Nothing stirred. As if Tavi had also gone deaf, perhaps, or they were sleeping like a log—maybe smitten with love for each other, the glorious silent-film couple Tavi and Tereza of Theresienstadt, fast asleep in their love's impenetrable armor of Krupp steel, *Sieg Heil*. He rang again, then several times in quick succession. He went downstairs and waited a little in front of the block. Then up again to the bell. Nobody, not a sound.

In the dim light of the corridor he now distinguished a note stuck to the door. He felt for the matches in his pocket. Dominic did not smoke, but he always had a box of matches on him. What with the energy crisis, you can find yourself at any time in need of the ancestral fire. A small sheet of paper from a notebook was fastened to the apartment door with a pretty little red Chinese pin. He stood closer and bent forward to decipher the tiny writing: *Away on holiday*.

Such notices were common enough on the doors of shops, dispensaries, post offices, everywhere. Not open due to a meeting. Shut for stock-taking. Closed due to management illness. Stocktaking. Meeting. Away on holiday. But in this case the handwritten note caused alarm. Tiny, delicate, barely legible, like a line from a letter—a feminine letter, concise, coded. He read it once more, rang once more. He went down the stairs, back up, down again. He waited in front of the building, climbed the stairs again, lit some more matches, read and reread the note. So this was it. Silence, nothingness.

He stopped in front of the Scampolo store, intending to enter but then giving up the idea. He headed listlessly for the bus stop.

COMRADE OREST,

As planned, I went to the reception at Central Army Headquarters. Modest food, rushed service. I wasn't too keen on the guys' mugs there, I have to say. The Source showed, in fact, but it didn't cheer me up. The engineer has good judgment, I must admit, but also a way of looking down on things from on high. He's not plugged into details, I know. And he's too evasive in anything to do with Narcissus. On the other hand, I liked his theory about paternalism. A basic human need—we both agreed. Guidance, order, stability, continuity. Many disasters of the modern world are, I know, a result of defying these needs. I know it well from my own life. When my uncle went through those investigations linked to his liberal past, I was also subjected to parallel hardships. On the face of it, the charges against him had no bearing on me. But my connections with the man who had become my father were already irreplaceable. So it was not unjust for me to be implicated in something with which, in reality, I had nothing to do. While he was in prison, things weren't easy for me either, as you know. But I didn't complain. And when the time came, I was prepared to do for him what I was asked to do, as you know. He was the focus of the whole of my unstable existence. The Source was also right so all those who pretend to be innocent only want to come to power themselves. I know that. It's not a question of ideals and principles. Power, power— that's what they want. And so it becomes important to guide, monitor, and protect the lives of our poor confused fellow citizens. I do it, too, in my modest functions and with the modest means at my disposal. Brilliantly, if I dare say so myself. That is: correctly, discreetly, in good faith. That's also why I prolonged my conversation with the engineer, although he didn't have a lot to offer. As I said, the Source wasn't in *great form at all. More interesting, perhaps, would have been the classic theme:* la femme. *But you told me not to get into that. Anyway, we're seeing each other again in a fortnight, at the football match with Italy. Tickets were sold out long ago, so the engineer couldn't resist the temptation of being given one.*

THIS TIME DOMINIC WAS determined to put little Marga in his place: I don't need your Irina! Stop playing the pimp: I've lost the patience for cuddling, unless you're prepared to accept other motives as well! The whole thing makes me puke, Doctor. I've had all I can take of your charitable tricks.

In the rear of the confessional was always Marga the professional, with his exercises in casuistry and therapy and ergo-psychotherapy: subterfuges, exotic spices! Nonsense, Father Marga. I'm the adolescent of long ago, immature and incurable, the hesitancy and the excess, trembling and secrecy. The intensity, Doctor, the intensity! Hypnosis, vertigo, on the bicycle saddle, on the back of the fairy-tale charger.

Whistling sorrows and face-pulling and bombshells, that's our answer! He will fling the truth in the face of the little Hippocrates, with all his stinking little secrets. Without any shame he'll do it, good and proper. Let Goody-Goody cover his ears and eyes; let him be struck dumb; let him learn a lesson for once.

The moment had come. Dominic was finally determined to bare himself before the friend of the family, who thought he was his friend as well. Determined, in front of the consulting-room door. Anatol Dominic Vancea Voinov was in front of the cabinet of mystification, determined to speak. He had come straight to the hospital, straight to the consulting room. To clear everything up at last: the removal from teaching, how he had escaped and what had followed, his youth, the schoolboy cyclist, the major's wife, the Model Association and the heroic photographer Tavi, the Hotel Tranzit informers, Argentina, absolutely everything. He had hurried there so as not to have time to change his mind. He was determined and prepared: he was in front of the door.

He had absentmindedly passed by those who were anxiously sitting on a bench in the waiting room. Quick: avoid any questions, avoid the danger of being lynched for jumping the queue. He also passed assistant Ortansa, who kept shouting: Where's your card, sir, who do you want to see, wait your turn, the doctor's busy, very busy, shouted little Mrs. Teodosiu, there are no urgent consultations, everyone waits his turn, no exceptions, that's how it is in a hospital, as in death, no exceptions; he also passed the madwoman, on and on. He had already pushed the door handle: he did not look left right or behind, he went in, yes, he went in.

In the consulting room was a sturdy gentleman in a white smock. The shorn head of an adult recruit.

"What do you want?"

"I'm looking for Dr. Marga."

The barracks-room head is wedged in a cup of coffee. His lips noisily slurp once, twice, nine times. He finally looks up again.

"Who did you say you was looking for?"

The visitor, unsure whether to reply in the same bumbling way, mentally counts the buttons on the starched white smock.

"Who was me looking for? For Gerbert. Saint Gerbert. I'm looking for Saint Gerbert of Aurillac. Pope Sylvester. Or Otto. Emperor Otto III."

The boxer raised his eyebrows, surprised but not all that surprised. He was used to anything. So he smiled, no more and no less.

"In a moment. He's just coming."

He pointed to a second cup of coffee, still full, at the other end of the table. The cup was steaming: that is, Saint Gerbert Marga was steaming and would soon appear from the magic cup, that was what the cranky doctor meant to say, fed up with the eccentricities of his patients. The coffee awaited the absent one, so Papa Goody-Goody would soon be back among us. The boxer had even vaguely gestured toward the chair by the door. Perhaps he was, perhaps he wasn't inviting the patient to take a seat. Dominic remained standing by the door for the eternity of a quarter of an hour. He lost the desire to chatter, to quarrel, to do anything. He was about to leave when Marga appeared. Plump and jolly, excitedly fluttering the tails of his smock. A pale face, however, made shadowy by a thin beard that continued his sideboards in a kind of black jaw bandage. He had blown into the room without noticing anybody. He sat down, took the cup, sipped from it, put it back in its place.

"Someone has been waiting for you, as you can see," muttered the tenor from behind the newspaper he was reading.

"You look like a romantic poet," Tolea attacked. "Like the Decembrists on the eve of arrest, or Bălcescu in Palermo. Like Pushkin before the duel."

Marga turned his glasses and his sound eye toward the door.

"Oh, what a surprise! To find you here. You've caught me at rather a— Sit down, Tolea. Commissions and committees, what can I do? We'll be through soon: there's not much left."

He stood up and brought the chair from the door next to his own.

"Let me introduce you. Florin, this is an old friend, Professor Vancea. My colleague, Dr. Florin Dinu."

Dr. Florin Dinu nodded and the professor sat down.

"Yes, that's right, make yourself comfortable. You'll be able to see us going about our business. Then I'll be free for a chat. It won't last long. We're nearly finished, aren't we, Florin?"

Florin agreed with a bow of the head. Their dumpy assistant appeared, with the voice and mouth of an angel.

"Did you enjoy the coffee, Doctor? Sweet and strong, as you like it. There's none around anywhere, you know. Not even on the black market; not even if you pay a month's wages for a kilo. What a blessing these patients are, these poor wretches, because they dig it up from under the ground, just so they can offer some to the doctor."

"Yes, yes, thank you, Ortansa. Be a dear and bring us another chair. Let me introduce a friend of mine, Professor Vancea. My assistant, Ortansa Teodosiu."

The dear went out, returned with a chair from the lobby, and put it by the door where the previous one had been.

"Show in Dumitrache Grigore."

Ortansa left and a short, stocky man came in. Big sweaty face, grayish curly hair. He sat on the chair obediently, with his hands on his knees.

"So, you've appealed against the disability grading we put you under. Instead of category three you are asking to be one—or even zero."

Marga looked sideways at Dr. Florin, who handed him a thick file.

"Mmm, yes, here are the results of the tests: EKG, X-rays. So, apart from the little bats in the belfry, you've got an ulcer, pain in your kidneys, and spleen. Yes, I see. I'm sorry, there's nothing we can do. Really."

The sick man looked humbly at the court, at the spy without a smock. He had made a snap decision. The stranger was the most important person there. Some inspector, or some kind of supervisor —one of those with power.

He stood up and moved toward Tolea. Then he undid the buttons on his fly and waist, until he was left in large underpants with a thick wide bandage as a belt. He untied the bandage and tried to gain Tolea's attention.

"They operated on me two months ago. But it's started running again. Or opening, or tearing open, or however you'd describe it."

"Yes, well—I can't do anything for you," Marga interrupted. "We put you in category two, but the inspectors came and said your diagnosis only fits into category three. That's it. There's nothing we can do."

"I'm an engine driver, a driver's companion. Moving around for ten, sometimes fourteen hours a day. I can't go on. But at our yard they won't agree to anything shorter," the patient went on explaining to Inspector Tolea.

"Well then, let's put here: Must not perform lengthy physical effort or travel out in the field. Is that okay?" Marga brightened up.

"They wouldn't take me back at my old job after I got ill. Then you reclassed me from two or three, and I had to get back in somewhere. I asked my brother-in-law to find me something. But it's hard with the illness, very hard. I've still got two years to go before I retire."

"Only the Institute for Manpower Recovery could authorize us to put you back in category two. Go and see them. Give it a try. Look, I'll give you a letter of recommendation. You'll find them there until three o'clock."

Marga wrote something on a sheet of paper. The patient did up his trousers and took the letter.

"Next. Bădulescu Coman."

A wan, shrunken old man. White hair parted down the middle, as in photos from the beginning of the century.

"How old are you?"

"Fifty-three."

He looked eighty: it was only just possible to make out his whispered words. He had perched on the edge of the chair and was looking at the floor.

"Mmm, yes. Tuberculosis, hepatitis," murmured Marga. "Bad EKG, signs of deterioration. How much do you weigh and how tall are you?"

"Forty-four kilos. One meter sixty-six," he whispered sluggishly.

"What work did you do?"

"Hairdresser."

"Okay. Wait outside."

The old man left the room holding on to the wall. Marga was hopping with irritation in his chair.

"What are we going to do with this poor wretch? He's completely washed out. Can hardly stand on his feet."

"Well, a hairdresser—it's not quite so bad. He might—" put in Marga's colleague, as he lit a long, gold-colored cigarette.

"What might he do, Florin? Didn't you see? He smells of death. We'll put him in category two and send him for a neurological examination. Do you agree?"

"I agree" came the smoke from Dr. Florin.

"Show in Costache Viorica," little Marga read out from his files.

Silence. Marga raised his head: his glasses turned to left and right.

"Ah, I forgot. Ortansa isn't here."

Dominic made as if to get up and play the usher, but Marga beat him to it. Before he could reach the door, however, it noisily banged against the wall. The room was invaded by a disheveled, elegant, garishly painted giant of a woman. She was waving about in a threatening manner her big black shiny handbag.

"What do you intend doing about my case? Another eight years of waiting? Eight years of chasing from one office to the next? Do you think I'm going to put up with another eight years? Is that really what you think, you bunch of eunuchs? More of the abuse you subject me to—more of your lies, disrespect, and ill breeding, you whoremongers? How much longer, you pimps, tell me how much longer."

The thick, powerful voice had still not peaked.

"What's your name?" ventured Marga dryly, leaning across the table to pull Florin's golden pack toward him. He took out a cigarette and lit it with a long mauve lighter that he had whipped from a pocket in his smock. Florin remained bent over the tailor's index card.

"Lawyer Olga Orleanu Buzău! I want a clear answer. None of your cock-and-bull stories. I'm not one of those you sweep up off the streets. I won't lick your paws, and not your cock either, I'm telling you. A clear answer. What am I supposed to do? That's all I want: to be given the right information. Where to go, who to ask."

"We don't have your file here. You'll have to inquire at the office, madam," the chivalrous Dr. Florin Dinu chimed in melodiously.

"What office? What are you talking about? For eight years you've been chasing me from one office to another. So he can have time for whores. Yes, he's been up to all kinds of debauchery, and you haven't done a thing. I picked him up off the streets and gave him the name of my ancestors, a name as old as our beloved fatherland. A name no one can touch! And lawyer Demostene Orleanu Buzău is off cruising around all the sewers. His head goes fuzzy as soon as he sees a hole—that's Screwy Spunky Buzău, I'm telling you. And you haven't done a thing. I'll report you to the Secretary General of the Party, you bunch of saboteurs. How right the Comrade was to ban abortion and divorce and venereal diseases. All you think about is fucking, you gang of cripples; you couldn't give a shit about our good hardworking people. You've ruined my personality, that's what you've done. You male-chauvinist degenerates! You've soiled me and degraded me, for eight long years. I'll tell the Secretary General of the Party, you'll see! So you'll have to account for your anti-socialist morality and justice. I'll tell our Party and state authorities. So they'll declare a general disaster, you bunch of microbes! You won't get away with it, I'm telling you. I'll go to the highest court in the land."

"Get out! Out!" screamed little Marga, leaping up together with his chair.

Somehow or other angel Ortansa had appeared, and she gently but firmly pushed the madwoman toward the door.

A moment of silence. Calm Florin muttered into his cigarette end: Well now . . .

"You want to have a dialogue with that one, do you, Florin? To get involved in all that?" said Goody-Goody as he mopped the perspiration from his forehead and his steamy glasses. "She's a well-known paranoiac. Every two or three weeks she goes for a stroll around town and drops in on us to play that number. Do you want to start telling her about files and offices?"

Nurse Ortansa Teodosiu went out. The next candidate was already standing in the door: Costache Viorica. Big eyes, elongated face, young and pale, hair going white at the temples.

"You are appealing against category three. But the diagnosis doesn't allow for anything else. What work do you do?"

"Technical drawing."

"It's not the hardest of jobs."

"I get tired quickly. I can't concentrate."

"The tests don't show any change since you were admitted last."

"I think they show—"

Her face narrowed, her eyes were burning.

"What you think or don't think is beside the point. We'll keep you in category three and send you to the institute for an expert's report."

Again he wrote a recommendation on a sheet of paper from his prescription pad. The woman went out, furiously slamming the door.

"Shall we have a break? Maybe you'd like a coffee, Tolea? No? Well then, let's see Vivi, Vivi Ionel."

A neatly dressed boy. Fearfully and listlessly swinging his hands about. A broad happy smile: perfect set of teeth. Behind him a supple, dark-haired woman with wrinkles on her face. Her soft, rarefied voice: "It's not possible anymore without someone to look after him. He's twenty-eight and needs to be watched all the time. I can't leave him alone for five minutes."

"Yes, it's probably something for the neurology department. We'll give him another appointment for Friday at neurology. Dr. Antoniu should also be there. Make a note of that, Florin. Dr. Antoniu, the neurologist, should be informed for Friday."

"Been, been Dr. Antoniu!" simpered the innocent. "Ha ha, I

been Antoniu. Dr. Antoniu, he say forward. Forward, forward, pioneers, say Antoniu." The child merrily skipped. Standing behind the beanstalk, the woman made signs so that they wouldn't take any notice.

"What work have you done, my boy?"

"Ha ha, waiter, Doctor."

"Bravo, Ionel, well done. So come on Friday. Vivi Ionel is coming back on Friday for a consultation. Show in Vlădescu Dragoș."

The door opens, shuts. Vlădescu Dragoș comes in: Gulliver's niece. Enormous risen face, round and damp. Big red mouth, bulging eyes. Rope-like hair tied in a loop. Her skirt up over her belly, baring the solid pillars of her swollen white legs. Sandals, a huge sole. Her foot a body to itself, independent.

"You are?"

"I'm here for my husband, Vlădescu Dragoș."

Dr. Marga looked for and found Vlădescu Dragoș's file, plunged into reading it, lifted his glasses from the papers, examined the massive shape in front of him, read some more, smiled, and finally delivered his conclusions.

"Pretty much opposites. You're poles apart, I understand. You and your husband, I mean—"

Mrs. Vlădescu blushed and silently dropped her eyes. She was holding a roll in her right fist.

"You didn't have patience. You went to the kiosk on the corner and bought yourself a roll."

"Er, I know I shouldn't. With these troubles—they take away your appetite. It was just for something to nibble. It's true: we can't sit still."

"What was your husband's job?"

"A locksmith."

"And how old is he?"

"Forty-six."

"And what do you do?"

"I'm a seamstress."

"Okay, you can leave. The decision will be mailed to you at home. He should stay calm, take the tablets, and stop starving himself. Make sure you feed him, even forcibly. You'll be sent the decision. He should stay calm. He'll be informed within a week."

"Thank you, Doctor. I wish you good health. May God look after you, Doctor!"

Suddenly she was leaning over the table. Madam Gulliver completely blocked the view of Goody-Goody: all that could be heard was some murmuring and frightened whispers. "Be serious, madam, let go of me. Take your envelope. Don't try any of those stunts. Take your money, madam, or you'll get into big trouble. You'll really be in for it, I'm telling you."

The woman of the snows took fright and vanished into thin air, envelope and all.

Florin laughed, Marga laughed, Dominic waited. Florin tidied the papers, Marga signed, Florin Dinu signed, Ortansa Teodosiu collected the cups and ashtrays. Kiss kiss, Florin, kiss kiss, Ortansa, Florin the gentleman bows, Ortansa the lady spins on her toes. Right, now we're alone: between us only the couch, which has become a chair, the tool of psychiatry.

"Did you like the carnival?"

"No comment."

"What made you come here, to the hospital? It must be something urgent. Has something happened? What's up?"

"Ah, no—nothing."

The doctor removed his glasses, passed his hand over his right eye, the sound one, then over his stitched-in eye, and then across his forehead. He picked the smoky glasses up again. He seemed weary.

"Do you want to be admitted, perhaps? Or a certificate, a prescription?"

"Like hell! Certificate, prescription, moonshine."

A long pause followed. Dominic put his delicate hands on the table, beside Dr. Marga's plump little hands with their nails trimmed at a manicurist's salon. Listen to this: You come here with the idea of confessing! You lose interest if you ever had any. Listen to him: certificate, prescription, admission. And how determined he had been when he came. Just like a child. He held his palms up, to examine his intricate lines of fate. He looked at his palms, his fortune, for a long time.

"I've dreamed of the letter," the patient said at some point.

"What letter?"

"*The* letter."

"Which one? Claudiu's letter?"

Dr. Marga adjusted his glasses on his nose and fidgeted about in his chair.

"What letter?"

"What do you mean? Weren't we talking about a letter?"

"One enchanted evening, long ago, as you know. A threatening letter. To my old man, to Papa."

The doctor gestured his distaste. So there was to be no consultation. Yes, that was what apeman Tolea wanted: entertainment and nonsense. So be it.

"Papa. So he threatens the old man but makes a beeline for the girl. The bachelor, nameless, intoxicated with love, had eyes only for my sister. The sender, the bachelor copies anyone's handwriting, so long as he's not caught. To undermine Papa's morals, do you understand? So, the fate of beautiful Sonia. He copies the handwriting of illiterates, of criminals with the Easter torch, the pogrom torch. You know: those with shouts and a belt and a cross and a revolver and green shirts like the grass of hell. He copies nothing else, you can bet. Forgery. To get his foot in the door. Or perhaps—"

"I don't understand."

"One evening, around nine-thirty, the maid enters the room and hands over a little letter. Who was the little letter from?"

"Who from?" squeaked Marga.

"You'll soon see. To Papa. To my father. We'll do this and that to you. The Easter torch, the Lord's revenge on those who crucified him. So that he'll hand over the business, the daughter—everything. Give everything up. Otherwise, bash! He imitated that bunch perfectly: maybe he was even one of them. You bet it was them. You know who I mean, in columns and belts. A forgery. To get a foot in the door, the rhinoceros. Or perhaps, you understand, bash! You should see the imitation, see the threat. Oh yes, you bet, nothing else! Anonymous, as if everyone had signed. The mourning envelope, with that emblem, you know. The addressee: Father. Who afterward—you know."

The doctor smiled: he was exhausted. He took a handkerchief from his pocket, gave up any thought of it, wanted to repeat that he was tired, but gave that up, too. So teenage Tolea moved back in for the attack.

"Let's bring in the former bachelor, dead or alive. That's what the gentleman in Buenos Aires wants. Crime, forgery, nightmares, revenge—he wants all of that. The full cast, with an honorarium guaranteed. He wants the truth. I want the truth and I'm afraid of the truth, and I don't know if I really want it."

"What truth?"

"What I sniffed out a long time ago."

"Well? What letter, what bachelor?"

"We all remember the suspect. The chatterlogue. The nihilist. The bachelor. The loverboy. Twisted, stuttering, like anyone in love. Because he was head over heels. And he felt he was losing that accursed beauty of the accursed people. That other one had come to take her away. And then bang!—the last attempt. He copied all those slogans from their filthy green newspapers. Was it courage? An anonymous letter, yes, but we all sign, so it's anonymous. He put that head in three parts instead of a signature."

"What head? What three parts?"

"The three-headed emblem! That's what gave him away, in fact. But Father didn't tell anyone. Maybe he wasn't even sure. Everything looked too much alike, and he was too afraid after a certain point. He, the philosopher, based himself on corruption. That's why he got involved in wine, to have money that would be of help in hard times. Because the barbarians were coming: he knew the hysterias of history and of this part of the world. And where there's no morality, not even corruption can always solve things. A society without principles! That's what Papa was afraid of: that in madness not even corruption would help any longer. Take our young man—that bachelor. Who would have expected it? Only he had heard Father talking about Macrobius, Giordano, the three-headed emblem. But you know Father."

"Come on, let's go. End of joke."

"Joke, you say. What am I? A child? This is called dreaming, not joking."

"Enough, enough! Let's go and eat: it's late. Jeny has cooked a wonderful meal."

The doctor stood up: he no longer heard the clown. Jeny had cooked something wonderful. No further delay was allowed.

"You'd do better to explain that business with the three-headed emblem. I don't understand."

"Is that all you don't understand, old man? Well, think of those paintings of yours. Holbein, Vermeer, Titian."

"On my wall? Are you mad? Titian?"

"That would have crowned it. They'd have arrested you and taken them away, in the name of the exemplary people thirsty for exemplary art. But the national masters—Pallady, Iser, Petraşcu—they're not exactly nothing. And a Brauner and a Pascin, if I'm not mistaken."

"What about the emblem? What's the connection?"

"The Egyptians, the Renaissance, Europe. The three-headed emblem. Triple superimposition: the emblem of prudence. That, I think, is what you talked to my father about when you were young. And he listened, the imprudent fool."

"Me? You think I gave lessons to the old philosopher Marcus? I was just a kid. I wouldn't have talked to him about something I didn't even know."

"No. Nor would there have been any point. Father was no great lover of art. It was a kind of desert for him. And he wasn't mad keen on deserts."

"So you see— What's all this larking around? You don't know what to cook up next to keep yourself amused, to fend off the boredom."

"You're right, Doctor. In fact, I came for another reason."

"Aha. So you did come for a reason."

"Yes. I couldn't say straight out or it would have irritated you. I came to ask you a question and to offer you a consultation."

"People ask me for a consultation, they don't offer one. But what's the question?"

"Why don't we all go to prison? That is the question. Why don't we have the courage? Explain to me, Goody-Goody, Mr. Psychoanalyst, why we don't all of us suddenly decide to go to prison?"

"Huh! And where are we now?"

"Ah, so we're already in prison, eh? Is that what you're saying? Well, in that case the question has even more point. If we're in prison anyway, what would be the difference?"

"There would be a difference. Jeny wouldn't be able to cook those delicious things of hers. That's just one example. I wouldn't have those pleasures, nor would I be able to look after her, and you wouldn't be able to play the detective. We don't all have the same interests simultaneously. Nor the same pleasures. Collective suicides are very rare indeed, my boy."

"Whom do you psychiatrists consult? Your stupid colleagues?

Listen, I'll offer you my fantasy. Or twaddle. Whatever you want to call it. Without charge."

"Okay, I've made a note of that. At the first dead-end I'll ask for you. For the moment I'm functioning satisfactorily."

"There are enormous advantages. When the imagination is probing the forbidden zone, the protective perimeter, the point of fissure—"

"Okay. Explain it to me over dinner."

"Crazy fantasy. And mine might tend toward such a performance; it may succeed where your medical torpor doesn't even make the effort!"

"I agree," sighed Dr. Marga. "But you actually came for something quite different from these speeches. Even an official psychiatrist like me can understand that much."

"Maybe. But I don't feel like it any longer. *C'est fini!* Not only a medical bureaucrat but even a thoughtless friend can grasp that. If he's not too hungry or greedy."

"Or too conscientious. Jeny is my patient. When the doctor's late for dinner, she panics and has a nasty attack. But for you, my dear boy, a special favor—one last quarter of an hour," and he looked at his watch.

"Goo-ood. Now, sir, what kind of country is ours?"

"Developing."

"What do you understand by that?"

"You bore me, Tolea. Surely you read the papers. Output per capita, productivity, national income, God knows."

"Yes, all that. And? Well, let's look at it in a different way. What about before the war, or during the war? Were we also developing then?"

"On the eve."

"Goo-ood. It's economics, then, just that filthy economics. Did you know that in the forty years since the war our Latin auntie,

France, has made an economic leap forward as great as that in the whole period from Louis XIV to the Second World War?"

"I don't believe it."

"I'll bring you the proof. Goo-ood. But what has France given the world in these forty years? Nothing. A few trifles. Substitutes. And what France gave in the period from Louis XIV to the Second World War we all know."

"It would have given now, too, don't you worry. But things were different in those days. Elites, great minds, extraordinary personalities."

"And now? Why don't we have extraordinary elites now? But that's not the point."

"Bravo! Just as well we're getting to the point. Seven minutes have passed."

Dr. Marga got up from his chair, took off his smock, and put it on the peg. He removed his jacket from the hanger and slipped into it. Then he came back and sat down facing the professor. In the position of a listener in a hurry. Tolea was not in a hurry.

"Do you remember the bachelor?"

"There you go again."

"Yes, the loverboy, the fool. Who wasn't at all dumb and wasn't going to be. But he was silent. I called him a fool. Who knows everything. He read, wrote, drew. You're not going to tell me he wasn't gifted. He was, the bastard. Even afterward he was never a simpleton. In the early postwar years he was a dogs' photographer. Maybe you didn't know. You see, you're finding a lot out from me today. You should have accepted the consultation: you'd have had some instructive surprises. Not any old photographer wants to take pictures of dogs. Did you know that? You need patience and skill. Like with children, in fact. Haven't you noticed how couples without children give birth to little curs? They adopt them, I mean. So the stutterer did that, too; the dog earned good money. Seven yellow folders with superb pictures of dogs. All breeds, all political convictions, all social classes, all erotic possibilities. Why are dogs photographed? Is that what you want to know? Well, as a souvenir—the sweet things. And to establish their breed. So many arguable cases, oho! There's terrible racism among dogs, Doctor. You should see their style of apartheid. But let's get back to the point. In his introverted youth, the dear boy was capable of holding forth about anything, agreed? He was capable, say, of talking about the iconography of the three-headed monster. About Poussin, Titian, the others, all the others; he was—tell me, eh?"

"I don't know. Leave me alone. I'm going anyway. You're having a bad day, Tolea. It's bad taste, Tolea. Bad taste, believe me."

"I believe you, don't worry. Good taste is what all those ladies have who strut around with their noses in the air. But the dear old boy really was capable of tackling any subject—that's what I mean. That evening Father received a letter. You know which evening I'm referring to. You knew my people well. Who did Marcu Vancea like most?"

"Your mother."

"Okay, but we're not talking about that side of things."

"You probably."

"Well, I think it was Sonia. And Mircea Claudiu didn't get a look in. An ice block, a calculating machine: he belonged to a different species. I'm the only one who knows about the threatening letter. Does that prove that Daddy loved me most? Maybe, if you say so. Is it really likely that I was the only one who knew about the letter? Yes, it is, you must confess. Let's say it had an emblem above the text. I was a greenhorn, I admit; I had no way of knowing what it meant. A three-headed image, let's say. Would that have been impossible? No. A man's head in those three tenses of the verb? Well, then—"

"What is all this? You're making things up and it's not funny. Listen, Tolea, Jeny and the stroganoff are waiting for me."

"You don't understand a thing! You'll only understand if you're forced to. Then you'll ask me for a consultation, Burschy. I'll give you one, Burschy, I will."

Marga went pale. No one knew about that nickname from his teenage years. He hadn't heard it himself for years. He turned gaping from the door, but Tolea appeared not to notice.

"What do you understand by prudence, Goody-Goody? Is it nothing other than the triple superimposition, which is a mark of submission? Past, present, and future urging you to be cautious? That is, to be wise? Is this wisdom? *Praesens prudenter agit?* The allegory of prudence? Memory—that is, the past and intelligence, understanding of the present—leading to this long rigmarole? But what of the project? The presentiment, the future, FUTURA, as the ancients used to say? I'm speaking to a doctor, listen to me! Listen to me, Doctor. You can't escape these truths!"

They were on the long drive that led up to the hospital gates. The hour of repose: the doctors had left, the patients were resting, the drive was deserted. The buffoon was waving his hands, nodding his bald head, and stamping his hooves to make his words seem more convincing. The fat little doctor was cleaning his glasses, finding it difficult to keep up with the rascal's nervous steps.

"The lion in the middle: the fierce, dominating present. On the right the cringing dog: the hypocritical smirk of the future, which wants to be liked by everyone, *benevolente, benedictinus.* On the left the wolf: the past devoured, devouring. The three-headed monster, I tell you, as the Egyptians of the desert and the Nile proposed it! It was the Renaissance, the European Renaissance, yes, our European Renaissance which introduced the snake. Snake, spiral, time. *Corpus serpentinum*—the three-headed monster acquired a snake's body. It's no longer the horror made to scare, no, no. The monster recovers the dimension of reality, at the feet of man. At the feet of man, Goody-Goody! Because the true divinity is yourself, Goody-Goody, vulnerable *homo*, brought to the center of the sequence, in the image of Apollo. That's how our Renaissance saw it. Ours,

Hippocrates! The European Mediterranean put you, Apollo, at the center of the sequence. You're Apollo, that's what you are, Goody-Goody! At your feet the monster recovers its true dimension."

Dominic did not calm down even in the taxi. The doctor sat in front, beside the swarthy young driver. Tolea was in the back, roaring away.

"Apollo or Christ: it doesn't matter. We've always found ourselves between beauty and creed, knowledge and belief. Athens and Jerusalem, well— Only then was a move made away from that tangled and naïve and exaggerated representation. So don't forget: those great painters of yours, obsessed with simplifying this image, were Europeans. Titian, Holbein—or the other, Pussy, as he was called, Poussin. Europeans, I tell you. Yes, the barbarians didn't use the human emblem. They aimed to be children of the monster. Fascinated with the anthropomorphic, coded, hooked, inaccessible image. The superman. Do you remember? The new man of the new times, the songs, the model, the Model Association, the uniforms, the howls, the promises. The rhythm, Herr Doktor, the rhythm. The two-headed three-headed beast, comrades, pam pam, with pomp and triumph, what a fine kettle of fish, tra-la-la."

The driver's eyes goggled and his ears dilated. These days you never know whom you've got in your taxi; you have to be very careful, all eyes and ears. The cab braked slowly, elegantly, in front of the villa. After such a speech, Mitică will show the gentlemen what the Bucharest drivers' art really means.

The doctor took out his wallet, but Tolea slapped him protectively on the back.

"Drop it, old boy. I'm paying."

"Be serious, Professor! You might say it was a consultation. An art lecture—or maybe it was philosophy. I think our friend at the wheel also enjoyed himself."

"Leave Mr. Bender out of this. I said I'm paying and I will. Otherwise it's not over: we'll keep going."

"What? Aren't you staying to eat? I would like that very much. Madam Jeny would be delighted. You're her soft spot."

"Thanks, but I'm already tied up. I can't even have a proper argument at your dinner table. The food's too good: it makes you feel weak and heavy—and bloated, to be quite honest."

Tolea snatched the money from the driver's fingers and gave it back to the doctor, who was just getting out of the car with all his baggage: raincoat, shopping bag, briefcase, umbrella.

The professor looked at his watch. "I'm sorry, I really can't. I've got to be back at home. A lady is waiting for me. You'll give way to that argument, from what I know of you."

"I will, and I won't even question it. But it's a pity. Okay, another time. Shall we say Friday? Call in the evening, or pick me up from the hospital. I see you know the address."

Tolea bent toward the driver. "To the Hotel Tranzit! You know where? On the Splai—"

The taxi turned around, took the first left back onto the boulevard, did a complete circle of Pache Park, and headed back.

"Ah, so you're not from Bucharest. You're staying at the hotel. Just passing through, are you?"

"Well, sure. Just passing through. The great passage. That's what we're all doing, my friend. But you're right, I am from the provinces —of course. Do people in Bucharest really have time to debate such important matters? They don't seem to: they're always in a hurry, always showing off! It's all froth. They haven't even got time to open a book. Yes, I'm a pure-blooded provincial, like my friends Ilf and Petrov, the doughnut sellers."

The driver seemed never to have heard the names before, but nothing surprised him after the previous speech. His Bucharest pride would not let him pass it by, however.

"Come on, sir, don't be that hard on us. I've met people here who—"

"Just a glossy surface, I can tell you! All they learn is chit-chat,

Mitică. Pinching words from here and there and giving them some spit and polish. But the provinces! That's where you'll find real greatness, in the smoldering boredom of provincial life. That's where the truth is, you know, Mr. Bender. Have you recently been in the main town of any county up in the mountains?"

The driver's hands tensed on the steering wheel: he managed to overtake the huge dump truck in front and shouted out a curse for the fun of it.

"Or why not try Mizil, for example. Just spend a hundred minutes in Mizil and you'll understand what mythology is. Homer? A nobody—nothing in him at all. *Niente.* So, how much? What do I give you, Mr. Bender, eh?"

Tolea leaned a long way toward the meter. The driver, taken aback by the unusual tip, no longer tried to explain anything, happy now with the provincial's babbling. The dry sound of the slamming door could be heard. Tolea jumped down crazily, youthfully, with his bag on his shoulder, and walked toward the Hotel Tranzit entrance.

THE DAY KEPT TO its usual repertoire, but the evening did not bring any soothing change. The stifling heat continued without respite.

A strange, unbearable infusion. Magnesium and iodine emissions lifted into the air multicolored peacocks, phosphorus rainbows. Pink smoky fog. Frozen sky, frozen time. Completely under the sway of the spring night, the hospitable sea, the great hospitable night which forgives our laughter and swallows up our dead bodies.

Suddenly the well-known shudder. A trembling of the shoulders.

At last, the night that takes us back, gives us back. At last, the oblivion in which we day laborers of hope have kept pumping the blood, the blood of a torn, bleeding self.

He really was shaking! A cold shiver on going out into the night. He found himself at the mouth of a metro station. He went down slowly, calmly, softly. Underground there was geometry, cool air, light. Pleasant. Why not admit it? The artificial concrete cave, an enclave purloined from nature.

He was a daylight creature. Night did not exist: it was a cunning, shapeless swamp. A barbaric, prehistoric sinking into the mud. And then all at once he forgot it: the day canceled it out, restoring energy and reflexes. When oh when did the constellation change and reduce everything to sameness? When did the blind, frozen gray establish itself?

Stifling. Larva unable to make it to the water's edge. Did everything break up and slide into the abyss and lose itself in the thick, skyless sky of the desert?

As he climbed the last steps from the metro's tunnel of light to the dark opening onto the street, he was still wearing his childish grin. Glad to be rejoining the great night of loneliness.

Happy pain, a moment lasting as long as we do. A moment, that's all.

Darkness. But the eye is watching. Nothing could be made out. Neither houses nor streets nor people. Everything in obscurity: saving on electricity, saving on life, saving on energy. The lethargy of submission and slumber and standardization, that's all.

And yet he sees them, he sees them very well. They are in the air, in the sky, among the street shadows. They come and pass hurriedly, wearing masks: the ones he met in the hospital waiting rooms, in lines for bread and meat and cigarettes, at selection committees, exemplary instruction meetings, exemplary festivities, and exemplary funerals.

Behold, he was the same age that old Marcu Vancea had been forty years before. In a similar spring he had suddenly lost contact with the earth and rambled through streets and fields beyond them, killing himself or being killed, in the night that was wasn't and was still continuing tirelessly, endlessly. If I were to assemble all Marga's patients tonight, lined up with a torch in their hand on the ridge sloping down to the sewer, to where it empties into the cold dark river, I would find him there among them. Yes, I'd recognize someone like him, like me. I ought to be capable of that much.

The switched-off city accepting the night. Lifeless buildings and streets in the nocturnal waste. Not a ghost, not one heart beating fraternally.

Occasionally steps could be heard. The night round, utopia's patrols, the idle rhythm of squalor's watchdogs.

All at once the darkness screeches. All at once bursts of light. Headlights, screeching cars, plate-metal wheels screws, an empty dilapidated bus staggering drunkenly, snatching from the night its sleeping walls and trees, rusting eaves, overflowing dustbins, the handlebars of a bicycle, an ax leaning against a broom, a silhouette. In the tall door frame the shape of an elegant gentleman. Bathed in the golden jet of the headlights, the man does not stir. Large forehead, metallic pate, fixed glassy eyes. A man from olden times, a gentleman out of interwar photo albums, frozen in the frame of the door.

The bus suddenly stops. The driver switches off its lights and the street disappears. Soon the engine and lights start up again. The dinosaur turns around and comes to a halt by the building, in front of the open door. The door is wide open, but there is no longer anyone in the wooden frame. The driver looks in astonishment through the dirty cabin window. The scar above his left eyebrow is burning painfully. He switches the lights off again. He is watching from the dark. His frightened breathing can be heard invading the street, covering it in darkness.

The round, the toxins, the muffled sounds, the spasm of the owl striking the television aerials. The dark air, its huge deceptive nets.

The airplane rocks gently. A clean, functional interior: geometry and luster. The passenger leans toward the window on his left, but he can see nothing, only the dense night. His big blue eyes turn to his neighbor. A thin, dark young man with a scar over his left eyebrow. The spitting image of the bus driver! The scar, the humble, malicious smile, the darting eyes. The old man leans over and says something, but his voice cannot be heard. The young man agrees, answering with a repetition of the tourist's words, but the sound does not take off. Then they both turn toward the stewardess. Standing straight, in a long voile dress. Naked beneath the transparent dress. She is holding out a tray and waiting. Colored bottles, colored glasses, colored labels. Straight, naked. Blond curls, long white hands, a suave, boyish appearance. Rings of bluish makeup. The long body of an ephebe. The gray-haired gentleman, the tourist, smiles at the androgyne. His lips are measuring words words words, but without any sound. The old man's pink face, starched collar, sky-blue shirt, dark-red tie, batrachian snout open shut open, soundless. His amphibian mouth jabbering soundless words. It moves rhythmically, and the little mustache of his young guide-minder is on patrol. The mannequin is awaiting orders, with the tray stretched out. Her voile blouse flutters so that you can see her boyish chest: the lightbulb in the middle, pink, electric, perfumed. Apollo Venus straightens her shoulders and bends toward the tourist. She again offers him glasses, bust, lips, anything. Clack-clack: the dry noise from his larynx, a red carp's mouth swallowing sounds. A flutter of his snake-tie, again the valve of his mouth, the beating of his crustacean mouth uselessly grinding time.

Suddenly a long screech. Endless screeching, like an alarm whistle. The guide's dark cheeks next to the tourist's senile baby cheeks.

They are jumping about with their arms in the air. Like all the other passengers, who are piling up on top of each other.

Dominic was jerkily groping around by the low sofa, his nerves suddenly shattered. Somewhere he could hear a whirl of alarmed voices, glassy birds' wings colliding with each other, and a long whistling or screeching, wavy, thin, vicious, and vivacious. Then, now, cascading peals of merry, red demented laughter. Hell's bells, the devil's cabaret.

He managed to get off the narrow worn sofa and headed blindly toward—toward nowhere. There wasn't a soul in the house. Only that long-drawn-out creaking of the cupboard doors, again and again. The doors gave an eerie, drawn-out sound: whrrr . . . ping . . . whrrr, and again. Until, after an eternity, Marcu Vancea reappeared at last.

The doors, the cupboards swung about crazily, creaking grating whistling. Maybe he had forgotten to close the cupboards. Old Vancea, the philosopher, had just appeared: how can you explain this madness to him of all people, so sensitive, so stern in his stern clothes, the philosopher–cum–wine dealer—explain now in such crazy, crazy surroundings?

Dominic nervously picked up one of the splendid leather gloves that had fallen by the sofa. Marcu Vancea did not speak, did not answer. He was as silent as the grave.

The son turned toward the creaking cupboard, but did not look up. His eyes were still where they had been when he had picked up the elegant glove of the elegant guest. He waited for the other one of the pair, which would be a sign that he could leave. But the waiting went on too long, and he turned toward the cupboards, advanced toward the door, mumbling all the time. He knew the ghost was behind him, dressed like himself to the minutest detail, ready to start out.

"What's this . . . what's this! There's nothing wrong with me, m'sieur. Just up to going to the meeting. That's why I summoned Goody-Goody's clients. I can't say I really care. That's my secret: indifference. That's what we need. Indifference is my best defense. I've learned that time and time again. Don't worry about me: that's the secret: indifference."

Tolea seemed disgusted with what he was saying. He was spitting the words out, happy that there were only a few of them, that he didn't have to say more. He remained with his eyes on the cupboard, but the gloved hand was in the pockets of the elegant coat, searching for the tablets.

Then he stroked his growth of beard with the glove. He had not shaved for several days, or even left the room. He had been preparing all the time for the decisive moment. At last he could set off. Splendid, flawless weather. A pleasure to breathe, a pleasure to walk, a pleasure to look around. But he couldn't tear himself away. He was waiting for the guest to leave first, to pave the way for him.

Look, it's already evening: how quickly night falls. I haven't even managed to summon all of them, but I'm sure the night will bring them together. The night is creative, isn't it? It's at night that we cook up our acts of deception and revenge.

Marcu Vancea had moved away, crossed the threshold, and gone out. He was no longer listening. But he had stopped before leaving. He had felt something and stopped. Tolea was standing with his back turned to avoid seeing him, but he could tell when the guest had a last moment of hesitation and stopped. Not even the doors were creaking any longer: everything had stopped. The doors were again creaking: the little light on the cassette player was lit up, as if the stranger's solemn steps were once more approaching.

Yes, the shadow had again reached his back, was again stuck to his back. It lasted a long short time. Hard to say. White as a sheet, he remained waiting like that, frozen to the spot, until he was sure no one was there beside him. There was no one in the room but he, Tolea, dressed in his brown English philosopher's raglan. A blue silk scarf around his neck. Long fluffy gloves. That fluffy raglan, with its left breast pocket under the lapel for a handkerchief. And in the breast pocket he did indeed have the starched letter, just right. On top of everything, stupid Tolea was even smiling, with those perfect big white teeth.

In the streets, desolation. Unbelievably he stopped at the little wooden bridge at the end of the village, to adjust his hat. The moon was golden and smooth, Mr. Dominic pallid and angular, his mission too tough for the strength he could command. The columns of slim torches, perhaps just extra-long candles. Lined up by the river, on the slope above where the town sewer emptied into the river.

He took the torch candle from the hands of the first person in the line. No one saw him, but he could see himself. He smiled as he took the torch. He breathed on it. The patient's disheveled head suddenly disappeared. With a smile on his face, Mr. Dominic approached the next one—a withered, red-haired peasant. He blew that one's face out as well. Then he gradually extinguished them all: candles, faces, they all vanished.

Dominic remained alone, holding his own torch, gentle and contented. The torch at the level of his coattails. A perfect dream silence.

That meow could be heard again—that irritating screech of rusty doors. The sky was on fire, the material had started to burn, as had the gloves and the silk around his neck. Mr. Dominic was still smiling when the howl of a night dog could be heard somewhere.

Smoke, magnetic visions. Only foolish Tolea could see them, and he did not have the strength to interrupt. No strength to blink in the face of the crumbling image.

COMRADE OREST,

Masterkey gave me the details about the hospitalization of Chatterbox. Nothing very much can be understood. Not even the doctor has been able to have a talk with him yet. For the time being they're shoving a handful of tablets down his throat every four hours. No improvement is likely in the near future, according to Masterkey. He hasn't been violent, nor has he uttered a word so far. Deaf-and-dumb. I know he won't have any memory of his offbeat investigations, or the Tranzit work team. The kid's unhinged, says Saint Veturia. One night ten days or so ago, when she was going to the bathroom, she saw a light on and heard the professor's voice. He was speaking to someone. She thought it odd. The tenant never had visitors, nor was there anywhere to receive any. His room was too small, I know. Especially at that time of night. Madam Pickle couldn't stop herself: she looked through the keyhole. In fact, she'd been looking all the time—not just that evening, I know. And it seems the receptionist was standing naked in front of the mirror. He was talking with someone called Tudor. Actually with his snipped little prick, which he couldn't take his eyes off. Can you imagine? Tudor! Tudor! Would you believe it! Madam Mushroom was right to be scared. They've stifled us, Tudor— that's what he was saying. They've squeezed us dry: we no longer get any pleasure from anything. We just feel sick at our own thoughts and body and soul, which are as full of holes as a Swiss cheese. We keep ourselves hidden, that's all we've learned to do. We shrink so much we can't even find ourselves. That's what Chatterbox was saying. He wasn't joking: he was serious, as if in tears. We don't have any bolt holes: all the orifices are traps, all of them, Tudor, he was saying. We'll die together, Tudor, because we are one and we are dead already.

There are no longer any fire hydrants, only sewage and death hydrants —that's what he said, according to Mrs. Veturia's agitated report, as if she'd learned it all by heart. It seems the creep was standing naked in front of the mirror and talking to his little Tudor. The old woman sneaked back into the marriage bed to wake up her old guide. Little old Marcel calmed her down: It's nothing, not important. That's what the professor's like, rather artistic. But the next morning the receptionist didn't go to work and the light remained on in his single room. The Gafton lovebirds talked it over in great secrecy and eventually rang One-Eye, the loonies' doctor. He came straightaway in an ambulance, I know that. The patient was naked on the sofa, staring up at the ceiling. Deaf-and-dumb. He didn't seem to recognize anyone. He didn't resist the ambulance men. But when they lifted him onto the stretcher, his little Tudor was awake. Madam Gafton put her hand to her mouth and seemed on the point of crossing herself, as if in the presence of the Unclean One, as if she both did and didn't feel like laughing. It seems that as they were moving the professor, little Tudor suddenly stood up for the salute. And that's how the villain betrayed himself: he could no longer hide his sinful origins. That's what I'd have liked to say to Potato-Head Veturia, but I let her and her old Master alone.

That's about it for the moment. I know Masterkey will keep us informed of any change.

HE DOZED OFF, LOST himself, then Ira appeared.

Her snow-white face, rising from the collar of a black dress. Her snow-white hands, out of dark billowing sleeves. Scarcely had the words been heard when—

There had to be maximum attention, maximum concentration. How can mere nothings tie you up like that, so that you forget the goal, the line? The secret line of fate, whispered Irina.

Forget fear and boredom, forget the day's ballast, the humiliating artifices. Let a single secret line accompany you. Not some stupid detail of the day. Nothing else, my little cricket—only the supreme principle. Only the flame, only the stake.

He was attentive, very attentive, too attentive. Neither blinking nor breathing, so as not to disturb the image or to let the words go astray.

But he was dozing again. He gripped the edge of the bench, almost crying from the tension of not blinking lest everything collapse. But the jamming had already begun: the day was already muttering its troubles. How could he silence it? How to ignore it? And the *fata morgana* is gone; the hypnosis has worn off—it's all over. Other voices nearby.

But they disappeared. He dozed off again from exhaustion, at peace with the torpor and the sun. He woke again and lost himself again and woke up and again shut his eyes. A movement. A heavy old shadow. It called for attention, maximum attention: someone or something was rustling nearby.

"What are you looking at? Why are you staring like that, young man?" The hoarse voice rushed at him from left and right, from all sides.

He did not blink. He still did not blink. He won't budge, he won't give in. Patience, patience, and curiosity and concentration. Indifference, only like this—attention, great attention, common sense, as much as possible. That's how sleep, dreams, come over you, like a faint. Indifference, insensitivity—

"What do you do in life, eh?" the bass voice returned on an authoritarian note.

"Well," the answer came.

"Okay, that's clear. I'm Titian." The voice continued to left and right, on all sides. Everything grew dimmer, clearer: nothing. Absolutely nothing. Just the intruder rambling on. He could see him at last, sitting beside him on the bench.

"Well, er—" muddled the muddlehead.

The old man really did look like—

"Well—I didn't quite get what you said."

"You heard, but you didn't understand. Well, I'm Titian. That's right. Titian. You ought to believe your ears, sonny. Am I being too familiar? Maybe you're not even a sonny boy. Hum, not the right words, eh? My eyesight—what can I do? It's my age. I'm ninety-nine."

Big dark eyes, slipping from their whitish sockets. Thin bluish nose. Deeply wrinkled cheeks. A thoughtful, still thoughtful expression on his face. A black felt skullcap concealed his forehead, hair, bald patch—whatever it was. An unkempt yellowing mustache, cracked lower lip. A white bushy beard. Huge, enormous ears.

"I do look like him, don't I? Well, I am him. I've been Titian for some twenty years now. Tiziano through and through! I'm ninety-nine, as I said. Close to death. The great Tiziano is close to death."

A woolen peasant coat, thick and black, with a nice fur collar from which his shirt was sticking out. His big hairy hands were trembling. Velvet trousers. Around his neck a metal pendant with a seashell. On his bare yellow feet a pair of sneakers.

"Well, you've been through a lot."

"Yes, I've done a lot, my boy. A lot of all sorts. I told you, I'm ninety-nine. I deserve a hundred. I deserved it, really I did. Now I'm dying, although I did deserve a hundred. I'm ninety-nine and on my way out. But I come here every day. On foot, from right out in the wilds. On foot, without a walking stick. I don't need one: I keep walking and don't get tired. But I haven't got long to go."

"Well, but you're very—how shall I put it?—in really excellent shape."

"Sure, excellent. The doctor said that as well. A little tubby one, with a glass eye. He hides the gap under his glasses, but there's no point: he's got a glass eye. And he's got quite a sense of humor—which is important with doctors, you know. Jokes are half the cure. I have my doubts about medicine. And that jokey doctor from the loony bin never seems to get anywhere either. I've caught it: it's a bad disease that I've caught. Old Titian has been infected by your dirty tricks. Just as he's getting to a hundred, his time has come. The great Titian is dying! That's what's written in the book: Tiziano Vecellio is dying. When you think—Charles V picked my brush up from the floor. A day like today—it was only yesterday. I'd dropped the brush, the Emperor bent over to pick it up. The Emperor! The highest power on earth. But in the presence of Tiziano he recognized he was a mere mortal."

"Yes, that's quite something. Etiquette counts for a lot at the court."

"I wasn't your scholarly Leonardo. Or your enchanting Raphael, or granite-block Michelangelo. I didn't respect the rules of composition, I presented unfinished canvases—or so they said. But the color! Well, the color gave them their unity. Intensity—that's what it's all about. Did you ever meet Pesaro? Have you heard of him?"

"Well . . . er . . . what shall I—"

"A patron—that's what he was. I had dealings with anyone I could. Have you seen the Pesaro family? That painting with the Virgin and saints. The Venetian noble Iacopo Pesaro. In that painting I directed Saint Peter's and the Madonna's gaze at the donor. Hmm, we're crafty all right. Crafty, but artists! You might think I'm just a dirty ass-licker. But to put a flag opposite the Holy Virgin no one is allowed to touch? A mere flag, of cloth and worldly sport. That took a lot of guts, I can tell you. That's why we are artists. But color! Color is the painter's impertinence, his virtuosity. Otherwise portraits—you know. Everyone wanted to pose for me, so they'd be immortal."

"But what about the allegory? *The Allegory of Time*," the dozer's voice started up. "You painted it ten years ago. You were already at a respectable age."

"They all wanted a portrait, I'm telling you," the old man continued. "Do you remember Pope Paul III? I didn't finish it, unfortunately. I wanted to get one up on Raphael. My Paul was going to be more alive. But I didn't finish it. Charles the Emperor called me to Rome unexpectedly. Charles summoned me!"

"But what about that *Allegory of Time*? Time. The three representations. Prudence. The allegory painted ten years ago," Tolea could hear his own bored voice saying. "I've heard there's a self-portrait among them. A self-portrait by Titian as an old man, it seems."

"Look, you've dropped an envelope there," the old man muttered in annoyance.

"You must remember it. The only time you didn't put your name on the painting. Not even the name of the models, as you used to do with portraits."

"What's in the envelope? Why have you hidden it? Love? Scented letters? Oh, how I used to love them, the devils. A long life and long glory also means—"

"There's no name in the allegory. But what about the Latin motto? *Ex praeterito . . . praesens prudentur agit . . . ni futura actione deturpet.* Do you remember? That is: The action of the present starts from the experience of the past. From the past, in other words. It acts with prudence. With pru-dence, you wrote. With prudence, not indifference. The present acts with prudence so as not to prejudice the future. Do you remember? The *Allegory of Prudence*— that's the painting. Maybe painted in a spring like this. Were you a prudent man, maestro?"

"What's up with this letter? Why are you hiding it?" continued the maestro. "It must be a dirty letter to entice you. I know what women are like! Read it, come on, read it out loud—to warm me up. Read the invitation for tonight. Come on—"

"Was it on a spring day like today that you began the *Allegory of Prudence*? A very old man in profile looking to his left. Your profile, I'm sure. Only two self-portraits were known: the one in Berlin and the one in the Louvre. This would be the third. The collection of Mr. Francis Howard. Later sold to Legatt. So, an old man looking to the left. Then, in the middle, a frontal view of a man in his maturity. Then a beardless profile on the right. Youth, maturity, old age. Future, present, past. Especially Prudence. Prudence, not indifference."

"Well, no, I haven't any rivals in portraiture. Even in my unfinished lifetime, I was a master of several generations. But what does it matter now? I'm ninety-nine, as I said before. I'm dying; I've been infected. No one will regret my passing. Only my housekeeper. A hell of a woman. A real beauty. Still young, my God! She takes care of me, do you understand? We look after each other from time to time. I'm still up to it, you know. Still got my strength. I haven't shaken off that sin of vigor. And the little she-devil takes advantage. She lets me take advantage, I mean. The strength of a madman. But now I've been infected and I'm ninety-nine. Filthy germs—filthy like the times we're living in. I won't pull through. I told you, I haven't got long to go."

"The three-headed monster comes from the East, but you took your lead from Europe. Not zoomorphic but anthropomorphic. Europe: does that mean Apollo and Christ? The ravenous wolf devouring memories. The omnipotent, majestic lion is the present. The future is hesitant like a groveling dog. Did you dream of Prudence, the symbol of the ages of man? Is prudence mute?"

"What do you want from me? I don't know what you're after with all this mad talk. Cut it out or I'll go crazy, you madman," Titian began to shout. "I'm going crazy, do you hear? Let me die, you madman. I'm dead as it is: I'm ninety-nine!"

He let himself slide to the ground, as if completely worn out. Nothing more was seen or heard. It was just a faint, from the hot wilting sun. But the voice returned.

"That one-eyed fatso doesn't know the cure. I'm going to die. They all lie to me. There's no cure for death. Believe Vecellio, you crazy man. Old Vecellio knows that whore all right. I told you, I'm Titian: I'm ninety-nine."

"But what about the painting in the collection of King Carol of Romania?" Sleepwalker Tolea could hear himself asking.

"Carol—Charles, of course. It's because of him that I broke off the Pope's portrait, as I told you. Charles V summoned me to Rome. I left the Pope in the lurch when Charles called me. Emperor Charles V. They all wanted to have their portrait done, to be immortal."

The midday sun had completely exhausted him. His bony red hands were lying on his chest. But the patient, Tolea, insisted, and his voice was clear and firm.

"A small painting. Saint Jerome kneeling. Maybe you don't know, but it is featured in a Bachelin catalogue. Another version is at the Balbi in Genoa, a copy is in the Louvre, and an alternative—"

The patriarch had dozed off, with his thick-veined hands hanging down over the pendant. But he started and opened his eyes. Enormous eyes, enormous ears.

"Altern— What altern? What is all this? What are you after? I told you: I'm dying, you fool. There is no alternative. Death, death! Phew!" And he spat profusely, with the repulsive cough of an old man, bending a long way toward the ground.

The word "death" revived him, and he repeated it with a burst of energy, as if suddenly risen from the dead.

"I'm not stupid, young man. I know what I'm leaving behind. The block has got to be dragged along by the teeth. Yes, as if it were made of precious stone! It's all we have, you know. Keep it safe from germs! You don't know when how— Look, I've been infected with your disease. I'll soon be dead. I caught it from you, I caught it from fools. Your disease is finishing me off. I'm ninety-nine: Tiziano Vecellio is dying, you know."

His big heavy head fell on the seashell pendant; the old man was exhausted. A huge, thick snore with matching convulsions filled the hospital grounds. Teenage Tolea started, opened closed opened his eyes, stretched out his arms, and touched the bench. He felt quite dizzy for a while. Then he got up, walked away, and found another single bench in a deserted corner of the park. He opened the envelope. It was familiar—yes, the old envelope, the awkward script, the irregular white spaces between the words.

The secret line, accompanying us to the end. Yes, that's it: to the end.

The pink smoky fog of the past all around, and the prisoner found himself lost. He returned, again set off, again returned: a chubby-faced and lisping boy. A chubby-faced angel with curls landed at the foot of the bench. Little blue denim trousers, a Tyrolean waistcoat. Huge cold eyes, short pink fingers. The trees were fluttering and the lake lay dozing. The blue-forested lake, the lilac in bloom, and the nightingales of an Eden swarming with sentinels where the spies' antennae whistled and the stench of the underground triumphantly spread out.

Fascinated by the glossy envelope and the letter, he pulled them toward him from the other end of the bench. For a moment he looked at them with disgust, then crumpled them up in his hand. He ran toward the sandy hillock, crouched down, fell, picked himself up, sat down sensibly in the sand. He began to tear the envelope and letter into tiny pieces, smaller and smaller, as small as possible, until they were dust. He carefully collected them all and began patiently to bury the little heap of ex-words in the sandy tomb, filling it again and again with a child's bucket and pail until not a trace remained.

He gazed at the tomb for another moment, after which he stood up contentedly. An image of waiting. Then the insane trilling broke out, the stormy, merry, irrepressible laughter. The heavenly garden filled with peals of childish laughter. Ever glassier, ever more sarcastic. Then the laughter became thicker and thicker, older and older.

A hoarse, choking laughter, as usual.

RINGING. SHE HAS NEITHER the strength nor the desire to pick up the receiver. She knows what will follow: a long silence. Recently she has been getting this mute call, more and more often, which she is careful not to decode.

The ringing comes back after a while. She jumps up from the chair, realizing that, in fact, it is the doorbell. This has happened to her before: yes, thoughts without thoughts, like a state of drowsiness; the one you keep calling without ever calling him now calls and does not call you. But it is a different sound, in fact, quite different.

She suddenly remembers that this afternoon she has invited around her old comrade in silence, Ianuli. Kir Ianuli, the friend with whom you can be silent for a few hours in difficult moments. Yes, she invited him round, fearing that she would not have the strength to be alone. The silent one, with his dark discretion. A good device: a substitute guest for a canceled celebration.

She looks through the peephole in the door. No, it's not the one she is expecting. She opens the door wide.

"Wow, what a surprise this is!"

The elegant guest remains in the doorway, holding out a huge bunch of red roses.

"The card index never seems to lie. So, if I'm not disturbing you, I've just come to say happy birthday."

"You're not disturbing me at all. It's just that I find it hard to cope with surprises. Come in, Doctor, come in."

Dr. Marga goes in.

"I won't stay long, don't worry. I'm just passing: to give you my greeting. I don't even know what I should be wishing you."

"Maybe you do know. You know enough, too much. But even

what you know wouldn't help you. Wish that I'll live in uninteresting times."

Irina looks at him. The cloudy green of her eyes makes him feel nervous, as does her hoarse and parched voice.

"That Eastern poet, as you know, used to pray for that every day. That the one up above should protect him from interesting times. How right he was, how right."

"Maybe you wouldn't be able to take it. You'll find it hard, believe me. As hard as our misery, which is actually too interesting. May I sit down?"

"Yes, of course, forgive me. Here in the armchair, right here. I'm sorry: I'm not dressed to receive guests."

The doctor makes no comment. He sits in one of the two green armchairs flanking a little white table, opposite a matching sofa.

"Do you have guests, Irina?"

"I wouldn't say so. I'm expecting a friend: he's not a guest," answers the hostess from the kitchen, where she is arranging the flowers in a vase.

"Oh. I don't think of myself as a guest either, although I wouldn't dare to claim the title of friend. Your friend—"

"No, I'm talking about someone else." Irina hastens to interrupt his reverie. She comes back into the room with a tall, cylindrical copper vase. "I asked an old friend round to have a chat. He doesn't know it's my birthday. Just like that. So as not to be alone. He calms me. His silence, his discretion, his tiredness. And his hidden, pent-up fury. Unflinching, yes."

She sits on the other armchair. She seems weighed down, unsure where to lead the discussion.

"He's been through a lot. He came to this country around 1950, I think, when he was still very young—almost a child. He'd been fighting in the mountains in Greece, as a young Communist, having broken off relations with his family. It was a well-to-do family. The father, a famous academic, committed suicide when he heard that his son had become a firebrand, an extremist. Yes, he gave up his family, his vocation, his homeland, and left everything behind. Everything in the end. Himself, too, perhaps."

"And now?"

"Withdrawn. Very withdrawn. He's become a kind of 'specialist' in linguistic problems, the philosophy of language. The study of dialects, or speech defects: I don't know exactly."

"And isn't he planning on going back? Greece is a free country nowadays. People live well there. A lot have returned in the last few years."

"He has no reason to. He's been through too much: he'd be a stranger now, with no links to the younger generation—or perhaps even the older one. He hasn't even been back to claim his inheritance, although his wife seems to keep pestering him to do it. Sudden changes, regrets, inheritances—none of that has any attraction for him."

"A rare case, I have to admit. These days—"

"Not only these days. But let's drink a glass or two together! Not in celebration, because there's no— Just for your visit. I trust you're not here on medical business."

"Certainly not. I just thought I'd give myself the pleasure of coming to see you, on a day when you can't turn guests away."

They walk out onto the terrace, Irina taking a bottle of red wine with her. They sit down in the large straw chairs. The doctor solemnly raises his glass and bows; the woman smiles and drinks in deeply.

Chit, chat: the conversation begins to slacken, then picks up again. They relax and joke like two old army comrades.

At eight o'clock the new guest appears. A sharply pointed face, thick long hair almost turned gray. He holds out a thin soft hand. He has a troubled look, probably because he didn't expect there to be a third person.

Marga appears invigorated by the strange apparition.

"I hope I'm not being indiscreet. Ira told me a little about you."

"Let's make it clear that we're not going to discuss politics!" Irina promptly breaks in. "Crowded buses, demagogic meetings, the Jabberer's jabbering, lines for salami and mineral water and cotton for sanitary napkins? No, no politics of any kind!"

"No, I was thinking of something quite different. Of Hellas! Athens: that is, art, science, beauty, reason. And you chose the opposite. Faith, the critical, combative spirit—the side of Jerusalem! That's what I wanted to say. It's a contradiction, no?"

Ianuli warms the glass of red wine in the palm of his hand. Slender hands, long nails. An intermittent shudder of thin, sticklike arms.

"Of the Hebrews, then! Do you know that poem? By your great modern poet."

All three rhythmically sip wine and munch biscuits.

" 'My most precious days are those when I drop my aesthetic studies,' " the doctor recites in a drawling voice. "Do you know the lines? 'My most precious days are those when I drop my aesthetic studies. When I abandon the harsh beauty of Hellenism / with its sovereign attachment / to perfect and fleeting white limbs. And I become what I have always wanted to remain: son of the Hebrews, of the sacred Hebrews.' A fantastic line, don't you think? 'Son of the Hebrews, of the sacred Hebrews.' It's by that Cavafy of yours."

Marga looks at Irina, lost somewhere or other. Then he turns to Ianuli, who is also looking at Irina. His long thin hands move backward and forward, over knees crammed into the narrow tubes of cheap, worn trousers.

They exchange a brief look of complicity. Irina is pale, her eyes burning as if with fever.

"And what about the conclusion?" resumes the excited tenor. " 'But nothing of it remained at all. Hedonism and Alexandrian Art had in him a devoted child.' What a magnificent ending! Like a cry of impotence, no? He was a great poet, that lonely man. Old and ill, exiled to the boiling mud of Alexandria."

He remains lost in his thoughts for a few moments. Then he turns again to Ianuli, having decided to change tactics.

Ianuli does not flinch, but goes on quietly sipping from his glass.

"Nowadays people keep chasing from one place to another. For money, or adventure, or freedom. When the exile is abruptly removed from his natural surroundings and his mother tongue, he also suddenly becomes simpler. Reduced to the elements: food, housing, illness, sleep, love. He once strove for something else, something—um—something meta-phys-i-cal. But your exile is obviously of another kind. 'For some a day comes when they have to say the great Yes or the great No.' Do you remember? 'I shall go to another country, on another sea.' Remember? Do you remember Cavafy?"

Irina gives a frightened glance, now at the doctor, now at Ianuli.

Ianuli's fixed, unwavering eyes. His dimmed expression, showing no reaction. And the garrulous doctor, always over the top.

" 'Nor will you find new places or other seas. / The city will follow as you circle and grow old in the same streets: / and under the same roof will your hair turn white. / Ever will you end up in this city. And as for leaving / have no hope / there is no ship and no highway for you. / As you have ruined your life in this corner / so have you laid waste the whole of the earth.' "

Irina stands up and looks at them both, without seeing either. In her dilated eyes is the fabled, odorous, magnificent spring of Alexandria. She goes onto the terrace, beneath the poisoned night sky, her eyes absorbed in Saturn and the Milky Way.

From time to time Goody-Goody's tireless voice keeps coming back, displaying on that evening an unnatural logorrhea and insistence.

"When I was young I also bravely marched in all kinds of columns. But I felt exiled in the end. One had the right to participate in evil, but not in the struggle against evil—what do you think? My work swallowed me up. Concrete, democratic suffering. There's no truer school."

But the telephone is ringing. Irina is in her room in one jump, hurrying to pick up the receiver.

"Hello. Ah, it's you! Thank you, thank you very much. No, it's not exactly a surprise. You're as thoughtful as ever. It's very nice. Yes, it was a cruel winter. A real cull, you're right. Unheated houses, I know, the schools, libraries, and cinemas as well. And how did your wife cope? You're right: yes, of course. No, you didn't disturb me. Yes, I'm with some friends. Ah, I haven't heard that joke before. Yes, the Jabberer's one quality is that he inspires good new jokes every day!" and Irina laughs merrily. When she hangs up she has a troubled, confused air. Afraid because of what she has said, or because she lifted the receiver too quickly, or because the expectation proved false, or because the wasted evening is treacherously dragging on and stifling her.

She turns around to explain. "Mr. Gafton! To wish me all the best. He's very thoughtful: he remembers every year."

"So you know Mauriciu! Marcel! Matei! I didn't realize that," the doctor mumbles, bending over to wipe his glasses but also taking care that his artificial left eye is not visible.

"We haven't seen each other for a long time. When they kicked him out of that national newspaper, they sent the poor man to work on the Association's paper. He was on his last legs, with only a little time to go before he retired. We made friends. He's a delicate man. He helped me quite a lot."

"You see, Mr. Ianuli," the doctor bursts out again, "this Marcel-Mauriciu is the best illustration. Coming from a very poor family, he studied day and night. Oho, what didn't he study! Serving the great cause! Honestly adding his bit to the great hotchpotch. What do you say? And that business with the changing of his name! As you know, you can't be a journalist in this country with some alien-sounding name. He took the name of his wife—the tainted and even dangerous name of a well-known family of legionaries. That was how he showed his courage, I ask you! How he, the victim, showed that there had to be an end to vengeance. By taking the name of the butcher. The silly man paid more than it was worth. Substitutions and substitutes, Mr. Ianuli. Is that world too picturesque, too interesting? Too boring in the end? Irina, did you know that Tolea lived at the Gaftons'?"

Irina pours some more wine into her glass. She does not answer: there is no need.

The doctor again turns in his chair to face Ianuli.

"I remember Tolea as a young man. A real dazzler, believe me. Serious and unaffected. Intelligent, polite, studious. You couldn't even tell when the change— Well, it would have been worth being patient with him. I've said it before: he needed patience. He paid for it in the end. It'll be hard for him to recover. It really wasn't worth the price: it's no joke. No, it's no joke this time. But what I wanted to say, what I actually wanted to ask—yes, you've become really interested in linguistics. In the language of seclusion. And suspicion? What about suspicion?"

Ianuli feels uncomfortable and remains silent. But this time he smiles, passing his hands very slowly through his hair. He hopes the doctor might resume his monologue and allow him to avoid answering.

And of course that is what happens. However, Marga seems increasingly tired of the role he has taken on. His sentences no longer gush out but are like a stammering in the darkness that spreads into every corner of the room. "I'm not young any longer. I'm skeptical of utopias: I know what they bring. But doesn't the collapse of great dreams spell disaster? Isn't suspicion worse? Are rapaciousness and bigotry and cynical egotism becoming more and more justified?" And after a while: "Yes, I'm interested in the psychology of seclusion: it's my obsession, yes." And again at some point: "Do you think there's something to be said for the isolation and impotence in which we are caught? Don't underdevelopment and apathy also have advantages, perhaps? Just think of all the comfortable habits! Siesta, family relations, reading, home-cooked food, domestic order, politely behaved children, friends. In the modern world there's no time for all that, is there? Whereas we hostages . . ."

But Dr. Marga is already gone. At a certain moment he stands up and disappears. The night is rapidly closing in. They suddenly feel more alone, more joined in complicity.

"Come out on the terrace"—and her rough voice seems to grow warmer.

Clear, untouchable sky. Smooth silence, ice packs, darkness over which the moon's sharp sickle is sliding.

Irina brings the bottle and glasses from inside and puts them on the cement, between the straw chairs.

"I didn't know today was your birthday"—and the shadow makes a bow and raises its glass. The sky is smoking—a long gray cloud. Irina also takes a short sip. The sky is smoking—the barbaric, gigantic smoke of the night cloud, like a body tensed up to seize the prey, to relieve its long wait.

"This spring! Irinia bursts out. "It's rotted our bones, hasn't it? Even the change of season frightens us. That's why I called you. When you are waiting all the time, you improvise solutions. Forgive me. And I'm sorry about Marga as well. He was in a bad mood, not his natural self at all—pathetically going on like that."

Ianuli bends forward to take his glass just as Irina is finally putting hers down, having pointlessly held it in her hand for so long. She looks at him closely, without seeing him—watching for imperceptible, delayed animation, his incapacity to assume the burden. She turns, ready to arouse him, provoke him, bring him back to life.

"Some time ago—a month or more, I don't remember—Comrade Orest Popescu, the head of the Association, read us all a sensational news item from some paper or other—I can't remember which one. It was a strange report, of the kind that's not usually allowed in our press. A woman had been attacked in her own apartment. Roughed up for no apparent reason. It's true she had a dog and some cats, but that was hardly a convincing pretext. The article gave off special vibes—a sort of menacing hum. Or maybe it was only an impression I had. We're not used to reading things like that in the papers. I began to realize the article was causing quite a stir. Lots of people were talking about it."

She speaks without pausing for breath, then gulps down the contents of her glass. Quickly, inattentively. Her deep voice seems to wipe out the hesitations: it requires an answer, a confirmation. She needs someone's voice and words, immediately, to give instant confirmation that the words really do exist, that this evening exists, that the terrace and the silences and the wine are real: words, headache, sky, death, everything.

"Well, yes, the text of the article seemed to condemn the attack. But its way of expressing itself was suspicious. So tough and vulgar and—complicitous. There seemed to be a complicity with the events, a profound affinity, even though it had the air of condemning them. The relationship between event and report showed that the rejection was only apparent. In reality there was a kind of complicity with what it rejected—with what it played at rejecting and combating. Will the real fighters ever come back to life? To clean out the filthy underground?"

Irina nervously stands up and lights a cigarette. Resting against the wooden balustrade, she looks with irritation at the combatant of days gone by.

"Fear of this spring. Of this stunted, ugly world that has been stifling for so long, drowsing for so long, missing for so long. The long winter of expectation. And now the pagan, illicit joy! Defiance that lacks the courage to defy. Something cunning and simple, prostrate before the elements, without the courage to become simple and elemental again. I am afraid! This outrageous appetite, disorder in the realm of order."

Translucent, Kir Ianuli, yellow and dark, with a narrow face beneath a head of graying hair. No, she doesn't see him, and that is good. Nor would he want to see her sorrowful eyes, or her greedy hands cutting the air with their burning fever.

The inky sky, the whitish moving patches in which she recognizes the nocturnal beast. A dizziness: her limbs and claws and desires become longer, her hair blows about, she feels sucked into the burned air, into the toxins of a huge alien being. She shakes herself, opens closes her eyes. Her mouth fills with a sticky, copious lava. A ravenous mouth in which tongue and teeth keep growing and growing. She tenses up, shakes herself, goes back into the room. Her small hand is trembling, with a cheap, foul-smelling cigarette between her pearly fingers. She tries to speak, faster and faster, whispering, stammering. Words would be a salvation. If she can manage to articulate the words, everything will become calmer and quieter. Remnants of a sentence she once heard: who was it who said there comes a moment for Yes or No.

Kir Ianuli is silent. But he is here, one step away, and does not see her: how good that he doesn't see her. He doesn't see her eyes burning, straining to stop the flow of tears, the hysteria. She tries to pull herself together, although her trembling hands are eager to grasp, to squeeze, to release.

Weighed down in his impenetrable silence, the believer of old is still alive. Kir Ianuli is still alive, but he does not hear and does not see the signs of change here, just one step away.

"The season is a trap," Irina manages to whisper. "An impatient time. People who are too patient, in an impatient time. Time impatient with those who are patient," Irina blurts out.

The screen of the window grows dark and then bright again. A flame replaces the darkness: the phosphorescent face, splendid Circe, the scumbag! Lioness, tigress, and sow majestically roaming the city, constantly crushing dainty little bones of her naïve male attendants. She is none other than the impatient consort of the patient gentleman Ianuli, his invaluable mare! Randy Emilia, known as Mila, Mila Ianuli, Megawhore. The goddess of substitutions and substitutes, Superwhore of the great pagan season, seductive mockery—yes, that was actually what she had wanted to ask the speechless combatant exiled to the moon. How do you manage with the sublime and soiled Superwhore? But does not have the time: her hands and tears and whimpers start up simultaneously, and the man is there a step away. A joke—of which nothing remains but a tearful grin, an angelic smile, sluggish and solitary on the entranced face. Her spluttering hands in the darkness. Trembling.

When she pulls herself together, the man is again in the same place, opposite her. They do not look at each other but gaze at the dark crater of the coffee paste left at the bottom of the cup: a chimera.

"Is the season a trap? What if we were to reverse the terms? What do you think? So that it is not the season but people who no longer have patience?"

The air is cool and dark—that's how she wants it to be. Her partner is somewhere close by, crouching and shrunken. He is asleep, or is just keeping his eyes shut. She does not disturb him. She just bows her tired head. This time, her waking mind rejects exaltation or nausea. It is nothing but rejection, the rejection that disguises her at last inside herself, like her ultimate mask that no longer accepts any disguise.

She looks up at the dark sky. The bells will find her ready, as required. The beginning of something new, the brink of a new age.

Alone—alone and in control.

At some point she sneaks into the house. On tiptoe, so as not to make any noise. She returns with a thick pink rug and wraps it around the absent man. He seems alive, although he does not stir or open his eyes. He does not move, but he isn't dead. No, not yet.

Irina remains on the terrace. The cool of morning gives her back to herself.

This is how she should be remembered, in this embrace of transition, beside a witness removed from the story.

Suddenly grown old, suddenly free. Revenge and joy: a sad triumph. Time is impatiently asking her for a sign. She is ready.